It was true. She was the mother of *triplets*.

"So, what's our plan for getting back our marriage license?" she asked. "I guess we can just drive out to Brewer first thing in the morning and ask for it back. If we get to the courthouse early and spring on them the minute they open, I'm sure we'll get the license back before it's processed."

"Sounds good," he said.

"And if we can't get it back for whatever reason, we'll just have to get the marriage annulled."

"Like it never happened," he said.

"Exactly," she said with a nod and smile.

Except it had happened, and Reed had a feeling he wouldn't shake it off so easily, even with an annulment and the passage of time. The pair of them had gotten themselves into a real pickle, as his grandmother used to say.

Their Triple Trouble

MELISSA SENATE

&

CATHY GILLEN THACKER

2 Heartfelt Stories

Detective Barelli's Legendary Triplets
and *Their Inherited Triplets*

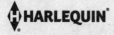 **HARLEQUIN**®

ISBN-13: 978-1-335-47329-5

Their Triple Trouble

Copyright © 2022 by Harlequin Enterprises ULC

Detective Barelli's Legendary Triplets
First published in 2018. This edition published in 2022.
Copyright © 2018 by Melissa Senate

Their Inherited Triplets
First published in 2019. This edition published in 2022.
Copyright © 2019 by Cathy Gillen Thacker

PLEASE RECYCLE
THIS PRODUCT IS RECYCLABLE

Recycling programs
for this product may
not exist in your area.

For questions and comments about the quality of this book, please contact us at CustomerService@Harlequin.com.

Harlequin Enterprises ULC
22 Adelaide St. West, 41st Floor
Toronto, Ontario M5H 4E3, Canada
www.Harlequin.com

Printed in U.S.A.

CONTENTS

Melissa Senate has written many novels for Harlequin and other publishers, including her debut, *See Jane Date*, which was made into a TV movie. She also wrote seven books for Harlequin Special Edition under the pen name Meg Maxwell. Her novels have been published in over twenty-five countries. Melissa lives on the coast of Maine with her teenage son; their rescue shepherd mix, Flash; and a lap cat named Cleo. For more information, please visit her website, melissasenate.com.

Visit the Author Profile page at
Harlequin.com for more titles.

Detective Barelli's Legendary Triplets

MELISSA SENATE

Dedicated to my darling Max.

Chapter 1

The first thing Norah Ingalls noticed when she woke up Sunday morning was the gold wedding band on her left hand.

Norah was not married. Had never been married. She was as single as single got. With seven-month-old triplets.

The second thing was the foggy headache pressing at her temples.

The third thing was the very good-looking stranger lying next to her.

A memory poked at her before panic could even bother setting in. Norah lay very still, her heart just beginning to pound, and looked over at him. He had short, thick, dark hair and a hint of five-o'clock shadow along his jawline. A scar above his left eyebrow. He was on his back, her blue-and-white quilt half covering him down by his belly button. An innie. He had an impressive six-pack. Very little chest hair. His biceps and triceps were something to behold. The man clearly worked out. Or was a rancher.

Norah bolted upright. Oh God. Oh God. Oh God. He wasn't a rancher. He was a secret service agent! She remembered now. Yes. They'd met at the Wedlock Creek Founder's Day carnival last night and—

And had said no real names, no real stories, no real anything. A fantasy for the night. That had been her idea. She'd insisted, actually.

The man in her bed was not a secret service agent. She had no idea who or what he was.

She swallowed against the lump in her parched throat.

She squeezed her eyes shut. What happened? *Think, Norah!*

There'd been lots of orange punch. And giggling, when Norah was not a giggler. The man had said something about how the punch must be spiked.

Norah bit her lower lip hard and looked for the man's left hand. It was under the quilt. Her grandmother's hand-me-down quilt.

She sucked in a breath and peeled back the quilt enough to reveal his hand. The same gold band glinted on his ring finger.

As flashes of memories from the night before started shoving into her aching head, Norah eased back down, lay very still and hoped the man wouldn't wake before she remembered how she'd ended up married to a total stranger. The fireworks display had started behind the Wedlock Creek chapel and everything between her and the man had exploded, too. Norah closed her eyes and let it all come flooding back.

* * *

A silent tester burst of the fireworks display, red and white just visible through the treetops, started when she and Fabio were on their tenth cup of punch at the carnival. The big silver punch bowl had been on an unmanned table near the food booths. Next to the stack of plastic cups was a lockbox with a slot and a sign atop it: Two Dollars A Cup/Honor System. Fabio had put a hundred-dollar bill in the box and taken the bowl and their cups under a maple tree, where they'd been sitting for the past half hour, enjoying their punch and talking utter nonsense.

Not an hour earlier Norah's mother and aunt Cheyenne had insisted she go enjoy the carnival and that they'd babysit the triplets. She'd had a corn dog, won a little stuffed dolphin in a balloon-dart game, which she'd promptly lost somewhere, and then had met the very handsome newcomer to town at the punch table.

"Punch?" he'd said, handing her a cup and putting a five-dollar bill in the box. He'd then ladled himself a cup.

She drank it down. Delicious. She put five dollars in herself and ladled them both two more cups.

"Never seen you before," she said, daring a glance up and down his six-foot-plus frame. Muscular and lanky at the same time. Navy Henley and worn jeans and cowboy boots. Silky, dark hair and dark eyes. She could look, but she'd never touch. No sirree.

He extended his hand. "I'm—"

She held up her own, palm facing him. "Nope. No real names. No real stories." She was on her own tonight, rarely had a moment to herself, and if she was going to talk to a man, a handsome, sexy, no-ring-on-his-finger man—something she'd avoided since becoming a mother—a little fantasy was in order. Norah didn't date and had zero interest in romance. Her mother, aunt and sister always shook their heads at that and tried to remind her that her faith in love, and maybe herself, had been shaken, that was all, and she'd come around. That was all? Ha. She was done with men with a capital *D*.

He smiled, his dark brown eyes crinkling at the corners. Early thirties, she thought. And handsome as sin. "In that case, I'm… Fabio. A…secret service agent. That's right. Fabio the secret service agent. Protecting the fresh air here in Wedlock Creek."

She giggled for way too long at that one. Jeez, was there something in the punch? Had to be. When was the last time she'd giggled? "Kind of casually dressed for a Fed," she pointed out, admiring his scuffed brown boots.

"Gotta blend," he said, waving his arm at the throngs of people out enjoying the carnival.

"Ah, that makes sense. Well, I'm Angelina, international flight attendant." Where had *that* come from? Angelina had a sexy ring to it, she thought. She picked up a limp fry from the plate he'd gotten from the burger booth across the field. She dabbed it in the ketchup on the side and dangled it in her mouth.

"You manage to make that sexy," he said with a grin.

Norah Ingalls, single mother of drooling, teething triplets, sexy? LOL. Ha. That was a scream. She giggled again and he tipped up her face and looked into her eyes.

Kiss me, you fool, she thought. *You Fabio. You secret service agent.* But his gaze was soft on her, not full of lascivious intent. Darn.

That was when he suggested they sit, gestured at

the maple tree, then put the hundred in the lockbox and took the bowl over to their spot. She carried their cups.

"Have more punch," she said, ladling him a cup. And another. And another. He told her stories from his childhood, mostly about an old falling-down ranch on a hundred acres, but she wasn't sure what was true and what wasn't. She told him about her dad, who'd been her biggest champion. She told him the secret recipe for her mother's chicken pot pie, which was so renowned in Wedlock Creek and surrounding towns that the *Gazette* had done an article on her family's pie diner. She told him everything but the most vital truth about herself.

Tonight, Norah was a woman out having fun at the annual carnival, allowing herself for just pumpkin-hours to bask in the attention of a good-looking, sexy man who was sweet and smart and funny as hell. At midnight—well, 11:00 p.m. when the carnival closed—she'd turn back into herself. A woman who didn't talk to hot, single men.

"What do you think the punch is spiked with?" she asked as he fed her a cold french fry and poured her another cup.

He ran two fingers gently down the side of her cheek. "I don't know, but it sure is nice to forget myself, just for a night when I'm not on duty."

Duty? *Oh, right*, she thought. He was a secret service agent. She giggled, then sobered for a second, a poke of real life jabbing at her from somewhere.

Now the first booms of the fireworks were coming fast and there were cheers and claps in the distance, but they couldn't see the show from their spot.

"Let's go see!" she said, taking his hand to pull him up.

But Fabio's expression had changed. He seemed lost in thought, far away.

"Fabio?" she asked, trying to think through the haze. "You okay?"

He downed another cup of punch. "Those were fireworks," he said, color coming back into his face. "Not gunfire."

She laughed. "Gunfire? In Wedlock Creek? There's no hunting within town limits because of the tourism and there hasn't been a murder in over seventy years. Plus, if you crane your neck, you can see a bit of the fireworks past the trees."

He craned that beautiful neck, his shoulder leaning against hers. "Okay. Let's go see."

They walked hand in hand to the chapel, but by the time they got there—a few missed turns on the path due to their tipsiness—the fireworks display was over. The small group setting them off had already left the dock, folks clearing away back to the festival.

The Wedlock Creek chapel was all lit up, the river behind it illuminated by the glow of the almost full moon.

"I always dreamed of getting married here," she said, gazing up at the beautiful white-clapboard building, which looked a bit like a wedding cake. It had a vintage Victorian look with scallops on the upper tiers and a bell at the top that almost looked like a heart. According to town legend, those who married here would—whether through marriage, adoption, luck, science or happenstance—be blessed with multiples: twins or triplets or even quadruplets. So far, no quintuplets. The town and county was packed with multiples of those who'd gotten married at the chapel, proof the legend was true.

For some people, like Norah, you could have triplets and not have stepped foot in the chapel. Back when she'd first found out she was pregnant, before she'd told the baby's father, she'd fantasized about getting married at the chapel, that maybe they'd get lucky and have multiples even if it was "after the fact." One baby would be blessing enough. Two, three, even four—Norah loved babies and had always wanted a houseful. But the guy who'd gotten her pregnant, in town on the rodeo circuit, had said, "Sorry, I didn't sign up for that," and left town before his next event. She'd never seen him again.

She stared at the chapel, so pretty in the moonlight, real life jabbing her in the heart again. *Where is that punch bowl?* she wondered.

"You always wanted to marry here? Then let's get married," Fabio said, scooping her up and carrying her into the chapel.

Her laughter floated on the summer evening breeze. "But we're three sheets to the wind, as my daddy used to say."

"That's the only way I'd get hitched," he said, slurring the words.

"Lead the way, cowboy." She let her head drop back.

Annie Potterowski, the elderly chapel caretaker, local lore lecturer and wedding officiant, poked her head out of the back room. She stared at Norah for a moment, then her gaze moved up to Fabio's handsome face. "Ah, Detective Barelli! Nice to see you again."

"You know Fabio?" Norah asked, confused. Or was his first name really Detective?

"I ran into the chief when he was showing Detective Barelli around town," Annie said. "The chief's my second cousin on my mother's side."

Say that five times fast, Norah thought, her head beginning to spin.

And Annie knew her fantasy man. Her fantasy groom! *Isn't that something*, Norah thought, her mind going in ten directions. Suddenly the faces of her triplets pushed into the forefront of her brain and she frowned. Her babies! She should be getting home. Except she felt so good in his arms, being carried like she was someone's love, someone's bride-to-be.

Annie's husband, Abe, came out, his blue bow tie a bit crooked. He straightened it. "We've married sixteen couples tonight. One pair came as far as Texas to get hitched here."

"We're here to be the seventeenth," Fabio said, his arm heavy around Norah's.

"Aren't you a saint!" Annie said, beaming at him. "Oh, Norah, I'm so happy for you."

Saint Fabio, Norah thought and burst into laughter. "Want to know a secret?" Norah whispered into her impending husband's ear as he set her on the red velvet carpet that created an aisle to the altar.

"Yes," he said.

"My name isn't really Angelina. It's Norah. With an *h*."

He smiled. "Mine's not Fabio. It's Reed. Two *e*'s." He staggered a bit.

The man was as tipsy as she was.

"I never thought I'd marry a secret service agent," she said as they headed down the aisle to the "Wedding March."

"And we could use all your frequent flyer miles for our honeymoon," Reed added, and they burst into laughter.

"Sign here, folks," Annie said as they stood at the altar. The woman pointed to the marriage license. Norah signed, then Reed, and Annie folded it up and put it in an addressed, stamped envelope.

I'm getting married! Norah thought, gazing into Reed's dark eyes as he stood across from her, holding her hands. She glanced down at herself, confused by her shorts and blue-and-white T-shirt. Where was her strapless, lace, princess gown with the beading and sweetheart neckline she'd fantasized about from watching *Say Yes to the Dress*? And should she be getting married in her beat-up slip-on sneakers? They were hardly white anymore.

But there was no time to change. Nope. Annie was already asking Reed to repeat his vows and she wanted to pay attention.

"Do you, Reed Barelli, take this woman, Norah Ingalls, to be your lawfully wedded wife, for richer and for poorer, in sickness and in health, till death do you part?"

"I most certainly do," he said, then hooted in laughter.

Norah cracked up, too. Reed had the most marvelous laugh.

Annie turned to Norah. She repeated her vows. Yes, God, yes, she took this man to be her lawfully wedded husband.

"By the power vested in me by the State of Wyoming, I now pronounce you husband and wife! You may kiss your bride."

Reed stared at Norah for a moment, then put his hands on either side of her face and kissed her, so tenderly, yet passionately, that for a second, Norah's mind cleared completely and all she felt was his love. Her new husband of five seconds, whom she'd known for about two hours, truly loved her!

Warmth flooded her, and when rice, which she realized Abe was throwing, rained down on them, she giggled, drunk as a skunk.

Reed Barelli registered his headache before he opened his eyes, the morning sun shining through the sheer white curtains at the window. Were those embroidered flowers? he wondered as he rubbed his aching temples. Reed had bought a bunch of stuff for his new house yesterday afternoon—everything from down pillows to coffee mugs to a coffee maker itself, but he couldn't remember those frilly curtains. They weren't something he'd buy for his place.

He fully opened his eyes, his gaze landing on a stack of books on the bedside table. A mystery. A travel guide to Wyoming. And *Your Baby's First Year.*

Your Baby's First Year? Huh?

Wait a minute. He bolted up. Where the hell was he? This wasn't the house he'd rented.

He heard a soft sigh come from beside him and turned to the left, eyes widening.

Holy hell. There was a woman sleeping in his bed.

More like he was in *her* bed, from the looks of the place. He moved her long reddish-brown hair out of her face and closed his eyes. Oh Lord. Oh no. It was her—Angelina slash Norah. Last night he'd given in to her game of fantasy, glad for a night to eradicate his years as a Cheyenne cop.

He blinked twice to clear his head. He wasn't a Cheyenne cop anymore. His last case had done him in and, after a three-week leave, he'd made up his mind and gotten himself a job as a detective in Wedlock Creek, the idyllic town where he'd spent several summers as a kid with his maternal grandmother. A town where it seemed nothing could go wrong. A town that hadn't seen a murder in over seventy years. Hadn't Norah mentioned that last night?

Norah. Last night.

He lifted his hand to scrub over his face and that was when he saw it—the gold ring on his left hand. Ring finger. A ring that hadn't been there before he'd gone to the carnival.

What the…?

Slowly, bits and pieces of the evening came back to him. The festival. A punch bowl he'd commandeered into the clearing under a big tree so he and Norah could have the rest of it all to themselves. A clearly heavily *spiked* punch bowl. A hundred-dollar bill in the till, not to mention at least sixty in cash. Norah, taking his hand and leading him to the chapel.

She'd always dreamed of getting married, she'd said.

And he'd said, "Then let's get married."

He'd said that! Reed Barelli had uttered those words!

He held his breath and gently peeled the blue-and-white quilt from her shoulder to look at her left hand—which she used to yank the quilt back up, wrinkling her cute nose and turning over.

There was a gold band on her finger, too.

Holy moly. They'd really done it. They'd gotten married?

No. Couldn't be. The officiant of the chapel had called him by name. Yes, the elderly woman had known him, said she'd seen the chief showing him around town yesterday when he'd arrived. And she'd seemed familiar with Norah, too. She knew both of them. She wouldn't let them drunk-marry! That was the height of irresponsible. And as a man of the law, he would demand she explain herself and simply undo whatever it was they'd signed. Dimly, he recalled the marriage license, scrawling his name with a blue pen.

Norah stirred. She was still asleep. For a second he couldn't help but stare at her pretty face. She had a pale complexion, delicate features and hazel eyes, if he remembered correctly.

If they'd made love, *that* he couldn't remember. And he would remember, drunk to high heaven or not. What had been in that punch?

Maybe they'd come back to her place and passed out in bed?

He closed his eyes again and slowly opened them. *Deep breaths, Barelli.* He looked around the bedroom to orient himself, ground himself.

And that was when he saw the framed photograph on the end table on Norah's side. Norah in a hospital bed, in one of those thin blue gowns, holding three newborns against her chest.

Ooh boy.

Chapter 2

"I'm sure we're not really married!" Norah said on a high-pitched squeak, the top sheet wrapped around her as she stood—completely freaked out—against the wall of her bedroom, staring at the strange man in her bed.

A man who, according to the wedding ring on her left hand—and the one on his—*was* her husband.

She'd pretended to be asleep when he'd first started stirring. He'd bolted upright and she could feel him staring at her. She couldn't just lie there and pretend to be asleep any longer, even if she was afraid to open her eyes and face the music.

But a thought burst into her brain and she'd sat up, too: she'd forgotten to pick up the triplets. As her aunt's words had come back to her, that Cheyenne didn't expect her to pick up the babies last night, that she'd take them to the diner this morning, Norah had calmed down. And slowly had opened her eyes. The sight of the stranger awake and staring at her had her leaping out of bed, taking the sheet with her. She was in a camisole and underwear.

Oh God, had they...?

She stared at Reed. In her bed. "Did we?" she croaked out.

He half shrugged. "I don't know. Sorry. I don't think so, though."

"The punch was spiked?"

"Someone's idea of a joke, maybe."

"And now we're married," she said. "Ha ha."

His gaze went to the band of gold on his finger, then back at her. "I'm sure we can undo that. The couple who married us—they seemed to know both of us. Why would they have let us get married when we were so drunk?"

Now it was her turn to shrug. She'd known Annie since she was born. The woman had waitressed on and off at her family's pie diner for years to make extra cash. How could she have let Norah do such a thing? Why hadn't Annie called her mother or aunt or sister and said, *Come get Norah, she's drunk off her butt and trying to marry a total stranger*? It made no sense that Annie hadn't done just that!

"She seemed to know you, too," Norah said, wishing she had a cup of coffee. And two Tylenol.

"I spent summers in Wedlock Creek with my grandmother when I was a kid," he said. "Annie may have known my grandmother. Do the Potterowskis live near the chapel? Maybe we can head over now and get this straightened out. I'm sure Annie hasn't sent in the marriage license yet."

"Right!" Norah said, brightening, tightening the sheet around her. "We can undo this! Let's go!"

He glanced at his pile of clothes on the floor beside the bed. "I'll go into the bathroom and get dressed." He stood, wearing nothing but incredibly sexy black boxer briefs. He picked up the pile and booked into the bathroom, shutting the door.

She heard the water run, then shut off. A few minutes later the door opened and there he was, dressed like Fabio from last night.

She rushed over to her dresser, grabbed jeans and a T-shirt and fresh underwear, then sped past him into the bathroom, her heart beating like a bullet train. She quickly washed her face and brushed her teeth, got dressed and stepped back outside.

Reed was sitting in the chair in the corner, his elbows on his knees, his head in his hands. How could he look so handsome when he was so rumpled, his hair all mussed? He was slowly shaking his head as if trying to make sense of this.

"So you always wanted to be a secret service agent?" she asked to break the awkward silence.

He sat up and offered something of a smile. "I have no idea why I said that. I've always wanted to be a cop. I start at the Wedlock Creek PD on Monday. Guess you're not a flight attendant," he added.

"I've never been out of Wyoming," she said. "I bake for my family's pie diner." That was all she'd ever wanted to do. Work for the family business and perfect her savory pies, her specialty.

The diner had her thinking of real life again, Bella's, Bea's and Brody's beautiful little faces coming to mind. She missed them and needed to see them, needed to hold them. And she had to get to the diner and let her family know she was all right. She hadn't called once to check in on the triplets last night. Her mom and aunt had probably mentioned that every hour on the hour. *No call from Norah? Huh. Must be having a good time.* Then looking at each other and saying *Not* in unison, bursting into laughter and sobering up fast, wondering what could have happened to her to prevent her from calling every other minute to make sure all was well with the babies.

Her phone hadn't rung last night, so maybe they'd just thought she'd met up with old friends and was having fun. She glanced at her alarm clock on the bedside table. It was barely six o'clock. She wouldn't be expected at the diner until seven.

Reed was looking at the photo next to the clock. The one of her and her triplets taken moments after they were born. He didn't say a word, but she knew what he was thinking. Anyone would. *Help me. Get me out of this. What the hell have I done? Triplets? Ahhhhh!* She was surprised he didn't have his hands on his screaming face like the kid from the movie *Home Alone.*

Well, one thing Norah Ingalls was good at? Taking care of business. "Let's go see Annie and Abe," she said. "They wake up at the crack of dawn, so I'm sure they'll be up."

His gaze snapped back to hers. "Good idea. We can catch them before they send the marriage license into the state bureau for processing."

"Right. It's not like we're really married. I mean, it's not *legal.*"

He nodded. "We could undo this before 7:00 a.m. and get back to our lives," he said.

This was definitely not her life.

* * *

Norah poked her head out the front door of her house, which, thank heavens, was blocked on both sides by big leafy trees. The last thing she needed was for all of Wedlock Creek to know a man had been spotted leaving her house at six in the morning. Norah lived around the corner from Main Street and just a few minutes' walk to the diner, but the chapel was a good half mile in the other direction.

"Let's take the parallel road so no one sees us," she said. "I'm sure you don't want to be the center of gossip before you even start your first day at the police station."

"I definitely don't," he said.

They ducked down a side street with backyards to the left and the woods and river to the right. At this early hour, no one was out yet. The Potterowskis lived in the caretaker's cottage to the right of the chapel. Norah dashed up the steps to the side door and could see eighty-one-year-old Annie in a long, pink chenille bathrobe, sitting down with tea and toast. She rang the bell.

Annie came to the door and beamed at the newlyweds. "Norah! Didn't expect to see you out and about so early. Shouldn't you be on your honeymoon?" Annie peered behind Norah and spied Reed. "Ah, there you are, handsome devil. Come on in, you two. I just made a pot of coffee."

How could the woman be so calm? Or act like their getting married was no big deal?

Norah and Reed came in but didn't sit. "Annie," Norah said, "the two of us were the victims of spiked punch at the festival last night! We were drunk out of our minds. You had to know that!"

Annie tilted her head, her short, wiry, silver curls bouncing. "Drunk? Why, I don't recall seeing you two acting all nutty and, trust me, we get our share of drunk couples and turn them away."

Norah narrowed her eyes. There was no way Annie hadn't known she was drunk out of her mind! "Annie, why would I up and marry a total stranger out of the blue? Didn't that seem weird?"

"But Reed isn't a stranger," Annie said, sipping her coffee. "I heard he was back in town to work at the PD." She turned to him. "I remember you when you were a boy. I knew your grandmother Lydia Barelli. We were dear friends from way back. Oh, how I remember her hoping you'd come live in Wedlock Creek. I suppose now you'll move to the ranch like she always dreamed."

Reed raised an eyebrow. "I've rented a house right in town. I loved my grandmother dearly, but she was trying to bribe me into getting married and starting a family. I had her number, all right." He smiled at Annie, but his chin was lifted. The detective was clearly assessing the situation.

Annie waved her hand dismissively. "Well, bribe or not, you're married. Your dear grandmother's last will and testament leaves you the ranch when you marry. So now you can take your rightful inheritance."

Norah glanced from Annie to Reed. What was all this about a ranch and an inheritance? If Reed had intended to find some drunk fool to marry to satisfy the terms and get his ranch, why would he have rented a house his first day in town?

The detective crossed his arms over his chest. "I have no intention of moving to the ranch, Annie."

"Oh, hogwash!" Annie said, waving her piece of

toast. "You're married and that's it. You should move to the ranch like your grandmamma intended, and poor Norah here will have a father for the triplets."

Good golly. Watch out for little old ladies with secret agendas. Annie Potterowski had hoodwinked them both!

Norah watched Reed swallow. And felt her cheeks burn.

"Annie," Norah said, hands on hips. "You did know we were drunk! You let us marry anyway!"

"For your own good," Annie said. "Both of you. But I didn't lure you two here. I didn't spike the punch. You came in here of your own free will. I just didn't stop you."

"Can't you arrest her for this?" Norah said to Reed, narrowing her eyes at Annie again.

Annie's eyes widened. "I hope you get a chance to leave town and go somewhere exotic for your honeymoon," she said, clearly trying to change the subject from her subterfuge. "New York City maybe. Or how about Paris? It's so romantic."

Norah threw up her hands. "She actually thinks this is reasonable!"

"Annie, come on," Reed said. "We're not *really* married. A little too much spiked punch, a wedding chapel right in our path, no waiting period required—a recipe for disaster and we walked right into it. We're here to get back the marriage license. Surely you haven't sent it in."

"We'll just rip it up and be on our way," Norah said, glancing at her watch.

"Oh dear. I'm sorry, but that's impossible," Annie said. "I sent Abe to the county courthouse in Brewer about twenty minutes ago. I'm afraid your marriage license—and the sixteen others from yesterday—are well on their way to being deposited. There's a mail slot right in front of the building. Of course, it's Sunday and they're closed, so I reckon you won't be able to drive over to try to get it back."

Reed was staring at Annie with total confusion on his face. "Well, we'll have to do something at some point."

"Yeah," Norah agreed, her head spinning. Between all the spiked punch and the surprise this morning of the wedding rings, and now what appeared to be this crazy scheme of Annie's to not undo what she'd allowed to happen…

"I need coffee," Reed said, shaking his head. "A vat of coffee."

Norah nodded. "Me, too."

"Help yourself," Annie said, gesturing at the coffeepot on the counter as she took a bite of her toast.

Reed sighed and turned to Norah. "Let's go back to your house and talk this through. We need to make a plan for how to undo this."

Norah nodded. "See you, Annie," she said as she headed to the door, despite how completely furious she was with the woman. She'd known Annie all her life and the woman had been nothing but kind to her. Annie had even brought each triplet an adorable stuffed basset hound, her favorite dog, when they'd been born, and had showered them with little gifts ever since.

"Oh, Norah? Reed?" Annie called as they opened the door and stepped onto the porch.

Norah turned back around.

"Congratulations," the elderly officiant said with a sheepish smile and absolute mirth glowing in her eyes.

* * *

Reed had been so fired up when he'd left Norah's house for the chapel that he hadn't realized how chilly it was this morning, barely fifty-five degrees. He glanced over at Norah; all she wore was a T-shirt and her hands were jammed in her pockets as she hunched over a bit. She was cold. He took off his jacket and slipped it around Norah's shoulders.

She started and stared down at the jacket. "Thank you," she said, slipping her arms into it and zipping it up. "I was so out of my mind before, I forgot to grab a sweater." She turned to stare at him. "Of course, now you'll be cold."

"My aching head will keep me warm," he said. "And I deserve the headache—the literal and figurative one."

"We both do," she said gently.

The breeze moved a swath of her hair in her face, the sun illuminating the red and gold highlights, and he had the urge to sweep it back, but she quickly tucked it behind her ear. "I'm a cop. It's my job to serve and protect. I had no business getting drunk, particularly at a town event."

"Well, the punch was spiked with something very strong. And you weren't on duty," she pointed out. "You're not even on the force till tomorrow."

"Still, a cop is always a cop. Unfortunately, by the time I realized the punch had to be spiked, I was too affected by it to care." He wouldn't put himself in a position like that again. Leaving Cheyenne, saying yes to Wedlock Creek—even though it meant he couldn't live in his grandmother's ranch—trying to switch off the city cop he'd been… He'd let down his guard and he'd paid for it with this crazy nonsense. So had Norah.

Damn. Back in Cheyenne, his guard had been so up he'd practically gotten himself killed during a botched stakeout. Where the hell was the happy medium? Maybe he'd never get a handle on *just right*.

"And you said you were glad to forget? Or something like that?" she asked, darting a glance at him.

He looked out over a stand of heavy trees along the side of the road. *Let it go*, he reminded himself. No rehashing, no what-ifs. "I'm here for a fresh start. Now I need a fresh start to my fresh start." He stopped and shook his head. What a mess. "Sixteen couples besides us?" he said, resuming walking. "It's a little too easy to get married in the state of Wyoming."

"Someone should change the law," Norah said. "There should be a waiting period. Blood tests required. Something, anything, so you can't get insta-married."

That was for sure. "It's like a mini Las Vegas. I wonder how many of those couples meant to get married."

"Oh, I'm sure all of them. The Wedlock Creek Wedding Chapel is famous. People come here because of the legend."

He glanced at her. "What legend?"

"Just about everyone who marries at the chapel becomes the parent of multiples in some way, shape or form. According to legend, the chapel has a special blessing on it. A barren witch cast the spell the year the chapel was built in 1895."

Reed raised an eyebrow. "A barren witch? Was she trying to be nice or up to no good?"

"No one's sure," she said with a smile. "But as the mother of triplets, I'm glad I have them."

Reed stopped walking.

She'd said it. It was absolutely true. She was the

mother of *triplets*. No wonder Annie Potterowski had called him a saint last night. The elderly woman had thought he was knowingly marrying a single mother of three babies! "So you got married at the chapel?" He supposed she was divorced, though that must have been one quick marriage.

She glanced down. "No. I never did get married. The babies' father ran for the hills about an hour after I told him the news. We'd been dating for only about three months at that point. I thought we had something special, but I sure was wrong."

Her voice hitched on the word *wrong* and he took her hand. "I'm sorry." The jerk had abandoned her? She was raising baby triplets on her own? One baby seemed like a handful. Norah had three. He couldn't even imagine how hard that had to be.

She bit her lip and forced a half smile, slipping her hand away and into her pocket. "Oh, that's all right. I have my children, who I love to pieces. I have a great family, work I love. My life is good. No complaints."

"Still, your life can't be easy."

She raised an eyebrow. "Whose is? Yours?"

He laughed. "Touché. And I don't even have a pet. Or a plant for that matter."

She smiled and he was glad to see the shadow leave her eyes. "So, what's our plan for getting back our marriage license? I guess we can just drive out to Brewer first thing in the morning and ask for it back. If we get to the courthouse early and spring on them the minute they open, I'm sure we'll get the license back before it's processed."

"Sounds good," he said.

"And if we can't get it back for whatever reason, we'll just have the marriage annulled."

"Like it never happened," he said.

"Exactly," she said with a nod and smile.

Except it had happened and Reed had a feeling he wouldn't shake it off so easily, even with an annulment and the passage of time. The pair of them had gotten themselves into a real pickle as his grandmother used to say.

"So I guess this means you really didn't secretly marry me to get your hands on your grandmother's ranch," Norah said. "Between renting a house the minute you moved here yesterday and talking about annulments, that's crystal clear."

He thought about telling her why he didn't believe in marriage but just nodded instead. Last night, as he'd picked her up and carried her into that chapel, he'd been a man—Fabio the secret service agent—who *did* believe in marriage, who wanted a wife and a house full of kids. He'd liked being that guy. Of course, with the light of day and the headache and stone-cold reality, he was back to Reed Barelli, who'd seen close up that marriage wasn't for him.

Reed envisioned living alone forever, a couple of dogs to keep him company, short-term relationships with women who understood from the get-go that he wasn't looking for commitment. He'd thought the last woman he'd dated—a funny, pretty woman named Valerie was on the same page, but a few weeks into their relationship, she'd wanted more and he hadn't, and it was a mess. Crying, accusations and him saying over and over *But I told you on the first date how I felt.* That was six months ago and he hadn't dated since. He missed sex like crazy, but he wasn't interested in hurting anyone.

They walked in silence, Norah gesturing that they should cross Main Street. As they headed down Norah's street, Sycamore, he realized they'd made their plan and there was really no need for that coffee, after all. He'd walk her home and then—

"Norah! You're alive!"

Reed glanced in the direction of the voice. A young blond woman stood in front of Norah's small, white Cape Cod house, one hand waving at them and one on a stroller with three little faces peering out.

Three. Little. Faces.

Had a two-by-four come out of nowhere and whammed him upside the head?

Just about everyone who marries at the chapel becomes the parent of multiples in some way, shape or form.

Because he'd just realized that the legend of the Wedlock Creek chapel had come true for him.

Chapter 3

Norah was so relieved to see the babies that she rushed over to the porch—forgetting to shove her hand into her pocket and hide the ring that hadn't been on her finger yesterday.

And her sister, Shelby, wasn't one to miss a thing. Shelby's gaze shifted from the ring on Norah's hand to Reed and his own adorned left hand, then back to Norah. "I dropped by the diner this morning with a Greek quiche I developed last night, and Aunt Cheyenne and Mom said they hadn't heard from you. So I figured I'd walk the triplets over and make sure you were all right." She'd said it all so casually, but her gaze darted hard from the ring on Norah's hand to Norah, then back again. And again. Her sister was dying for info. That was clear.

"I'm all right," Norah said. "Everything is a little

topsy-turvy, but I'm fine." She bent over and faced the stroller. "I missed you little darlings." She hadn't spent a night away from her children since they were born.

Shelby gave her throat a little faux clear. "I notice you and this gentleman are wearing matching gold wedding bands and taking walks at 6:30 a.m." Shelby slid her gaze over to Reed and then stared at Norah with her "tell me everything this instant" expression.

Norah straightened and sucked in a deep breath. Thank God her sister was here, actually. Shelby was practical and smart and would have words of wisdom.

"Reed Barelli," Norah said, "this is my sister, Shelby Mercer. Shelby, be the first to meet my accidental husband, Detective Reed Barelli of the Wedlock Creek PD...well, starting tomorrow."

Shelby's green eyes went even wider. She mouthed *What?* to Norah and then said, "Detective, would you mind keeping an eye on the triplets while my sister and I have a little chat?"

Reed eyed the stroller. "Not at all," he said, approaching warily.

Norah opened the door and Shelby pulled her inside. The moment the door closed, Shelby screeched, *"What?"*

Norah covered her face with her hands for a second, shook her head, then launched into the story. "I went to the carnival on Mom and Aunt Cheyenne's orders. The last thing I remember clearly is having a corn dog and winning a stuffed dolphin, which I lost. Then it's just flashes of the night. Reed and I drinking spiked punch—the entire bowl—and going to the chapel and getting married."

"Oh, phew," Shelby said, relief crossing her face.

"I thought maybe you flew to Las Vegas or something crazy. There's no way Annie or Abe would have let you get drunk-married to some stranger. I'm sure you just *think* you got married."

"Yeah, we'd figured that, too," Norah said. "We just got back from Annie's house. Turns out she knows Reed from when he spent summers here as a kid. Apparently she was friends with his late grandmother. She called him a saint last night. Annie married us with her blessing! And our marriage license—along with sixteen others—is already at the county courthouse."

"Waaah! Waah!" came a little voice from outside.

"That sounds like Bea," Norah said. "I'd better go help—"

Shelby stuck her arm out in front of the door. "Oh no, you don't, Norah Ingalls. The man is a police officer. The babies are safe with him for a few minutes." She bit her lip. "What are you two going to do?"

Norah shrugged. "I guess if we can't get back the license before it's processed, we'll have to get an annulment."

"The whole thing is nuts," Shelby said. "Jeez, I thought my life was crazy."

Norah wouldn't have thought anything could top what Shelby had been through right before Norah had gotten pregnant. Her sister had discovered her baby and a total stranger's baby had been switched at birth six months after bringing their boys home from the Wedlock Creek Clinic. Shelby and Liam Mercer had gotten married so that they could each have both boys—and along the way they'd fallen madly in love. Now the four of them were a very happy family.

"You know what else is crazy?" Norah said, her

voice going shaky. "How special it was. The ceremony, I mean. Me—even in my T-shirt and shorts and grubby slip-on sneakers—saying my vows. Hearing them said back to me. In that moment, Shel, I felt so…safe. For the first time in a year and a half, I felt safe." Tears pricked her eyes and she blinked hard.

She was the woman who didn't want love and romance. Who didn't believe in happily-ever-after anymore. So why had getting married—even to a total stranger—felt so wonderful? And yes, so safe?

"Oh, Norah," her sister said and pulled her into a hug. "I know what you mean."

Norah blew out a breath to get ahold of herself. "I know it wasn't real. But in that moment, when Annie pronounced us husband and wife, the way Reed looked at me and kissed me, being in that famed chapel…it was an old dream come true. Back to reality, though. That's just how life is."

Shelby squeezed her hand. "So, last night, did the new Mr. and Mrs. Barelli…?"

Norah felt her cheeks burn. "I don't know. But if we did, it must have been amazing. You saw the man."

Shelby smiled. "Maybe you can keep him."

Norah shook her head. Twice. "I'm done with men, remember? *Done*."

Shelby let loose her evil smile. "Yes, for all other men, sure. Since you're married now."

Norah swallowed. But then she remembered this wasn't real and would be rectified. Brody let out a wail and once again she snapped back to reality. She was no one's bride, no one's wife. There was a big difference between old dreams and the way things really were.

"I'd better go save the detective from the three little screechers."

Norah opened the door and almost gasped at the sight on the doorstep. Brody was in Reed's strong arms, the sleeves of his navy shirt rolled up. He lifted the baby high in the air, then turned to Bea and Bella in the stroller and made a funny face at them before lifting Brody again. "Upsie downsie," Reed said. "Downsie upsie," he added as he lifted Brody again.

Baby laughter exploded on the porch.

Norah stared at Reed and then glanced over at Shelby, who was looking at Reed Barelli in amazement.

"My first partner back in Cheyenne had a baby, and whenever he started fussing, I'd do that and he'd giggle," Reed explained, lifting Brody one more time for a chorus of more triplet giggles.

Bea lifted her arms. Reed put Brody back and did two upsie-downsies with Bea, then her sister.

"I'll let Mom and Aunt Cheyenne know you might not be in today," Shelby said very slowly. She glanced at Reed, positively beaming, much like Annie had done earlier. "I'll be perfectly honest and report you have a headache from the sweet punch."

"Thanks," Norah said. "I'm not quite ready to explain everything just yet."

As her sister said goodbye and walked off in the direction of the diner, Norah appreciated that Shelby hadn't added a "Welcome to the family." She turned back to Reed. He was twisting his wedding ring on his finger.

"So you were supposed to work today?" he asked.

"Yes—and Sundays are one of the busiest at the Pie Diner—but I don't think I'll be able to concentrate. My mom and aunt will be all over me with questions. And now that I think about it, with the festival and carnival continuing today, business should be slow. I'll just make my pot pies here and take them over later, once we're settled on what to say if word gets out."

"Word will get out?" he said. "Oh no—don't tell me Annie and Abe are gossips."

"They're *strategic*," Norah said. "Which is exactly how we ended up married and not sent away last night."

"Meaning they'll tell just enough people, or the right people, to make it hard for us to undo the marriage so easily."

"She probably has a third cousin at the courthouse!" Norah said, throwing up her hands. But town gossip was the least of her problems right now, and boy did she have problems, particularly the one standing across from her looking so damned hot.

She turned from the glorious sight of him and racked her brain, trying to think who she could ask to babysit this morning for a couple hours on such short notice so she could get her pies done and her equilibrium back.

Her family was out of the question, of course. Her sister was busy enough with her own two kids and her secondhand shop to run, plus she often helped out at the diner. There was Geraldina next door, who might be able to take the triplets for a couple of hours, but her neighbor was another huge gossip and maybe she'd seen the two of them return home last night in God knew what state. For all Norah knew, Reed Barelli had carried her down the street like in *An Officer and a Gentleman* and swept her over the threshold of her house.

Huh. Had he?

"You okay?" he asked, peering at her.

Her shoulders slumped. "Just trying to figure out a sitter for the triplets while I make six pot pies. The usual suspects aren't going to work out this morning."

"Consider me at your service, then," he said.

"What?" she said, shaking her head. "I couldn't ask that."

"Least I can do, Norah. I got you into this mess. If I remember correctly, last night you said you'd always wanted to get married at that chapel and I picked you up and said 'Then let's get married.'" He let out a breath. "I still can't quite get over that I did that."

"I like being able to blame it all on you. Thanks." She smiled, grateful that he was so…nice.

"Besides, and obviously, I like babies," he said, "and all I had on my agenda today was re-familiarizing myself with Wedlock Creek."

"Okay, but don't say I didn't try to let you off the hook. Triplet seven-month-olds who are just starting to crawl are pretty wily creatures."

"I've dealt with plenty of wily creatures in my eight-year career as a cop. I've got this."

She raised an eyebrow and opened the door, surprised when Reed took hold of the enormous stroller and wheeled in the babies. She wasn't much used to someone else…being there. "Didn't I hear you tell Annie that you had no intention of ever getting married? I would think that meant you had no intention of having children, either."

"Right on both counts. But I like other people's kids. And babies are irresistible. Besides, yours already adore me."

Brody was sticking up his skinny little arms, smil-

ing at Reed, three little teeth coming up in his gummy
mouth.

"See?" he said.

Norah smiled. "Point proven. I'd appreciate the help.
So thank you."

Norah closed the door behind Reed. It was the strang-
est feeling, walking into her home with her three babies—and her brand-new husband.

She glanced at her wedding ring. Then at his.

Talk about crazy. For a man who didn't intend to
marry or have kids, he now had one huge family, even if
that family would dissolve tomorrow at the courthouse.

As they'd first approached Norah's house on the way
back from Annie and Abe's, Reed had been all set to
suggest they get in his SUV, babies and all, and find
someone, anyone, to open the courthouse. They could
root through the mail that had been dumped through
the slot, find their license application and just tear it up.
Kaput! No more marriage!

But he'd been standing right in front of Norah's door,
cute little Brody in his arms, the small, baby-shampoo-
smelling weight of him, when he'd heard what Norah
had said. Heard it loud and clear. And something inside
him had shifted.

*You know what else is crazy, how special it was. The
ceremony, I mean. Me—even in my T-shirt and shorts
and grubby slip-on sneakers—saying my vows. Hearing
them said back to me. In that moment, Shel, I felt so...
safe. For the first time in a year and a half, I felt safe.*

He'd looked at the baby in his arms. The two little
girls in the stroller. Then he'd heard Norah say something about a dream come true and back to reality.

His heart had constricted in his chest when she'd said she'd felt safe for the first time since the triplets were born. He'd once overheard his mother say that the only time she felt safe was when Reed was away in Wedlock Creek with his paternal grandmother, knowing her boy was being fed well and looked after.

Reed's frail mother had been alone otherwise, abandoned by Reed's dad during the pregnancy, no child support, no nothing. She'd married again, more for security than love, but that had been short-lived. Not even a year. Turned out the louse couldn't stand kids. His mother had worked two jobs to make ends meet, but times had been tough and Reed had often been alone and on his own.

He hated the thought of Norah feeling that way—unsteady, unsure, alone. This beautiful woman with so much on her shoulders. Three little ones her sole responsibility. And for a moment in the chapel, wed to him, she'd felt safe.

He wanted to help her somehow. Ease her burden. Do what he could. And if that was babysitting for a couple hours while she worked, he'd be more than happy to.

She picked up two babies from the stroller, a pro at balancing them in each arm. "Will you take Bea?" she asked.

He scooped up the baby girl, who immediately grabbed his cheek and stared at him with her huge gray-blue eyes, and followed Norah into the kitchen. A playpen was wedged in a nook. She put the two babies inside and Reed put Bea beside them. They all immediately reached for the little toys.

Norah took an apron from a hook by the refrigerator. "If I were at the diner, I'd be making twelve pot pies—

five chicken and three turkey, two beef, and two veggie—but I only have enough ingredients at home to do six—three chicken and three beef. I'll just make them all here and drop them off for baking. The oven in this house can't even cook a frozen pizza reliably."

Reed glanced around the run-down kitchen. It was clean and clearly had been baby-proofed, given the covered electrical outlets. But the refrigerator was strangely loud, the floor sloped and the house just seemed…old. And, he hated to say it, kind of depressing. "Have you lived here long?"

"I moved in a few months after finding out I was pregnant. I'd lived with my mom before then and she wanted me to continue living there, but I needed to grow up. I was going to be a mother—of three—and it was time to make a home. Not turn my mother into a live-in babysitter or take advantage of her generosity. This place was all I could afford. It's small and dated but clean and functional."

"So a kitchen, living room and bathroom downstairs," he said, glancing into the small living room with the gold-colored couch. Baby stuff was everywhere, from colorful foam mats to building blocks and rattling toys. There wasn't a dining room, as far as he could see. A square table was wedged in front of a window with one chair and three high chairs. "How many bedrooms upstairs?"

"Only two. But that works for now. One for me and one for the triplets." She bit her lip. "It's not a palace. It's hardly my dream home. But you do what you have to. I'm their mother and it's up to me to support us."

Everything looked rumpled, secondhand, and it probably was. The place reminded him of his apartment as a kid. His mother hadn't even had her own room. She'd slept on a pull-out couch in the living room and folded it up every morning. She'd wanted so much more for the two of them, but her paycheck had stretched only so far. When he was eighteen, he'd enrolled in the police academy and started college at night, planning to give his mother a better standard of living. But she'd passed away before he could make any of her dreams come true.

A squeal came from the playpen and he glanced over at the triplets. The little guy was chewing on a cloth book, one of the girls was pressing little "piano" keys and the other was babbling and shaking keys.

"Bea's the rabble-rouser," Norah said as she began to sauté chicken breasts in one pan, chunks of beef in another, and then set a bunch of carrots and onions on the counter. "Bella loves anything musical, and Brody is the quietest. He loves to be read to, whereas Bea will start clawing at the pages."

"Really can't be easy raising three babies. Especially on your own," he said.

"It's not. But I'll tell you, I now know what love is. I mean, I love my family. I thought I loved their father. But the way I feel about those three? Nothing I've ever experienced. I'd sacrifice anything for them."

"You're a mother," he said, admiring her more than she could know.

She nodded. "First and foremost. My family keeps trying to set me up on dates. Like any guy would say yes to a woman with seven-month-old triplets." She glanced at Reed, then began cutting up the carrots. "I sure trapped you."

He smiled. "Angelina, international flight attendant,

wasn't a mother of three, remember? She was just a woman out having a good time at a small-town carnival."

She set down the knife and looked at him. "You're not angry that I didn't say anything? That I actually let you marry me without you knowing what you were walking into?"

He moved to the counter and stood across from her. "We were both bombed out of our minds."

She smiled and resumed chopping. "Well, when we get this little matter of our marriage license ripped up before it can be processed, I'll go back to telling my family to stop trying to fix me up and you'll be solving crime all over Wedlock Creek."

"You're not looking for a father for the triplets?" he asked.

"Maybe I should be," she said. "To be fair to them. But right now? No. I have zero interest in romance and love and honestly no longer believe in happily-ever-after. I've got my hands full, anyway."

Huh. She felt the same way he did. Well, to a point. Marriage made her feel safe, but love didn't. Interesting, he thought, trying not to stare at her.

As she pulled open a cabinet, the hinge broke and it almost hit her on the head. Reed rushed over and caught it before it could.

"This place is falling down," he said, shaking his head. "You could have been really hurt. And you could have been holding one of the triplets."

She frowned. "I've fixed that three times. I'll call my landlord. She'll have it taken care of."

"Or I could take care of it right now," he said, surveying the hinge. "Still usable. Have a power drill?"

"In that drawer," she said, pointing. "I keep all the tools in there."

He found the drill and fixed the hinge, making sure it was on tight. "That should do it," he said. "Anything else need fixing?"

"Wow, he babysits *and* is handy?" She smiled at him. "I don't think there's anything else needing work," she said, adding the vegetables into a pot bubbling on the stove. "And thank you."

When the triplets started fussing, he announced it was babysitting time. He scooped up two babies and put them in Exersaucers in the living room, then raced back for the third and set Brody in one, too. The three of them happily played with the brightly colored attachments, babbling and squealing. He pulled Bea out—he knew she was Bea by her yellow shirt, whereas Bella's was orange—and did two upsie-downsies, much to the joy of the other two, who laughed and held up their arms.

"Your turn!" he said to Bella, lifting her high to the squeals of her siblings. "Now you, Brody," he added, putting Bella back and giving her brother his turn.

They sure were beautiful. All three had the same big cheeks and big, blue-gray eyes, wisps of light brown hair. They were happy, gurgling, babbling, laughing seven-month-olds.

Something squeezed in his chest again, this time a strange sensation of longing. With the way he'd always felt about marriage, he'd never have this—babies, a wife making pot pies, a family. And even in this tired old little house, playing at family felt...nicer than he expected.

Brody rubbed his eyes, which Reed recalled meant he was getting tired. Maybe it was nap time? It was barely seven-thirty in the morning, but they'd probably woken before the crack of dawn.

"How about a story?" he asked, sitting on the braided rug and grabbing a book from the coffee table. *"Lulu Goes to the Fair."* A white chicken wearing a baseball cap was on the cover. "Your mother and I went to the fair last night," he told them. "So this book will be perfect." He read them the story of Lulu wanting to ride the Ferris wheel but not being able to reach the step until two other chickens from her school helped her. Then they rode the Ferris wheel together. The end. Bella and Brody weren't much interested in Lulu and her day at the fair, but Bea was rapt. Then they all started rubbing their eyes and fussing.

It was now eight o'clock. Maybe he'd put the babies back in the playpen to see if he could help Norah. Not that he could cook, but he could fetch.

He picked up the two girls and headed back into the kitchen, smiled at Norah, deposited the babies in the playpen and then went to get Brody.

"Thank you for watching them," she said. "And reading to them."

"Anytime," he said. Which felt strange. Did he mean that?

"You're sure you didn't win Uncle of the Year or something? How'd you get so good with babies?"

"Told you. I like babies. Who doesn't? I picked up a few lessons on the job, I guess."

Why had he said "anytime" though? That was kind of loaded.

With the babies set for the moment, he shook the thought from his scrambled head and watched Norah cook, impressed with her multitasking. She had six tins covered in pie crust. The aromas of the onions and chicken and beef bubbling in two big pots filled the kitchen. His stomach growled. Had they eaten breakfast? He suddenly realized they hadn't.

"I made coffee and toasted a couple of bagels," she said as if she could read his mind. She was so multi-talented, he wouldn't be surprised if she could. "I have cream cheese and butter."

"You're doing enough," he said. "I'll get it. What do you want on yours?"

"Cream cheese. And thanks."

He poured the coffee into mugs and took care of the bagels, once again so aware of her closeness, the physicality of her. He couldn't help but notice how incredibly sexy she was, standing there in her jeans and maroon T-shirt, the way both hugged her body. There wasn't anywhere to sit in the kitchen, so he stood by the counter, drinking the coffee he so desperately needed.

"The chief mentioned the Pie Diner is the place for lunch in Wedlock Creek. I'm sure I'll be eating one of those pies tomorrow."

She smiled. "Oh, good. I'll have to thank him for that. We need to attract the newcomers to town before the burger place gets 'em." She took a long sip of her coffee. "Ah, I needed that." She took another sip, then a bite of her bagel. She glanced at him as if she wanted to ask something, then resumed adding the pot pie mixtures into the tins. "You moved here for a fresh start, you said?"

He'd avoided that question earlier. He supposed he could answer without going into every detail of his life.

He sipped his coffee and nodded. "I came up for my grandmother's funeral a few months ago. She was the last of my father's family. When she passed, I suddenly wanted to be here, in Wedlock Creek, where I'd spent those good summers. After a bad stakeout a few weeks ago that almost got me killed and did get my partner injured, I'd had it. I quit the force and applied for a job in Wedlock Creek. It turns out a detective had retired just a few weeks prior."

"Sorry about your grandmother. Sounds like she was very special to you."

"She was. My father had taken off completely when I was just a month old, but my grandmother refused to lose contact with me. She sent cards and gifts and called every week and drove out to pick me up every summer for three weeks. It's a three-hour drive each way." He'd never forget being seven, ten, eleven and staring out the window of his apartment, waiting to see that old green car slowly turn up the street. And when it did, emotion would flood him to the point that it would take him a minute to rush out with his bag.

"I'm so glad you had her in your life. You never saw your dad again?"

"He sent the occasional postcard from all over the west. Last one I ever got was from somewhere in Alaska. Word came that he died and had left instructions for a sea burial. I last saw him when I was ten, when he came back for his dad's funeral—my grandfather."

"And your mom?"

"It was hard on her raising a kid alone without much money or prospects. And it was just me. She remarried, but that didn't work out well, either, for either of us." He took a long slug of the coffee. He needed to change the subject. "How do you manage three babies with two hands?"

She smiled and lay pie crust over the tins, making some kind of decoration in the center. "Same way you did bringing the triplets from the kitchen to the living room. You just have to move fast and be constantly on guard. I do what I have to. That's just the way it is."

An angry wail came from the playpen. Then another. The three Ingalls triplets began rubbing their eyes again, this time with very upset little faces.

"Perfect timing," she said. "The pies are assembled." She hurried to the sink to wash her hands, then hurried over to the playpen. "Nap time for you cuties."

"I'll help," Reed said, putting down his mug.

Brody was holding up his arms and staring at Reed. Reed smiled and picked him up, the little weight sweet in his arms. Brody reached up and grabbed Reed's cheek, like his sister had, not that there was much to grab. Norah scooped up Bea and Bella. They headed upstairs, the unlined wood steps creaky and definitely not baby-friendly when they would start to crawl, which would probably be soon.

The nursery was spare but had the basics. Three cribs, a dresser and changing table. The room was painted a pale yellow with white stars and moons stenciled all over.

"Ever changed a diaper?" she asked as she put both babies in a crib, taking off their onesies.

"Cops have done just about everything," he said. "I've changed my share of diapers." He laid the baby on the changing table. "Phew. Just wet." He made quick work of the task, sprinkling on some cornstarch powder and fastening a fresh diaper.

"His jammies are in the top drawer. Any footsie ones."

Reed picked up the baby and carried him over to the dresser, using one hand to open the drawer. The little baby clothes were very neatly folded. He pulled out the top footed onesie, blue cotton with dinosaurs. He set Brody down, then gently put his little arms and legs into the right holes, and there Brody was, all ready for bed. He held the baby against his chest, Brody's impossibly little eyes drooping, his mouth quirking.

He tried to imagine his own father holding him like this, his own flesh and blood, and just walking away. No look back. No nothing. How was it possible? Reed couldn't fathom it.

"His crib is on the right," Norah said, pointing as she took one baby girl out of the crib and changed her, then laid her down in the empty crib. She scooped up the other baby, changed her and laid her back in the crib.

He set Brody down and gave his little cheek a caress. Brody grabbed his thumb and held on.

"He sure does like you," Norah whispered.

Reed swallowed against the gushy feeling in the region of his chest. As Brody's eyes drifted closed, the tiny fist released and Reed stepped back.

Norah shut off the light and turned on a very low lullaby player. After half a second of fussing, all three babies closed their eyes, quirking their tiny mouths and stretching their arms over their heads.

"Have a good nap, my loves," Norah said, tiptoeing toward the door.

Reed followed her, his gold band glinting in the dim light of the room. He stared at the ring, then at his surroundings. He was in a nursery. With the woman he'd accidentally married. And with her triplets, whom he'd just babysat, read to and helped get to nap time.

What the hell had happened to his life? A day ago he'd been about to embark on a new beginning here in Wedlock Creek, where life had once seemed so idyllic out in the country where his grandmother had lived alone after she'd been widowed. Instead of focusing on reading the WCPD manuals and getting up to speed on open cases, he was getting his heart squeezed by three eighteen-pound tiny humans.

And their beautiful mother.

As he stepped into the hallway, the light cleared his brain. "Well, I guess I'd better get going. Pick you up at eight thirty tomorrow for the trip to Brewer? The courthouse opens at nine. Luckily, I don't report for duty until noon."

"Sounds good," she said, leading the way downstairs. "Thanks for helping. You put Brody down for his nap like a champ."

But instead of heading toward the door, he found himself just standing there. He didn't want to leave the four Ingalls alone. On their own. In this falling-down house.

He felt…responsible for them, he realized.

But he also needed to take a giant step backward and catch his breath.

So why was it so hard to walk out the door?

Chapter 4

At exactly eight thirty on Monday morning, Norah saw Reed pull up in front of her house. He must be as ready to get this marriage business taken care of as she was. Yesterday, after he'd left, she'd taken a long, hot bubble bath upstairs, ears peeled for the triplets, but they'd napped for a good hour and a half. In that time, a zillion thoughts had raced through her head, from the bits and pieces she remembered of her evening with Fabio to the wedding to waking up to find Detective Reed Barelli in her bed to how he played upsie-downsie with the triplets and read them a story. And fixed her bagel. And the cabinet.

She couldn't stop thinking about him, how kind he'd been, how good-natured about the whole mess. It had been the man's first day in town. And he'd found himself married to a mother of three. She also couldn't stop thinking about how he'd looked in those black boxer briefs, how tall and muscular he was. The way his dark eyes crinkled at the corners.

After the triplets had woken up, she'd gotten them into the stroller and moseyed on down to the Pie Diner with her six contributions. She'd been unable to keep her secret and had told her mother and aunt everything, trying to not be overheard by their part-time cook and the two waitresses coming in and out. She'd explained it all and she could see on her sister's face how relieved Shelby was at not having to keep her super-juicy family secret anymore.

"That Annie!" Aunt Cheyenne had said with a wink. "Always looking out for us."

Arlena Ingalls had had the same evil smile. "Handsome?"

"Mom!" Norah had said. "He's a stranger!"

"He's hardly that now," her mother had pointed out, glancing at an order ticket and placing two big slices of quiche Lorraine on a waitress's tray.

Aunt Cheyenne had laughed. "I have to hand it to you. We send you to the carnival for your first night out in seven months and you come home married. And to the town's new detective. I, for one, am very impressed."

After talk had turned to who had possibly spiked the punch, Norah, exasperated, had left. Her mother had offered to watch the triplets this morning so that Norah could get her life straightened out and back together. "If you absolutely have to," her mother had added.

Humph, Norah thought now, watching Reed get out of his dark blue SUV. As if marriage was the be-all and end-all. As if a good man was a savior. They didn't even know if Reed was a good man.

But she did, dammit. That had been obvious from the get-go, from the moment he'd stuffed that hundred in the till box to pay what he'd thought was fair for swiping all the punch to picking her up and taking her into the chapel to fulfill her dream of getting married there. He was a good man when bombed out of his ever-loving mind. He was a good man stone-cold sober, who played upsie-downsie with babies, making sure each got their turn. He'd fixed her broken cabinet.

And damn, he really was something to look at. His thick, dark hair shone in the morning sun. He wore charcoal-colored pants, a gray button-down shirt and black shoes. He looked like a city detective.

In the bathtub, as she'd lain there soaking, and all last night in bed, in between trips to the nursery to see why one triplet or another was crying or shrieking, she'd thought about Reed Barelli and how he'd looked in those boxer briefs. She was pretty sure they hadn't had sex. She would remember, wouldn't she? Tidbits of the experience, at least. There was no way that man, so good-looking and sexy, had run his hands and mouth all over her and she hadn't remembered a whit of it.

Anyway, their union would be no more in about a half hour. It was fun to fantasize about what they might have done Saturday night, but only because it was just that—fantasy. And Reed would be out of her life very soon, just someone she'd say hi to in the coffee shop or grocery store. Maybe they'd even chuckle at the crazy time they'd up and gotten married by accident.

She waited for the doorbell to ring, but it didn't. Reed wouldn't be one to wait in the car and honk, so she peered out the window. He stood on the doorstep, typing something into his phone. Girlfriend, maybe.

The man had to be involved with someone. He'd probably been explaining himself from the moment he'd left Norah's house this morning. Poor guy.

Her mom had already come to pick up the babies, so she was ready to go. She wore a casual cotton skirt and top for the occasion of getting back their marriage license, but in the back of her mind she was well aware she'd dolled up a little for the handsome cop. A little mascara, a slick of lip gloss, a tiny dab of subtle perfume behind her ears.

Which was all ridiculous, considering she was spending her morning undoing her ties to the man!

A text buzzed on her phone.

Not sure if the cutes are sleeping, so didn't want to ring the doorbell.

Huh. He hadn't been texting a girlfriend; he'd been texting *her*. Maybe there was no girlfriend.

She glanced at the text again. The warmth that spread across her heart, her midsection, made her smile. The cutes. An un-rung doorbell so as not to disturb the triplets. If she needed more proof that Reed Barelli was top-notch, she'd gotten it.

She took a breath and opened the door. Why did he have to be so good-looking? She could barely peel her eyes off him. "Morning," she said. "My mom has the triplets, so we're good to go."

"I got us coffee and muffins," he said, holding up a bag from Java Joe's. "Light, no sugar, right? That's how you took your coffee yesterday."

She smiled. "You don't miss much, I've been noticing."

"Plight of the detective. Once we see it, it's imprinted."

"What kind of muffins?" she asked, trying not to stare at his face.

"I took you for a cranberry-and-orange type," he said, opening the passenger door for her.

She smiled. "Sounds good." She slid inside his SUV. Clean as could be. Two coffees sat in the center console, one marked *R*, along with a smattering of change and some pens in one of the compartments.

"And I also got four other kinds of muffins in case you hate cranberry and orange," he said, handing her the cup that wasn't marked regular.

Of course he had, she thought, her heart pinging. She kept her eyes straight ahead as he rounded the hood and got inside. When he closed his door, she was ridiculously aware of how close he was.

"Thanks," she said, touched by his thoughtfulness.

"So, it's a half hour to the courthouse, we'll get back our license and that's that." He started the SUV and glanced at her.

She held his gaze for a moment before sipping her coffee to have something to do that didn't involve looking at him.

Would be nice to keep the fantasy going a little longer, she thought. *That we're married, a family, my mom is babysitting while we go off to the county seat to... admire the architecture, have brunch in a fancy place.* Once upon a time, this was all she'd wanted. To find her life's partner, to build a life with a great guy, have children, have a family. But everything had gotten turned on its head. Now she barely trusted herself, let alone anyone she wasn't related to.

Ha, maybe that was why she seemed to trust Reed. He was related to her. For the next half hour, anyway.

By the time they arrived at the courthouse, a beautiful white historic building, she'd finished her coffee and had half a cranberry-and-orange muffin and a few bites of the cinnamon chip. Reed was around to open her door for her before she could even reach for the handle. "Well, this is it—literally and figuratively."

"This is it," she repeated, glancing at him. He held her gaze for a moment and she knew he had to be thinking, *Thank God. We're finally here. Let's get this marriage license ripped up!*

They headed inside. The bronze mail slot on the side of the door loomed large. She could just imagine sneaky, old Abe Potterowski racing over and shoving all the licenses in. As they entered through the revolving door, Norah glanced at the area under the mail slot. Just an empty mail bucket was there.

Empty. Of course it was. Every step of this crazy process was going to be difficult.

After getting directions to the office that handled marriage licenses, they took the elevator to the third floor.

Maura Hotchner, County Clerk was imprinted on a plaque to the left of the doorway to Office 310. They went in and Norah smiled at the woman behind the desk.

"Ms. Hotchner, my name is Norah—"

"Good morning!" the woman said with a warm smile. "Ms. Hotchner began her maternity leave today. I'm Ellen Wheeler, temporary county clerk and Ms. Hotchner's assistant. How may I help you?"

Norah explained that she was looking for her marriage license and wanted it back before it could be processed.

"Oh dear," Ellen Wheeler said. "Being my first day and all taking over this job, I got here extra early and processed all the marriage licenses deposited into the mail slot over the weekend. Do you believe there were seventeen from Wedlock Creek alone? I've already put the official decrees for all those in the mail."

Norah's heart started racing. "Do you mean to tell me that my marriage to this man is legally binding?"

The county clerk looked from Norah to Reed, gave him a "my, you're a handsome one" smile, then looked back at Norah. "Yes, ma'am. It's on the books now. You're legally wed."

Oh God. Oh God. Oh God. This can't be happening.

She glanced at Reed, whose face had paled. "Can't you just erase everything and find our decree and rip it up? Can you just undo it all? I mean, you just processed it—what?—fifteen minutes ago, right? That's what the delete key is for!"

The woman seemed horrified by the suggestion. "Ma'am, I'm sorry, but I most certainly cannot just 'erase' what is legally binding. The paperwork has been processed. You're officially married."

Facepalm. "Is this the correct office to get annulment forms?" Norah asked. At least she wouldn't walk out of there empty-handed. She would get the ball rolling to undo this…crazy mistake.

Ellen's face went blank as she stared from Norah to Reed to their wedding rings and then back at Norah. "I have them right here."

Norah clutched the papers and hurried away. She could barely get to the bench by the elevators without collapsing.

Reed put his hand on her shoulder. "Are you all right? Can I get you some water?"

"I'm fine," she said. "No, I'll be fine. I just can't believe this. We're married!"

"So we are," he said, sitting beside her. "We'll fill out the annulment paperwork and I'm sure it won't take long to resolve this."

She glanced at the instruction form attached to the form. "Grounds for annulment include insanity. That's us, all right."

He laughed and held her gaze for a moment, then shoved his hands into his pockets and looked away.

"I guess I'll fill this out and then give it to you to sign?" she said, flipping through the few pages. She hated important forms with their tiny boxes. She let out a sigh.

He nodded and reached out his hand. "Come on. Let's go home."

For a split second she was back in her fantasy of him being her husband and having an actual home to go to that wasn't falling down around her with sloping floors and a haunted refrigerator. She took his hand and never wanted to let go.

She really was insane. She had to be. What the hell was going on with her? It's like she had a wild crush on this man.

Her husband!

As Reed turned onto the road for Wedlock Creek, he could just make out the old black weather vane on top of his grandmother's barn in the distance. The house wasn't in view; it was a few miles out from here, but that weather vane, with its arrows and mother and baby buffalo, had always been a landmark when that old green car would get to this point for his stay at his grandmother's.

"See that weather vane?" he said, pointing.

Norah bent over a bit. "Oh yes, I do see it now."

"That's my grandmother's barn. When I was a kid heading up here from our house, I'd see that weather vane and all would be right in the world."

"I'd love to see the property," she said. "Can we stop?"

He'd driven over twice Saturday morning, right after he'd arrived in Wedlock Creek, but he'd stayed in the car. He loved the old ranch house and the land, and he'd keep it up, but it was never going to be his, so he hadn't wanted to rub the place in his own face. Though, technically, until his marriage was annulled, it *was* his. His grandmother must be mighty happy right now at his situation. He could see her thinking he'd finally settle down just to be able to have the ranch, then magically fall madly in love with his wife and be happy forever. Right.

He pulled onto the gravel road leading to the ranch and, as always, as the two-story, white farmhouse came into view, his heart lurched. Home.

God, he loved this place. For some of his childhood, when his grandfather had been alive, he'd stayed only a week, which was as long as the grouchy old coot could bear to have him around. But when he'd passed, his grandmother had him stay eight weeks, almost the whole summer. A bunch of times his grandmother had told his mother she and Reed could move in, but his mother had been proud and living with her former mother-in-law had never felt right.

Norah gasped. "What a beautiful house. I love these farmhouses. So much character. And that gorgeous red door and the black shutters…"

He watched her take in the red barn just to the left of the house, which was more like a garage than a place for horses or livestock. Then her gaze moved to the acreage, fields of pasture with shade trees and open land. A person could think out here, dream out here, *be* out here.

"I'd love to see inside," she said.

He supposed it was all right. He did have a key, after all. Always had. And he was married, so the property was out of its three-month limbo, since he'd fulfilled the terms of the will.

He led the way three steps up to the wide porch that wrapped around the side of the house. How many chocolate milks had he drunk, how many stories had his grandmother told him on this porch, on those two rocking chairs with the faded blue cushions?

The moment he stepped inside, a certain peace came over him. Home. Where he belonged. Where he wanted to be.

The opposite of how he'd felt about the small house he'd rented near the police department. Sterile. Meh. Then again, he'd had the place only two days and hadn't even slept there Saturday night. His furniture from his condo in Cheyenne fit awkwardly, nothing quite looking right no matter where he moved the sofa or the big-screen TV.

"Oh, Reed, this place is fantastic," Norah said, looking all around. She headed into the big living room with its huge stone fireplace, the wall of windows facing the fields and huge trees and woods beyond.

His grandmother had had classic taste, so even the

furniture felt right to him. Brown leather sofas, club chairs, big Persian rugs. She'd liked to paint and her work was hung around the house, including ones of him as a boy and a teenager.

"You sure were a cute kid," Norah said, looking at the one of him as a nine-year-old. "And I'm surprised I never ran into you during your summers here. I would have had the biggest crush on that guy," she added, pointing at the watercolor of him at sixteen.

He smiled. "My grandmother didn't love town or people all that much. When I visited, she'd make a ton of food and we'd explore the woods and go fishing in the river just off her land."

The big, country kitchen with its white cabinets and bay window with the breakfast nook was visible, so she walked inside and he followed. He could tell she loved the house and he couldn't contain his pride as he showed her the family room with the sliders out to a deck facing a big backyard, then the four bedrooms upstairs. The master suite was a bit feminine for his taste with its flowered rose quilt, but the bathroom was something—spa tub with jets, huge shower, the works. Over the years he'd updated the house as presents for his grandmother, happy to see her so delighted.

"I can see how much this place means to you," Norah said as they headed back downstairs into the living room. "Did it bother you that your grandmother wrote her will the way she did? That you had to marry to inherit it?"

"I didn't like it, but I understood what she was trying to do. On her deathbed, she told me she knew me better than I knew myself, that I did need a wife and children and this lone-wolf-cop nonsense wouldn't make me happy."

Maybe your heart will get broken again, but loss is part of life, Lydia Barelli had added. *You don't risk, you don't get.*

Broken again. Why had he ever told his grandmother that he'd tried and where had it gotten him? Those final days of his grandmother's life, he hadn't been in the mood to talk any more about the one woman he'd actually tried to be serious about. He'd been thinking about proposing, trying to force himself out of his old, negative feelings, when the woman he'd been seeing for almost a year told him she'd fallen for a rich lawyer— sorry. He hadn't let himself fall for anyone since, and that was over five years ago. Between that and what he'd witnessed about marriage growing up? Count him out.

Reed hadn't wanted to disappoint his beloved grandmother and had told her, "Who knows what the future holds?" He couldn't outright lie and say he was sure he'd change his mind about marriage. But he wouldn't let his grandmother go on thinking no one on this earth would ever love him. She wouldn't have been able to abide that.

"*Have* you been happy?" Norah asked, glancing at him, then away as if to give him some privacy.

He shrugged. "Happy enough. My work was my life and it sustained me a long time. But when I lost the only family I had, someone very special to me, I'll tell you, I *felt* it."

"It?" she repeated.

"Loss of…connection, I guess."

She nodded. "I felt that way when my dad died, and I had my mother, aunt and sister crying with me. I can't imagine how alone you must have felt."

He turned away, looking out the window. "Well, we should get going. I have to report to the department for my orientation at noon. Then it's full-time tomorrow."

"Thanks for showing me the house. I almost don't want to leave. It's so…welcoming."

He glanced around and breathed in the place. They had to leave. *He* had to leave. Because this house was never going to be his. And being there hurt like hell.

Chapter 5

Reed sat in his office in the Wedlock Creek Police Department, appreciating the fact that he had an office, even if it was small, with a window facing Main Street, so he could see the hustle and bustle of downtown. The two-mile-long street was full of shops and restaurants and businesses. The Pie Diner was just visible across the street if he craned his neck, which he found himself doing every now and again for a possible sighting of Norah.

His wife for the time being.

He hadn't seen her around today since dropping her off. But looking out the window had given him ideas for leads and follow-ups on a few of the open cases he'd inherited from his retired predecessor. Wedlock Creek might not have had a murder in over seventy years—knock on wood—but there was the usual crime, ranging from the petty to the more serious. The most pressing involved a missing person's case that would be his focus. A thirty-year-old man, an ambulance-chasing attorney named David Dirk who was supposed to get married this coming Saturday, had gone missing three days ago. No one had heard from him and none of his credit cards had been used, yet there was no sign of foul play.

David Dirk. Thirty. Had to be the same guy. When Reed was a kid, a David Dirk was his nearest neighbor and they'd explore their land for hours during the summers Reed had spent at his grandmother's. David had been a smart, inquisitive kid who'd also had a father who'd taken off. He and Reed would talk about what jerks their dads were, then laud them as maybe away on secret government business, unable to tell their wives or children that they were really saving the world. That was how much both had needed to believe, as kids, that their fathers were good, that their fathers did love them, after all. David's family had moved and they'd lost touch as teenagers and then time had dissolved the old ties.

Reed glanced at the accompanying photo stapled to the left side of the physical file. He could see his old friend in the adult's face. The same intense blue eyes behind black-framed eyeglasses, the straight, light brown hair. Reed spent the next hour reading through the case file and notes about David's disappearance.

The man's fiancée, Eden Pearlman, an extensions specialist at Hair Palace on Main Street, was adamant that something terrible had happened to her "Davy Darling" or otherwise he would have contacted her. According to Eden, Davy must be lying gravely injured in a ditch somewhere or a disgruntled associate had hurt him, because marrying her was the highlight of his life. Reed sure hoped neither was the case. He would interview Ms. Pearlman tomorrow and get going on the investigation.

In the meantime, though, he called every clinic and hospital within two hours to check if there were any John Does brought in unconscious. Each one said no. Then Reed read through the notes about David's last case, which he'd won big for his client a few days prior to his disappearance. A real-estate deal that had turned ugly. Reed researched the disgruntled plaintiff, who'd apparently spent the entire day that David was last seen at a family reunion an hour away. Per the notes, the plaintiff was appealing and had stated he couldn't wait to see his opponent and his rat of a lawyer in court again, where he'd prevail this time. Getting rid of David in some nefarious way certainly wouldn't get rid of the case; Reed had his doubts the man had had anything to do with David's disappearance.

So where are you, David? What the heck happened to you?

Frustrated by the notes and his subsequent follow-up calls getting him nowhere, Reed packed up his files at six. Tomorrow would be his first full day on the force and he planned to find David Dirk by that day's end. Something wasn't sitting right in his gut about the case, but he couldn't put his finger on it. He'd need to talk to the fiancée and a few other people.

As he left the station, he noticed Norah coming out of a brick office building, wheeling the huge triple stroller. He eyed the plaque on the door: Dr. Laurel McCray, Pediatrician. Brody in the front was screaming his head off. Bella was letting out shrieks. Or was that Bea? All he knew for sure was that one of the girls, seated in the middle, was quiet, picking up Cheerios from the narrow little tray in front of her and eating them.

He crossed the street and hurried up to her. "Norah? Everything okay?"

She looked as miserable as the two little ones. "I just came from their pediatrician's office. Brody was tugging at his ear all afternoon and crying. Full-out ear infection. He's had his first dose of antibiotics, but they haven't kicked in yet."

"Poor guy," Reed said, kneeling and running a finger along Brody's hot, tearstained cheek. Brody stopped crying for a moment, so Reed did it again. When he stood, Brody let out the wail of all wails.

"He really does like you," Norah said, looking a bit mystified for a moment before a mix of mom weariness came over her. "Even Bella has stopped crying, so double thank you."

As if on cue, Bella started shrieking again and, from the smell of things, Reed had a feeling she wasn't suffering from the same issue as her brother. People walking up and down the street stared, of course, giving concerned smiles but being nosey parkers.

Norah's shoulders slumped. "I'd better get them home."

"Need some help?" he asked. "Actually, I meant that rhetorically, so don't answer. You do need help and I'm going home with you."

"Reed, I can't keep taking advantage of how good you are with babies."

"Yes, you can. I mean, what are husbands for if not for helping around the house?"

She laughed. "I can't believe you actually made me laugh when I feel like crying."

"Husbands are good for that, too," he said before he could catch himself. He was kidding, trying to lighten her load, but he actually *was* her husband. And there was nothing funny about it.

"Well, you'll be off the hook in a few days," she said. "I filled out the annulment form and all you have to do is sign it and I'll send it in. It's on my coffee table."

She hadn't wasted any time. Or Norah Ingalls was just very efficient, despite having triplet babies to care for on her own. He nodded. "Well, then, I'm headed to the right place."

Within fifteen minutes they were in Norah's cramped, sloping little house. He held poor Brody while Norah changed Bella, who'd stopped shrieking, but all three babies were hungry and it was a bit past dinnertime.

Reed was in charge of Brody, who was unusually responsive to him, especially when his little ears were hurting, so he sat in front of Brody's high chair, feeding him his favorite baby food, cereal with pears. Norah was on a chair next to him, feeding both girls. Bella was in a much better mood now that her Cheerios had been replenished and she was having pureed sweet potatoes. Bea was dining on a jar of pureed green beans.

Reed got up to fill Brody's sippy cup with water when he stopped in his tracks.

On the refrigerator, half underneath a Mickey Mouse magnet, was a wedding invitation.

Reed stared at it, barely able to believe what he was seeing.

Join Us For
The Special Occasion of Our Wedding
Eden Pearlman and David Dirk...

Norah was invited to the wedding? He pulled the invitation off the fridge. "Bride or groom?" he asked, holding up the invitation.

Norah glanced up, spoon full of green bean mush midway to Bea's open mouth. "Groom, actually. I'm surprised he invited me. I dated David Dirk for two weeks a couple years ago. He ditched me for the woman he said was the love of his life. She must be, because I got that invitation about six weeks ago."

"You only dated for two weeks?" Reed asked.

She nodded. "We met at the Pie Diner. He kept coming in and ordering the pot pie of the day. I thought it was about the heavenly pot pies, but apparently it was me he liked. He asked me out. We had absolutely nothing in common and nothing much to talk about over coffee and dinner. But I'll tell ya, when my sister, Shelby, needed an attorney concerning something to do with her son Shane, I recommended David based on his reputation. He represented her in a complicated case and she told me he did a great job."

He tucked that information away. "No one has seen or heard from him in three days. According to the case notes, his fiancée thinks there was foul play, but my predecessor found no hint of that."

"Hmm. David was a real ambulance chaser. He had a few enemies. Twice someone said to me, 'How could you date that scum?'"

His eyebrow shot up. "Really? Recall who?"

"I'll write down their names for you. Gosh, I hope David's okay. I mean, he was a shark, but, like I said, when Shelby *needed* a shark, he did well by her. I didn't get to know him all that well, but he was always a gentleman, always a nice guy. We just had nothing much to say to each other. Zero chemistry."

He was about to put the invitation back on the fridge. "Mind if I keep this?" he asked.

She shook her head. "Go right ahead." She turned back to her jars of baby food and feeding the girls. "Brody seems calmer. The medicine must have kicked in." She leaned over and gave his cheek a gentle stroke. "Little better now, sweet pea?"

Brody banged on his tray and smiled.

"Does that mean you want some Cheerios?" Reed asked, sitting back down. He handed one to Brody, who took it and examined it, then popped it in his mouth, giving Reed a great gummy smile, three little jagged teeth making their way up.

Bea grabbed her spoon just as Norah was inching it toward her mouth and it ended up half in Bea's hair, half in Norah's.

"Oh, thanks," Norah said with a grin. "Just what I wanted in my hair." She tickled Bea's belly. "And now the three of you need a bath." She laughed and shook her head.

By eight o'clock, Norah had rinsed the baby food from her hair, all three babies had been fed, bathed, read to and it was time for bed. Reed stood by the door as Norah sang a lullaby in her lovely whispered voice. He almost nodded off himself.

"Well, they're asleep," she said, walking out of the nursery and keeping the door ajar. "I can't thank you enough for your help tonight, Reed."

"It was no trouble."

For a moment, as he looked into her hazel eyes, the scent of pears clinging to her shirt, he wanted to kiss her so badly that he almost leaned forward. He caught himself at the last second. What the hell? He couldn't kiss Norah. They weren't a couple. They weren't even dating.

Good Lord, they were married.

And he wanted to kiss her, passionately, kiss her over to that lumpy-looking gold couch and explore every inch of her pear-smelling body. But he couldn't, not with everything so weird between them. And things were definitely weird.

He was supposed to sign annulment papers. But those papers on the coffee table had been in his line of vision for the past two hours and he'd ignored them. Even after Norah had mentioned them when they'd first arrived tonight. "There are the papers," she'd said, gesturing with her chin. Quite casually.

But he'd bypassed the forms and fed Brody instead. Rocked the little guy in his arms while Norah gave his sisters a bath. Changed Brody into pajamas and sang his own little off-key lullaby about where the buffalos roamed.

And all he could think was *How can I walk away from this woman, these babies? How can I just leave them?*

He couldn't. Signing those annulment papers would mean the marriage never happened. They'd both walk away.

He didn't want to. Or he couldn't. One or the other. He might not want love or a real marriage, but that didn't mean he couldn't step up for Norah.

And then the thought he'd squelched all day came right up in Technicolor.

And if you stay married to Norah, if you step up for

*her, you can have your grandmother's ranch. You can
live there. You can go home. You can all go home, far
away from this crummy little falling-down house.*

Huh. Maybe he and his new bride could make a deal.
They could *stay* married. She'd feel safe every day.
And he could have the Barelli ranch fair and square.

She'd said she was done with romance, done with
love. So was he.

He wondered what she'd think of the proposition. She
might be offended and smack him. Or simply tell him
the idea was ludicrous. Or she might say, "You know
what, you've got yourself a deal" and shake on it. Instead of kiss. Because it would be an arrangement, not
anything to do with romance or feelings.

He'd take these thoughts, this idea, back to the sterile rental and let it percolate. A man didn't propose a
romance-less marriage without giving it intense consideration from all angles.

But only one thought pushed to the forefront of his
head: that he wasn't walking away from Norah and the
triplets. No way, no how. Like father, *not* like son.

Norah was working on a new recipe for a barbecue
pot pie when the doorbell rang. Which meant it wasn't
Reed. He'd just left ten minutes ago and wouldn't ring
the bell knowing the triplets were asleep. Neither would
her sister, mother or aunt.

Please don't be someone selling something, she
thought as she headed to the front door.

Amy Ackerman, who lived at the far end of the
street, stood at the door, holding a stack of files and
looking exasperated. "Oh, thank God, you're here,
Norah. I have to ask the biggest favor."

Norah tried to think of the last time someone had asked a favor of her. Early in her pregnancy, maybe. Before she started showing for sure. People weren't about to ask favors from a single mother of triplets.

"Louisa can't teach the zero-to-six-month multiples class and it starts Wednesday!" Amy shrieked, balancing her files in her hands. "Sixteen people have signed up for the class, including eight pregnant mothers expecting multiples. I can't let them down."

Amy was the director of the Wedlock Creek Community Services Center, which offered all kinds of classes and programming for children and adults. The multiples classes were very popular—the center offered classes in preparing for and raising multiples of all ages. How to feed three-week-old twins at once. How to change triplets' diapers when they were all soaked. How to survive the terrible twos with two the same age. Or three. Or four, in several cases.

During her pregnancy, Norah had taken the prep class and then the zero-to-six-month class twice herself. At the time, she'd been so stressed out about what to expect that she'd barely retained anything she'd learned, but she remembered being comforted by just being there. She'd been the only one without a significant other or husband, too. She'd gotten quite a few looks of pity throughout and, during any partner activities, she'd had to pair up with the instructor, Louisa.

"Given that you just graduated from the real-life course now that the babes are seven months," Amy said, "will you teach it? You'll get the regular fee plus an emergency bonus. The class meets once a week for the next six weeks."

Norah stared at Amy, completely confused. "Me? Teach a class?"

"Yes, you. Who better? Not only do you have triplets, but you're a single mom. You're on your own. And every time I see you with those three little dumplings, I think, 'There goes a champ.'"

Huh. Norah, champ. She kind of liked it.

She also knew she was being buttered up big-time. But still, there was sincerity in Amy's eyes and the woman had always been kind to her. In fact, the first time Norah had signed up for the zero-to-six-month class, Amy had waived the course fee for her, and it wasn't cheap.

But how could she teach a class in anything? She was hardly a pro at being the mother of triplets. Last week Norah had made the rookie mistake of guiding her shopping cart in the grocery store a little too close to the shelves. Bella had managed to knock over an entire display of instant ramen noodles and either Bea or Brody had sent a glass jar of pickles crashing to the floor, blocking the path of a snooty woman who'd given Norah a "control your spawn" dirty look.

Then there was the time Norah had been waiting for a phone call from the pediatrician with test results, couldn't find her phone in her huge tote bag with its gobs of baby paraphernalia and had let go of the stroller for a second to dig in with both hands. The stroller had rolled away, Norah chasing after it. She'd caught someone shaking his head at her. Then there were all the times Norah had been told her babies should be wearing hats, shouldn't have pacifiers and "Excuse me, but are you really feeding your child nonorganic baby food? Do you know what's in that?"

Not to mention all the secret shame. How Brody had almost fallen off the changing table when she'd raced to stop Bea from picking up the plastic eye from a stuffed animal that had somehow come off in her crib. Norah could go on and on and on. She was no Super Mom of Multiples, ages zero to six months.

Thinking of all that deflated her, despite the fact that a minute ago, just being asked to teach the course had made her feel almost special, as though she had something to share with people who could use her help.

"Amy, I'm sorry, but I don't think—" Norah began.

Amy held up a hand. "If anyone is qualified to teach this class, it's you, Norah. And I promise you, I'm not just saying that because I'm desperate. Though I am desperate to find the right instructor. And that's you."

Norah frowned. "I make so many mistakes. All the time."

"Oh. You mean you're human? It's *not* easy taking care of baby triplets? Really?"

Norah found herself smiling. "Well, when you put it like that."

"There's no other way to put it."

"You know what, Amy? Sign me up. I will teach the class." Yeah, she would. Why not? She most certainly *had* been taking care of triplet babies—on her own—for seven months.

But she would have to hire a sitter or ask her mom or aunt to watch the triplets while she taught.

The fee for teaching was pretty good; paying a sitter every week would still leave a nice little chunk left over, and now she'd be able to afford to buy a wall-unit air conditioner for the downstairs. Norah had a feeling her mom and aunt would insist on watching the babies, though; both women had taken the class when Norah was in her ninth month. And even Shelby had signed up when she'd found herself the mother of not one but two six-month-old babies and needed to learn how to multitask on the quick.

The relief that washed over Amy's face made Norah smile. "You've saved me! Here's Louisa's syllabus and notes. You don't have to use her curriculum, though. You may have different ideas. It's your class now, so you make it your own."

That sounded good. "I'm looking forward to it," she said. "And thanks for asking me."

As Amy left, Norah carried the folder into the kitchen and set it down beside the bowl containing her special barbecue sauce, which wasn't quite there yet. Norah's regular barbecue sauce was pretty darn good, but she liked creating specials for the pot pies and wanted something with more of a Louisiana bite. She'd try a new batch, this time with a drop more cayenne pepper and a smidge less molasses. She'd just have to keep trying bits and dashes until she got it just right, which, now that she thought about it, was sometimes how parenting went. Yeah, there were basics to learn, but sometimes you had to be there, doing it, to know what to do.

As she headed to the coffeepot for a caffeine boost, she noticed the manila envelope on the counter. The annulment papers were inside. A yellow Post-it with Reed's name on the outside. Tomorrow she'd drop it off at the station and he'd sign them and she'd send them in or he would. And that would be the end of that.

No more Reed to the rescue, which had been very nice today.

No more fantasy husband and fantasy father.

No more sexy man in her kitchen and living room.

More than all that, she liked the way Reed made her feel. Despite his offers to help, he never looked at her as though she was falling apart or unable to handle all she had on her plate. He made her feel like she could simply use another hand…a partner.

Could the annulment papers accidentally fall behind the counter and disappear? She smiled. She liked this new and improved Norah. Kicking butt and teaching a class. Suddenly wanting her accidental husband to stick around.

Maybe because she knew he wouldn't?

Anyway, one out of two wasn't bad, though. At least she had the class.

Tomorrow she'd be out a husband.

Chapter 6

Norah had filled her tenth pulled pork pot pie of the morning when she noticed Reed Barelli pacing the sidewalk that faced the back windows of the Pie Diner's kitchen. He seemed to be deep in thought. She was dying to know about what. His missing person's case? Or maybe even…her? The annulment papers he'd forgotten to sign last night on his way out?

It's not like I reminded him, she thought. The way he'd come to her rescue last night like some Super Husband had brought back all those old fantasies and dreams. Of someone having her back. Someone to lean on, literally and figuratively. And, oh, how she would love to lean on that very long, sexy form of his, feel those muscular arms wrapped around her.

Focus on your work, she admonished herself. She topped the pot pie with crust and made a design in the center, then set the pie on the tray awaiting the oven for the first of the lunch rush.

"Norah?" a waitress named Evie called out. "There's someone here to see you."

Had to be Reed. He was no longer out back. She quickly washed her hands and took off her apron, then left the kitchen. Reed sat at the far end of the counter. Since it was eleven, late for breakfast and early for lunch, the Pie Diner had very few customers. He was alone at the counter except for their regular, Old Sam, who sat at the first spot just about all day, paying for one slice of pie and coffee and getting endless refills and free pot pie for lunch, which had been the case for over a decade. Norah's mom had a soft spot for the elderly widower who reminded her of her late dad, apparently.

Reed looked...serious. Her heart sank. He must be there to sign the papers.

"I have the papers in my bag," she said. "Guess we both forgot last night. Follow me to the back office and you can sign them there if you want."

He glanced around, then stood and trailed her into the kitchen. The large office doubled as a kiddie nook and the triplets were napping in their baby swings.

She grabbed her tote bag from where it hung on the back of the desk chair and pulled out the annulment papers from the manila envelope.

But Reed wasn't taking the papers. He was looking at the babies.

"I'm glad they're here," he said. "Because I came to say something kind of crazy and seeing the triplets re-inforces that it's actually not crazy. That *I'm* not crazy."

She stared at him, no idea what he could be talking about.

He took the papers from her and set them down on the desk. "Instead of signing those, I have a proposition for you."

Norah tilted her head and caught her mother and aunt and sister all staring at them. She could close the door and give them some privacy, but then she'd only have to repeat what he'd said to her family, so they might as well get the earful straight from him. Besides, they'd never forgive her if she shut them out of this juicy part.

"A proposition?" she repeated.

Out of the corner of her eye, she could see her mother, sister and aunt all shuffle a step closer to the office.

He nodded. "If I sign those papers and you return them to the county clerk, poof, in a week, we're not married anymore. Never happened. Drunken mistake. Whoops. Except it *did* happen. And the intensive couple of days I've been a part of your life makes me unable to just walk away from you and Bella, Bea and Brody. I can't. A man doesn't do that, Norah."

Did she hear a gasp or two or three coming from the kitchen?

She stared at him. "Reed. We got married by accident. By drunken mistake, as you perfectly put it."

"Maybe so. But we also got married. We both stood up there and said our vows. Drunk off our tushes or not, Norah, we got married."

She gaped at him. "So you feel you have to stand by vows you made under total insanity and drunken duress? Why do you think both of those are grounds for annulment?"

"I stand by you and the triplets. And if we're married, if we stay married, I also get to have the Barelli ranch fair and square. I was never planning on getting married. You said you weren't, either. We're both done with love and all that nonsense about happily-ever-after. So why not partner up, since we're already legally bound, and get what we both need?"

"What do I need exactly?" she asked, narrowing her eyes on him.

"You need a safe home, for one. A place big enough for three children growing every single day. You need financial stability and security. You need someone there for you 24/7, having your back, helping, sharing the enormous responsibility of raising triplets. That's what you need."

No kidding. She did need that. She *wanted* that more than she could bear to admit to herself. She also wanted to take responsibility for her own life, her own children, and do it on her own. And it was harder than she even imagined it would be, than her mother had warned her it would be when she'd been so set on moving out and going it alone.

She couldn't be stubborn at the triplets' expense. She would focus on that instead of on how crazy Reed's proposal was. Because when it came right down to it, he was absolutely right about what she needed.

And what *he* needed was his grandmother's ranch. She'd witnessed just how great that need was when they'd been together at the house. The ranch meant so much to him. It was home. It was connection to his family. It was his future. And his being able to call the ranch home came down to her saying yes to his proposition.

Hmm. That proposition was a business deal of sorts. She thought, at least. "I get stability and security and you get the Barelli ranch."

He eyed her and she could tell he was trying to read

her. She made sure she had on her most neutral expression. She had no idea what she thought of his proposal. Stay legally married to a man she'd known for days? For mutual benefit?

"Right," he said. "I need it more than I ever realized. It's home. The only place that's ever felt like home. You could move out of that falling-down, depressing little place and move to the ranch with room and wide-open spaces for everyone."

Her house *was* falling down and depressing. She hated those steep, slippery wooden stairs. And the lease was month to month. It would be a snap to get out of.

But the man was talking about serious legal stuff. Binding. He was talking about keeping their marriage on the books.

She looked up at him. "So we just rip up the papers and, voilà, we're married?"

"We are truly married, Norah. Yeah, we can go through with the annulment. Or we can strike a bargain that serves us both. Neither of us is interested in a real marriage about love and all that jazz. We've both been burned and we're on the same page. Our marriage would be a true partnership based on what we need. I think we'll be quite happy."

Quite happy? She wasn't so sure she'd be even close to happy. Comfortable, maybe. Not afraid, like she was almost all the time.

And what would it be like to feel the way she had during the ceremony? Safe. Secure. Cherished. Sure, the man "promising" those things had been drunk off his behind, but here he was, sober as a hurricane, promising those things all over again.

Maybe not to cherish her. But to stand at her side.

God, she wanted that. Someone trustworthy at her side, having her back, being there.

But what did Reed Barelli, bachelor, know about living 24/7 with babies? What if she let herself say yes to this crazy idea, moved to that beautiful homestead and breathed for the first time in over seven months, and he couldn't handle life with triplets after a week? He had no idea what he was in for.

She raised an eyebrow. "What makes you think you want to live with three seven-month-old, teething babies? Are you nuts?"

He smiled. "Insane, remember?"

He had to be. She had to be. But what did she have to lose? If the partnership didn't work out, he would sign the papers and that would be that.

She could give this a whirl. After all, they were already married. She didn't have to do anything except move into a beautiful ranch house with floors that didn't creak or slope and with an oven that worked all the time. Of course, she would be living with Reed Barelli. Man. Gorgeous man. What would *that* be like?

"Let's try," he whispered.

She looked up at him again, trying to read him. If she said, "Yes, let's try this wild idea of yours," he'd get his ranch. If she said no, he'd never have the only place that had ever felt like home. Reed wouldn't marry just to get the ranch; she truly believed that. But because of a big bowl of spiked punch, he had his one chance. He'd been so kind to her, so good to the triplets.

Brody let out a sigh and Norah glanced over at her son. His little bow-shaped mouth was quirking and a hand moved up along his cheek. The partnership would benefit the triplets and that was all she needed to know.

"I was about to say 'Where do I sign?' but I guess I'm not signing, after all." She picked up the papers and put them back in her tote bag.

The relief that crossed Reed's face didn't go unnoticed. Keeping that ranch meant everything to him. Even if it meant being awakened at 2:00 a.m. by one, two or three crying babies. And again at 3:00 a.m.

Out of the corner of her eye, Norah caught her mother hurrying back over to her station, pretending to be very busy whisking eggs. She poked her head out of the office. "Did y'all hear this crazy plan of his?"

"What? No, we weren't eavesdropping," her mother said. "Okay, we were. And I for one think his crazy plan isn't all that crazy."

"Me, too," Cheyenne said from in front of the oven. "You each get what you need."

Even if it's not what we really want, Norah thought. Reed didn't want to be married. Just as she didn't. Sure, it felt good and safe. But even a good man like Reed couldn't be trusted with her stomped-on heart. No one could. It wasn't up for grabs, hadn't been since the day after she'd found out she was pregnant and had been kicked to the curb.

Shelby sidled over and took Norah's hand. "You don't mind if I borrow your wife, do you?" she asked Reed.

What also didn't go unnoticed? How Reed swallowed, uncomfortably, at the word *wife*.

Wife. Norah was someone's wife. Not just someone's—this man's. This handsome, kind, stand-up man.

"Of course," he said. "I'll keep an eye on the triplets."

Shelby gave him a quick smile, then led Norah by the hand to the opposite end of the kitchen. "Don't forget to figure out the rules."

"The rules?" Norah repeated.

"Just what kind of marriage will this be?" her sister asked. "He used the word *partnership*, but you're also husband and wife. So are you sharing a bedroom?"

Norah felt her face burn. She was hardly a prude, but the thought of having sex with Reed Barelli seemed... sinful in a very good way. They'd hardly worked up to the level of sex. Even if they were married. They weren't even at the first-kiss stage yet.

Norah pictured Reed in his black boxer briefs. "I guess we'll need to have a conversation about that."

"Yeah, you will," Shelby said. "Been there, done that with my own husband back when we first got together. Remember, Liam and I only got married so we could each have both our babies—the ones we'd raised for six months and the ones who were biologically ours."

Norah would never forget that time in Shelby's life. And the fact that all had turned out very well for her sister was a bonus. It wasn't as if Norah and Reed Barelli were going to fall in love. She had zero interest in romance. Yes, Reed was as hot as a man got, but nice to look at was different than feeling her heart flutter when she was around him. That wasn't going to happen. Not to a woman who'd been burned. Not to a busy mother of baby triplets. And it certainly wouldn't happen to Reed. He was even more closed to the concept of love and romance than she was. And as if he'd fall for a woman who'd lost all sex appeal. She smelled like strained apricots and spit-up and baby powder when she wasn't smelling like chicken pot pie. She wasn't exactly hot stuff these days.

"No matter what you're thinking, Norah, don't forget one thing," Shelby said.

Norah tilted her head. "What's that?"

Shelby leaned in and whispered, "He's a man."

"Meaning?"

"What's the statistic about how many times per second men think about sex?" Shelby asked.

Norah let out a snort-laugh and waved a hand down the length of herself. "Oh yeah, I am irresistible." She was half covered in flour. Her hair was up in a messy bun. She wore faded overalls and yellow Crocs.

"Trust me," Shelby said. "The issue will arise." She let out a snort herself. "Get it? *Arise.*" She covered her mouth with her hand, a cackle still escaping.

"You're cracking jokes at a time like this?" Norah said, unable to help the smile.

"I'm just saying. You need to be prepared, Norah. Your life is about to change. And I'm not just talking about a change in address."

That was for sure. She'd be living with a man. Living with Reed Barelli. "Your words of wisdom?" she asked her sister.

"Let what happens happen. Don't fight it."

Norah narrowed her eyes. "What's gonna happen?"

"Let's see. Newlyweds move in together..."

Norah shook her head. "You can stop right there, sistah. We may be newlyweds, but like Reed said, this is a partnership. No hanky-panky. This isn't about romance or love. Nothing is *arising.*"

"We'll see. But just know this, Norah. It's nice to be happy. Trust me on that."

Norah loved that her sister was happy. But the pursuit of happiness wasn't why Norah was saying yes to Reed's proposition.

"I'm finally at a good place, Shel," Norah said. "It

took me a long time to bounce back from being abandoned the way I was. Lied to. Made a fool of. I might not be skipping all over town, but I'm not *un*happy. And I'm not throwing away my equilibrium when my first and foremost job is to be a good mother. I will not, under any circumstances, fall for a guy who's made it crystal clear he feels the same way I do—that love is for other people."

Shelby squeezed her hand. "Well, just know that anytime you need a sitter for an evening out with your husband, I'm available."

"I no longer need sitters because I'll have a live-in sitter."

"Answer for everything, don't you?" Shelby said with a nudge in Norah's midsection. She threw her arms around her and squeezed. "Everything's going to be fine. You'll see."

Norah went back into the office and stared hard at her sleeping babies, then at Reed, who leaned against the desk looking a bit…amused, was it?

"Your sister is right," he said. "Everything *is* going to be fine."

Norah wasn't so sure of that.

And had he heard *everything* they'd said?

Chapter 7

Thanks to the Wedlock Creek PD going digital, copies of all the case files were now a click away and on Reed's smartphone. He was almost glad to have a confounding case to focus on for the next couple of hours while Norah packed for herself and the triplets.

For a while there he'd thought she might say no. The idea *was* crazy. To stay married? As a business partnership? Nuts. Who did that?

People like him whose wily grandmother had him over a barrel.

People like her who could use a solid place to land.

When he'd left the Pie Diner, the annulment papers back in the envelope, unsigned, the ranch rightfully his after a visit to his grandmother's attorney, an unfamiliar shot of joy burst inside him to the point he could have been drunk on spiked punch. The ranch was home for real. He'd wake up there every day. Walk the land he'd explored as a child and teenager. Finally adopt a dog or two or three and a couple of black cats that he'd always been partial to. He was going home.

But right now he was going to find David Dirk, who hadn't been seen or heard from in days. Reed sat in his SUV and read through the notes on his phone. Dirk's fiancée, Eden Pearlman, twenty-five, hair stylist, never before married, no skeletons in the closet, per his predecessor's notes, had agreed to meet with him at her condo at the far end of Main Street.

He stood in front of the building and took it in: five-story, brick, with a red canopy to the curb and a part-time doorman who had seen David Dirk leave for his office four days ago at 8:45 a.m., as usual, briefcase in one hand, travel mug of coffee in the other. He'd been wearing a charcoal-gray suit, red-striped tie. According to his predecessor's notes, David had had a full day's appointments, meetings with two clients, one prospective client, but had mostly taken care of paperwork and briefs. His part-time administrative assistant had worked until three that day and noted that David had seemed his usual revved-up self. Except then he vanished into thin air instead of returning home to the condo he shared with his fiancée of eight months.

Looking worried, sad and hopeful, Eden closed the door behind Reed and sat on a chair.

Reed sat across from her. "Can you tell me about the morning you last saw Mr. Dirk?"

Eden pushed her light blond hair behind her shoulders and took a breath. "It was just a regular morning. We woke up, had breakfast—I made him a bacon-and-cheese omelet and toast—and then David left for his office. He texted me a Thinking about you, beautiful at around eleven. That's the last time I heard from him. Which makes me think whatever went wrong happened soon after because he would have normally texted a cute little something a couple hours later and he didn't. He always texted a few times a day while at work. I just know something terrible happened! But I don't want that to be true!" She started crying, brown streaks under her eyes.

Reed reached for the box of tissues on the end table and handed it to her. She took it and dabbed at her eyes. "I know this isn't easy, Ms. Pearlman. I appreciate that you're talking to me. I'm going to do everything I can to find your fiancé. I knew David when I was a kid. We used to explore the woods together when I'd come up summers to stay with my grandmother. I have great memories of our friendship."

She sniffled and looked up at him. "So it's personal for you. That's good. You'll work hard to find my Davy Doo."

He wondered if any old girlfriend of his had ever referred to him as Reedy Roo or whatever. He hoped not. "What did you talk about over breakfast?" he asked.

"The wedding mostly. He was even trying to convince me to elope to Las Vegas—he said he wanted me to be his wife already and that we could even fly out that night. He's so romantic."

Hmm, making a case for eloping? Had Dirk wanted to get out of town fast? Was there a reason he'd wanted to go to Las Vegas in particular? Or was there a reason he'd wanted to marry Eden even faster than the weekend? "Did you want to elope?"

She shook her head. "My mother would have my

head! Plus, all the invitations were out. The wedding is this Saturday!"

"Where?" he asked, trying to recall the venue on the invitation.

"The Wedlock Creek chapel—this Saturday night," she said, sniffling again. "What if he's not back by then?"

"I'm going to go out there and do my job," he said. "I'll be in touch as soon as I have news."

She stood and shook his hand. "Thanks, Detective. I feel better knowing an old friend of David's is on the case."

Back in his SUV, Reed checked David Dirk's financials again. None of his credit cards had been used in the past twenty-four hours. Reed's predecessor had talked to five potential enemies of David's from opposing cases, but none of the five had struck the retired detective as holding a grudge. Reed flipped a few more pages in the man's notes. Ah, there it was. "According to friends and family, however, David wouldn't have just walked out on Eden. He loved her very much."

So what did happen to you, David Dirk? Reed wondered.

Reed had sent a small moving truck with two brawny guys to bring anything Norah wanted from the house to the ranch, but since the little rental had come furnished, she didn't have much to move. Her sister had given her way too many housewarming gifts from her secondhand shop, Treasures, so Norah had packed up those items and her kitchen stuff and everything fit into a small corner of the moving truck. It was easier to focus on wrapping up her picture frames than on actually setting them on surfaces in Reed's home.

She was moving in with him? She was. She'd made a deal.

Norah had never lived with a man. She'd lived on her own very briefly in this little dump, just under a year, and while she liked having her own place and making her way, she'd missed hearing her mom in the kitchen or singing in the shower. Did Reed sing in the shower? Probably not. Or maybe he did. She knew so little about him.

She gave the living room a final sweep. This morning she'd done a thorough cleaning, even the baseboards because she'd been so wired, a bundle of nervous energy about what today and tomorrow and the future would be like. She was taking a big leap into the unknown.

"We're all set, miss," the big mover in the baseball cap said, and Norah snapped out of her thoughts.

She was about to transfer the triplets from their playpen to their car seats, then remembered her mom had them for the day to allow Norah a chance to settle in at Reed's. She stood in the doorway of her house, gave it a last once-over and then got in her car. She pulled out, the truck following her.

In fifteen minutes they were at the farmhouse. Reed told the movers to place all the items from the truck in the family room and that Norah would sort it all later. Once the movers were gone and it was just Norah and Reed in the house, which suddenly seemed so big and quiet, it hit her all at once that this was now her home. She *lived* here.

"I want you to feel comfortable," he said. "So change anything you want."

"Did we talk about sleeping arrangements?" she asked, turning away and trying to focus on an oil painting of two pineapples. They hadn't, she knew that full well.

"I'll leave that to you," he said.

"As if there's more than one option?"

He smiled. "Why don't you take the master bedroom? It's so feminine, anyway." He started for the stairs. "Come, I'll give you more of a tour."

She followed him to the second level. The first door on the left was open to the big room with its cool white walls and huge Oriental rug and double wood dresser and big round mirror. A collection of old perfume dispensers was on a tray. A queen-size four-poster was near the windows overlooking the red barn, the cabbage-rose quilt and pillows looking very inviting. Norah could see herself falling asleep a bit easier in this cozy room. But still. "I feel like you should have the master suite. It's your house, Reed."

"I'd really rather have the room I had as a kid. It's big and has a great view of the weeping willow I used to read under. My grandmother kept it the same for when I'd come visit through the years. I'm nostalgic about it. So you take the master."

"Well, if you insist that I take the biggest room with the en suite bath, who am I to say no?" She grinned and he grinned back. She walked inside the room and sat on the bed, giving it a test. "Baby-bear perfect. I'll take it." She flopped back and spread out her arms, giving in to this being home.

"Good, it's settled."

A vision of Reed Barelli in his black boxer briefs and nothing else floated into her mind again, the way he'd looked lying next to her, all hard planes and five-o'clock shadow, long, dark eyelashes against his cheeks. She had a crazy thought of the two of them in bed.

And crazy it was, because their marriage was platonic. Sexless.

Focus, Norah. Stop fantasizing, which is bad for your health, anyway. Men can't be trusted with any part of your anatomy. That little reminder got her sitting up. "My sister says we need to talk about how this is going to work."

"Your sister is right. I made a pot of coffee before you came. Let's go talk."

She followed him downstairs and into the kitchen. On the refrigerator was a magnet holding a list of emergency numbers, everything from 9-1-1 to poison control to the clinic and closest hospital. His work and cell numbers were also posted, which meant he'd put up this sheet for her.

He poured coffee and fixed hers the way she liked, set them both on the round table in front of the window and sat down. "I have a feeling we'll just have to deal with things as they come up."

She sat across from him, her attention caught by the way the light shone on the side of his face, illuminating his dark hair. He was too handsome, his body too muscular and strong, his presence too…overwhelming.

"But I suppose the most important thing is that you feel comfortable here. This is now your home. Yours and the triplets. You and they have the run of the place. The crawl of the place."

She smiled. "I guess that'll take some getting used to." She glanced out the window at the fields she could imagine Bella, Bea and Brody running like the wind in just several months from now.

"No rush, right?" he said.

I could do this forever, she finished for him and realized that really was probably the case for him. He seemed to be at ease with the situation, suddenly living with a woman he'd accidentally slash drunk-married, appointing himself responsible for her and her three children. Because he wasn't attracted to her physically, most likely. Or emotionally. Men who weren't interested in marriage generally went for good-time girls who were equally not interested in commitment. Norah Ingalls was anything but a good-time girl. Unless you counted their wedding night. And you couldn't because neither of them could remember it.

Detective Reed Barelli's job was to serve and protect and that was what he was doing with his accidental wife. That was really what she had to remember here— and not let her daydreams get a hold on her. The woman he'd thought he was getting was Angelina, international flight attendant. Not Norah.

There was no need to bring up her sister Shelby's bedroom questions again or exactly what kind of marriage this was. That was clear. They were platonic. Roommates. Sharing a home but not a bed. Helping each other out. Now that she had that square in her mind, she felt more comfortable. There were boundaries, which was always good. She could ogle her housemate, stare at his hotness, but she'd never touch, never kiss and never get her heart and trust broken again.

"Anything else we should cover?" he asked.

She bit her lip. "I think you're right. We'll deal with

whatever comes up. Right now we don't know what those things might be."

"For instance, you might snore really loud and keep me awake all night and I'll have to remember to shut my door every night to block out the freight train sounds."

She smiled. "I don't snore."

"Not an issue, then," he said, and she realized that, again, he was trying to break the ice, make her feel more comfortable.

She picked up her mug. "You know who might keep you awake, though? The three teething seven-month-olds you invited to live here with you."

"They're supposed to do that, so it's all good."

"Does anything rattle you?" she asked, wondering if anything did.

"Yes, actually. A few things. The first being the fact that we're married. Legally married."

Before she could even think how to respond to that, he changed the subject.

"So what's on your agenda for today?" he asked.

"I figure I'll spend the next couple of hours unpacking, then I'll be working this afternoon. It's Grandma's Pot Pie Day, so I'll be making about fifty classics—chicken, beef, vegetable—from my grandmother's recipes. Oh—and I'll be writing up a class syllabus, too."

He took a sip of his coffee and tilted his head. "A class syllabus?"

She explained about the director of the community services center asking her to teach the multiples class for parents and caregivers of zero-to-six-month-olds. "I tried to get out of it—I mean, I'm hardly an expert—but she begged."

"You *are* an expert. You're a month out of the age

group. Been there, done that and lived to tell the tale. And to teach the newbies what to do."

She laughed. "I guess so!"

Norah always thought of herself as barely hanging on, a triplet's lovie falling out of the stroller, a trail of Cheerios behind them on the sidewalk, a runny nose, a wet diaper. Well-meaning folks often said, "I don't know how you do it," when they stopped Norah on the street to look at the triplets. Most of the time she didn't even feel like she *was* doing it. But all three babies were alive and well and healthy and happy, so she must be. She could do this and she would. She *did* have something to offer the newbie multiples moms of Wedlock Creek.

She sat a little straighter. She had graduated from the zero-to-six-month age range, hadn't she? And come through just fine. She was a veteran of those first scary six months. And yeah, you bet your bippy she'd done it alone. With help from her wonderful family, yes. But alone. She could teach that class blindfolded.

He covered her hand with his own for a moment and she felt the two-second casual touch down to her toes.

"Well, I'd better start unpacking," she said, feeling like a sixteen-year-old overwhelmed by her own feelings.

"If you need help, just say the word."

He was too good. Too kind. Too helpful. And too damned hot.

She slurped some more coffee, then stood and carried the mug into the family room, where the movers had put her boxes. But she wanted to be back in the kitchen, sitting with…her husband and just talking.

Her husband. She had a husband. For real. Well, sort of for real.

She didn't expect it to feel so good. She'd just had an "I'm doing all right on my own" moment. But it was nice to share the load. Really, really nice.

After walking Norah to the Pie Diner and taking a slice of Grandma's Classic Beef Pot Pie to go, Reed was glad the diner was so busy, because he kept seeing Norah's mom and aunt casting him glances, trying to sneak over to him for news and information about how Norah's move-in had gone. Luckily, they'd kept getting waylaid by customers wanting more iced tea and "could they have sausage instead of bacon in their quiche Lorraine?" and "were the gluten-free options really gluten free?"

Move-in had gone just fine. He was comfortable around Norah for some reason he couldn't figure out. He'd never lived with a woman, despite a girlfriend or two dumping him over his refusal for even that, let alone an engagement ring.

As far as tonight went, he'd simply look at his new living arrangement the way he would with any roommate. They were sharing a home. Plain and simple. The snippets he'd overheard from Norah's conversation with her sister wouldn't apply. There would be no sex. No kissing. No romance. As long as he kept his mind off how pretty and sexy she was and remembered why they were staying married, he'd be fine.

That settled in his head, he hightailed it out of the Pie Diner with his to-go bag and took a seat at a picnic table edging the town green, waving at passersby, chatting with Helen Minnerman, who had a question about whether it was against the law for her neighbor's Chihuahua to bark for more than a minute when outside—no, it was not—and helping a kid around ten or eleven up from under his bike when he slid from taking a turn too fast.

Life in Wedlock Creek was like this. Reed could get used to this slower pace. A man could think out here in all this open space and fresh air, which was exactly what he was doing, he realized. Too much thinking. About his new wife and what it would be like to wake up every morning knowing she was in bed down the hall. In the shower, naked under a spray of steamy water and soap. Making waffles in his kitchen. Their kitchen. Caring for babies who had him wrapped around their tiny fingers after just a few days of knowing them.

But all his thinking hadn't gotten him closer to finding David Dirk. In fifteen minutes he was meeting Dirk's closest friend, a former law associate, so hopefully the man would be able to shed some light.

Reed finished the last bite of the amazing beef pot pie, then headed for Kyle Kirby's office in a small, brick office building next to the library.

Kirby, a tall, lanky man with black eyeglasses, stood when Reed entered, then gestured for him to sit. "Any luck finding David?"

Reed sat. "Not yet. And to be honest, not much is making sense. I've looked into all the possibilities and I'm at a loss."

Kirby was chewing the inside of his lip—as if he knew more than he wanted to say. He was looking everywhere but at Reed.

Reed stared at him. "Mr. Kirby, if you know where David is or if he's okay or not, tell me now."

Was that sweat forming on the guy's forehead despite the icy air-conditioning?

"I wish I could help. I really do." He stood. "Now, if those are all your questions, I need to get back to work."

Reed eyed him and stood. This was strange. Reed had done his homework on Kyle Kirby's relationship with David and the two were very close friends, had been since David had moved back to Wedlock Creek to settle down after graduating from law school. Kirby had no skeletons in his closet and there was no bad blood between him and David. So what was the guy hiding?

Frustrated, Reed put in a couple more hours at the station, working on another case—a break-in at the drugstore. A promising lead led to a suspect, and another hour later, Reed had the man in custody. The solid police work did nothing to help his mood over his inability to figure out what had happened to David. It was as if he had just vanished into thin air.

One staff meeting and the receptionist's birthday cake celebration later, Reed headed home. He almost drove to the house he'd rented and would need to find a new tenant for. It still hadn't sunk in that the Barelli ranch was his, was home, and that when he arrived, he wouldn't walk into an empty house. Norah would be there. Bella, Bea and Brody would be there. And tonight he was grateful for the company. Company that wouldn't be leaving. *That* would definitely take some getting used to.

He pulled up at the ranch, glad to see Norah's car. Inside he found her in the kitchen, the triplets in their big playpen near the window. Bella was chewing on a cloth book, Brody was banging on a soft toy piano and Bea was shaking a rattling puppy teether. The three looked quite happy and occupied.

"Something sure smells good," he said, coming up

behind Norah and peeking into the big pot on the stove. "Pot pies for the diner?"

"Meatballs and spaghetti for us," she said. "I remember you mentioned you loved meatballs and spaghetti the night we met, so I figured it would be a good first dinner for us as—"

He smiled. "Official husband and wife."

"Official husband and wife," she repeated. She turned back to the pot, using a ladle to scoop out the meatballs and fragrant sauce into a big bowl. Was it Reed's imagination or did she look a little sad?

"You okay?" he asked.

She didn't answer. She picked up the pot of spaghetti and drained it into a colander over the sink, then added it to the bowl of meatballs and stirred it. Before he could say another word, the oven timer dinged and she took out heavenly smelling garlic bread.

"Well, can I at least help with anything?" he asked.

"Nope. The babies have eaten. Dinner is ready. The table is set. So let's eat."

She'd poured wine. There was ice water. A cloth napkin. He hadn't been treated to this kind of dinner at home in a long, long time, maybe not since he'd last visited his grandmother just weeks before she'd died.

"This is nice. I could get used to this," he said. "Thank you."

"You will get used to it because I love to cook and, given everything you're doing for me and the triplets, making dinner is the least I can do."

But as they chatted about their days and the triplets and she filled him in on some upcoming events in town, Norah seemed to get sadder. And sadder. Something was wrong.

"Norah. This marriage is meant to be a true partnership. So if something is bothering you, and something clearly is, tell me. Let's talk about it."

She poked at her piece of garlic bread. "It's silly."

"I'm sure it's not."

"It's just that, there I was, cooking at the stove in this beautiful country kitchen, my dream kitchen, the triplets happily occupied in the playpen, and my husband comes home, except he's not really my husband in the way I always thought it would go. I'm not complaining, Reed. I'm just saying this is weird. I always wanted something very different. Love, forever, growing old together on the porch. The works."

"It's not quite what I expected for myself, either," he said, swirling a bite of spaghetti. "It'll take some getting used to. But we'll get to know each other and soon enough we'll seem like any other old married couple."

"Kind of backward to have to get to know your spouse." She gave him a wistful smile and took a sip of wine.

"The triplets' father—you wanted to marry him?"

Norah put down her fork as though the mention of him cost her her appetite. "I just don't understand how someone could seem one way and truly be another way. I got him so wrong. I thought he was crazy about me. He was always talking about us and the future. But then the future presented itself in the form of my pregnancy and everything changed. I'll never forget the look on his face when I told him I was pregnant. A combo of freaked out and horrified."

"Sorry."

"And now everything I wanted—the loving husband, the babies, a home for us—is right here and it's all…"

He touched her hand. "Not like the old dreams."

She lifted her chin and dug her fork into a meatball with gusto. "I'm being ridiculous. I'm sitting here moping over what isn't and what wasn't. My life is my life. Our deal is a good one. For both of us. And for those three over there," she added, gesturing at the playpen. She focused on them for a moment and then turned back to him. "Okay, full speed ahead on the marriage partnership. My head is back in the game."

The meatball fell off her fork and plopped back onto her plate, sending a splatter of sauce onto both of them—her cheek and his arm. They both laughed and then he reached out and dabbed away the sauce from her cheek as she did the same to his arm.

"Anytime you need to talk this through, just tell me," he said. "And we'll work it out."

"You, too, you know."

He nodded. "Me, too."

As she pushed around spaghetti and twirled it but never quite ate any more, he realized she had the same funny pit in the middle of her stomach that he had in his, just maybe caused by a different emotion. She'd wanted something so much more—big passion, real romance, everlasting love—and had to settle for plain ole practical for a good reason. He'd planned on going it alone, never committing, but he had committed in a huge way, even if his heart wasn't involved. He was responsible for this family of four. Family of five now, including him.

He wouldn't let Norah down. Ever. But he knew he'd never be able to give her what she wanted in the deepest recesses of her heart.

Chapter 8

There was no way Reed was getting any sleep tonight. Not with Norah down the hall, sleeping in who knew what. Maybe she slept naked, though he doubted she'd choose her birthday suit for her first night in her new home with her new partnership-husband. Twice he'd heard her get out of bed—the floor creaked a bit in that room—and go into the nursery. One of the babies had been fussing a bit and she sang a lullaby that almost had him drifting off. Almost. Norah had a beautiful voice.

He glanced at the clock: 2:12 a.m. He heard a faint cry. Then it grew louder. If he wasn't mistaken, that was Brody. He waited a heartbeat for the telltale creak of the master bedroom floor, but it didn't come. Only another cry did.

Reed got out of bed, making sure he was in more than his underwear. Check. A T-shirt and sweats. He headed to the nursery and gently pushed the door open wider. One frustrated, red-faced little one was sitting up in his crib, one fist around the bar.

"Hey there, little guy," Reed said in his lowest voice to make sure he wouldn't wake Brody's sisters. "What's going on? What's with the racket?"

Brody scrunched up his face in fury that Reed wasn't picking him up fast enough. His mouth opened to let loose a wail, but Reed snatched him up and, as always, the sturdy little weight of him felt like pure joy in his arms. Brody wore light cotton footie pajamas and one sniff told Reed he was in the all clear for a middle-of-the-night, heavy-duty diaper change. He brought the baby over to the changing table and took off the wet diaper, gave Brody a sprinkle of cornstarch, then put on a new diaper like a pro. All the while, Brody looked at him with those huge slate-blue eyes.

Reed picked him up and held him against his chest, walking around the nursery while slightly rocking the little guy. Brody's eyes would flutter closed, then slowly open as if making sure Reed hadn't slipped him inside his crib and left. This went on four more times, so Reed sat in the rocker and Brody let out the sigh of all sighs and closed his eyes, his lips quirking and then settling.

"Guess that means you're comfortable, then," Reed whispered. He waited a few seconds, then stood, but the baby opened his eyes. Reed almost laughed. "Busted. You caught me." Reed sat back down, figuring he might be there awhile. Maybe all night. "Want to hear a story?"

Brody didn't make a peep in response, but Reed took that for a yes anyway.

"Once upon a time, there was a little boy named Beed Rabelli. That's not me, by the way."

Did Brody believe him? Probably not. But it made the story easier to tell.

"Well, this little kid, Beed, did everything to try to win his father's approval. His father's interest. But no matter what Beed did, pretending to be interested in things he really didn't even like, his father barely paid attention to him. He only came around every now and then as it was. But one day, Beed's dad never came around again and Beed started getting postcards from far-off places."

Brody moved his arm up higher by his ear and Reed smiled at how impossibly adorable the baby was. And what a good listener.

"So one day, Beed and his friend David Dirk were riding bikes and exploring the woods and they got to talking about how even though they pretty much had the same type of not-there dad, it didn't mean their dads didn't love them or care about them. Their dads were just…free spirits who had to follow the road in their souls. Or something like that. Anyway, Brody, I just want you to know that your father is like that and that's why he's not here. I don't want you to spend one minute wondering why he doesn't care about you, because I'm sure he does. He's just following that road that took him far away from here and—"

Reed stopped talking. Where the hell was this coming from? Why was he saying anything of this to Brody?

Because he cared about this little dude, that was why. And it was important to know because at some level it was very likely true.

He heard a sniffle and glanced toward Bea's and Bella's cribs. They were both fast asleep. He heard the sound again and realized it was coming from outside. Reed put Brody gently back inside his crib, and *booyah*—the baby did not open those eyes again. Either Reed had bored him to sleep or a story worked like it always had since time began.

He tiptoed out to investigate the sound of the sniffle. Was Norah so upset about her lost dreams that she was crying in the middle of the night?

He froze at the sight of her standing to the left of the nursery door, tears in her eyes.

"Norah? What's wrong?"

She grabbed him, her hands on the sides of his face, and pulled him close, laying one hell of a kiss on him. Damn, she smelled so good and her skin was so soft. Everything inside him was on fire. He backed her up against the wall and pressed against her, deepening the kiss, his hands roaming her neck, into her hair, down along her waist. He wanted to touch her everywhere.

"So you're not upset," he whispered against her ear, then trailed kisses along her beautiful neck.

"I was touched enough that you'd gotten up at a baby crying," she said. "And then as I was about to walk in, I heard you talking to Brody and couldn't help eavesdropping. I can't tell you how anxious I've been about the questions that would be coming my way someday, maybe at age three or four. 'Where's my father? Why doesn't Daddy live with us? Why doesn't Daddy ever see us? Doesn't he care about us?'"

Norah wiped under her eyes and leaned the front of her luscious body against Reed's. "I had no idea what I would say, how I could possibly make it okay for them. And one 2:00 a.m. diaper change later, you've settled it."

"Eh, I didn't say anything I hadn't worked out over the past twenty-nine years."

She smiled and touched his face, and he leaned his cheek against it. Then he moved in for another kiss, hoping reality and the night-light in the hallway wouldn't ruin the moment and make her run for her room.

She didn't. She kissed him back, her hands on his chest, around his neck, in his hair. He angled them down the hall toward his room and they fell backward onto his bed, the feel of her underneath him, every part of her against him, almost too much to bear.

He slid his hands under her T-shirt and pulled it over her head, then tugged off his own shirt and flung it behind him. He lay on top of her, kissing her neck, her shoulder, between her luscious breasts.

And then he felt her shift. Just slightly. The equivalent of a bitten lower lip. A hesitation.

He pulled back and looked at her. "Too fast?"

"Way too fast," she said. "Not that I'm not enjoying it. Not that I didn't start it."

He laughed. "That was hot. Trust me."

Her smile faded. "You've made it very clear what this marriage is, Reed. 'Friends with benefits' when we're married is too weird. Even for us. I think we need to keep some very clear boundaries."

She turned away from him and quickly put her T-shirt back on. He did the same.

"An emotional moment, the middle of the night, then there's me, still probably highly hormonal. Of course I jumped your bones."

She's trying to save face. Let her. "Believe me, if you hadn't kissed me, I would have kissed you first."

"Oh," she said, a bit of a smile back on her pretty face. "I guess we know where we stand, then. We're foolishly attracted to each other on a purely physical level, and we went with the moment, then wised up. We'll just keep our hands to ourselves from now on. So that this partnership has a fighting chance."

She was right. If they screwed this up with great sex, that could lead to who knew what, like other expectations, and suddenly she would be throwing annulment papers at him, all his plans to stand by her and the triplets would fall to pot. And so would this ranch—home.

He nodded. Twice to convince himself of just how right she was. "We both know where romance leads. Trouble. Heartache. Ruin."

"Well, at least the mystery is gone. You've seen my boobs."

He had to laugh. But he sobered up real fast when he realized the mystery was hardly gone. He had yet to truly touch her.

"So if I let what happens happen and then we realize it's a bad idea, what does that mean?" Norah asked Shelby the next morning as they sat at a corner table for two in Coffee Talk, their favorite place to catch up in Wedlock Creek. Their huge strollers against the wall behind them, triplets asleep and Shelby's toddler sons drifting off after a morning running around the playground, the sisters shared a huge slice of delicious crumbly coffee cake. Of course they'd never have pie anywhere but at their own family restaurant.

"Ooh, so something happened?" Shelby asked, sipping her iced mocha.

"In the middle of the night last night, I thought I heard one of the babies crying, but when I went to the nursery, Reed was sitting in the rocker with Brody in his arms, telling him a story about himself and relating it to Brody. I stood there in tears, Shel. This is going to sound crazy, but in that moment, my heart cracked open."

Shelby's mouth dropped open. "You're falling in love!"

"Oh God, I think I am. I was so touched and so hormonal that I threw myself at him. But then I realized what an idiot I was being and put the kibosh on that."

"What? Why?"

"Shelby, he's made it crystal clear he married me for his ranch. And because he feels some kind of chivalrous duty toward me, as if annulling our marriage means he's walking away from his responsibilities. He's not responsible for us!"

"He feels he is," Shelby said. "The man's a police officer. Serve and protect. It's what he does."

Maybe that was a good reminder that Reed was operating on a different level—the cop level, the responsibility level. His father had walked away from him and his mother, the triplets' father had walked away from them and Norah, and Reed couldn't abide that, couldn't stand it. So he was stepping in. Attracted to her physically or not, Reed's feelings where she was concerned weren't of the romantic variety. He was trying to right wrongs.

"Um, excuse me?" a woman asked as she approached the table.

"Hi," Norah said. "Can we help you?"

"I noticed your triplets," she said, looking at Bella, Bea and Brody, who were all conked out in their stroller wedged up against the wall. "So it's true? If you get married at the Wedlock Creek chapel, you'll have multiples?"

"I didn't get married at the chapel and still had triplets," Norah said.

"And I did get married at the chapel and had one baby," Shelby said, "but ended up with twins, sort of." At the woman's puzzled expression, she added, "It's a long story."

Norah took a sip of her iced coffee. "Well, the legend does say if you marry at the chapel you'll have multiples in some way, shape or form. Are you hoping for a houseful of babies all at the same time?" she asked the woman.

"My fiancé is a twin and so we have a good chance of having twins ourselves, but he wants to increase our luck. I just figure the legend is just that—a silly rumor."

"No way," Shelby said. "Last year alone, there were five multiple births—two sets of triplets and three twins. The year before, four sets of twins and one set of triplets. The year before that, one set of quadruplets and two sets of twins. And that's just in Wedlock Creek."

The woman paled. She truly seemed to lose color. "Oh. So the legend is actually true?"

"Well, as true as a legend can be," Shelby said. "But this town is full of multiples. We can both personally attest to that."

"Um, is that a bad thing?" Norah asked gently.

"Well, twins just seem like a lot," the woman said. "One seems like a lot. I want to be a mother, but two at once? I don't know. I don't think I want to help our chances, you know?"

Norah smiled. "Then you definitely don't want to marry at the Wedlock Creek chapel." She upped her chin out the window. "See that woman? Pregnant with triplets. All boys!"

The woman swallowed. "I think we'll marry at the Brewer Hotel. Thanks!" she said and practically ran out.

Shelby laughed. "One baby *is* a lot of work. She's not wrong."

"But the more the merrier," Norah said, lifting her iced coffee for a toast.

"Got that right," Shelby said and tapped her cup. "Of course, you know what this means."

"What what means?"

"You and Reed got married at the chapel. You're going to have more multiples. Omigod, Norah, you're going to have, like, ten children."

She imagined three babies that looked like Reed Barelli. The thought made her smile.

"Jeez, you are far gone," Shelby said.

"Heaven help me. But I am."

She was falling in love with her business partner of a husband. She had to put the brakes on her feelings. But how did you do that when the floodgates just opened again?

Chapter 9

That night, Norah arrived at the Wedlock Creek Community Services Center with her stack of handouts, her laptop, for her slideshow on her favorite baby products, and a case of the jitters. As she stood at the front of the room, greeting students as they entered, she took a fortifying gulp of the coffee she'd brought in a thermos. As she'd left the ranch, she was surprised by how much she wished Reed had been there to see her off and give her a "you've got this" fist bump or something. She was beginning to need him a little too much for comfort. But he was working late, following up on a promising lead about David Dirk, who was still missing.

A woman's belly entered the room before she did. "If my water breaks while I'm sitting down, here's my husband's cell number," she said to Norah with a smile. "I'm not due for another month, but you never know."

You never know. No truer words ever spoken.

Norah smiled and took the card with the woman's husband's information. "I'm glad you're here. And if your water does break, I've got my cell phone at the ready and a list of emergency medical numbers."

"Pray I don't give birth until after the last class!" the woman said on a laugh. "I need to learn everything!" she added and slowly made her way over to the padded, backed benches that had been brought in specifically for women in her condition.

There were several pregnant women with their husbands, mothers, mothers-in-law and various other relatives all wanting to learn the basics of caring for newborn multiples. Several women had infant multiples already. Norah glanced around the room, seeing excitement and nerves on the faces. That was exactly how she'd felt when she'd shown up for the first class.

She was about to welcome her students when the door opened and Reed walked in. "Sorry I'm a minute late," he said, handing her a printout of his online registration form. He took an empty seat next to one of the husbands, giving the man a friendly nod.

Reed was taking her class?

Of course he was.

Norah smiled at him and the smile he gave her back almost undid her. *Don't think about what happened in the hallway last night*, she ordered herself. *Stop thinking about his hands on your bare skin. You're standing in front of a room full of people!*

She sucked in a breath, turned her attention away from Reed and welcomed her students. "Eight months ago, I was all of you," she said. "I was nine months' pregnant with BGG triplets—that's boy, girl, girl—and

I was a nervous wreck. Not only was I about to give birth to three helpless infants who would depend on me for everything, but I was a single mother. I will tell you right now that the most important thing I have learned about being the mother of triplets, particularly in my position, is to ask for help."

Norah looked around the room. All eyes were on her, interested, hanging on her every word, and some were actually taking notes.

So far, so good, she thought. "Ladies, don't expect your husbands to read your minds—if you want him to change Ethan while you change Emelia, ask him! No passive-aggressive stewing at the changing table while he's watching a baseball game. Speak up. Ask for what you need!"

"She's talking to you, Abby," the man next to Reed said and got a playful sock in the arm from his wife.

The students laughed. This was actually going well! She was standing there giving advice. People were responding! "And men, while you have infant twins or triplets or quadruplets, you're not going to be watching the game unless you have a baby or two propped in your arms, one hand on a bottle, the other burping another's little back."

A guy got up and headed for the door. "Just kidding," he said with a grin. More laughter.

Norah smiled. "And you grandmothers-to-be…what I learned from my mother? You're the rock. You're going to be everything to the mother and father of newborn multiples. Not only do you have experience, even if it's not with multiples yourselves, but you've been there, done that in the parenting department. You love those little multiples and you're there to help. Sometimes your brand-new mother of a daughter or daughter-in-law may screech at you that she's doing it her way. Let her. Maybe it'll work, maybe it won't. But what matters is that you're supporting one another. You're there."

She thought of her mother and her aunt Cheyenne and her sister. Her rocks. She couldn't have done it without them—their love and support and good cheer.

"So that's my number one most valuable piece of information I can offer you. Ask for help when you need it. When you think you'll need it. Because you will need it. If some of you don't have a built-in support system, perhaps you can create one when you go home tonight. Friends. Caring neighbors. Folks from your house of worship. Think about the people you can turn to."

From there, Norah started up her slideshow of products she'd found indispensable. She talked about cribs and bassinets. Feeding schedules and sleep schedules. How laundry would take over entire evenings.

"You did all that on your own?" a woman asked.

"I lived on my own, but I have a fabulous mother, fabulous aunt and fabulous sister who were constantly over, taking shifts to helping me out, particularly that first crazy month. So when I tell you help is everything, I mean it. Just don't forget that thank-yous, hugs and homemade pies go a long way in showing appreciation for their support."

Fifty-five minutes later the class was winding down. Norah let them know that in two weeks she'd be bringing in her triplets for show-and-tell with her mom as a volunteer assistant, demonstrating how to perform necessary tasks with three babies. After a question-and-answer session, Norah dismissed the students.

Huh. She'd really done it. She'd taught a class! And she was pretty darn good at it.

One of the last to pack her notebook and get up was a woman who'd come to the class alone. Early thirties with strawberry blond hair, she looked tired and defeated and hadn't spoken much during the period. She walked up to Norah with tears in her eyes.

Oh no. This woman had the look of multiple-itis.

"I have twin six-week-olds," the woman said. "My mother is with them now, thank God. They're colicky and I'm going to lose my mind. My husband and I argue all the time. And I only have twins—the bare minimum to even have multiples—and I'm a falling-apart wreck!"

Norah put her hand on the woman's arm. "I totally hear you." She offered the woman a commiserating smile. "What's your name?"

"Sara Dirk."

Norah noticed Reed's eyebrows shoot up at the name Dirk.

"Welcome, Sara. I'm really glad you're here. I haven't personally dealt with colic, but I've known colicky babies, and let me tell you, you might as well have sextuplets."

Sara finally smiled. "They don't stop crying. Except to breathe. I don't know how my mother does it—the screeching doesn't even seem to bother her. She just walks up and down with one baby while she watches the other in the vibrating baby swing, then switches them. I hear those cries that go on forever and I just want to run away."

Reed walked over and sat in the chair at the side of the desk, collecting Norah's handouts. She knew he was intently listening.

"That's wonderful that your mom is so supportive, Sara. I tell you what. Stop by the Pie Diner tomorrow and let anyone there know that Norah said they're to give you two of your and your mom's favorite kinds of pies on the house."

"I love the Pie Diner's chocolate peanut butter pie. It always cheers me up for a good ten minutes."

Norah smiled. "Me, too. And I'll research some tips for dealing with colic," she said. "I'm sure you have already, but I'll talk to the mothers I know who've dealt with it and survived. I'll email you the links."

"Thanks," she said. "I really appreciate it."

Reed stood with Norah's folders and laptop. He extended his hand to Sara. "Did I hear you say your last name is Dirk?"

Sara nodded.

"Are you related to David Dirk?" he asked.

Sara nodded. "My husband's first cousin."

"I'm Reed Barelli, a detective with the Wedlock Creek Police Department. I also knew David when I was a kid. I'm trying to find him."

"I sure hope he's okay," Sara said. "We just can't figure out what could have happened. The night before he went missing, he stopped by for a few minutes to drop off a drill he'd borrowed from my husband and he seemed so happy."

"Any particular reason why—besides the upcoming wedding, I mean?" Reed asked.

"He said something had been bothering him but that he'd figured out a solution. And then the twins started screaming their heads off, as usual, and there went the conversation. He left and that was the last time I saw him."

"Do you know what was bothering him?" Reed asked.

"No idea. I know he's madly in love with Eden. Things are going well at work, as far as I know."

"When did you see him before that last time?" Reed asked.

"Hmm, maybe a couple nights before. We—my husband and I—needed a sitter for an hour and my mother couldn't do it, so we begged David. He and Eden watched the twins. Do you believe that after babysitting our little screechers, that woman is hoping for triplets or even quadruplets? Craziest thing. She loves the idea."

"More power to her," Norah said.

"Well, I'd better get back and give my mother a break. See you next week, Norah. Oh, and, Detective Barelli, I do hope you find David. Eden must be out of her mind with worry."

Norah watched Reed wait until Sara had left, then hurried to the door and closed it.

"Are you thinking what I'm thinking?" he asked.

"I have so many thoughts running through my head that it could be any number of them."

"About David Dirk. And why he suddenly went missing."

Norah tilted her head and stared at Reed. "What do you mean?"

"Well, let's recount the facts and evidence. David Dirk has a cousin with colicky twins. David Dirk and his fiancée babysit said colicky twins. Despite the screeching in their ears for over an hour, Eden is hoping for multiples."

Norah wasn't sure where he was going with this.

"Okay," she said. "What does that have to do with his disappearance?"

"Well," he continued, "she and David are to be married at the Wedlock Creek chapel, where legend says those who marry will be blessed with multiples. The night before he went missing, David told Sara something was bothering him but he'd figured out a solution. Cut to David's fiancée telling me that on the morning he disappeared, he'd asked her to elope. But she reminded him how badly she wanted to marry at the chapel."

Ah. Now she was getting it. "Oh boy."

"Exactly. Because why would David want to elope instead of marrying at the Wedlock Creek chapel?

"The only reason folks in this town don't get married there is because they don't want multiples." But was David really so freaked out by his cousin's colicky babies and his fiancée wanting sextuplets that he ran away? No way. Who would do that? She herself had dated him, and he'd seemed like a stand-up guy, even if they'd had zero to talk about other than the weather and which restaurants they liked in town.

She remembered the woman who'd approached her and Shelby in the coffee shop yesterday. She'd wanted to avoid that legend like the ole plague. So maybe it was true. David had run!

"I'm thinking so," Reed said. "It's the only thing that makes sense. Yesterday I spoke with a friend of his who seemed nervous, like he was hiding something. Maybe he knew the truth—that David took off on his own—and had been sworn to secrecy."

"What a baby David is," Norah said.

"Pun intended?"

Norah laughed. "Nope. He's just really a baby. Why

not tell Eden how he felt? He has family and friends scared that something terrible happened to him. He had a friend lie to a police officer."

"Based on everything I've heard, I'm ninety-nine percent sure he took off on his own. I just have to find him. Maybe the friend can shed some light. I doubt he'll tell me anything, though."

"So how will you find David, then?"

"The right questions," Reed said. "And maybe my own memories of where David would go when his world felt like it was crashing down. I might know where he is without even realizing it. I need to do some thinking."

She nodded. "So let's go home, then."

"Home to the ranch. I like the sound of that."

Norah smiled and took his hand before she realized they weren't a couple. Why did being a couple feel so natural, then?

"Tell me more about the legend of the Wedlock Creek chapel," Reed said to Norah as they sat in the living room with two craft beers and two slices of the Pie Diner's special fruit pie of the day—Berry Bonanza.

"Well, as far as I know, back in the late 1800s, a woman named Elizabeth Eckard, known for being a bit peculiar, married her true love at the chapel."

"Peculiar how?"

"Some say she was a witch and could cast spells," Norah explained. "It was just rumor, but most shunned her just in case they got on her bad side."

Reed raised an eyebrow. "Apparently her true love wasn't worried."

Norah smiled. "Legend says he was so in love with

Elizabeth, he married her against his parents' wishes, who refused to have anything to do with them."

"Jeez. Harsh."

"Yup. But he loved her and so he married her at the beautiful chapel that she had commissioned to be built. Elizabeth had inherited a bit of money and wanted the new town of Wedlock Creek to have a stately chapel for services of all kinds."

Reed took a bite of the pie. "That must have buttered up the townspeople. Did his family come around?"

"Nope. And the townspeople still shunned her. Some even avoided services at the chapel. But some started noticing that those who attended church seemed luckier than those who didn't. And so everyone started going."

Reed shook his head. "Of course."

"Well, the luck didn't extend to Elizabeth. All she wanted was children—six. Three boys and three girls. But she never did get pregnant. After five years of trying, her husband told her there was no point being married to her if she couldn't give him a family, and he left her."

"That's a terrible story," Reed said, sipping his beer.

Norah nodded. "But Elizabeth loved children and ended up turning her small house into a home for orphans. She had the children she'd always wanted so much, after all. But when her only sister found herself in the same position, not getting pregnant, her sister's husband went to the officiants of the chapel and demanded an annulment. That night, Elizabeth crept out to the chapel at midnight and cast a spell that those who married at the chapel would not only be blessed with children, but multiples."

"Come on," Reed said.

Norah shrugged. "Nine months later, Elizabeth's sister had twin girls. And all the couples who married at the church that year also had multiples. Whispers began that Elizabeth had blessed the church with a baby spell."

"Did she ever marry again? Have her own multiples?"

Norah shook her head. "No, but she took in orphans till her dying day, then hired people to keep the home going. It was going strong until the 1960s, when foster care became more prominent."

"It's crazy that I actually think that David Dirk, reasonable, intelligent, suspicious of everything, believes in this legend to the point that he fled town to avoid marrying at the chapel. It's just an old legend. There's no blessing or spell."

"Then what accounts for all the multiples?" Norah asked.

"A little help from science?" he asked.

"Maybe sometimes," she said. "But I know at least ten women who married at the chapel and had multiples without the help of a fertility doctor."

"Don't forget me," he said.

"You?"

"I married at the chapel and now I have triplets."

She smiled, but the beautiful smile faded. "Are you their father, Reed? I mean, we didn't actually ever talk about that. You said you felt responsible for them and me. You said you would help raise them and help support them and be there for them. But are you saying you want to be their father?"

He flinched and realized she caught it. "I—" He grabbed his beer and took a swig, unsure how to answer. *Did* he want to be the triplets' father? He was their mother's husband—definitely. He was doing all the things Norah said when it came to caring for Bella, Bea and Brody. He was there for them. But was he their *father*?

That word was loaded.

"This is a partnership," she said, her voice formal as she sat straighter. "Of course you're not their *father*." She waved a hand in the air and made a strange snorting noise, then cut a forkful of berry pie. "It was silly of me to even use the term." A forced smile was plastered on her face. "So where do you think David Dirk is?"

Should he let her change the subject? If he were half the person she thought he was, he wouldn't. They'd talk this out. But he had no idea how he felt about this. Their *father*? Was he anyone's father? Could he be? Did he *want* to be?

"Norah, all I know for sure is that I want to take care of the four of you. I'm responsible for you all."

Her lips were tightly pressed. "Because you drunk-married me."

"I'm legally wed to you. It might have been because of spiked punch, but being married serves us both."

"You got your ranch," she said, staring at him. "And I got some security. I just have to keep reminding myself of that. Why we're here. Why we did this. Crazy as it really is."

Was it all that crazy? No. They both got what they needed.

He wasn't anyone's father. Reed Barelli? A father? With his craptastic model of paternity?

"It's good to know, to remember, what we are," she said, her voice higher pitched.

Higher pitched because she was upset? Or because

she was stating a fact? They'd almost had sex, but she'd called a halt and wisely so. She knew messing around with their partnership could have terrible consequences. Anything that could put conflict between them could ruin a good thing. And this marriage was a good thing. For both of them.

He was no one's father. He was Norah's husband and caretaker of her children. Guardian of them all.

None of this sounded right. Or felt right. His shoulders slumped and he slugged down the rest of the beer.

"Maybe I should go pick up the babies," she said. "My mom wants to keep them overnight, but I'm sure she'd rather have a solid night's sleep."

She wanted—needed—a buffer, he realized. And so did he.

"I'll go with you," he said. "Tell you the truth, I miss their little faces."

She bit her lip and lifted her chin, and he also realized he'd better stop saying things like that, despite the fact that it was the truth. His affection for the triplets was also a good thing—the fact that they had his heart meant he'd be a good provider, a good protector.

And that was what he'd vowed to be.

Chapter 10

The next morning, Norah woke very early and made twelve pot pies to deliver to the Pie Diner, the need to keep her eyes and mind on the various pots and timers a help in keeping her mind off Reed. But as she slid the last three pies from the oven, the smell of vegetable pot pie so comforting and tantalizing that she took out a frozen one to heat up for her breakfast, she couldn't stop hearing him say he wasn't the triplets' father.

She knew that. And of course, he didn't say it outright because he was Reed Barelli. But she'd been under the impression that fatherhood was part of the deal. Until she'd heard what had come stumbling out of her own mouth last night. He'd said again that being married, spiked punch or not, served them both. And she'd said something like, "Right, you got your ranch, I got some security."

Security. That was very different than "a father for my children."

Her shoulders slumped. Maybe she hadn't thought this through quite far enough. A father for her kids should have been first on her list, no?

Except you weren't looking for a father for your kids, dummy, she reminded herself. *You weren't looking for anyone. You got yourself in a situation and you didn't undo it so that you and your babies could have that security: a safe house, another caring adult, the financial burden lifted a bit, one more pair of hands. All that in a kind, supportive—and yes, sexy as all get-out—husband.*

No one, certainly not Reed Barelli, had used the word *father.*

Okay. She just had to let it sink in and accept it. Her marriage was platonic. Her husband was not her children's father. She had a good setup. It was good for the both of them.

"Do people eat pot pie for breakfast?" Reed asked as he walked into the kitchen in a T-shirt and navy sweats. Even his bare feet were sexy. His hair was adorably rumpled and as the sunlight illuminated half his face, he looked so beautiful she just stood there and stared at him until he tilted his head.

"Pot pie is appropriate for all meals," she said. "Seven a.m. Three p.m. Six p.m."

"Good, because this kitchen smells so good I'm now craving it."

"You're in luck because I have six frozen in the freezer. Just pop one in the oven for a half hour. It'll be ready when you're out of the shower." She glanced at her watch. "I'm going to drop these off at the Pie Diner and pick up the babies, bring them home and then go to Sara Dirk's with some frozen pot pies. I think she could use a freezer full of easily reheatable meals."

"That's thoughtful of you. Tell you what. Why don't you go to Sara's and I'll deliver the pies and pick up the rug rats and bring them home. I'm not on duty till noon."

"I can pick up the triplets," she said, her stomach twisting. "They're my children and I—"

"Norah," he said, stepping closer. He took both her hands and held them. "That's why I'm here. That's why you're here. I'm now equally responsible for them. So go."

He sure did use the word *responsible* a lot. She had to keep that in mind. *Responsible* was how he'd gotten himself married to her in the first place. He'd heard the plaintive, wistful note in her voice—*I've always dreamed of getting married here*—and instead of running for the hills, he'd felt responsible for her lost dreams and picked her up in his arms and carried her inside the chapel and vowed to love, honor and cherish her for the rest of his days.

She glanced down at their entwined hands. Why did it have to feel so good? Why did she have to yearn for more than the deal they'd struck? "Thank you, then," she managed to say, moving to the freezer to pull out six pot pies for Sara. The icy blast felt good on her hot, Reed-held hands and brought her back to herself a bit. "I'll pop one in the oven for you. Thirty minutes, okay?"

"Got it. See you back at home in a bit."

Back at home. Back at home. As she carried her bag to the door, she looked around and realized this ranch didn't feel like home, that she wasn't quite letting herself feel that it was hers, too. It wasn't. Not really. Just like Reed wasn't the triplets' father.

Because he was holding back just as she was. For self-preservation.

Stop thinking, she ordered herself as she got into her car and turned on the radio, switching the station until she found a catchy song she couldn't resist singing along to. A love song that ended up reminding her of the hot guy taking a shower right now. Grr, why did everything always come back to Reed Barelli?

"So how's married life?" Norah's mother, Arlena, asked as she set a slice of apple pie in front of Reed at the counter of the Pie Diner.

"Things are working out great," Reed said quite honestly.

"It's nice having someone to come home to, isn't it?" Cheyenne said, sidling up with a coffeepot in each hand. She refilled two tables behind them, then poured Reed a fresh cup.

"You two," Shelby chided. "Leave the poor detective alone. We all know theirs isn't a real marriage."

Reed stiffened, glancing at Shelby. Norah's sister was sharp and cautious, a successful business owner, and had held her own against one of the wealthiest and most powerful businessmen in Wedlock Creek, Liam Mercer, whom she'd eventually married. He felt like Shelby was trying to tell him something. Or trying to get across a message. But what?

Their marriage *was* real. They might not be loving and cherishing, but they were honoring each other's deepest wishes and needs.

But still, he couldn't shake what she'd said. *Not a real marriage. Not a real marriage. Not a real marriage.*

If their union wasn't real, then why would he feel such responsibility for her children? And he did. He had from day one when he'd woken up with the wedding ring and seen that photo of Norah and her triplets on the day they were born.

"Well, everyone's happy, including my beloved little grandbabies, so that's what matters," Arlena said, taking away Reed's empty plate.

Cheyenne nodded.

Shelby nodded extra sagely.

Arlena returned with the stroller, parking it beside Reed. "Look who's here to take you home," she cooed to the triplets. She frowned, then looked at him. "What do they call you?"

"Call me?" he repeated.

"Call you," Norah's mother repeated. "Da-da? Papa? Reed? Mama's husband?"

He felt his cheeks sting. Had Norah talked to her mom about their conversation? He doubted there'd been time. "They don't talk yet, so, of course, they don't call me anything."

"They'll be taking any day," she said, clearly uninterested in letting this line of questioning go. He should suggest detective work on the side for Arlena Ingalls.

He swallowed and got up from the bar stool, refusing to take the twenty Cheyenne tried to foist back at him. He put the bill under his empty coffee mug and got out of there fast with the giant stroller. Or as fast as anyone could make their way around tables in a diner while pushing a three-seat stroller with a yellow-and-silver polka-dotted baby bag hanging off the handle.

Anyway, what he'd said in regard to "how married life was" was true: things *were* great. He and Norah had to get used to each other—that was all. Yes, he'd made a mistake in not being clear about the father title, but the subject hadn't come up even though it was really the root and heart of staying married in the first place.

What the hell was wrong with him? How could he be so damned dense sometimes?

And what *were* the triplets going to call him?

He didn't like the idea of them calling him Reed.

Humph.

Frowning again, he settled the babies in their car seats, got the stroller in the trunk of his SUV and drove to the ranch, grateful, as always, that he was making this drive, that he was going home to the ranch. The summer sun lit the pastures through the trees and, as expected, the sight of the homestead relaxed Reed in a way nothing could. He remembered running out to the crazy weeping willow, which always looked haunted, with David Dirk when they were nine, David talking about his uncle who'd just won a quarter million dollars in Vegas and "was so lucky" that their lives were changing. He remembered David saying that if only his mother could win that kind of money, they'd have everything and wouldn't need anything else. As if money alone—

Wait a minute. Reed pulled the car over and stared hard at that weeping willow.

Could David have gone to Las Vegas? To try to win a pot of money to make having multiples more palatable? Or just easier? Or maybe he'd gone there to hide out for a few days before the wedding, to think through what he wanted?

He pulled out his phone and called David's bank. In seconds he was switched over to the manager and reintroduced himself as the detective working on the Dirk disappearance. Reed's predecessor had noted that David hadn't taken out a large sum of cash before he'd gone missing. But David had never been a gambler. He wouldn't risk more than five hundred bucks on slots and tables, even for the chance of a big payday. "Can you tell me if David withdrew around five hundred dollars the week of the tenth?"

"He withdrew two hundred and fifty dollars on the eleventh. Then another hundred on the twelfth."

Well, hardly enough cash for even a cheap flight, a cheap motel and quarters for a few slot machines. But he might have had cash socked away, too.

It was just a hunch. But Reed would bet his ranch that David Dirk was in Vegas, sitting at a slot machine and freaking out about what he was doing—and had done.

Before Norah even got out of her car, she could hear the loud, piercing wails from inside Sara Dirk's house. Screeching babies.

Norah rang the bell and it was a good minute before Sara opened the door, a screaming baby against her chest and frazzled stress etched on her tired face. Behind Sara, Norah could see the other twin crying in the baby swing.

"I thought you could use some easy meals to heat up," Norah said, holding up the bag of pies. "I brought you every kind of pot pie we make at the Pie Diner."

Sara looked on the verge of tears. "That's really nice of you," she managed to say before the baby in her arms let out an ear-splitting wail.

"Could you use a break?" Norah asked, reaching out her arms.

"Oh God, yes," Sara said, handing over the baby girl. "This is Charlotte. And that's Gabrielle," she added, rushing over to the crying one in the swing. She scooped her out and rocked her, and the baby quieted.

Norah held Charlotte against her chest, rubbing the baby's back and murmuring to her.

"A few minutes' reprieve," Sara said. "They like the change, but then they'll start up again."

"Is your husband at work?" Norah asked, giving Charlotte's back little taps to burp her.

Sara nodded. "He works at the county hospital and starts at 5:00 a.m. But the poor guy was up for a couple hours before then. He's such a great dad. He calls and texts as often as he can to check to see if I'm okay, if they're okay."

Norah smiled. "Support is everything."

Sara nodded. "It really is. David's fiancée said she'd come over this morning to help out. I feel so bad for her. Is there still no word on David?"

"Not that I know of."

The doorbell rang and there was Eden, her blond hair in a ponytail. Norah knew Eden from the Pie Diner, like just about everyone in town, so no introductions were necessary. And since David had done his share of dating among the single women in town, Norah's two weeks as David's girlfriend hardly merited a second thought. There wouldn't be any awkwardness in that department with Eden, thank heavens.

Eden burst into tears. "You know what I think?" she asked, taking Gabrielle from Sara and rocking the baby in her arms while sniffling. "I think David up and left.

I think he changed his mind about me and didn't want to break my heart. But—" She let out a wail. "He broke it anyway." She cried, holding the baby close against her, her head gentle against Gabrielle's head.

"That man loves you to death," Sara said. "Everyone knows that."

"Well, he's either dead in a ditch somewhere or he left on his own because he doesn't want to marry me," Eden said, sniffling.

Norah handed her a tissue. It wasn't her place to mention Reed's theory. But maybe she could work in the subject of the chapel to see if Eden brought up whether or not David wanted multiples the way she did.

Before Norah could even think about how to pose a question about marrying at the chapel, Eden's phone rang. Sara took Gabrielle as Eden lunged for her phone in her bag, clearly hoping it was her fiancé.

"It's him!" Eden shrieked. "It's David!"

Norah stared at Eden as she screamed, "Hello, Davy Doo?" into her phone and then realized she should at least pretend to give the woman some privacy.

Eden was listening, her blue eyes narrowing with every passing second, her expression turning murderous. "*What?* I was kidding when I got to your cousin's house today and said I was sure you left on your own because of me! I just said that so everyone would say 'Of course that's not true.' But it is!" she screamed so loudly that both babies startled and stopped fussing entirely.

Whoa boy. So Reed's theory was right.

"Yes, I hear the twins crying again, David. I'm in the same house with them. It's what babies do!" Silence. Eyes narrowing some more. Death expression. And then she said through gritted teeth, "I don't want just *one* baby. I want triplets! Or even quadruplets! Twins at the least!" More listening. More eyes narrowing. "Well, fine! Then I guess we're through!" She stabbed at the End Call button with her finger, threw the phone in her bag, then stormed out. A second later she was back. "I'm sorry you had to hear that. Apparently I was engaged to a weenie twerp! No offense to your husband or his family, Sara," she added, then stormed out again.

Norah stared at Sara, who looked as amazed as Norah felt.

"Omigod," Sara said. "What was that?"

Norah shifted little Charlotte in her arms. "A little miscommunication in expectations before the wedding."

"A little?" Sara shook her head. "And I don't know if I'd classify that as miscommunication. Eden has been talking about getting married at the chapel and having triplets from the first family dinner she was invited to. David knew what she wanted. He probably didn't think too much about it until his cousin had twins—colicky twins—and he realized what he'd be in for. David has witnessed some whopper arguments between me and my husband. He probably just ran scared with the wedding coming so close."

"Well, I'm glad he's okay—that he wasn't hurt or anything like that," Norah said, realizing something had changed. She gasped—Charlotte had fallen asleep in her arms. She glanced at Sara, who was beaming. Sara pointed to the nursery and Norah tiptoed into the room and laid the baby in her crib. The little creature didn't even stir.

"I owe you," Sara said. "Thank you!"

They glanced at Gabrielle, who was rubbing her eyes

and yawning. Easily transferred to the vibrating swing, she, too, was asleep a few seconds later.

"I get to have coffee!" Sara said. "Thank you so much for staying to help."

"Anytime," Norah said. "See you at the next class. Oh, and if your husband hears from David, will you let Reed know?"

"Will do," Sara said.

As Norah headed home, eager to see her own baby multiples, she wondered if she was the one with the problem. She'd picked three men who didn't want to be fathers. She'd dated David, albeit for two weeks. Then her babies' father. Now Reed.

She was chewing that over when she opened the front door to find Reed sitting in the family room with all three babies in their swings, cooing and batting at their little mobiles. He was reading them a story from a brightly colored book with a giraffe on the cover.

Not a father, huh? Sure. The man was father material whether he liked it or not. Knew it or not.

"Have I got news for you," she said and then told him the whole story about Eden and the phone call from David.

Reed shook his head. "At least he's not dead—yet, anyway. Once Eden gets her hands on him…"

"I didn't get the sense he told her where he was or when or if he was coming home."

"I'm ninety-nine percent sure I know where he is— Las Vegas. But it's a big place, and since he's not using his credit cards, he could be at any super-cheap hole-in-the-wall motel. Though now that he's let the cat out of the bag that he's alive and well and afraid of triplets, he might start using his cards and check in somewhere cushy while he lets Eden digest the news."

Not a minute later a call came in from the station. An officer reporting that David Dirk had finally used his MasterCard to check into the fancy Concordia Hotel on the Strip.

"I have to say, Detective. You're good."

"Does that mean you're coming to Vegas with me?" he asked.

Chapter 11

Just like that, Norah found herself on a plane to Las Vegas, a city she'd never been to, with Reed beside her, studying the floor plans of the Concordia Hotel and the streets of Vegas on his iPad.

As she stared out at the clouds below, she knew the answer she should have given was "No. Of course not. I'm not going." But what had come out of her mouth, with barely any hesitation was "Yes." This trip wasn't a honeymoon. Or a vacation. But it wasn't strictly business, either. Or Wedlock Creek police business. David Dirk had every right to disappear; once Reed knew for sure that the man had willingly left town, the case had been closed. But Reed wanted to find David and talk to him old friend to old friend. Bring him home. And Norah wanted some time away from real life with her…husband.

Why, she wasn't quite sure. What would be different in a new environment? They were the same people with the same gulf between them.

Still, the trip was a chance. To experience Reed off duty, away from home, where neither of them had any of their usual responsibilities. To see who they were together in a completely different environment. Maybe there would be nothing between them and Norah could just start to accept that their relationship was exactly what she'd agreed to. A platonic marriage slash business partnership for mutual benefit.

The only problem with that was the fact that just sitting this close to Reed, their sides practically touching, she'd never been so aware of a man and her physical attraction to him in her entire life.

"Of course, I booked us separate rooms," Reed said, turning to glance at her. "Right across the hall from each other."

Too bad the Concordia wasn't completely booked except for one small room with a king-size bed, she thought, mesmerized by the dark hair on his forearms and how the sunlight glinted on his gold wedding band, the one that symbolized their union.

Before she knew it, the plane had landed and they were checking in at the front desk, then being shown to their rooms. Reed had 401. Norah was in 402.

"Meet you in the hallway in twenty minutes?" he asked. "I don't have much of a plan to find David other than to sit in the lobby for a while to see if he passes through. We might get lucky. I tried calling David's friend Kyle Kirby, the one who seemed to be withholding, but he didn't answer his phone or my knock at his door. We're gonna have to do this the boring way."

"It's my chance to see you doing surveillance work," she said. "Not boring at all. See you in twenty," she added and hurried inside her room with her weekend bag.

The room was a bit fancier than she'd expected. King-size bed, wall of windows and a fuzzy white robe hanging on the bathroom door. She called her mom to check on the triplets, who were fine and having their snack, then she freshened up and changed into a casual skirt, silky tank top and strappy sandals.

Twenty minutes later, when she went into the hallway, Reed was standing there and she caught his gaze moving up and down the length of her. He liked strappy, clearly. Good.

He was amazingly handsome, as always. He wore dark pants and a dark buttoned shirt, no tie. He looked like a detective.

They sat in the well-appointed lobby for forty minutes, pretending to be poring over maps of the Strip and brochures and dinner menus. No sign of David. Many people came through the lobby, all shapes and sizes and nationalities. Norah noticed a coffee bar across the lobby and had a hankering for an iced mocha. She definitely needed caffeine.

"Want something?" she asked Reed, who was glancing over the lobby, his gaze shooting to the chrome revolving doors every time they spun.

"Iced coffee, cream and sugar. And thanks."

"Coming right up," she said and sauntered off, wondering if he took his eyes off his surveillance to watch her walk away. She turned back to actually check and almost gasped. He *was* watching her. But then he darted his eyes back to the revolving door. Busted!

This meant that no matter what he had to say about

ignoring their attraction to each other, he ignored it only when he had to. There was hope to change things between her and the detective. And she was going for it. What happened in Vegas didn't have to stay in Vegas all the time, right?

Her mood uplifted with her secret plan, Norah stood behind a group of women who had very high-maintenance drink orders—double no whip this and no moo that—and studied the board to see if she wanted to try something besides her usual iced mocha when someone said, "Norah?"

She whirled around.

And almost gasped again.

David Dirk himself was staring at her, his mouth agape. "Holy crap, it *is* you," he said, walking over to her. Tall and lanky with light brown hair and round, black glasses, he held an iced coffee in one hand and a small white plate with a crumb cake in the other. "I never took you for a Vegas type."

What did *that* mean? That she couldn't let loose and have fun? Let down the ole hair and have a cocktail or three? Throw away a couple hundred bucks? Okay, maybe fifty at most.

I'm actually here with the detective who's been searching for you for days, she wanted to say. But who knew what David's frame of mind was? He might bolt.

"I'm here with my husband," she said, holding up her left hand and giving it a little wave. She turned and looked toward where Reed was sitting, staring at him hard for a second until she caught his attention. When he looked up and clearly saw David, his eyes practically bugged out of his head.

She turned back to David, who was staring at her ring.

"Oh, wow, congrats!" David said, a genuine smile on his face. "I didn't know you got married. Good for you. And good for your triplets." He bit his lip, looked at the ring again and then promptly burst into tears. He put the drink and the crumb cake down on the counter beside them and slashed each hand under his eyes. "I'm supposed to be getting married tomorrow night. At the chapel," he added, looking stricken.

He sniffled and Norah reached into her bag for her little packet of tissues. He took the whole packet and noisily blew his nose.

"But…?" she prompted, despite knowing exactly what the *but* was.

Tears slipped down his cheeks. Had he always been such a crier? They'd gone to two movies during the two weeks they'd dated, action flicks with very little pathos, so she hadn't had a chance to see him show much emotion.

"I…" He dabbed at his eyes with a wadded-up tissue.

"Whoa, David? David Dirk?" Reed asked with great feigned surprise as he walked up to them.

David stared at Reed, clearly trying to place him. His mouth dropped open, then curved into a grin. "No way. No flipping way! Reed Barelli? Who I last saw when I was thirteen?"

"It's me, man," Reed said, extending his hand.

Instead of taking his hand, David pulled Reed into a hug and sobbed. "You're probably wondering how my life is after all these years. I'll tell you. It sucks. I've ruined everything. Destroyed the best thing that ever happened to me." He pulled a few tissues from the packet and dabbed at his eyes again.

"Why don't we go get a beer?" Reed said, his arm

slung around David's shoulders. "We'll catch up." He turned to Norah. "You'll be all right on your own for a couple of hours, honey?"

Honey. It was for show, but it warmed her heart nonetheless.

"Sure," she said. "I'll hit the shops. Maybe get a massage."

"Wait," David said. "*You two* are married? How'd you even meet?" he asked, looking from Reed to Norah.

"Long story," Reed said. "I'll tell you all about it over a cold one. And you can fill me in on what's going on with you."

David nodded, his shoulders slumped. "I let the best thing that ever happened to me get away."

"There's always a second chance if you don't screw it up," Reed said as they headed toward the bar.

Here's hoping so, Norah thought. *For everyone.*

The waiter placed two craft beers and a plate of nachos with the works on the square table in front of Reed and David. David took a chug of his beer, then said, "Okay, you first. How'd you meet Norah?"

He told David the entire story. The truth and nothing but the truth. He and Norah had talked about being generally tight-lipped about their story of origin, but he had a feeling David could use the information and apply it to himself.

Now it was David's eyes that were bugging out of his head.

"Oh man," David said, chugging more beer. "So you'll get it. You got married at the chapel. And now you're the father of triplets."

There was that word again. *Father.*

"What I can't believe is that you actually proposed *staying* married," David said. "The woman handed you annulment papers, man! You were home free."

"I couldn't just walk away from Norah and the babies. How could I?" He knew he didn't need to add, "You of all people should know that." He was sure David had heard it loud and clear. And from his old friend's expression, Reed was certain.

"I don't want to walk away from Eden," David said. "I love her. I know I screwed up by running away. But I had to think. I had to get my head on straight. Spending time with my cousin and those screaming colicky twins of his made me realize I'm not ready for that. I don't want that."

"You don't want *what*, exactly?" Reed asked. "A colicky baby? Twins? Or kids at all?"

David pulled a nacho onto his plate but just stared at it. "I don't know."

How could such a smart guy know so little? "Why not just tell Eden the truth?"

David frowned. "I did when I called her yesterday. She was so angry at me she hung up." Tears glistened in the guy's eyes and he ate the loaded nacho chip in one gulp.

"I think you should call Eden. FaceTime her, actually. And tell her exactly how you feel. Which sounds to me like you love her very much and want to marry her, but you're not ready for children and certainly not ready for multiples."

"That's it, exactly. I want kids someday. Just not now. And not all at once."

"Tell her. You need to have faith in your relationship with her, David. And remember, that showing her you didn't have faith in her, in your relationship, by running, is probably what is stinging her the most."

David seemed to think about that. He nodded, then took a sip of his beer. "So is it as awful as I think?"

Reed took a swig of his beer. "Is what?"

"Living with three screaming babies."

"Actually, I love those little buggers." The minute he said it, he felt his smile fade. He'd do anything for them. Of course he loved them. He had since the day he'd first upsie-downsied Bea on the rickety porch of Norah's old rental house.

"Really?" David asked, eyes wide behind the black-framed glasses.

"Yeah. Huh. I guess being a father can be more instinctive than I thought. There's really nothing to it other than caring and showing up and doing what needs to be done."

David nodded. "Right. I guess I don't want to do any of that—yet."

Reed laughed. "Then you shouldn't. And don't have to. Not everyone is ready for parenthood at the same time." He thought about Norah, who'd had to be ready. And him, too, in a way. But something told Reed he'd been ready for a long time. Waiting to give his heart to little humans in the way his own father hadn't been willing.

So. He *was* their father. Father. Daddy. He laughed, which made David look at him funny.

"Just thinking about something," Reed said.

David got up and polished off his beer, putting a twenty on the table. "I'm gonna go FaceTime Eden. Wish me luck. I'm gonna need it."

"Go get her," Reed said.

But as he sat there, finishing his beer and helping

himself to the pretty good nachos, he realized something that twisted his gut.

Maybe he'd been focusing on the father thing as an excuse not to focus on the marriage thing. Maybe it was only *husband* he had the issue with. *Husband* that he didn't want to be.

Deep down he knew it was true. Of course it was true; it was the whole reason he'd proposed what he'd proposed. A sham of a marriage. So he'd get what he really wanted. His ranch. And a chance to still be the father he'd never had. A chance to do right.

But he also knew deep down that it wasn't what Norah wanted. At all. And she was so independent-minded and used to being on her own that he was pretty sure she wouldn't give up her dreams so soon. She'd tell him the plan wasn't working, that she needed more and she'd hold out for a man who could be a father and a husband.

She deserved that.

Reed sat there long after his beer was gone, his appetite for the nachos ruined. What the hell was going to happen to him and Norah?

If Norah wasn't mistaken, Reed was being…distant.

While Reed had been with David at the bar, she'd gone into the hotel's clothing boutique and bought herself a little black dress she'd have no use for at home. It wasn't cheap and she'd likely wear it every few years, since it was kind of a classic Audrey Hepburn sleeveless with just the right amount of low neckline to make Norah feel a bit more daring than her usual mom-of-three self.

She and Reed had agreed to meet at six thirty for dinner at an Italian restaurant in their hotel that was supposed to have incredible food. But when she came out of her room at six thirty on the nose, all dolled up, including a light dab of perfume in the cleavage, Reed seemed surprised. And kept his eyes on her face. Not even a peek at her in the hotsy-totsy dress.

Instead, he filled her in on what had happened with David, how he'd texted his old buddy an hour ago to ask if he'd spoken to Eden and how things had gone. David hadn't gotten back to him.

Love, marriage, parenthood, life. Why was it so complicated? Why did wanting one thing mean you had to give up another thing? Compromise was everything in life and relationships.

Can I give up wanting what I used to dream about? she asked herself as they walked into Marcello's, so romantic and dimly lit and full of candles and oil paintings of nudes and lovers that Norah figured Reed hadn't known what they were in for. *Can I stay married to a man I'm falling in love with when it's platonic and he wants to keep it that way forever?*

Maybe not forever. Maybe just till the triplets were grown and off starting their lives and he could finally take a breath from the sense of responsibility he felt. Oh, only eighteen years. No biggie.

Face-palm. Could she live this way for eighteen years?

Norah had just noticed a sign on an easel by the long zinc bar that said Closed For Private Event when a woman rushed up to them. The restaurant was closed? Or the bar?

"Oooh," the woman said, ushering them inside the restaurant "You two had better hurry. There's only one table left. Otherwise you'll have to eat standing at the counter along the back."

Huh? She glanced at Reed, who shrugged, and they followed the hostess to a small round table for two. A man and a woman sat a table on a platform in the center of the dining room, a candle between them, wineglasses and a plate of bruschetta.

Hmm, bruschetta, Norah thought. She definitely wanted some of that. "Maybe it's their anniversary," she told Reed. "And they're high rollers or something, so they get a platform."

"You never know in Vegas," he said, his dark eyes flashing in the dimly lit room. He looked so damned hot, this time all in black, again tieless but wearing a jacket and black shoes.

They were seated and Norah couldn't help but notice the fortyish couple at the table beside theirs. The woman sat with her arms crossed over her chest, looking spitting mad. The man was gobbling up Italian bread and slathering it with butter.

"How can you even eat when I'm this upset!" the woman hiss-whispered.

The man didn't quite roll his eyes, but he didn't stop buttering the bread or popping it in his mouth.

"Welcome!" said the woman at the platform table.

Norah turned her attention to her. She and the man beside her stood. They had microphones. Gulp. This was clearly the "special event." Had she and Reed crashed a wedding or something?

Should they get up now and slink out? While all eyes were focused on the couple and it was dead quiet otherwise?

"We'll slip out when she stops talking, when it's less noticeable," Reed whispered.

Norah nodded. *Awk*ward.

"I know it's not easy for you to be here," the woman continued, turning slowly around the room to speak to all tables. "And because you are here, you've taken the first step in your relationship recovery."

Okay, what? Relationship recovery?

Reed raised an eyebrow and looked at Norah; now it was her turn to shrug.

"My name is Allison Lerner," the woman on the platform said. "My husband, Bill, here, and I have been married for thirty-six years. Yes, we got married at eighteen—*badump!* No, seriously, ladies and gents, we have been married for thirty-six years. Some of those years were so bumpy we threatened each other with divorce every other day. Some months were good. Some days were amazing. Do you want to know *why* we didn't divorce despite the arguments, problems, issues, this, that and the other?"

"Yes!" a woman called out.

Allison smiled. "We didn't divorce because—and this is the big secret—we *didn't want* to. Not really. Even when we hated each other. We didn't want to not be married to each other. Not really."

"What the hell kind of special event is this?" Reed whispered. "They're the entertainment?"

"God, I hope not," Norah whispered back.

"All of you taking tonight's Relationship Recovery seminar are here because you don't want to divorce or separate or go your separate ways, either. So enjoy a glass of wine, folks, order your appetizers and entrées, and once the waiters are off in the kitchen, we'll start the hard work of saving our relationships. Because we want to!"

Norah glanced around. The woman with the arms

crossed over her chest had tears in her eyes. Her husband was rubbing her arm—half-heartedly, but hey, at least he was doing something. The entire restaurant must be booked for the seminar.

"I sure got this one restaurant choice wrong," Reed said. "Shall we?" he asked, throwing down his napkin.

"Sir, you can do this," Allison Lerner said from behind them as she put a hand on Reed's arm. She and her husband must have been on the lookout for runners. "You deserve this. You both do. Give yourselves—and your marriage," she added, glancing at their wedding rings, "a chance."

"No, I—" Reed started to say.

"Allison is right," Norah said to Reed. "We need to learn how to fight for our marriage instead of against it."

As Reed gaped at her, she realized how true that was. Reed was fighting against it without even knowing it because he didn't want a real marriage. Norah was fighting against it because she wanted more when she'd agreed to less. Did that even make sense? No wonder she was so confused about her feelings.

"We need to figure out how to make this work, right?" Norah said. "Let's stay."

Reed stared at her, then glanced at Allison's patiently kind face. He sat back down.

"I'm thinking of pasta," Norah said, opening her menu.

He raised his eyebrow at her. Scowled a bit. Then she saw the acquiescence in his eyes and the set of his shoulders. "Okay, okay. I'm in." He opened his menu.

They ordered a delicious-sounding seafood risotto as an appetizer. Norah chose the four-cheese-and-mushroom ravioli for an entrée; Reed went with the stuffed filetto mignon. Norah sure hoped he'd offer her a bite.

"Everyone, take a sip of your beverage—wine, soda, water, what have you," Bill Lerner said from the platform.

Norah and Reed picked up their glasses, clinked and took a sip. The woman next to them frowned. There was no clinking at their table.

"Okay, now put down your drinks," Bill said. "Turn to your partner. Look at your partner and say the first nice thing that comes to you in reference to your partner. Ladies, you begin."

Norah turned to Reed. This was an easy one. "I love how you are with the triplets. I love how you read to them and blow raspberries on Brody's and Bea's arms but not Bella's because you know she doesn't like it. I love that you know which of them likes sweet potatoes and which hates carrots. I feel like I can relax as a parent in my own home…well, *your* home, for the first time since they were born because you're there. Really, really there. It's a good feeling. Better than I even hoped it would be."

Norah felt tears spring to her eyes. She hadn't meant to say all that. But every word was true. Oh hell. That was the entire reason she'd agreed not to rip up the annulment papers—so that exactly what had happened would happen. And she wanted things to change? She wanted more? She was being selfish. Demanding more of Reed than he wanted to give. Putting the triplets' good new fortune in jeopardy. Mommy's love life had to come second. Period.

Reed took her hand and held it. "Thank you. That means a lot to me. Those babies mean a lot to me."

She almost burst into tears but held back the swell of emotion by taking a sip of wine.

"Okay, gentlemen," Allison said from the platform.

"Your turn. Say the first true and nice thing you feel about your partner."

Reed took a sip of his wine and then looked at Norah. "I admire you. You've got your act together. You're lovely. You're kind. You're funny. I like seeing you around the house."

Norah laughed. She liked what he'd said. Maybe it wasn't quite as personal as what she'd said, but it came down to him liking her, really liking her, as a person. And liking having her around.

"Okay, gentlemen," Bill said into the mic. "Now look at your partner and tell her how you felt about what she said."

Reed put down his glass of wine, which from his expression, he clearly wanted to gulp. "Maybe I am the triplets' father, after all."

Norah did feel tears sting her eyes this time and she didn't wipe them away. She was also speechless.

"I realized it before you said what you said. I realized it from talking to David Dirk. I love those babies, Norah. They have my heart. I am their father. If they'll have me."

Norah bit her lip. "They'll have you." *I'll have you.*

"Okay, ladies, now tell your partner how the nice thing he said about you made you feel."

Norah took Reed's hand and squeezed it. "You'll never say anything that I'll treasure more than what you just did. The triplets come first. That's just how it is with me."

He tilted his head as if considering something. But he didn't say anything. He just nodded.

"Whew!" Allison said from the platform. "That is quite a bit of work we did all before the entrées were served! Feel free to talk about what we just did or change the subject and enjoy dinner. Once you've had a chance to eat, we'll resume with the next exercise. Of course, after dinner, we'll get into the heavy lifting."

"Luckily we've got plans," Reed whispered. "So we'll have to skip the heavy lifting."

Norah smiled. "Oh?"

"There's something I want to show you. Something more fun than heavy lifting."

"I feel like my head was put back on straight," she said. "So I'd say this Relationship Recovery seminar was a huge success. In just one exercise."

He squeezed her hand but again didn't say anything and cut into his delicious-looking filetto mignon. He cut a bite and instead of lifting the fork to his mouth, reached it out to hers. "Ladies first."

She smiled, feeling her moment-ago resolve to focus on the partnership and not her heart start to waver. How was she supposed to avoid her feelings for Reed Barelli when he was so wonderful?

She took the bite and closed her eyes at how tender and delicious the steak was. "Amazing," she said. "Thank you."

She scooped a ravioli onto his plate. "For you."

And then they ate, drank and didn't talk more about the exercise, which the poor woman at the next table was trying to get her husband to do.

"So you really like my hair this way?" she'd said three times.

The husband shoveled his pasta into his mouth and barely looked up. "Honestly, Kayla, with your hair blonder like that, you look just like you did the day I got the nerve to talk to you after earth science class junior year of high school. Took me a month to get the courage."

The woman gasped and looked like she might faint. Pure joy crossed her face and she reached out her hand and squeezed her husband's. "Oh, Skip."

Sometimes people knew how to say the right things at the right time.

Reed glanced over at the Lerners on the platform. They had their arms linked and were feeding each other fettuccine. Norah's and Reed's plates were practically empty, both of them having just declared they couldn't eat another bite. "I say we slip out now."

Norah smiled. "Let's go."

Reed put a hundred-dollar bill and a fifty on the table, then took her hand and made a point of asking a waiter where the restrooms were, pointing and gesturing for show. They dashed over to the entrance and then quickly ran up the hall. They were free.

"That was unexpected," Norah said on a giggle as they stopped around the corner of the lobby. Her first giggle since her wedding night.

"But worthy," Reed said. "Our marriage feels stronger. We actually did some good work in there."

Norah smiled. "We did. So what did you want to show me?"

"Follow me." He pressed the elevator button. Once they were inside, he pressed the button marked Roof. They rode up forty-two floors and exited into a hallway without any doors except one with a sign that said Roof. Reed pushed open the door and she followed.

It was a roof deck, with couches and chairs and flowers and a bar staffed with a waiter in a tuxedo. Reed took her hand and led her over to the other side of the deck, away from the small groups gathered. She gasped at the view of the Strip, sparkling lights everywhere, all underneath a canopy of stars.

"Something else, huh?" he asked, looking up and then around at the lights.

"Yeah," she said. "Something else. You sure don't see a view like this in Wedlock Creek."

Would she appreciate it even more if Reed were standing a drop closer? With his arm around her? Or behind her, pressed against her, both of his strong arms wrapped around her? Yes, she would. But hadn't she said she wasn't going to be greedy and selfish? She knew what was important. She had to remember that and not want more.

Reed's phone buzzed in his pocket. He pulled it out and read the screen. "It's David Dirk," he whispered. He turned toward the view. "Hey, David." He listened, then smiled. "Great news. And yes, we'd love to. See you in two hours."

Norah's eyebrows shot up. "We'd love to what?"

"Seems we're invited to be David and Eden's witnesses at their wedding at the Luv U Wedding Chapel."

Norah was surprised. "Wait. Eden flew here? She's giving up the Wedlock Creek chapel and her dream of triplets?"

"I guess she did some soul-searching and decided what she wanted most."

Norah nodded. "That's the key. What you want most. You have to follow that even if it involves some compromise."

And what she wanted most was a good life for her children, the security and safety Reed would provide, the love and kindness, the role model he'd be. She wanted that for her triplets more than she wanted anything. Even if her own heart had to break to get it.

He'd be there, right? Even if he was a million miles away at the same time.

"Wow," Norah said. "She must really love him."

"Well, she's still getting some assurance. Turns out there's a legend associated with the Luv U Wedding Chapel."

"And what would that be?"

"Eden's parents eloped there the summer after high school, scandalizing both sets of parents. Twenty-five years later the Pearlmans are happy as can be. According to Pearlman family legend, if you marry at the Luv U Wedding Chapel in Las Vegas, you're pretty much guaranteed happily-ever-after."

Norah laughed. "That's a really good legend."

Reed nodded. "This has turned out to be a pretty busy day for us. First a marriage counseling seminar over dinner and now we're witnesses at a legend-inspired wedding that almost didn't happen."

"Like ours," she said. "It's pretty crazy that it happened at all."

He looked into her eyes and squeezed her hand. "I'm glad it did happen, Norah. Our insane wedding changed my life. For the much, much better."

She squeezed his hand back. "Mine, too."

Because I'm in love with my husband. A good thing *and* exactly what wasn't supposed to happen.

I love you, Reed Barelli, she shouted in her head. *I love you!*

She wondered what he was shouting in his head.

Chapter 12

"Well, it's not the Wedlock Creek Wedding Chapel," Eden said, reaching for her "something borrowed," her grandmother's seed-pearl necklace. "But if getting married here blessed my parents with twenty-five so-far happy years and four children, I'll take it."

Norah clasped the pretty necklace for Eden and looked at her reflection in the standing mirror in the bridal room of the Luv U Wedding Chapel. The bride looked absolutely lovely in her princess gown with more lace and beading than Norah had ever seen on one dress. "I love it. Your own family legend."

Eden bit her lip and looked at Norah in the mirror. "Do you really believe in the Wedlock Creek legend? I mean, you had triplets without getting married there."

"Well, actually, I did get married there, just after the fact. So maybe the fates of the universe knew that down the road I'd be getting married at the chapel and so I got my triplets. Just early." She rolled her eyes. "Oh, who the hell knows? I think Reed will tell you the legend is true, though. He got married at the chapel and voilà— father of triplets."

Eden laughed. "Poor guy." Her smile faded as she stared at herself. "Do you think I'm an idiot for forgiving David and marrying him on his terms after what he pulled?"

"I think you know David best and you know what's right and what feels right. No one else can tell you otherwise."

Eden adjusted her long, flowy veil. "I know he loves me. But he did a real bonehead thing just running away. I mean, I *really* thought something happened to him." She frowned. "Maybe he's too immature to get married. I know I'm not about to win Person of the Year or anything, but still."

"Well, he got scared and he didn't know how to deal with it, so he fled. He didn't want to lose you by telling you how he really felt. In the end, though, he did call you and tell you the truth. You two worked it out, because here you are."

Eden's smile lit up her pretty face. "It'll make one hell of a family story, huh? I'll be telling my grandkids about the time Grandpa ran for the hills to avoid having quadruplets."

Norah laughed. "You just might have quadruplets anyway. You never know."

"Mwahaha," Eden said, doing her best evil-laugh impersonation. She turned around to face Norah. "So is this your honeymoon? Is that why you and Reed are here?"

Honeymoons were for real newlyweds. She sighed inwardly. There she went again, wanting more.

Was it wrong to want more when it came to love? If your heart was bursting?

Eden was eyeing her, so she'd better say something reasonable. She had no idea what Reed had told David about the two of them and how they'd ended up married. Probably the truth. She knew Reed Barelli well enough to know that he didn't lie.

"I suppose it's like a mini honeymoon. Reed just started at the police department, so he can't take off any real time." She kind of liked saying that. It was true—in a way. This was like their honeymoon. And since they *were* newlyweds, they should have this time away.

"He must really love you," Eden said, turning back to the mirror to freshen her pink-red lipstick. "He married a single mother of seven-month-old triplets."

Norah felt her heart squeeze. How she wished that were true. Of course, they couldn't go backward and fall in love and then get married. They'd already done the backward thing by getting married first, then actually getting to know each other. She smiled, her heartache easing just a bit. There was hope there, no? If you started out backward, you could only go forward. And forward was love and forever.

Unless your husband was Reed "No Romance" Barelli.

Did a man who didn't believe in romance bring his dry-eyed deal of a wife to see a breathtaking view forty-two flights above the city? Did he do any of the sweet and wonderful things Reed had done? Including offering her the first bite of his incredible filetto mignon?

"He's a great guy," Norah said. He sure was.

Eden smiled and checked that her pearl drop earrings were fastened. "You're so lucky. You have your triplets and your hot new detective husband who's madly in love with you. You have everything."

Oh, if only.

After tearing up a time or two at the wedding and doing her official job as Witness One, Norah watched as David Dirk, looking spiffy in a tuxedo, lifted his bride and carried her out of the Luv U chapel. Reed threw rice and then it was time for the next couple to say their I Do's, so Norah and Reed headed out into the balmy July Las Vegas air.

"Case closed with a happy ending," Reed said. "The best kind of case."

"I think they're going to be just fine," she agreed. "But he'll probably keep doing dumb things."

Reed laughed. "No doubt." He looked over at her. "So should we head back to the hotel? Have a nightcap on the terrace?"

"Sounds good," she said. And too romantic. But there was nothing she'd rather do than continue this night of love and matrimony with her own husband.

They passed a lot of couples holding hands. Brides and grooms with their heads popped out of limo sun-roofs, screaming, "I did!" The happy, drunken energy reminded her of her wedding night.

In ten minutes they were back at the Concordia, taking the elevator to the fourth floor. Reed's room was just like hers. The king-size bed in the center of the room had her attention. Suddenly all she could think about was waking up the morning after her wedding, the shock of seeing Fabio-Reed in her bed, half-naked except for the hot, black boxer briefs, the hard planes of his chest and rippling muscles as he shifted an arm, the way his long eyelashes rested on his cheeks.

"Do you think that on our wedding night we...?" She trailed off, staring at the bed.

"We what?"

"Had sex," she said, turning to face him.

He placed his key card on the dresser, took off his jacket and folded it over the desk chair, then went over to the minibar. "No. In fact, I'm ninety-nine percent sure."

"How?"

He poured two glasses of wine from the little bottles. "Because if I made love to you, Norah, I never would have forgotten it." He held her gaze and she felt her cheeks burn a bit, the warmth spreading down into her chest, to her stomach, to her toes.

She took the wineglass he held out and took a sip, then moved over to the windows, unable to stand so close to him or to look directly at him without spontaneously combusting. Being in his room, the bed, images of him, the very thought of his gorgeous face and incredibly hot body... She wanted him with a fierceness she couldn't remember ever experiencing. She wanted to feel his hands and mouth all over her. She wanted him to be her husband—for real.

Maybe she could show him how it could be, how good it could be between them. That if she of all people could let go of mistrust and walls and actually let herself risk feeling something, then he could, too, dammit. There was no way she could be married to this man, share a home and life with him, and not have him in every sense of the word. And the fact that he was clearly attracted to her gave her the cojones to take a long sip of her wine, put down the glass and sit on the edge of the bed.

He was watching her, but he stayed where he was. On the other side of the bed, practically leaning against the wall.

So now what? Should she throw herself at him? No way was she doing that.

Ugh, this was stupid. Forget it. She wasn't going to beg this man—any man—to want her; all of her, heart, mind, soul, body. Hadn't her smart sister told her to let what would happen just happen? She shouldn't be forcing it.

She sighed a wistful sigh and stood. "Well, I guess I'll head to my room, maybe watch a movie. Something funny." She needed funny. A good laugh.

"Sounds good," he said. "I could go for funny." He grabbed the remote control off the desk and suddenly the guide was on the screen. "Hmm, *Police Academy 3*, *Out of Africa*, *Jerry Maguire* or *Full Metal Jacket*?"

Uh-oh. She hadn't meant they watch together. They were going to lie down on the bed, inches apart, and watch a movie? Really?

"Unless you were hinting that you're sick of me and don't want company," he said with a smile. "I could never get tired of you, so I forget not everyone is dazzled by me 24/7."

She burst out laughing. Hot *and* funny. Who needed the movie? She'd just take him.

"I've seen *Jerry Maguire* at least five times, but you really can't see that enough," she said.

"Really? I've never seen it."

You. Complete. Me, she wanted to scream at him and

then grab him down onto the bed and kiss him every-where on his amazing body.

"Wait, we can't watch a movie without popcorn," he said, picking up the phone. Was the man really order-ing from room service? Yes, he was. He asked for a big bowl of popcorn, freshly popped, two sodas, a bottle of a good white wine and two slices of anything chocolate.

Amazing. "You really know how to watch a movie," she said.

He grinned. "The way I see it, you might as well do everything right."

Yup. That was why he hadn't rushed the annulment papers to the county clerk's too-efficient replacement. Because he did things right. Like stay married to a mother of teething seven-month-old triplets who'd lived in a falling-down dump and made her living by the pot pie.

Twenty minutes later, their little movie feast delivered, they settled on the bed, on top of the blanket, the big bowl of popcorn between them, to watch *Jerry Maguire*.

"Oh, it's the *Mission Impossible* dude," he said, throwing some popcorn into his mouth. They were both barefoot and Norah couldn't stop looking at Reed's sexy feet.

"Don't see many movies, huh?" she asked.

"Never really had much time. Hopefully now in Wedlock Creek, I will. Slower pace of life and all that."

She nodded and they settled down to watch. Reed laughed a lot, particularly at the scenes with Cuba Gooding Jr. By the time Renée Zellweger said Tom Cruise had her at hello, Norah was mush and teary-eyed.

"Softy," Reed said, slinging his arm over so that she could prop up against him. She did.

Great. Now they were cuddling. Sort of. His full attention was on the movie. Norah found it pretty difficult to keep her mind on the TV with her head against Reed's shoulder and him stretched out so close beside her. She ate popcorn and dug into the chocolate cake to take her mind off Reed and sex.

But as the credits rolled, Reed turned onto his side to face her. "Do you believe in that 'you complete me' stuff?"

She turned onto her side, too. "Believe in it? Of course I do."

"So someone else can complete you?" he asked. "You're not finished without a romantic partner?"

"What it *means* is that your romantic partner brings out the best in you, makes you realize and understand the depth of your feelings, makes you feel whole in a way you never did before, that suddenly nothing is missing from your life."

He smiled. "I don't know, Norah. I think it was just a good line."

She shook her head. "Nope. She completes him and he knows it."

He reached out to move a strand of hair that had fallen across her face, but instead of pulling his hand back, he caressed her cheek. "You're a true romantic."

"You are, too. You just don't know it," she said. It was so true. Everything he did was the mark of a romantic. His chivalry. His code of honor. His willingness to watch *Jerry Maguire*. The man had ordered popcorn and chocolate cake from room service, for God's sake. He was a romantic.

The thought made her smile. But now he was staring at her mouth.

His finger touched her lip. "Popcorn crumb," he said. "Does popcorn have crumbs?"

"Yes," he whispered, his face just inches away. He propped up on his elbow and moved another strand of hair away from her face. There was a combination of tenderness and desire in his eyes, in his expression.

He was *thinking*, she realized, fighting the urge to move his head down and kiss her. *Win out, urge*, she telepathically sent to his brain. *Do it. Kiss her. Kiss. Her.*

And then he did. Softly at first. Passionately a second later.

He moved on top of her, his hands in her hair, his mouth moving from her lips to her neck. She sucked in a breath, her hands roaming his back, his neck, his hair. Thick, silky hair. "Tell me to stop, Norah. This is nuts."

"I don't want you to stop. I want you to make love to me."

He groaned and tore off his shirt, then unzipped her dress. She sat up and flung the dress off before he could change his mind. His eyes were on her lacy bra. Her one sexy, black undergarment with panties to match, chosen for this possibility.

And it was happening. Mmm. Yes, it was happening! She lay back, his eyes still on her cleavage. That was good. He was not thinking. He was only feeling. And the moment her hands touched the bare skin of his chest, he was hers. He groaned again and his mouth was on hers, one hand undoing his pants and shrugging out of them while the other unsnapped her bra like a pro.

Suddenly they were both naked. He lay on top of her and propped up on his forearms. "I can't resist you, Norah. I don't have *that* much self-control."

She smiled. "Good."

By the time he reached for the foil-wrapped little packet in his wallet, she was barely able to think for the sensations rocketing every inch, every cell, of her body. But she was vaguely aware that he'd brought a condom. Probably a whole box. Which meant he'd anticipated that something could happen between them.

Her husband *wasn't* lost to her behind that brick wall he'd erected between him and love, him and *feeling*. There was hope for them. That was all she needed to know. In that moment her heart cracked wide-open and let him in fully, risks be damned.

And then he lay on top of her and suddenly they were one, all thought poofing from her head.

Reed's phone was on silent-vibrate, but as a cop he'd long trained himself to catch its hum. He must have drifted off to sleep after two rounds of amazing sex with Norah. His wife. Sex that they weren't supposed to have. Not part of the deal.

He glanced over at her. She lay next to him, turned away on her side, asleep, he figured from her breathing. Her long reddish-brown hair flowed down her sexy bare shoulders. Just looking at her had him stirring once more, wanting her like crazy, but then his phone vibrated again on the bedside table. Then again. And again. What the hell could this be at almost one thirty in the morning?

David Dirk was what it was. A series of texts.

I owe u, man. Good talk we had earlier.

I'm lying here next to my gorgeous wife, feeling so lucky.

I might as well have won a mil downstairs, bruh.

I'm realizing the depth of my love for this woman means she comes 1st.

The selfish crap is stopping. I love Eden 2 death and I'm putting her needs above my own.

Double-date back in the Creek, dude?

Well, good for David Dirk. And Eden. The guy had flipped out, fled town in a spectacularly immature fashion, but had worked it out with himself and laid his heart bare to the woman he loved. And they'd both ended up getting what they'd wanted: each other—still with a hearty dose of legend on their side.

So why was Reed feeling so…unsettled? He put the phone back on the table and lay very still, staring up at the ceiling.

Because he wasn't putting Norah's needs above his own? She wanted the whole shebang—love, romance, snuggles while watching *Jerry Maguire*, a shared, true partnership. And what was he giving her? Just the partnership. Fine, he threw in some snuggles while watching the biggest date-night movie of all time.

And then made mad, passionate love to his wife of "convenience." His life-plan partner.

He shook his head at himself.

He got to feel like a better man than his father was when he was too much of a coward to marry and plan a family of his own. He got to have his ranch when his grandmother would be sorely disappointed at the "marriage" he'd engineered to have the Barelli homestead.

Meanwhile he was keeping Norah from finding what she really wanted. She'd agreed to the marriage deal; she herself had said she wanted nothing to do with love or romance or men. But something had changed for her. Because her heart had opened up. Somehow. Married to a brick wall like him.

Whereas he was still unbreakable and unblastable.

He turned his head and looked at Norah, reaching for a silky strand of her hair. Sex with her was everything he'd thought it would be; they fit perfectly together, they were in rhythm. But afterward, part of him had wanted to hit the streets and just breathe it out. He'd stayed put for her, like he was doing her some kind of big favor. Which had made him feel worse about what he could and couldn't give her.

There was only one thing to do, he realized as he lay there staring back up at the ceiling.

One way out of the mess he'd created by thinking this kind of marriage could work, could be a thing.

Yes. The more he thought about what he needed to do, the more he knew it was the right thing. He'd have to take an hour off work in the morning, but he'd make up the time and then some.

Decision made, he turned over and faced the beige-and-white-striped wallpaper until he realized Norah was a much better sight to fall asleep to. He wanted to reach out and touch her, to wrap his arms around her and tell her how much he cared about her, for her, but he couldn't.

Nothing about Reed Barelli escaped Norah's notice. So she'd caught on to his distance immediately. It had started in the hotel room when she'd woken up five minutes ago. All the warmth from the night before was gone, replaced by this…slight chill. He was polite. Respectful. Offering to run out for bagels or to call room service.

She sat up in bed, pulling the top sheet and blankets up to her chest. *Keep it light, Norah*, she warned herself. "All that hot sex does have me starving," she said with a smile, hoping to crack him.

Instead of sliding back into bed for another round, he practically raced to the phone. "I'll call room service. Omelet? Side of hash browns?"

Deep endless sigh. If she couldn't have him, she may as well eat. She hadn't been kidding. She *was* starving. "Western omelet. And yes to hash browns. And a vat of coffee."

He ordered two of that.

She could still feel the imprint of his lips on hers, all over her, actually. The scent of him was on her. He was all over her, inside her, with her. She felt like Cathy in *Wuthering Heights—"I am Heathcliff!"*

Maybe not the most hopeful reference for the Barellis of Wedlock Creek.

"Here you go," he said, handing her the fluffy terry robe, compliments of the Concordia. "Use mine."

Either he didn't want to see her naked anymore or he was just being kind and polite and respectful. She knew it was all the latter. Last night, everything he did had shown how much he'd wanted to see her naked, how much he'd wanted *her*. And now it was all over. Light of day and all that other back-to-Cinderella, back-to-a-pumpkin reality.

They ate on the terrace, making small talk. He asked how the triplets were, since of course she'd already called to check in on them. They were all fine. The Pie Diner was fine. The police station was fine. Eden and David were fine. Everything was fine but them. What had changed so drastically overnight?

He pushed his hash browns around on his plate. "Norah, we need to talk. Really talk."

Oh hell. She put down her coffee mug. "Okay."

He cleared his throat, then took a long sip of his coffee. Then looked out at the view. Then, finally, he looked at her. "I will stand by you, beside you, and be a father to Bella, Bea and Brody. I want to be their father."

"But…?" she prompted, every nerve ending on red alert.

"But I sense—no, I *know*—that you want more. You want a real marriage. And I'm holding you back from that. If you want to find a man who will be both husband and father, I don't want to hold you back, Norah. You deserve everything."

"I deserve everything, but you won't give me everything," she said, pushing at her hash browns. Anything to avoid directly looking into his eyes.

"I wish I could, Norah. I don't have it in me. I guess it's been too long, too many years of shutting down and out. My job made it easy. I swore off all that stuff, said 'no more,' and I guess I really meant it."

Crud. She wished there was something lying around on the floor of the terrace that she could kick. A soda can. Anything. "So I'm supposed to decide whether I want half a marriage or to let you go so I can find everything in one man."

He glanced out toward the Strip, at the overcast sky. "Yes."

Half of him or the possibility of everything with another? She'd take a quarter of Reed Barelli.

Oh, really, Norah? That's all you deserve? A man who can't or won't give more of himself?

He wanted to serve and protect the community and his family. Same thing to him. She shook her head, trying to make sense of this, trying to make it work for her somehow. But she wasn't a town. She wasn't a bunch of houses or people. She was his *wife*.

"And if I hand you the annulment papers to sign, you're prepared to give up the Barelli ranch? Your heart and soul?"

His expression changed then, but she couldn't quite read it. There was pain, she was pretty sure.

"Yes, I'm fully prepared to give it up."

God. She sucked in a breath and turned away, trying to keep control of herself. "Well, then. If you're willing to give up the ranch that means so much to you, I think we both know we need to get those annulment papers over to the courthouse."

She slid off her wedding ring, her heart tearing in two. "Here," she managed to croak out, handing it to him. "I don't want it."

He bit his lip but pocketed it. Then she pushed out of her chair, ran back into the room, grabbed her clothes off the floor and rushed across the hall into her room.

She sat on the edge of her bed and sobbed.

Chapter 13

"What? You're just gonna let him go?" Aunt Cheyenne said with a frown.

Norah stirred the big pot of potatoes on the stove in the kitchen of the Pie Diner. She'd asked herself that very question on the flight back home and all night in her bedroom at the ranch. Reed had packed a bag and had gone to the one hotel in town to give her "some privacy with your thoughts."

She'd wanted to throw something at him then. But she'd been too upset. When the door had closed behind him, she was just grateful the triplets were with her mother so that she could give in to her tears and take the night to get it out of her system. Come morning, she'd known she'd have to turn into a pot pie baker and a mother and she wouldn't have the time or the luxury of a broken heart.

"Not like I have much choice," she said.

"Uh, Norah, a little more gently with that spoon," her mother said from her station across the kitchen. "The potatoes aren't Reed."

Norah took a deep breath and let up on the stirring. She offered her mom a commiserating smile. "I'll be okay. The potatoes will be okay. The only one who won't be okay is that stubborn brick wall I married by accident."

"Fight for him!" Cheyenne said. "The man is so used to being a lone wolf that he doesn't feel comfortable having a real-life partner. He's just not used to it. But he likes being married or he wouldn't have suggested staying married—no matter what."

Norah had thought of that. Her mind had latched on to so many hopeful possibilities last night. But then she'd come back to all he'd said on the terrace in Las Vegas. "He's giving up the ranch to undo it," Norah reminded her aunt.

"Because he thinks you're losing out," her mother said, filling six pie crusts with the fragrant beef stew she and Cheyenne had been working on this morning. "He wants you to have everything you deserve. The man loves you, Norah."

She shook her head. "If he loved me, he'd love me. And we wouldn't have had that conversation in Vegas." Tears poked her eyes and she blinked them back. The triplets were in the office slash nursery having their nap and she needed to think about them. In Reed, they'd have a loving father but would grow up with a warped view of love and marriage because their parents' lack of love—kisses, romance, the way a committed couple acted—would be absent. They would be roommates, and her children would grow up thinking that was how married people behaved. No sirree.

The super annoying part? She couldn't even go back to the old Norah's ways of having given up on love and romance. Because she'd fallen hard for Reed and she knew she was capable of that much feeling. She did want it. She wanted love. She wanted a father for her babies. She wanted that man to be the same.

She wanted that man to be Reed.

He didn't want to be that man. Or couldn't be. Whatever!

Being Fabio was his fantasy, though, she suddenly realized. A man who *did* want to marry. Fabio had suggested it, after all. Fabio had carried her into that chapel.

Could there be hope?

A waitress popped her head into the kitchen "Norah? There's someone here to see you. Henry Peterfell." The young woman filled her tray with her order of three chicken pot pies and one beef and carried it back out.

"Henry Peterfell is here to see me?" She glanced at her mother and aunt. Henry Peterfell was a pricey attorney and very involved in local government. What could he want with Norah?

She wiped her hands on her apron and went through the swinging-out door into the dining room. Fiftysomething-year-old Henry, in his tan suit, sat at the counter, a Pie Diner yellow to-go bag in front of him. "Ah, Ms. Ingalls. I stopped in to pick up lunch and realized I had some papers for you to sign in my briefcase, so if you'd like, you can just John Hancock them here. Or you can make an appointment to come into the office. Whatever is more convenient."

Panic rushed into her stomach. "Papers? Am I being sued?"

Oh God. Was Reed divorcing her? Perhaps he figured they couldn't annul the marriage because they'd made love. *You're the one who gave him back your ring,* she reminded herself, tears threatening again. *Of course he's divorcing you.*

"Sued? No, no, nothing like that." He set his leather briefcase on the counter and pulled out a folder. "There are three sets. You can sign where you see the neon arrow. There, there and there," he said, pointing at the little sticky tabs.

Norah picked up the papers. And almost fell off the chair.

"This is a deed," she said slowly. "To the Barelli ranch."

"Yes," the lawyer said. "Everything is in order. Lovely property."

"Reed turned the ranch over to me? The ranch is now mine?"

"That's right. It's yours. Once you sign, of course. There, there and there," he said, gesturing.

Norah stared at the long, legal-size papers, the black type swimming before her eyes. *What?* Why would Reed do this?

"Mr. Peterfell, would it be all right if I held on to these to read first?"

"Absolutely," he said. "Just send them to my office or drop them off at your convenience."

With that, he and his briefcase of unexpected documents were gone.

Reed had deeded the ranch to her. His beloved ranch. The only place that had ever felt like home to him.

Because he didn't feel he deserved it now that they were going to split up? That had to be the reason. He wasn't even keeping it in limbo in case he met someone down the road, though. He was that far gone? That sure he was never going to share his heart with anyone?

A shot of cold swept through her at the thought. How lonely that would be.

She wasn't letting him get away that easily. Her aunt and mother were right. She was going to fight for him. She was going to fight for Fabio. Because there was a chance that Reed did love her but couldn't allow himself to. And if the feeling was there, she was going to pull it out of him till he was so happy he made people sick.

The thought actually made her smile.

Reed stood in the living room of his awkward rental house—the same old one, which of course was still available because it was so blah—trying to figure out why the arrangement of furniture looked so wrong. Maybe if he put the couch in front of the windows instead of against the wall?

This place would never look right. Or feel right. Or be home.

But giving Norah the ranch had been the right thing to do. Now she'd have a safe place to raise the triplets with enough room for all of them, fields to roam in, and she'd own it free and clear. She'd never have to worry about paying rent again, let alone a mortgage or property taxes—he'd taken care of that in perpetuity.

And he had a feeling his grandmother was looking down at him, saying, *Well, you tried. Not hard enough, but you tried and in the end you did the right thing. She should have the ranch, you dope.*

He *was* a dope. And Norah should have the ranch.

The doorbell rang. He had a feeling it was Norah, coming to tell him she couldn't possibly accept the ranch. Well, tough, because he'd already deeded it to her and it was hers. He'd even talked over the legalities with his lawyer; he'd married, per his grandmother's will, and the ranch was his fair and square. His to hand over.

He opened the door and it was like a gut punch. Two days ago they'd still had their deal. Two nights ago they'd been naked in bed together. And then yesterday morning, he'd turned back into the Reed he needed to be to survive this thing called life. Keeping to himself. No emotional entanglements.

And yet his first day in town he'd managed to get married and become a father to three babies. He was really failing at no emotional entanglements.

"I can't accept this, Reed," she said, holding up a legal-size folder.

"You have no choice. It's yours now. The deed is in your name."

She scowled. "It's your home."

"I'd rather you and the triplets have it. My grandmother would rather that, too. I have no doubt."

"So you get married, get your ranch and then give up the ranch, but the wife who's not really your wife gets to *keep* the ranch. That makes no sense."

"Does anything about our brief history, Norah?" An image floated into the back of his mind, Fabio and Angelina hand in hand, him scooping her up and carrying her into the chapel with its legend and sneaky, elderly caretakers slash officiants.

She stared at him hard. "I'll accept the ranch on one condition."

He raised an eyebrow. "And that would be?"

"I need your help for my multiples class. I'd like you to be a guest speaker. Give the dad's perspective."

No, no, no. What could *he* contribute? "I've only been a dad for a little while," he said. "Do I really have anything to truly bring to the class? And now with things so…up in the air between us."

Up in the air is good, she thought. Because it meant things could go her way. Their way. The way of happiness.

"You have so much to contribute," she said. "Honestly, it would be great if you could speak at all the remaining classes," she said. "Lena Higgins—she's the one expecting all boy triplets—told me her husband wasn't sure he felt comfortable at the class last week and might not be joining her for the rest because the class seemed so mom-focused. Poor Lena looked so sad. A male guest speaker will keep some of the more reluctant dads and caregivers comfortable. Especially when it's Reed Barelli, detective."

He didn't quite frown, so that was something. "I don't know, Norah. I—"

"Did you see how scared some of those dads looked?" she asked. "For dads who are shaking over the responsibility awaiting them—you could set their minds at ease. I think all the students will appreciate the male perspective."

Some of the guys in the class, which had included fathers, fathers-to-be and grandfathers, had looked like the ole deer in the headlights. One diaper was tough on some men who thought they were helpless. Two, three, even four diapers at the same time? Helpless men would poof into puddles on the floor. He supposed he could be a big help in the community by showing these guys they weren't helpless, that they had the same instincts—and fears—as the women and moms among them.

Step up, boys, he thought. That would be his mission.

Ha. He was going to tell a bunch of sissies afraid of diaper wipes and onesies and double strollers to step up when he couldn't step up for the woman he'd do anything for?

Anything but love, Reed?

He shook the thought out of his weary brain. His head ran circles around the subject of his feelings for Norah. He just couldn't quite get a handle on them. Because he didn't want to? Or because he really was shut off from all that? Done with love. Long done.

She was tilting her head at him. Waiting for an answer.

"And if I do this, you'll accept the ranch as yours?" he said.

She nodded.

He extended a hand. "Deal."

She shook his hand, the soft feel of it making him want to wrap her in his arms and never let her go.

"We make a lot of deals," she said. "I guess it's our thing."

He smiled. "The last one failed miserably." He failed miserably. Or had Norah just changed the rules on him by wanting more? They'd entered their agreement on a handshake, too. He wasn't really wrong here. He just wasn't…right.

"This one has less riding on it," she said. "You just have to talk about how you bonded with the triplets.

How you handle changing time. Feeding time. Bedtime. What's it like to come home from work and have three grumpy, teething little ones to deal with. How you make it work. How it's wonderful, despite everything hard about it. How sometimes it's not even hard."

He nodded and smiled. "I'll be there," he said. He frowned, his mind going to the triplets. "Norah, how are things going to work now? I mean, until you find the right man, I want to be there for you and the babies. I want to be their father."

"Until I find a father who can be that and a real husband?"

"Okay, it's weird, but yes."

She frowned. "So you're going to get all enmeshed in their lives, give a hundred percent to them, and then I meet someone who fits the bill and you'll just back off? Walk away? Bye, triplets?"

Hey, wait a minute.

"Look, Norah, I'm not walking away from anything. I want to be their father. I told you that. But I want you to have what you need, too. If I can't be both and someone else can…"

Someone else. Suddenly the thought of another man touching her, kissing her, doing upsie-downsie with his babies…

His babies. Hell. Maybe he should back off now. Or he'd really be done for. Maybe they both needed a break from each other so they could go back to having what they wanted. Which was all messed up now.

She lifted her chin. "Let's forget this for now. Anytime you want to see Bella, Bea and Brody, you're welcome over. You're welcome at the ranch anytime."

He nodded, unable to speak at the moment.

She peered behind him, looking around the living room. "The couch should go in front of the windows. And that side table would be better on that wall," she said, pointing. "The mirror above the console table is too low. Should be slightly above eye level."

"That should help. Thank you. I can't seem to get this place right."

"I'm not sure I want it to feel right," she said. "Wait, did I say that aloud?" She frowned again. "Everything is all wrong. I don't like that you left your home, Reed. That place is your dream."

"That place is meant for a family. I want you to have it."

She looked at him for a long moment. He could see her shaking her head without moving a muscle. "See you in class."

He watched her walk to her car. The moment she got in, he felt her absence and the weight of one hell of a heavy heart.

Chapter 14

Word had spread that Detective Reed Barelli, who'd become de facto father to the Ingalls triplets by virtue of marrying their mother at the Wedlock Creek chapel with its Legend of the Multiples, would be a guest speaker at tonight's zero-to-six-month multiples class. There were more men than women this time, several first-timers to the class who practically threw checks at Norah. At this rate, she'd be raking it in as a teacher.

She hadn't even meant to invite him to speak—especially not as a condition of her keeping the ranch. The sole condition, no less. But it had been the best she could come up with, just standing there, not knowing what to say, how to keep him, how to get him to open up the way she had and accept the beautiful thing he was being offered: love. She did want him to be a speaker in her class, and it would get them working together, so that was good. She couldn't try to get through to him if they were constantly apart now that he'd moved out.

They hadn't spent much time together in three days.

He'd come to the ranch to see the triplets every day since their return from Las Vegas. He'd help feed them, then read to them, play with them. Blow raspberries and do upsie-downsies. And then he'd leave, taking Norah's heart with him.

Now here he was, sitting in the chair beside her desk with his stack of handouts, looking so good she could scream.

"Welcome, everyone! As you may have heard through the grapevine, tonight we have a guest speaker. Detective Reed Barelli. When Reed and I got married, he became the instant father of three seven-month-old teething babies. Was he scared of them? Nope. Did he actually want to help take care of them? Yes. Reed had never spent much time around babies and yet he was a natural with my triplets. Why?"

She looked at Reed and almost didn't want to say why. Because it proved he could pick and choose. The triplets. But not her.

She bit back the strangled sob that rose up from deep within and lifted her chin. She turned back toward the class. "Because he wanted to be. That is the key. He *wanted* to be there for them. And so he was. And dads, caregivers, dads-to-be, grandfathers, that's all you have to know. That you want to be there for them. So, without further ado, here is Detective Reed Barelli."

He stood, turned to her and smiled, then addressed the class. "That was some introduction. Thank you, Norah."

She managed a smile and then sat on the other side of the desk.

"Norah is absolutely right. I did want to be there for the triplets. And so I was. But don't think I had a clue of how to take care of one baby, let alone three. I know how to change a diaper—I think anyone can figure that out. But the basics, including diapers and burping and sleep schedules and naps? All that, you'll learn here. What you won't learn here, or hell, maybe you will because I'm talking about it, is that taking care of babies will tell you who you are. Someone who steps up or someone who sits out. Be the guy who steps up."

A bunch of women stood and applauded, as did a few guys.

"Is it as easy as you make it sound?" Tom McFill asked. "My wife is expecting twins. I've never even held a baby before."

"The first time you do," Reed said, "everything will change. That worry you feel, that maybe you won't know what you're doing? It'll dissipate under the weight of another feeling—a surge of protection so strong that you won't know what hit you. All you'll know is that you're doing what needs to be done, operating by instinct and common sense, Googling what you don't know, asking a grandmother. So it's as hard and as easy as I'm making it sound."

A half hour later Norah took over, giving tutorials on feeding multiples, bathing multiples and how to handle sleep time. Then there was the ole gem: what if both babies, or three or four, all woke up in the middle of the night, crying and wet and hungry. She covered that, watching her students taking copious notes.

Finally the class was over. Everyone crowded around Reed, asking him questions. By the time the last student left and they were packing up to go, it was a half hour past the end of the class.

"You were a big hit," she said. "I knew I called this one right."

"I'm happy to help out. I knew more than I thought on the subject. I'd stayed up late last night doing research, but I didn't need to use a quarter of it."

"You had hands-on training."

"I miss living with them," he said, and she could tell he hadn't meant to say that.

She smiled and let it go. "Most people would think you're crazy."

"I guess I am."

Want more, she shouted telepathically. *Insist on more! You did it with the babies, now do it with me. Hot sex every night, fool!* But of course she couldn't say any of that. "Well, I'd better get over to the diner to pick up the triplets."

"They're open for another half hour, right? I could sure go for some beef pot pie."

She stared at him. Why was he prolonging the two of them being together? Because he wanted to be with her? Because he really did love the triplets and wanted to see them?

Because he missed her the way she missed him?

"I have to warn you," she said as they headed out. "My family might interrogate you about the state of our marriage. Demand to know when we're patching things up. *If* we will, I should say."

"Well, we can't say what we don't know. That goes for suspects and us."

Humph. All he had to do was say he'd be the one. The father and the husband. It was that easy!

On the way to their cars, she called her mom to let her know she and Reed would be stopping in for beef pot pies so they'd be ready when they arrived. Then she got in her car and Reed got in his. The whole time he trailed her in his SUV to the Pie Diner, she was so aware of him behind her.

The diner was still pretty busy at eight thirty-five. Norah's mom waved them over to the counter.

"Norah, look who's here!"

Norah stared at the man sitting at the counter, a vegetable pot pie and lemonade in front of him. She gasped as recognition hit. "Harrison? Omigod, Harrison Atwood?" He stood and smiled and she threw her arms around him. Her high school sweetheart who'd joined the army and ended up on the east coast and they'd lost contact.

"Harrison is divorced," Norah's mom said. "Turns out his wife didn't want children and he's hoping for a house full. He told me all about it."

Norah turned beet red. "Mom, I'm sure Harrison doesn't want the entire restaurant knowing his business."

Harrison smiled. "I don't mind at all. The more people know I'm in the market for a wife and children, the better. You have to say what you want if you hope to get it, right?"

Norah's mother smiled at Norah and Reed, then looked back at Harrison. "I was just telling Harrison how things didn't work out between the two of you and that you're available again. The two of you could catch up. High school sweethearts always have such memories to talk over."

Can my face get any redder? Norah wondered, shooting daggers at her busybody mother. What was she trying to do?

Get her settled down, that was what. First Reed and now a man she hadn't seen in ten years.

Norah glanced at Reed, who seemed very stiff. He was stealing glances at Harrison every now and then.

Harrison had been a cute seventeen-year-old, tall and gangly, but now he was taller and more muscular, attractive, with sandy-brown hair and blue eyes and a dimple in his left cheek. She'd liked him then, but she'd recognized even then that she hadn't been in love. To the point that she'd kept putting him off about losing their virginity. She'd wanted her first time to be with a man she was madly in love with. Of course, she'd thought she was madly in love with a rodeo champ, but he'd taken her virginity and had not given her anything in return. She'd thought she was done with bull riders and then, wham, she'd fallen for the triplets' father. Maybe she'd never learn.

"Harrison is a chef. He studied in Paris," Aunt Cheyenne said. "He's going to give us a lesson in French cooking. Isn't that wonderful? You two must have so much in common," she added, wagging a finger between Norah and Harrison.

"Well, I'd better get going," Reed said, stepping back. "I have cases to go over. Nice to see you all."

"But, Reed, your pot pie just came out of the oven," Norah's mother said. "I'll just go grab it."

Norah watched him give Harrison the side-eye before he said, "I'll come with you. I want to say goodnight to the triplets."

"They are so beautiful," Harrison said with so much

reverence in his voice that Norah couldn't help the little burst of pride in her chest. Harrison sure was being kind.

Reed narrowed his gaze on the man, scowled and disappeared into the kitchen behind her mother.

And then Aunt Cheyenne winked at Norah and smiled. Oh no. Absolutely not. She knew what was going on here. Her mother and aunt realized they had Norah's old boyfriend captive at the counter and had been waiting for Norah and Reed to come in so they could make Reed jealous! Or, at least, that was how it looked.

Sneaky devils.

But they knew Reed wasn't in love with her and didn't want a future with her. So what was the point? Reed would probably push her with Harrison, tell her to see if there was anything to rekindle.

But as cute and nice as Harrison was, he wasn't Reed Barelli. No one else could be.

Every forkful of the pot pie felt as if it weighed ten pounds in his hand. Reed sat on his couch, his lonely dinner tray on the coffee table, a rerun of the baseball game on the TV as a distraction from his thoughts.

Which were centered on where Norah was right now. *Probably on a walking date with Harrison*, he said in his mind in a singsong voice. High school sweethearts would have a lot to catch up on. A lot to say. Memories. Good ones. There were probably a lot of firsts between them.

Reed wanted to throw up. Or punch something.

Just like that, this high school sweetheart, this French chef, would waltz in and take Reed's almost life. His wife, his triplets. His former ranch, which was now Norah's. A woman who wanted love and romance and

a father for her babies might be drawn to the known—
and the high school sweetheart fit that bill. Plus, they
had that cooking thing in common. They might even
be at the ranch now, Harrison standing behind Norah
at the stove, his arms around her as he showed her how
to Frenchify a pot pie. You couldn't and shouldn't! Pot
pies were perfect as they were, dammit.

Grr. He took a swig of his soda and clunked it down
on the coffee table. What the hell was going on here?
He was jealous? Was this what this was?

Yes. He was jealous. He didn't want Norah kissing
this guy. Sleeping with this guy. Frenchifying pot pies
with this guy.

He flung down his fork and headed out, huffing into
his SUV. He drove out to the ranch, just to check. And
there was an unfamiliar car! With New York plates!

Hadn't Norah's mother said Harrison had lived on
the east coast?

He was losing her right now. And he had let it happen.

*This is what you want, dolt. You want her to find
everything in one man. A father for her triplets. A husband for herself. Love. Romance. Happiness. Forever.
You don't want that. So let her go. Let her have what
she always dreamed of.*

His heart now weighing a thousand pounds, he
turned the SUV around and headed back to his rental
house, where nothing awaited him but a cold pot pie
and a big, empty bed.

"Upsie-what?" Harrison said, wrinkling his nose in
the living room of the Barelli ranch. Correction. The
Ingalls ranch. The Norah Ingalls ranch.

Norah frowned. "Upsie-downsie," she repeated.

"You lift her up, say 'Upsie' in your best baby-talk voice, then lower her with a 'downsie'!"

They were sitting on the rug, the triplets in their Exersaucers, Bella raising her hands for a round of upsie-downsie. But Harrison just stared at Bella, shot her a fake smile and then turned away. Guess not everyone liked to play upsie-downsie.

Bella's face started to scrunch up. And turn red. Which meant any second she was about to let loose with a wail. "Waaaah!" she cried, lifting her arms up again.

"Now, Bea, be a good girl for Uncle Harrison," he said. "Get it, *Bea* should *be* a good girl. LOL," he added to no one in particular.

First of all, that was Bella. And did he just LOL at his own unfunny "joke"? Norah sighed. No wonder she hadn't fallen in love with Harrison Atwood in high school. Back then, cute had a lot to do with why she'd liked him. But as a grown-up, cute meant absolutely nothing. Even if a man looked like Reed Barelli.

"I'd love to take you out to a French place I know over in Brewer," he said. "It's not exactly Michelin-starred, but come on, in Wyoming, what is? I'm surprised you stuck around this little town. I always thought you'd move to LA, open a restaurant."

"What would give you that idea?" she asked.

"You used to talk a lot about your big dreams. Wanting to open Pie Diners all across the country. You wanted your family to have your own cooking show on the Food Network. Pot pie cookbooks on the *New York Times* bestseller list."

Huh. She'd forgotten all that. She did used to talk about opening Pie Diners across Wyoming, maybe even in bordering states. But life had always been busy enough. And full enough. Especially when she'd gotten pregnant and then when the triplets came.

"Guess your life didn't pan out the way you wanted," Harrison said. "Sorry about that."

Would it be wrong to pick up one of the big foam alphabet blocks and conk him over the head with it?

"My life turned out pretty great," she said. *I might not have the man I love, but I have the whole world in my children, my family, my job and my little town.*

"No need to get defensive," he said. "Jeez."

God, she didn't like this man.

Luckily, just then, Brody let loose with a diaper explosion, and Harrison pinched his nostrils closed. "Oh boy. Something stinks. I guess this is my cue to leave. LOL, right?"

"It was good to see you again, Harrison. Have a great rest of your life."

He frowned and nodded. "Bye." He made the mistake of removing his hand from his nose, got a whiff of the air de Brody and immediately pinched his nostrils closed again.

She couldn't help laughing. "Buh-bye," she said as he got into his car.

She closed the door, her smile fading fast. She had a diaper to change. And a detective to fantasize about.

Chapter 15

Reed kept the door of his office closed the next morning at the police station. He was in no mood for chitchat and Sergeant Howerton always dropped in on his way from the tiny kitchen to talk about his golf game and Officer Debowski always wanted to replay any collars from the day before. Reed didn't want to hear any of it.

He chugged his dark-brew coffee, needing the caffeine boost to help him concentrate on the case he was reading through. A set of burglaries in the condo development. Weird thing was, the thief, or thieves, was taking unusual items besides the usual money, jewelry and small electronics. Blankets and pillows, including throw pillows, had been taken from all the hit-up units.

Instead of making a list of what kind of thief would go for down comforters, he kept seeing Norah and the high school sweetheart with their hands all over each other. Were they in bed right now? He had to keep blinking and squeezing his eyes shut.

He wondered how long the guy had stayed last night. Reed should have made some excuse to barge in and interrupt them a bunch of times. Checking on the boiler or something. Instead, he'd reminded himself that the reason the French chef was there was because of Reed's own stupidity and stubbornness and inability to play well with others. Except babies.

He slammed a palm over his face. Were they having breakfast right now? Was Norah in his button-down shirt and nothing else? Having pancakes on the Barelli family table?

Idiot! he yelled at himself. *This is all your fault.* He'd stepped away. He'd said he couldn't. He'd said he wouldn't. And now he'd lost Norah to the high school sweetheart who wanted a wife and kids. They were probably talking about the glory days right now. And kissing.

Dammit to hell! He got up and paced his office, trying to force his mind off Norah and onto a down-feather-appreciating burglar. A Robin Hood on their hands? Or maybe someone who ran a flea market?

He's going to give us lessons in French cooking, Norah's mother had said. Suddenly, Reed was chopped liver to the Ingalls women, having been replaced by the beef bourguignon pot pie.

So what are you going to do about this? he asked himself. *Just let her go? Let the triplets go? You're their father!*

And he was Norah's husband. Husband, husband, husband. He tried to make the word have meaning, but the more it echoed in his head, the less meaning it had.

Husband meant suffering in his memories. His mother had had two louses and his grandfather had been a real doozy. He thought of his grandmother trying to answer Reed's questions about why she'd chosen such a grouch who didn't like anyone or anything. She'd said that sometimes people changed, but even so, she knew who he was and, despite his ways, he'd seemed to truly love her and that had made her feel special. She'd always said she should have known if you're the only one, the exception, there might be a problem.

So what now? Could he force himself to give this a real try? Romance a woman he had so much feeling for that it shook him to the core? Because he was shaken. That much he knew.

His head spinning, he was grateful when his desk phone rang.

"Detective Barelli speaking."

"Reed! I'm so glad I caught you. It's Annie. Annie Potterowski from the chapel. Oh dear, I'm afraid there's a bit of a kerfuffle concerning your marriage license. Could you come to the chapel at ten? I've already called Norah and she's coming."

"What kind of kerfuffle?" he asked. What could be more of a kerfuffle than their entire wedding?

"I'll explain everything when you get here. 'Bye now," she said and hung up.

If there was one good thing to come from this kerfuffle, it was that he knew Norah would be apart from the high school sweetheart, even for just a little while.

"Annie, what on earth is going on?" Norah asked the elderly woman as she walked into the chapel, pushing the enormous stroller.

"Look at those li'l dumplings!" Abe said, hurrying over to say hello to the triplets. He made peekaboo faces and Bea started to cry. "Don't like peekaboo, huh?" Abe said. "Okay, then, how about silly faces?" He scrunched up his face and stuck out his tongue, tilting his head to the left. Bea seemed to like that. She stopped crying.

"I'm just waiting for Detective Barelli to arrive," Annie said without looking at Norah.

Uh-oh. What was this about?

"Ah, there he is," Annie said as Reed came down the aisle to the front of the chapel.

Reed crossed his arms over his chest. "About this kerfuffle—"

"Kerfuffle?" Norah said. "Anne used the words *major problem* when she called me."

Annie bit her lip. "Well, it's both really. A whole bunch of nothing, but a lot of something."

Reed raised an eyebrow.

"I'll just say it plain," Abe said, straightening the blue bow-tie that he wore almost every day. "You two aren't married. You spelled your names wrong on the marriage license."

"What?" Norah said, her head spinning.

"The county clerk's temporary replacement checked her first week's work, just in case she made rookie errors, and discovered only one. On your marriage license. She sent back the license to you and Reed and to the chapel, since we officiated the ceremony. You didn't receive your mail yet?"

Had Norah even checked the mail yesterday? Maybe not.

"I was on a case all day yesterday and barely had

time to eat," Reed said. "But what's this about spelling our names wrong?"

Anne held up the marriage license. "Norah, you left off the *h*. And, Reed, you spelled your name *R-e-a-d*. I know there are lots of ways to spell your name, but that ain't one of them."

"Well, it's not like you didn't know we were drunk out of our minds, Annie and Abe!" Norah said, wagging a finger at them.

"I didn't think to proofread your names, for heaven's sake!" Annie said, snorting. "Now we're supposed to be proofreaders, too?" she said to Abe. "Each wedding would take hours. I'd have to switch to my reading glasses, and I can never find them and—"

"Annie, what does this mean?" Reed asked. "You said we're not married. Is that true? We're not married because our names were spelled wrong?"

"Your legal names are not on that document or on the official documents at the clerk's office," Abe said.

"So we're not married?" Norah repeated, looking at Reed. "We were never actually married?"

"Well, double accidentally, you were," Annie said. "The spiked punch and the misspelling. You were married until the error was noted by the most efficient county clerk replacement in Brewer's history."

I'm not married. Reed is not my husband.

It's over.

Her stomach hurt. Her heart hurt. Everything hurt.

Reed walked over to Norah and seemed about to say something. But instead he knelt down in front of the stroller. "Hey, little guys. I miss you three."

Brody gave Reed his killer gummy smile, three tiny teeth poking up.

She glanced at his hand. He still wore his wedding ring even though she'd taken hers off. Guess he'd take it off now.

"We'll leave you to talk," Annie said, ushering Abe into the back room.

Norah sat in a pew, a hand on the stroller for support. She wasn't married to Reed. How could she feel so bereft when she never really had a marriage to begin with?

"We can go back to our lives now," she said, her voice catching. She cleared her throat, trying to hide what an emotional mess she was inside. "I'll move out of the ranch. Since we were never legally married, I'm sure that affects possession of the ranch. You can't deed me something you didn't rightfully inherit."

She was babbling, talking so she wouldn't burst into tears.

He stood, giving Bea's hair a caress. "I guess Harrison will be glad to hear the news."

"Harrison?"

"Your high school sweetheart," he said. "The one you spent the night with."

She narrowed her eyes at him. "What makes you think we spent the night together?"

"I drove by the house to see if his car was there."

"Why? Why would you even care? You don't have feelings for me, Reed."

He looked away for a moment, then back at her. "I have a lot of feelings for you."

"Right. You feel responsible for me. You care about me. You're righting wrongs when you're with me."

He shook his head but didn't say anything.

"I should get back to work," she said.

"Me, too," he said.

She sucked in a breath. "I guess when we walk out of here, it's almost like none of it ever happened. We were never really married."

"I felt married," he said. Quite unexpectedly.

"And you clearly didn't like the feeling." She waited a beat, hoping he'd say she was wrong.

She waited another beat. Nothing.

"There's nothing between me and Harrison," she said without really having to. What did it matter to Reed anyway? His urge to drive by the ranch had probably been about him checking up on her, making sure she'd gotten back okay, the detective in him at work. "He did come over for a bit and was so insufferable I couldn't wait for him to leave."

He looked surprised. "But what about all the firsts you two shared?"

"Firsts? I had my first kiss with someone else. I lost my virginity to someone else. I did try sushi for the first time with Harrison. I guess that counts."

"So you two are *not* getting back together," he said, nodding.

"We are definitely not."

"So my position as father of the triplets still stands."

"That's correct," she said even though she wanted to tell him no, it most certainly did not. This was nuts. He was going to be their father in between semi-dates and short-term relationships until the real thing came along for her?

"I'd like to spend some time with them after work, if that's all right," he said. "I have presents for them for their eight-month birthday."

Her heart pinged. "It's sweet that you even know that."

"You only turn eight months once," he said with a weak smile.

And you find a man like Reed Barelli once in a lifetime, she thought. *I had you, then lost you, then didn't ever really have you, and now there's nothing.* Except his need to do right by the triplets, be for them what he'd never had.

"Time to go, kiddos," she said, trying to inject some cheer in her voice. "See you later, then," she said, wondering how she'd handle seeing him under such weird circumstances. Were they friends now?

"I'll get the door," he said, heading up the aisle to open it for her. He couldn't get rid of her fast enough.

Her heart breaking in pieces, she gripped the stroller and headed toward the Pie Diner, knowing she'd never get over Reed Barelli.

"Your grandmother would have loved Norah."

Reed glanced up at the voice. Annie Potterowski was walking up the chapel aisle toward where he sat in a pew in the last row. He'd been sitting there since Norah had left, twenty minutes or so. He'd married her in this place. And been unmarried to her here. He couldn't seem to drag himself out.

"Yeah, I think she would have," Reed said.

Annie sat beside him, tying a knot in the filmy pink scarf around her neck. "Now, Reed, I barely know you. I met you a few times over the years when you came to visit Lydia. So I don't claim to be an expert on you or anything, but anyone who's been around as long as I have and marries people for a living knows a thing or two about the human heart. Do you want to know what I think?"

He did, actually. "Let me have it."

She smiled. "I think you love Norah very much. I think you're madly in love with her. But this and that happened in your life and so you made her that dumb deal about a partnership marriage."

He narrowed his eyes at her. "How'd you know about that?"

"I listen, that's how. I pick up things. So you think you can avoid love and feeling anything because you were dealt a crappy hand? Pshaw," she said, adding a snort for good measure. "We've all had our share of bad experiences."

"Annie, I appreciate—"

"I'm not finished. You don't want to know the upbringing I had. It would keep you up at night feeling sorry for me. But when Abe Potterowski came calling, I looked into that young man's eyes and heart and soul, and I saw everything I'd missed out on. And so I said yes instead of no when I was scared to death of my feelings for him. And it was the best decision I ever made."

He took Annie's hand in his and gave it a gentle squeeze.

"I was used to shutting people out," she continued. "But you have to know when to say yes, Reed. And your grandmother, God bless her sweet soul, only ever wanted you to say yes to the right woman. Don't let her get away." Annie stood and patted his shoulder. "Your grandmother liked to come in here and do her thinking. She sat in the back row, too, other end, though."

With that, Annie headed down the aisle and disappeared into the back room.

Leaving Reed to do some serious soul-searching.

Chapter 16

"Not married?" Shelby repeated, her face incredulous as she cut up potatoes for the lunch-rush pot pies.

Norah shook her head, recounting what Annie and Abe had said.

"Oh hell," her mother said. "I really thought you two would work it out."

"You pushed Harrison on me last night!" Norah complained even though she knew why.

"Yeah, but I only did that because he was here when you called and said you and Reed were stopping in for pot pies. I wanted Reed to know he had competition for your heart."

"Well, he doesn't. Harrison was awful. He freaked the minute one of the triplets did number two in his presence."

"Norah, you and Reed belong together," Aunt Cheyenne said as she filled six pie tins with beef stew. "We can all see that."

"I thought we did," Norah said, tears threatening her eyes. "But he never wanted a real relationship. He wanted to save me. And he wanted the ranch."

"The ranch he gave up for you?" her mother asked. "You do something crazy like that when you love someone so much they come first."

"There's that responsibility thing again," Norah said, frowning. "Putting me first. Everything for me, right? He wants me to have 'everything I deserve.' Except for him."

"Coming through," called a male voice.

Norah glanced up at her handsome brother-in-law, Liam Mercer, walking into the kitchen, an adorable toddler holding each of his hands. Despite being in the terrible twos, Norah's nephews, Shane and Alexander, were a lot of fun to be around.

Liam greeted everyone, then wrapped his wife in a hug and dipped her for a kiss, paying no mind to the flour covering her apron. Norah's heart squeezed in her chest as it always did when she witnessed how in love the Mercers were.

You should hold out for that, she told herself. *For a man who loves you like Liam loves Shelby. Like Dad loved Mom.*

Like I love Reed, she thought with a wistful sigh.

In just a few hours he'd be at the ranch, which they'd both have to give up, and the wonderful way he was with the triplets would tear her heart in two. She could have everything she'd ever wanted if Reed would just let go of all those old memories keeping him from opening his heart.

Hmm, she thought. Since being around the triplets did have Reed Barelli all mushy-gushy and as close to his feelings as he could get, maybe she could do a little investigative detective work of her own to see if those "feelings" he spoke of having for her did reach into the recesses of his heart. She knew he wanted her—their night in Las Vegas had proved that, and she knew he cared for her. That was obvious and he'd said it straight-out. But could he enter into a romantic relationship with her and hold nothing back?

The man was so good at everything. Maybe she could get him to see that he could be great at love, too.

"Something smells amazing," Reed said when Norah opened the door. For a moment he was captivated by the woman herself. She wore jeans and a pale yellow tank top, her long, reddish-brown hair in a low pony-tail, and couldn't possibly be sexier. His nose lifted at the mouth-watering aroma coming from somewhere nearby. "Steak?"

"On the grill with baked potatoes and asparagus at the ready."

"Can't wait. I'm starving." He set a large, brown paper bag down by the closet. "Where are the brand-new eight-month-olds?"

She smiled. "In their high chairs. They just ate."

"Perfect. It's party time." He trailed her into the kitchen carrying the bag. He set it on the kitchen table and pulled out three baby birthday hats, securing one on each baby's head.

"Omigod, the cutest," Norah said, reaching for her phone to take pictures. She got a bunch of great shots. Including Reed in several.

"For the eight-month-olds," Reed said, putting a chew rattle on Bea's tray. And one on Bella's and one on Brody's. "Oh, I set up a college fund for them today. And got them these new board books," he added, pulling out a bunch of brightly colored little hardcovers. At first he'd gone a little overboard in the store, putting three huge stuffed animals in his cart, clothing and all kinds of toys. Then he'd remembered it wasn't even their first birthday and put most of the stuff back.

"Thank you, Reed," she said. "From the bottom of my heart, thank you. I can't tell you how much it means to me that they're so special to you."

"They're very special to me. And so are you, Norah." With the babies occupied in their chairs with their new rattles, he moved closer to their mother and tilted up her chin. "I'm an idiot."

"Oh?" she asked. "Why is that?"

"Because I almost lost you to that French chef. Or any other guy. I almost lost you, Norah."

"What are you talking about? I'm alive." She waved a hand in front of herself.

"I mean I almost lost out on being with you. Really being with you."

"But I thought—"

"I couldn't get the triplets gifts and not get you something, too," he said. "This is for you." He handed her a little velvet box.

"What's this?" she asked.

"Open it."

She did—and gasped. The round diamond sparkled in the room. "It's a diamond ring. A very beautiful diamond ring."

He got down on one knee before her. "Norah, will you marry me? For real, this time? And sober?"

"But I thought—"

"That I didn't love you? I do. I love you very much. But I was an idiot and too afraid to let myself feel anything. Except these little guys here changed all that. They cracked my heart wide-open and I had to feel everything. Namely how very deeply in love with you I am."

She covered her mouth with her hands. "Yes. Yes. Yes. Yes."

He grinned and stood and slid the ring on her finger. "She said yes!" he shouted to the triplets, then picked her up and spun her around.

"I couldn't be happier," she said.

"Me, either. I get you. I get the triplets. And, hey, I get to live in the ranch because the owner is going to be my wife."

She smiled and kissed him and he felt every bit of her love for him.

"So the Luv U Wedding Chapel?" she asked. "That would be funny."

He shook his head. "I was thinking the Wedlock Creek Wedding Chapel."

Her mouth dropped open. "Wait. Are you forgetting the legend? You *want* more multiples?"

"Sure I do. I think five or six kids is just about perfect."

She laughed. "We really must be insane. But you'll be in high demand to teach the multiples classes. You'll never have a minute to yourself."

"I'll be too busy with my multiples. And my wife."

"I love you, Reed."

"I love you, too."

After calling her mother, aunt and sister with the news—and Reed could hear the shrieks and cheers from a good distance away, Reed called Annie Potterowski at the chapel.

"So, Annie… Norah and I would like to book the chapel for an upcoming Saturday night for our wedding ceremony. We're thinking a month from now if there are any openings."

Now it was Annie's turn to shriek. "You're making your grandmother proud, Reed. How's the second Saturday in August? Six p.m.?"

"Perfect," he said. Norah had told him a month would be all she'd need to find a wedding dress and a baby tux for Brody and two bridesmaids' dresses for Bella and Bea. Her family was already all over the internet.

"And we'll spell our names right this time," he added.

A few hours later the triplets were in their cribs, the dishes were done and Reed was sitting with his fiancée on the sofa, stealing kisses and just staring at her, two glasses of celebratory champagne in front of them.

"To the legend of the Wedlock Creek chapel," he said, holding up his glass. "It brought me my family and changed my life forever."

Norah clinked his glass and grinned "To the chapel—and the very big family we're going to have."

He sealed that one with a very passionate kiss.

Epilogue

One year later

Reed stood in the nursery—the twins' nursery—marveling at tiny Dylan and Daniel. Five days ago Norah had given birth to the seven-pounders, Dylan four ounces bigger and three minutes older. Both had his dark hair and Norah's perfect nose, slate-blue eyes that could go Norah's hazel or his dark brown, and ten precious fingers and ten precious toes.

Norah was next door in the triplets' nursery, reading them their favorite bedtime story. Soon they'd be shifting to "big kid" beds, but at barely two years old they were still smack in the middle of toddlerhood. He smiled at the looks they'd gotten as they'd walked up and down Main Street yesterday, Norah pushing the twins' stroller and him pushing the triplets'.

"How do you do it?" someone had asked.

"Love makes it easy," Reed had said. "But we have *a lot* of help."

They did. Norah's family and the Potterowskis had set up practically around-the-clock shifts of feeding them, doing laundry and entertaining the triplets the first couple of days the twins were home. Many of their students from the past year had also popped by with gifts and offers to babysit the triplets, couples eager to get some first-hand experience at handling multiples.

Even the Dirks had come by. David and a very pregnant Eden—expecting twins without having ever said "I do" at the Wedlock Creek chapel.

"I've got this," David had said, putting a gentle hand on his wife's belly. "I thought I'd be scared spitless, but watching you two and taking your class—easy peasy."

Reed had raised an eyebrow. David might be in for the rude awakening he'd been trying to avoid, but Reed wasn't about to burst his bubble. They'd have help just like the Barellis did. That was what family and friends and community were all about.

Norah came in then and stood next to him, putting her arm around him. "The triplets are asleep. Looks like these guys are close."

"Which means we have about an hour and a half to ourselves. Movie?"

She nodded. "*Jerry Maguire* is on tonight. Remember when we watched that?"

He would never forget. He put his arms around her and rested his forehead against hers. "Did I ever tell you that you complete me?"

She shook her head. "You said it was nonsense."

"Didn't I tell you I was an idiot? You. Complete. Me.

And so do they," he added, gesturing at the cribs. "And the ones in the room next door."

She reached up a hand to his cheek, her happy smile melting his heart. Then she kissed him and they tiptoed out of the nursery.

But Dylan was up twenty minutes later, then Daniel, and then the triplets were crying, and suddenly the movie would have to wait. Real life was a hell of a lot better, anyway.

* * * * *

Cathy Gillen Thacker is a married mother of three. She and her husband reside in North Carolina. Her stories have made numerous appearances on bestseller lists, but her best reward is knowing one of her books made someone's day a little brighter. A popular Harlequin author, she loves telling passionate stories with happy endings and thinks nothing beats a good romance and a hot cup of tea! Visit her at cathygillenthacker.com for information on her books, recipes and a list of her favorite things.

Books by Cathy Gillen Thacker

Harlequin Special Edition

Lockharts Lost & Found

His Plan for the Quadruplets
Four Christmas Matchmakers
The Twin Proposal
Their Texas Triplets

Texas Legends: The McCabes

The Texas Cowboy's Quadruplets
His Baby Bargain
Their Inherited Triplets

Visit the Author Profile page at
Harlequin.com for more titles.

Their Inherited Triplets

CATHY GILLEN THACKER

Chapter 1

"What are *you* doing here?" Lulu McCabe rose to her feet and gaped at the big, strapping cowboy with the wheat-blond hair and the mesmerizing gold-flecked eyes. Even with a good ten feet and a huge table between them, just the sight of him made her catch her breath.

Sam Kirkland strolled into the conference room at their Laramie, Texas, lawyers' office in his usual commanding way. He offered her a sexy half smile that warmed her from the inside out. "I could ask the same of you, darlin'."

With a scowl, Lulu watched as he came around the table to stand beside her.

Clad in jeans, a tan shirt and boots, his Resistol held politely against the center of his broad chest, he was the epitome of the highly successful, self-made rancher.

The way he carried himself only added to his inherent masculine appeal.

Ignoring the shiver of awareness pooling inside her, Lulu looked him square in the eye. "So, you don't know what this is about, either?" she guessed finally.

"Nope." He gave her a leisurely once-over, then narrowed his eyes at her, as always appearing to blame her for every calamity that came their way. "I figured you engineered it."

Anger surged through her, nearly as strong as the attraction she'd worked very hard to deny.

Lulu drew a breath and inhaled the brisk, masculine fragrance of his cologne and the soapy-fresh scent of his hair and skin. Determined to show him just how completely she had gotten over him, she stepped closer, intentionally invading his space. "Why would I want to do that?"

He held her eyes deliberately. Gave her that slow smile, the one that always turned her legs to jelly. "Honestly, darlin'," he taunted in a low tone, "I don't know why you want to do *lots* of things."

Really? He was going to go back to their last argument, claiming she was not making any sense? Again? Slapping both her hands on her hips, she fumed, "Listen, cowboy, you know exactly why I want to join the Laramie County Cattleman's Association!"

His gaze drifted over her before she could make her proposal again. "And you know exactly why, as organization president, I'm not about to let you."

She had a good idea. And it had a lot to do with what had secretly happened between them a little over a decade ago. With exaggerated sweetness, she guessed,

"Because you're not just a horse's behind, but a stubborn, sexist mule, too?"

Finally, his temper flared, as surely as her own. He blew out a frustrated breath, then lowered his face to hers. "It's not enough to just own a ranch in Laramie County, Lulu," he reiterated.

Both hands knotted at her sides, she glared up at him, aware her heart was pounding, and lower still, there was a building heat. "Well, it should be!" she argued right back.

"You have to raise cattle. Not honeybees."

"Okay, you two, calm down." Family law attorney Liz Cartwright Anderson breezed into the conference room, her husband and law partner right behind her.

"Or someone might think something besides a show of heat is going on with you," Travis Anderson quipped.

"The only thing we share is an immense dislike of each other," Lulu grumbled. *Well, that, and an unwillingness to forgive.* Because if they had been able to do that…things might be different now. But they hadn't… So…

Liz sent a questioning look at Sam. He lifted an amiable hand. "What she says," he quipped.

An awkward silence fell.

"We could meet with you separately," Travis offered finally. "Since Sam is my client, and Lulu is Liz's."

Lulu shook her head. They wouldn't have been called in together unless the matter involved them both. "Let's just get it over with," she groused.

"Okay, then." Liz smiled. "Travis and I called you both here together because we have some very important things to discuss," she began, as a somber-looking man with buzz-cut silver hair walked in to join them.

He was dressed in a suit and tie, carrying a briefcase and appeared to be in his late fifties.

Travis made the formal introductions. "This is Hiram Higgins. He's an estate attorney from Houston. He's enlisted our help in making what we hope will be a smooth transition."

"*Transition?* For what?" Lulu blurted, glancing over at Sam. For once, the big, sexy cowboy looked as clueless as she was. Unsure whether to take comfort in that or not, she opened her mouth to speak again.

Liz lifted a hand. "It will all become clear in a moment. Why don't we all sit down?" she suggested kindly.

Everyone took the chair closest to them, which put Sam and Lulu on one side of the table and Liz and Travis opposite them.

Hiram took a chair at the head of the table and opened up his briefcase. "There's no easy way to say this," he said, "so I am going to plunge right in. I'm handling the estate of Peter and Theresa Thompson. They were killed in an auto accident in Houston two months ago."

Lulu sucked in a breath. She hadn't seen her sophomore year roommate, Theresa, and her husband, Peter—one of Sam's old college friends—since the two had eloped years before, but shock and sorrow tumbled through her. Sam seemed equally taken aback by the tragic loss. He reached over and put his hand on top of hers.

Normally, Lulu would have resisted his touch. But right now, she found she needed the warm, strong feel of his fingers draped over hers.

She actually needed more than that.

Given the grief roiling around inside her, a hug wouldn't have been out of bounds...

Had the person beside her been anyone but the man who had stomped her heart all to pieces, of course.

Unobtrusively, Lulu withdrew her hand from his.

Hiram continued, "Peter and Theresa left three sons, two-year-old triplets."

Lulu struggled to take this all in. Regretting the fact they'd all lost touch with each other, she asked hoarsely, "Where are the children now?"

"In Houston."

"With family?" Sam ascertained.

Hiram grunted in the affirmative. "And friends. Temporarily. We're keeping them together, of course. Which is where the two of you come in." He paused to give both Lulu and Sam a long, steady look.

"Peter and Theresa came to see me shortly after their children were born. They wanted to make out wills, but sadly, were never able to agree on who should take care of their children in the event something happened to them. So, they did what a lot of people do when it comes to thorny guardianship issues. They agreed to discuss it some more...and put off finalizing anything with my office."

He cleared his throat. "In the meantime, they went on one of those do-it-yourself legal websites and made out practice wills. They never had those notarized, so they aren't official and may or may not hold up in probate court. But thanks to the copies they left behind, we do have their wishes on record, which is what we are using to guide us now."

"And those wishes are...?" Sam prodded.

After a long silence, Hiram finally said, "Sam, you

were Peter's third choice for legal guardian. And Lulu, you were Theresa's fourth choice."

Third! And fourth! "Who was first?" Lulu asked, curious.

Hiram looked down at his notes. "Theresa chose the great-aunt who raised her. Mabel had the boys for about two weeks, before she fell and broke her hip."

Sam and Lulu exchanged concerned looks.

"From there, they went to Peter's first choice—his best friend, Bob, who is also a father of three, all under age five."

Sam nodded, listening.

"The kids all got along great, even if it was something of a madhouse. Unfortunately, Bob's wife is pregnant and had to go on bed rest for the duration of her pregnancy."

Lulu sighed in dismay.

"So, the triplets then went to Theresa's second choice—a cousin of hers who is a flight attendant." Hiram frowned. "Olivia had them for a week and a half before deciding there was no way she was cut out for this."

He looked up. Adding in concern, "From there, they went to Peter's second cousin. Aaron's engaged and wants a lot of kids, but his fiancée is not on board with the idea of a ready-made family. So that trial run also didn't work out."

"And now…?" Lulu asked, her heart going out to the children for all they had been through.

"They are with Theresa's business colleague and her husband. Unfortunately, although they adore the boys and vice versa, they both travel a lot for work, so permanent guardianship is not a viable option there, either. Which brings us to Sam, the last person on Peter's list."

"Or…actually, me," Lulu interjected with her usual gung ho enthusiasm for all things family. She was more than ready to take on the challenge. "If you just want to cut to the chase."

Sam didn't know why he was surprised Lulu was jumping headlong into a situation neither of them was cut out for. She'd always been romantic and impulsive. Never more so, it seemed, than when she was around him.

The trouble was, he felt passionate and impractical around her, too.

Part of it was her looks. She really was drop-dead gorgeous, with that thick mane of sun-kissed, honey-brown hair, those long-lashed turquoise blue eyes, elegant cheekbones and cute, determined chin. And she had impeccable fashion sense, too. Her five-foot-eight-inch frame was currently decked out in a short-sleeved black polo, bearing the Honeybee Ranch logo above one luscious breast, a snug-fitting dark denim skirt that made the most of her trim hips and long, lissome legs, and a pair of Roper boots that were as sturdy as they were feminine. She had movie-star sunglasses on top of her head, a leather-banded watch on her left wrist and four handmade bracelets, probably made by her four nieces, pushed high on the other.

But it was the skeptical twist of her soft, kissable lips as she leaned toward him and shot him a disdainful look that captivated him the most.

"Let's be real here," she said, inundating him with the scent of her signature fragrance, an alluring combination of flowers and citrus, along with a heady dose of that saucy attitude he recalled so well. "There's no way you're going to take on two-year-old triplets for more than a week or so without changing your mind, too, the way everyone else who's had them already has."

The fact she had such a low opinion of him stung. Unable to keep the growl out of his voice, he challenged, "What makes you think that?"

"Because." Lulu shrugged, her eyes taking on a turbulent sheen. "You're a man…and you're busy running a big cattle ranch…and you're single…"

All of which, last time he'd heard, were facts in his favor. "And you're a woman. And you're busy running a honeybee ranch and now a food truck, too. And you're single."

Lulu's mouth dropped into an O of surprise. She squared her shoulders and tried again. "The point is, *cowboy*—" she angled her thumb at her chest "—I'm cut out for this."

He let his glance sift over her from head to toe before returning, with even more deliberation, to her eyes. "Really?" he countered softly. As always, when they were together, the world narrowed to just the two of them. "'Cause I am, too."

Indignant color flooded her cheeks. "Sam, come on, be reasonable!" She gave him a look he was hardpressed to reject. "I've wanted a family forever."

He cocked his head to one side, once again forcing himself to do what was best, instead of letting his emotions get the better of him. "Mmm-hmm. Well, so do I, darlin'."

She stared at him. He stared back. Years of pent-up feelings entered the mix and combined with the ever-encompassing grief and sense of loss. Both feelings she seemed to be struggling with, too. Then, breaking the silent standoff, she pushed her chair back from the table and pivoted to face him. As always, when overwrought, she let her temper take charge. "You're just volunteering to do this in order to be difficult."

Actually, he was trying to honor their late friends' wishes, and keep them all from being hurt any more than they already had been. "You couldn't be more wrong, Lulu."

"Is that right? Then please, enlighten me."

With a grave look, hoping to get through to her once and for all, he said, "I'm taking this on because Peter was once a very good friend of mine, and he trusted me to care for his sons, if the worst ever happened. Since it has…" Sam's voice caught. Pushing his sorrow aside, he went on huskily, "I will."

Hiram interjected, "Y'all understand. The request isn't binding. You both are free to say no."

Lulu turned back to the children's lawyer. "And if we *were* to do so?" she asked in concern.

Hiram said, "Then we'd notify social services in Houston and have the agency start looking for suitable adoptive parents."

Not surprisingly, Sam noted, Lulu looked as upset by the thought of leaving the kids at the mercy of the system as he was. Once again, without warning, the two of them were on the exact same page.

"And in the meantime?" he asked gruffly.

Hiram explained, "They'll be put in foster care."

"Together?" Lulu queried.

Hiram's face took on a pained expression. "I would

hope so. But honestly, there's no guarantee a placement like that could be found, at least right away."

Lulu sighed, appearing heartbroken. "Which would likely devastate the children."

Hiram nodded.

She swung back toward Sam, and concluded sadly, "So, it's either going to be you, or it's going to be me, taking these three kids on and raising them." She gave him a long, assessing look. "And you have to know, deep down, which one of us is better suited for parenting toddlers."

He did.

Although he doubted they agreed.

"Which is why, given the options that are left," Sam said, pushing aside his own welling grief, and ignoring the pleading in her soft turquoise blue eyes, "I think I'm the right one to assume responsibility."

"Okay, then," Hiram declared, looking happy everything had been resolved so very quickly. He reached into the folder in front of him and brought out a file of paperwork. "I'll make arrangements to have the boys brought to Laramie County as soon as possible. All you'll need to do is sign here—"

"Whoa! Wait! *That's it?*" Lulu sputtered. "You're not even going to ask me if I'm interested in being the triplets' legal guardian?"

Hiram paused, papers still in hand. "Are you?"

"Yes! Very!" Hands clasped tightly, she leaned toward the estate lawyer urgently. "I would love to do this for Peter and Theresa's boys!"

"Until it starts to get hard and reality sinks in," Sam muttered, thinking of their torrid past, and knowing there was no way he would visit such a reversal of fortune on those boys. "Then we both know where you will be, don't we, darlin'?" he returned bitterly. "Out the door. Without so much as a look back."

Lulu glared at him. "I'm not a quitter, Sam," she told him fiercely.

Wasn't she? It seemed like that was exactly what she had done ten years ago, albeit in a roundabout way. He regarded her skeptically. "But you are still very emotional. And impetuous." Two character traits that were intensified by their mutual sense of loss.

Lulu winced. "And you're overbearing and hopelessly set in your ways, so—"

Travis let out a referee-style whistle, signaling everyone needed to stop before anyone else said anything regrettable, no matter how upset they were. He turned to his wife, giving her the floor.

"Obviously," Liz interjected gently but firmly, "this has been a tremendous shock, and we're all feeling a little emotional and overwrought right now."

"Which is why, on second thought," Hiram concurred, putting the papers back in his briefcase before leveling a look at Sam, "I'm going to ask you to take a little more time to think about this." After a beat, Hiram continued, "If, after due consideration, you still feel inclined to accept temporary guardianship, you can call me and let me know, and I'll arrange to have the boys and their belongings driven here. The guardianship papers can be signed when you take custody of them."

"What about me?" Lulu said, clearly hurt and disappointed.

Hiram stood. "As I said, you're next in line if things don't go well with Sam and the boys. But for right now," the lawyer said firmly, "he is the one being tapped to take care of the triplets."

The meeting broke up.

Sam and Lulu walked outside.

As they reached their respective vehicles, she studied him with wary reserve. "How are you going to do this?"

It irked him to realize she did not think he could. He squinted down at her. "One step at a time."

"I'm serious, Sam!"

He shrugged. "Obviously," he drawled, "I'll need help."

Lulu opened her mouth to respond just as her cell phone went off. She plucked it out of her purse and stared disbelievingly at the text message.

Concerned, Sam stepped closer. "What is it?" he asked.

Her brow furrowed. In a dumbfounded tone, she admitted, "The sheriff's department has been called to my ranch!"

Chapter 2

An hour and a half later, Lulu stood at the entrance of the apiary on her ranch, staring at the empty field. Bare spots where the boxes and pallets had been. A few wooden lids scattered here and there. The occasional honeybee buzzing around, wondering where in the world the hives had gone.

"Are you okay?" Sam asked, standing next to her, looking more solid and imperturbable than ever.

Was she?

Resisting the urge to throw herself into his arms and ask for the comfort only he could give, Lulu turned away from his quiet regard. Her heart aching, she watched the patrol car leave her ranch. The only time she had ever felt this devastated was when Sam had walked away from her years ago in Tennessee. But she had survived heartbreak then, she told herself steadfastly. And she would survive it now.

"Lulu?" he prompted again.

She pivoted back toward him and lifted her chin, hating that he had to see her at her most vulnerable. "Of course I'm all right," she muttered. Although the devastation might have been easier to bear had he not gallantly insisted on accompanying her to the scene of the crime. And then, once amid the devastation, done his best to assist her and the sheriff's deputy who'd been sent to investigate. Because that had made her want to lean on him, the way she once had. And she knew she could never do that again.

Oblivious to the morose direction of her thoughts, Sam put a staying hand on her shoulder. Moved so she had no choice but to look into his face. Solemnly, he reminded her, "It's been a hell of a day, darlin'. First, we found out about the death of our close friends. Learned their boys had been orphaned. And found out we had both been tapped as potential guardians. Now, you just had all three hundred of your bee boxes, as well as your entire stockpile of honey, stolen."

Which left her with exactly nothing, she realized miserably. Seven years of hard work, building up her hives, gone. The only thing she had left of her business, aside from her small 150-acre ranch property, was her Honeybee Ranch food truck, and without her signature honey, the food she served out of that wasn't going to be the same, either.

His gaze drifting over her with unexpected gentleness, Sam told her, "I called the other officers of the Laramie County Cattleman's Association while you were talking to the deputy, and put out the word. Everyone's offered to do whatever they can to help."

Lulu was grateful for the assistance. Even if she

wasn't entirely sure it would do much good now, after the theft. With a grimace, she stepped back. Despite her efforts to the contrary, she was unable to control the emotions riding roughshod inside her.

Bitter tears misting her eyes, she blurted out, "If only you had made that offer prior to today, cowboy, I might not be in such a mess."

Recognition lit his gold-flecked eyes. "Wait…" He touched her arm and surveyed her. "Is *that* why you were so determined to join the Laramie County Cattleman's Association? Because you were *afraid* something like this could happen?"

Shoulders stiff, she shrank from his touch. "What did you think?" she scoffed. "That it was for your charming company?"

Stepping closer, he cupped her shoulders between his large palms, preventing her escape. "Why didn't you just tell me this?"

As if it had been that easy, given his resistance to cutting her even the slightest bit of slack, after what had happened between them.

His tranquil manner grating on her nerves as much as his chivalrous attitude, Lulu broke free from his hold and spun away. Her pulse skittering, she headed toward the barn. "I would have, had I felt you would be the least bit sympathetic or helpful." She tossed the words over her shoulder, then turned her glance forward again. "But you weren't…so…" An ache rose in her throat.

Sam caught up with her, matching her stride for indignant stride. "Come on, Lulu," he said. "It's not as if you've ever been afraid to fight any battle with me."

Lulu stopped dead in her tracks. He was right. She wasn't afraid to go toe-to-toe with him. Never had been.

With effort, she forced herself to be honest. Wearily, she said, "In the end, I didn't come to you with my fears because even though I knew it was happening in other parts of the state, big-time, I wasn't really sure something like this could ever happen here in Laramie County." She sighed. "Or maybe I just didn't want to believe that it would. Especially since I'm the only beekeeper who runs—or did run, anyway—a big commercial operation."

"And the other beekeepers?" Sam didn't take his eyes off her.

Lulu felt the heat of his gaze like a caress. "Are simply hobbyists, with one or two hives, so it really wouldn't be worthwhile for anyone to go in and try to locate and then steal their boxes."

She went into the barn, came out with a wooden pallet and carried it over to the apiary. She wanted any remaining bees in the area to have a place to go.

Sam kept pace with her, inundating her with his brisk, masculine scent. He watched her set down the pallet in the middle of the barren field. "Why would they want to do that, anyway? I mean, given the risk of getting caught?"

She returned to the barn for a brand-new wooden bee box bearing the Honeybee Ranch brand and a metal water pan. Already thinking about getting a new queen for the hive. "Because adding hives to orchards can increase the yield up to four hundred percent." At his look of amazement, she added, "I've had offers to rent out my bees to almond orchards in California, watermelon fields in south Texas and cranberry bogs in Wisconsin."

His large frame blocking out the late-afternoon June

sunshine, Sam stood back and gave her room to work. "And you said no?"

Acutely aware of his fiercely masculine presence, she carried both items over to the pallet inside the apiary. Set the lidded box down, filled a water pan from the outdoor faucet and left it nearby. "Every time."

His brow furrowed. She could see he didn't understand.

Sighing, she explained, "I could earn money that way, but it'd be hard on my bees, and it would bring with it risk of mites and disease and infection to the hives. Which would not be worth it in my opinion, since I already have a very good market for my honey. Or had."

Briefly, guilt and remorse etched the handsome features of his face. "I'm so sorry, darlin'."

Again. Too little, too late.

Arms folded, she moved even farther away.

Gruffly, he promised, "We'll find your bees, Lulu."

She dug in her heels. Now was not the time for idle comfort, just as earlier had not been the time for idle promises. "And if we don't?" The tears she'd been holding back flooded her eyes. "Then what?" She blotted the moisture with her fingertips. "I'm going to have to start my honey business *all over*, Sam."

He shook his head, stubbornly nixing even the possibility of that outcome. "Someone had to have seen something unusual, even if they didn't put it together at the time. With the sheriff's department and the cattleman's association both working on finding answers ASAP, we should know something soon."

Would they? Lulu wished she could be as certain of that as Sam. Heck, she wished she had even a tenth of his confidence.

"In the meantime," he continued in an agreeable tone that warmed her through and through, "I'd like to help you in whatever way I can."

Lulu studied him. "Do you mean that?" she asked thickly, turning her attention to the other big challenge currently facing her. The one with even more potential to break her heart. "Because if you do," she said slowly, "I've got a proposition for you." She paused, bracing for battle. "I'd like to be the children's nanny."

Sam had known that Lulu would not accept him as the triplets' guardian when she was next on the list. And hence she would continue to fight the decision, in one way or another.

But he hadn't expected her to offer this.

"*You*...want to be the triplets' nanny?" he repeated in disbelief, staring down into her pretty face.

Lulu tossed her head, her dark hair flowing over her shoulders in soft, touchable waves. And as she stepped closer, tempting him with the scent of her perfume, it took every ounce of self-control he had not to haul her into his arms and simply breathe her in.

"Well, I'm right in my assumption, aren't I?" she demanded. "You are planning on hiring one to help you with the three little boys."

"Yes." He intended to call a five-star service as soon as he got home and have them send someone out. Hopefully, by tomorrow evening. "I was."

"Well, I'm telling you there is no need for that," she went on sweetly, "when you have *me*, volunteering for the position."

Actually, there were a lot of reasons, Sam thought. Starting with the fact he had never really gotten over

Lulu. Or the way their relationship had ended. Or the fact that, even now, he found himself wanting to take her to bed and make love to her over and over again.

Was she feeling the same damning pull of attraction? And if so, where would that lead them? "Why do you want to do this?" he asked.

She shrugged, suddenly holding back as much as he was. She spread her hands wide. "Well, at the moment, it's not like I have anything else to do."

Uh-huh. "And if I believe that, you have some prime swampland to sell me."

"Okay." She flushed guiltily and her tongue snaked out to wet her lower lip. "You're right." A small sigh. "I do have an ulterior motive."

Now they were talking.

"I want to be there for the children in case things don't work out with the four of you."

"Except…they're going to work out, darlin'," he promised, just as persuasively.

At his assertion, an inscrutable veil slipped over her eyes. Her slender body stiffened and he took in the gentle rise and fall of her breasts.

"You seem sure of that," she said finally.

Sam nodded. Trying to keep his own latent anger and disappointment at bay, he replied, "When *I* make a commitment, Lulu, I keep it." Their eyes locked, held. Memories came flooding back.

Reminded of their falling-out all those years ago, and the reason for it, the color in her cheeks grew even rosier.

"Even if they do work out just fine with you…as their *single* daddy…you're going to need loving backup for them. And what better person for that role than their next, and *only remaining*, named legal guardian?"

She had a point. What she was suggesting did sort of make sense. At least when it came to doing what was best for the three little ones.

"You'd have to come to my ranch," he warned.

"Obviously."

"And be available to help whenever, wherever, however I need you."

He expected her to resist. Instead, she did not so much as flinch. She rocked forward on the toes of her cowgirl boots, patient and ready. "I can make plenty of sacrifices, when necessary."

There had been a time, he thought irritably, when that wasn't the case.

"In fact, if you'll let me take charge of them, you won't even have to pay me or be anything more than an admirable father figure in their lives. I'm perfectly willing to handle everything on my own."

She was deliberately calling the shots and shutting him out. He frowned, warning her, "I intend to be a lot more hands-on than that, darlin'. And if you take this on, I will pay you the going rate."

"Okay. Well, then, if you want, I'll do the days while you're out working. When you get home at night, you could take over completely in the evening."

As much as he wanted that to be the case, he knew that might be a little much for him. Especially in the beginning, until the kids got settled in and developed a routine.

As if sensing that, she continued, "Or you could have me stay and help you until they're all in bed for the night. And then I could still head home to my place.

After all…" Lulu sighed, pausing to look him in the eye, letting him know that nothing essential would ever change between the two of them, even if two-year-old triplets were involved, "…like oil and water, you and I will never really mix." She pivoted and headed for the barn. "Not for long, anyway."

We could, Sam thought, with a ferocity that surprised him, *if you would ever give us even half a chance.*

But Lulu wouldn't, he realized, watching her long legs eat up the ground. Not back then, when they had loved each other, and clearly not now, given the lingering animosity between them.

He caught up with her, overwhelmed yet again with the desire to sweep her into his arms and kiss her until she melted against him. Pushing the impulse aside, he retorted gruffly, "We need to think about what is right for the kids, Lulu." *Not what either of us wish could happen in some fantasy world.*

She shut one barn door, then the other. Over her shoulder, she sent him a contemplative look and said, "I am thinking, Sam." She brushed past him and headed for the porch of her small and tidy cottage-style home.

She settled on one of the cozy wicker chairs on the front porch. With a gesture, she invited him to make himself comfortable, too. "In fact, I haven't stopped mulling over what to do since the moment I heard about the triplets being orphaned. Which is why I know in my heart that the boys need to be here in Laramie County, where they will be well cared for and loved. Not just by you or me but by the whole community."

Sam wasn't surprised Lulu was feeling protective. She had always been sweetly maternal. An emotion that as of late had been bestowed upon her bees.

She had also switched gears pretty quickly. From cantankerous ex slash opponent, to heartbroken business owner, to ferociously determined nanny-to-be. He couldn't help but wonder if they were moving too fast, if they shouldn't ask for an extra few days to think about what they wanted to do, before they gave Hiram their answer.

Able to see how Lulu might take such a suggestion, however, he said only, "You're really willing to go all out to lend a hand, even after what happened here at the Honeybee Ranch today?" A theft that had left her devastated?

She gave him a look that said, *Especially after this.* "First of all, Sam," she reflected sadly, "we owe it to our friends to do everything we can to protect and nurture their three little boys."

Renewed grief wafted over him, too. "I agree," he said gruffly.

"Second, it'll keep me busy until I see *if* my hives will ever be recovered." As she seemed to fear they wouldn't be. "Third, to make this work, you're going to need help. Lots of it."

He leaned against a post on the porch and studied her. Aware the impulsive, reckless, romantic side of her was simultaneously the most thrilling and the most irritating. Which made him wonder just how long she would last, in what was likely to be a very challenging—and potentially heartbreaking—situation.

He sauntered toward her. "I don't half do anything, Lulu." A fact he'd made perfectly clear ten years before.

Her lower lip slid out in a delicious pout. She rose with elegant grace to face off with him. "Unlike me, I suppose?"

He let his gaze drift over her, taking in her luscious curves and lithe frame, her elegant arms and long sexy legs. "I wasn't talking about our previous big mistake."

She sent her glance heavenward. Sighed, with what seemed like enormous regret. "It was that, all right."

He jammed his hands on his waist and lowered his face to hers, wishing she had realized that a whole lot sooner. Like at the beginning of their spring break, instead of the end. "It was your idea in the first place."

She glared back at him. "Yeah, well, you went along with me, cowboy. At least initially."

Until she'd begun to panic. And suffer regret. Then, well, it had been clear their relationship was all over.

Emotion rose as their stare-down continued.

Realizing she had almost goaded him into losing his cool, Sam shoved a hand through his hair and stepped away. Deciding it might be best to be more direct, he said honestly, "This is what worries me, darlin'. The fact we can hardly be around each other without quarreling."

Lulu nodded. Sober now. "It would worry me, too, if we didn't have something much more important to worry about. The health and welfare and happiness of Theresa and Peter's three boys."

She released a soft, empathetic sigh and compassion gleamed in her eyes. "You heard what Hiram said. They're at the end of the line of the named guardians. If we don't want them to end up separated and in foster care, you and I are going to *have* to find a way to make it all work." She paused to draw a deep, enervating breath that lifted the curves of her breasts against her polo shirt. "I don't think, under the circumstances, that this is too much to ask of us. Do you? Especially since Peter and Theresa named both of us in their wills?"

"All right," Sam said, deciding he could be as selfless as she was being and more. "I'll agree to this arrangement for one month." *Which should be enough time for you to realize how unworkable a situation this is going to be for the two of us, and then decide to simply take on the role of close family friend.* "At the end of that time," he said sternly, "we reassess. And if we need to find a professional nanny, we will."

"Agreed. Although I have to warn you, I'm not going to change my mind."

That, Sam thought, remained to be seen. From what he'd observed, one two-year-old could be a lot. Three… at one time…who were also in mourning…? But in the short-term, there were other important things they needed to worry about, too. Her personal safety being paramount.

"Where are you going to be this evening?" he asked, guessing she hadn't yet told her family what had happened. Otherwise her cell phone would have been ringing off the hook and the place would have been inundated with McCabes.

But they would know, as soon as the ranchers in the family got the alert from the cattleman's association. "Are you going to stay with your parents?"

She blinked, confused. "Why would I want to do that?"

"In case the rustlers come back."

She pooh-poohed the notion, fearless as always. "They already took everything of value."

She had a point. They hadn't touched her house. And they certainly could have looted it, too, if they had wanted to do so. Still… He gazed down at her. "I think until we know more about who did this and why, you'll be safer elsewhere, Lulu."

"And I think I'll be just fine right here." She took hold of his biceps and steered him toward the porch steps, clearly done with this topic.

But he was not satisfied. Not in the least. Because the need to protect her was back, stronger than ever. "Lulu…"

She peered up at him from beneath a fringe of dark lashes. "You just worry about contacting Hiram and getting the triplets here as soon as possible. I'll handle the rest." She went into the house and shut the door behind her.

Chapter 3

"Sam's *still* out there?" Lulu's mother, Rachel, asked during the impromptu family phone call an hour later.

Grimacing, Lulu peeked out the window of her living room, catching a glimpse of the ornery cowboy through the dusky light. Cell phone still pressed to her ear, she confirmed, "He's sitting in his pickup truck, talking on the phone and doing something on what appears to be a laptop." Looking as devastatingly handsome and sexy as ever with his hat tossed off and his sleeves rolled up, another button of his shirt undone. Not that she was noticing the effect the summer heat might be having on him...

"Good for him," growled her father. He had heard all about the theft from other members of the cattleman's association before she'd even managed to call home to tell them. "Since Sam obviously doesn't think you should be left alone right now, either."

But Sam had once, Lulu thought. When the two of them had been at odds, he'd had no problem issuing an ultimatum. When he'd become deeply disappointed in her and walked away.

"Now, Frank," her mother warned, "Lulu can make her own decisions."

On the other end of the connection, her father harrumphed.

Lulu didn't want what she saw as her problems bringing conflict to her family. "It's not that I don't appreciate the offers made by you and my brothers," she said soothingly. All five of whom wanted to help out by either temporarily taking her into their home or standing guard over her and her property. "It's just that I need some alone time right now."

She needed time to think, to figure out how she and Sam were going to manage the triplets. Without continually bringing up any of their former angst.

With uncanny intuition, her mother asked, "Is there anything else going on?"

Glad she had opted not to FaceTime or speak with her parents in person, at least not until after Sam had formally become the triplets' guardian and she their nanny, Lulu tensed. "Like what?" She feigned innocence. Knowing her folks, they were going to have a lot of opinions about her decision to become a parent this way, too.

"I'm not sure." Her mother paused.

Lulu's heartbeat accelerated as she saw Sam get out of his pickup truck and stride through the twilight. He still had his cell phone and a laptop in his big hands. "Listen, Mom, Dad, I've gotta go. Talk to you soon." She hung up before they had a chance to reply.

The doorbell rang.

Her body thrumming with a mixture of impatience and anticipation, she switched on the porch light and opened the door. She stood, blocking him, and gave him a deadpan look. "Yes?"

His legs were braced apart, broad shoulders squared. Looking as confident and determined as ever, he turned his ruggedly handsome face to hers. "I wanted to tell you what the cattlemen have unearthed thus far," he said in the low, masculine voice she knew so well.

Lulu blinked in surprise and glanced at her watch. "It's only been a few hours."

A stubble of evening beard, a shade darker than his wheat-blond hair, lined his jaw. A matter-of-fact smile turned up the corners of his sensual lips. But it was the compelling intensity of his eyes that unraveled her every time. No matter how fiercely she determined that he would not get to her. Not again. "When it comes to rustlers, it's important to strike before the trail gets cold," he explained.

She couldn't argue that.

Their eyes met for one brief, telling moment, that—however fleeting—had them on the exact same page.

Gratitude oozing through her and figuring they might as well sit down for this, she ushered him in. He followed her past the cozy seating area and over to the kitchen island, where she'd been working on her own laptop, notifying fellow beekeepers of what had transpired.

Sam set his belongings down but remained standing. "First," he said, "I want to tell you that I phoned Hiram and told him you and I were going to be jointly caring for the boys, at least in the interim. Me as their permanent legal guardian, you as their nanny. He was on board with the idea of the two of us joining forces during the kids' transition, so the triplets are being brought to my ranch tomorrow afternoon around 3:30 p.m."

Wow, Sam worked fast. On multiple fronts. But then he always had. His ability to really get things done was one of the things she admired most about him.

He paused to check an incoming text on his phone, then turned his attention back to her. "Apparently, they are going to have everything they need with them for the short-term, and the rest of their belongings will be delivered by movers the following day."

She nodded, trying not to think about how attracted to him she still was.

His gaze roving her head to toe, he continued, "So, if you would like to be at Hidden Creek with me to greet them…"

There were times when he made her feel very comfortable, and then there were others, like now, when he made her feel very off-kilter. Lulu moved around to the other side of the island. "I would." She busied herself, putting a few dishes away.

He smiled. "Great. And second of all…" He settled his six-foot-three-inch frame on the bar stool, opened up his laptop and, eyes locked on hers, continued, "I know that you gave some of this information to the sheriff's department regarding the theft, but I want to make sure I didn't miss anything, if that's okay."

Ribbons of sensation ghosting down her spine, Lulu dipped her head in assent. He nodded back at her, then typed in a few words. "The burglary happened sometime this morning."

His manner was so businesslike, Lulu began to realize she could lean on Sam, at least in this situation, if only she allowed herself to do so.

Determined to keep him at arm's length, she fought the waves of sexual magnetism that always existed between them. "Sometime between eight o'clock, when I left for town to set up my lunch service for my food truck," she confirmed. "And when the sheriff's department notified me at around five o'clock, to let me know there had been a break-in."

Which left a huge nine-hour window.

His big hands paused over the keys. "A customer reported it?"

Aware she was suddenly feeling shaky again, Lulu moved around the island in search of a place to sit down. "Lucille Lockhart came out to buy some honey. She hadn't read my social media page advertising the location of my food truck today, so she didn't know I wasn't here." But the thieves likely had.

Sam made a low, thoughtful sound. "And everything was gone when Mrs. Lockhart arrived?"

She settled in the high-backed stool next to him and swiveled to face him. The sincerity in his gaze was almost as unnerving as his unexpected, unrelenting kindness. "The entire apiary was emptied, and so were the storehouse shelves. Panic-stricken, Mrs. Lockhart tried to call me, and when she couldn't reach me, she notified the sheriff. We don't know much more than that right now."

"Actually, we do." He swiveled toward her, too, and braced one elbow on the counter next to his laptop. His other hand rested on his rock-hard thigh. Nodding tersely once again, he added, "I put out the word when we got here. I've heard back from almost all our members."

She caught her breath at the worry in his eyes.

"Apparently two trucks were spotted on the farm-to-market road that goes by here around one o'clock this afternoon. They seemed to be traveling together and were headed north. One was a white refrigeration truck, the other a flatbed loaded with two off-road forklifts." His lips compressed, and his gruff tone registered his disappointment. "We didn't get an actual license number, but someone noticed the plates were from Wisconsin."

Hope mingling with dread, Lulu laid her hand across her heart. "They're sure it was a refrigeration truck?"

"It had the cooling unit on top of the cab."

Relief filtered through her. She didn't know whether to shout hallelujah or sob with relief. In truth, she felt like doing both. "Oh, thank heavens," she whispered finally.

"That's important?" Sam guessed.

Lulu swallowed around the ache in her throat. "Very. The bees wouldn't survive in their boxes if they were transported a long way in this kind of heat." She ran her hand over the side seam of her denim skirt. Sam's glance followed her reflexive move. Realizing the fabric had ridden up, Lulu did her best to surreptitiously tug it down. Yet, maddeningly, the hem remained several inches above her bare knees.

Knees he had once caressed with devastating sensuality.

Pushing aside her rush of self-consciousness, she added, "Moving bees is hard on them as it is."

Sam lifted his glance and locked eyes with her yet again. He regarded her with the respect of a fellow rancher. "Makes sense they'd do better if they were kept cool." He rubbed his jaw. "That kind of truck will also make the thieves easier to find."

Glad he had taken it upon himself to help her, even when she had preferred he leave her to handle everything on her own, Lulu drew a breath. It would be so easy to lean on him again. Too easy, maybe, given how acrimoniously they had once parted. "So what now?" she asked quietly.

Sam sobered, the corners of his lips slanting down. "I've already notified the sheriff's department with all the information I was able to compile, and they in turn have put out an APB and will be checking with truck stops and weighing stations for any vehicles fitting the description."

Feeling her first concrete ray of hope, Lulu asked, "You really think we might find them?"

He nodded. "Trucks like that can't stick to country roads without drawing a lot of attention. On the highway, they'll be a lot easier to find. Hopefully, we'll know something soon."

He shut the lid on his laptop and stood.

Feeling surprisingly reluctant to see him go, Lulu rose, too. "Sam…" She touched his arm, delaying him. He turned to gaze down at her and her heart rate kicked up another notch.

"I really… I don't know how to thank you," she continued sincerely. "A few hours ago, I had very little hope I'd ever see my beehives again. Now, well." She struggled to put her gratitude into words. As she gazed up at him, she pushed through the wealth of conflicting emotions suddenly racing through her and tried again. "I never would have expected you to...help."

Something dark and turbulent flashed in his eyes. "Well, you should have," he said, as if fighting his own inner demons.

The next thing Lulu knew, she was all the way in his arms. His head was lowering, his lips capturing hers. His kiss was everything she remembered, everything she had ever dreamed of receiving, everything the wildly impulsive and romantic part of her still wanted. From him...

Because the truth was, no one had ever affected her like Sam did. No one had ever made her want, wish, need... And as his lips ravished hers, she moaned at the sweet, enervating heat. The touch of his tongue against hers sent her even further over the edge. Wreathing her arms about his neck, she shifted closer. Nestling the softness of her breasts against the solid, unyielding warmth of his broad chest. His hand swept lower, bringing her even nearer. And, just like that, the walls she'd erected around her began to crumble and her heart expanded, tenfold.

One kiss melded into another. And then another... and another. Until he had her surrendering to the firm, insistent pressure of his mouth as never before. She clung to him, soaking up everything about him. His strength, his scent. His warmth and tenderness. Years of pent-up emotion poured out of her as she rose on tiptoe and pressed her body even closer against the hardness of his.

And still he kissed her. Slowly and thoroughly. Softly

and sweetly. With building need. Until a low, helpless moan escaped her throat. And she recalled everything that had once brought them together…and had ultimately torn them apart…

Sam hadn't meant to kiss her. Hadn't thought he would even come close. But when Lulu had looked up at him with such sweet surprise in her expression, well, it triggered something in him. Something primitive and hot and wild.

It had made him want to claim her again.

As his woman.

As his…

He cut off the thought before it could fully form. Knowing there was no way either of them could go back to that tumultuous period of time, even if the hot, intense connection that had always been between them was definitely still there. And she knew it, too, as he felt her begin to tense the way she always did when she began to have second thoughts.

With a sigh, he drew back. Sure of what he was going to see.

She gazed up at him, eyes awash with the kind of turbulent emotion that had always signaled trouble for them. Lower lip trembling, she flattened her hands over his chest and pushed him away. "We can't do this again."

And once again, the need to possess her got the better of his common sense.

"Why not?" he demanded gruffly.

"Because we already proved it will never work between us," she whispered, the shimmering hurt back in her pretty eyes, "and I really don't want to go there again."

* * *

To Lulu's relief, after a moment's consideration, Sam seemed to concede it wouldn't be wise to complicate their situation any further.

And when he greeted her at the door of his sprawling ranch house the following afternoon, his manner was appropriately circumspect.

Which left her free to forget about the heady aftermath of their passionate embrace and concentrate on the changes made to the Hidden Creek cattle ranch since she had last been there.

The thousand-acre spread was as tidy and filled with good-looking cattle as ever, the barns, stables, bunkhouse and other buildings meticulously well kept. He had updated the main house with dark gray paint on the brick, white trim and black shutters. She admired the beautifully landscaped front lawn and the circular drive directing guests to the covered porch and inviting front door. A quartet of dormer windows adorned the steeply pitched roof.

Most arresting of all, though, was the ruggedly handsome rancher who ushered her inside. The corners of his sensual lips lifted in an appraising smile. He came close enough she could smell the soap and sun and man scent of his skin. "A little early, aren't you?"

Her heart panged in her chest. "I wanted to make sure I was here when they arrived, but if you'd like me to wait in my SUV..." Aware she was fast becoming a bundle of nerves, she gestured at the Lexus in the driveway.

"Don't be ridiculous." He ushered her inside.

Aware the atmosphere between them was quickly becoming highly charged and way too intimate, Lulu turned her attention elsewhere. There'd been a lot of changes since she'd been here last, she noted as she followed him. The ecru walls and dark wide-plank wood floors were the same, but the fancy upholstered pieces and heavy custom draperies favored by his late mother had been exchanged for large leather couches, mahogany furniture and modern plantation shutters. A lot of the knickknacks and elegant paintings were gone, replaced by a handsomely redone white brick fireplace and mantel, a complete wall of built-in bookshelves and a state-of-the-art entertainment center.

His gaze dropped to the hamper in her hand "Planning a picnic?" he drawled.

Lulu's hands curled around the wicker handle. "I'm open to whatever the kids need, although I don't really know what to expect when they do arrive." Which was one of the reasons she was so uncharacteristically on edge.

Evidently that was something they had in common. Sam sighed. "Me, either." He led the way down the hall to the back of the ranch house, where changes also abounded. The kitchen's flowered wallpaper and frilly curtains were gone, replaced by stainless steel appliances and concrete countertops and sleek white walls washed in sunlight. The breakfast room table and eight captain chairs were the same, although all had been refinished with a glowing golden-oak stain. The family room had become a work space, with file cabinets, a U-shaped computer desk, scanner/copier phone and printer.

He squinted at her. "Meet your approval?"

With effort, she met his probing gaze. She set the

hamper on the island—also new—in the center of the large square kitchen. "It's very nice. You've outdone yourself," she said.

He shrugged, all affable male again. "Can't take all the credit. My sister Lainey is an interior designer now, so she helped. Tara, the computer expert, set up all my business systems for me. Liza, the chef, taught me how to cook. Betsy, the innkeeper, showed me how to properly stock a pantry and freezer."

Like the McCabes, the Kirklands always had each other's backs. "Your sisters are scattered all over now, aren't they?"

"Yep." He lounged against the counter, arms folded. "I'm the only one left in Texas."

Trying not to notice how well he filled out his ranching clothes, she asked, "You miss them?"

His gaze skimmed her appreciatively. "They visit."

Not an answer. But then, he had never been one to own up to anything that hurt. He just moved on.

As he was about to do now...

He inclined his head. "So what's in there?" he asked.

"I wasn't sure what you had on hand or what they were sending with the kids, so I brought some toddler favorites like applesauce and kid-friendly mac and cheese for their dinner, just in case."

Another nod. "Thanks," he said, as a big, sleepy-looking Saint Bernard came around the corner. The brown patches of fur over the pet's eyes and back and chest contrasted with the fluffy white coat everywhere else. An extremely feminine flowered pink collar encircled her neck.

Lulu watched the big dog pad gracefully over to

stand beside Sam. She sat down next to him, pressing her body up against his sinewy leg and hip. Tail wagging, she gazed up at Sam adoringly. Waited, until he petted her head, then let out a long, luxuriant sigh that Lulu understood all too well.

Pushing aside the memory of Sam's gentle, soothing touch, she asked, "Who is this?"

"Beauty. As in *Beauty and the Beast*."

Unable to resist, Lulu guessed, "And you're the Beast?"

Although he tried, he couldn't quite contain a smile. "Very funny."

Lulu chuckled. "I thought so."

Although, the moniker fit. The 120-pound dog was absolutely gorgeous. And not really the type of canine she would have expected a rough-hewn rancher like Sam to choose.

"When did you get her?" Lulu smiled and made eye contact with Beauty, who appreciated her right back.

Tilting his head, Sam paused, calculating. "A little over four years ago."

"As a puppy?"

"She was about six months old at the time."

Lulu paused. "I didn't know you wanted a dog." He certainly hadn't mentioned it when they were together. Back then, all he'd talked about were horses and cattle. And of course the importance of keeping one's commitments. Which he definitely did not think Lulu had done.

He smiled as his dog stood again and then stretched her front legs out in front of her, dipping her tummy close to the floor in a play bow. "She's not mine. She belongs to my sister Hailey."

Hence, the romantic pet name.

Lulu turned back to him, confused. "But…you're keeping her?" She watched Beauty rise again and turn back to Sam for one last pet on the head.

His big hand sank into the soft, luxuriant fur on the top of Beauty's head, massaging it lightly in a way that made Lulu's own nerve endings shudder and her mouth go dry.

"It was never the intention," Sam admitted, oblivious to the effect his tender ministrations were having on Lulu. "But Beauty was too big for Hailey's apartment, and she suddenly had to travel internationally for her job. Constantly boarding Beauty didn't seem fair. My sister asked me to help out temporarily, since I have plenty of room. I agreed."

Lulu observed the free-flowing affection between man and pet. "Looks like you made the right decision."

And possibly, Lulu thought as Beauty lumbered over to stand next to her, the right decision regarding the three kids, as well.

Because if Sam wouldn't turn out a dog who had come to live with him, she knew he would never abandon three little orphaned boys. And that meant if she was going to form a permanent, loving connection with Theresa and Peter's triplets, she would have to forget the difficulties of their past and find a way to forge an enduring, *platonic* connection with Sam, too.

The next twenty minutes passed with excruciating slowness. Sam settled down to do something at his desk while Lulu paced, looking out one front window, then the next.

Finally, a large dark green van made its way up the

lane. It stopped next to the ranch house. The doors opened. Hiram Higgins and three other adults stepped out. And even though there was no sign of the children they were going to care for just yet, Lulu's heartbeat quickened.

"Sam! They're here!" she exclaimed.

He rose and strode briskly through the hall to her side.

Together, they walked out the front door and down the porch steps. Hiram introduced his wife, Winnifred, a kind-faced woman with gray hair, and Sandra and Jim Kelleher, the thirtysomething couple who had been looking after the triplets.

Seeing that Lulu and Sam were chomping at the bit to meet the kids, the Kellehers proceeded to unfasten safety harnesses and bring the children out, one by one. All three were holding stuffed animals and clutching well-loved blue baby blankets. In deference to the shimmering June heat, they were wearing blue plaid shorts and coordinating T-shirts, sandals, plaid bucket hats and kiddie sunglasses. All appeared shy and maybe even a little dazed. As if they'd been napping and were still trying to wake up.

"This is Theo," Winnifred introduced the most serious-looking toddler.

Sandra brought forward the one with the trembling lower lip. "And Ethan."

"And Andrew," Jim said, shifting the weight of the only one starting to fidget.

"Hello, Theo, Ethan and Andrew," Lulu greeted them in turn.

They simply stared at her, then eventually turned away.

Her heart sank. She was a McCabe. She'd been around

children all her life. Not once had one responded to her with such indifference.

But then, these children had been through hell. It was probably no surprise they'd become…numb.

Hiram retrieved his briefcase and inclined his head at Sam. "We probably should sign the papers first and then unload the belongings they brought with them today."

"Lulu," Sam said, "you want to take them all on in?"

"Sure." She led the way inside as Sam and Hiram adjourned to a corner of the front porch. Winnifred and the Kellehers took a seat in the living area, a child on each lap. Once they were all settled, Lulu sat down, too, and they got down to business.

"I brought a folder with me of everything I've been able to piece together about the children's previous routines, plus everything that did or did not work for us, in terms of their care," Sandra said.

Jim exhaled, then turned to look at Lulu. "I hope Sam has better luck with them. It's good you're going to be helping out, too."

Winnifred chimed in, "Hiram and I can both attest to that. They can be a handful."

Suddenly feeling a little unsure they were up to the task, Lulu nodded her understanding. Had she and Sam underestimated the task of helping the orphaned triplets?

Sam and Hiram walked in. After Sam set the papers on the entry table, Jim handed the still-fidgety Andrew to Lulu and all three men headed back outside. Short minutes later, a trio of car seats, travel beds, booster seats, suitcases, and a big box of toys were stacked in a corner of the living room.

"Probably best we be on our way," Hiram said.

Lulu expected the kids to wail in protest at the impending departure of yet another set of guardians. Instead, they took it stoically in stride. Too stoically, in fact, to be believed.

Chapter 4

"How long do you think they're going to sit there like that, before they decide to get comfy and stay awhile?" Sam quipped to Lulu a good half hour later. Although he was the one with legal responsibility for them, she was the one who seemed to inherently understand what was going on with them. That put them all in the awkward position of really needing her soothing maternal presence in a way Sam hadn't expected. And that he wasn't sure how to deal with, given his ever-present desire for her.

Oblivious to his chaotic thoughts, Lulu looked up from the toy fort she was building in the center of the living room floor and turned her glance in the direction Sam indicated.

The triplets were right where they'd initially settled. Cuddled together in the middle of his big leather sofa.

All still wore their hats and sunglasses. Their blankets and stuffed animals were on their laps. Thumbs in their mouths. All previous attempts, and there had been three thus far, to gently separate them from their head-wear had failed.

"I don't know." With a shrug, Lulu continued pulling toys from the box. Unlike him, she was completely at ease, despite the fact that, like him, she'd been rebuffed at every attempt to get acquainted with the children, too. Her turquoise eyes sparkled with amusement and her soft lips curved into a sweet, contented smile. "Until they're ready to do something else?"

Sam edged closer and caught a whiff of her signature fragrance. With effort, he concentrated on the problem at hand. Helping the boys acclimate.

"With those sunglasses on, this place has to look dark to them, even though we opened up the blinds and turned the lights on." He wondered if they were scared.

Lulu dusted off her hands and stood. Looking incredibly fetching in a pretty floral sundress and casual canvas flats, she came close enough to go up on tiptoe and whisper in his ear, "Would you relax, cowboy?" Her hand curved over his biceps. "I think your anxiety is making them tense."

Was it his imagination or was it getting hot in here? "I'm not anxious."

Clearly, she didn't believe him.

She let go of him for a moment and stepped back to study him from beneath a fringe of thick, dark lashes, then lightly clasped one of his forearms just above his wrist. "Let's just give them a moment to acclimate without us staring at them, okay?" She gave a little tug when he didn't budge. "Come on. You can help me set their booster seats up at the kitchen table. Maybe set out a snack or…" she glanced at her watch, noting that it was nearly five o'clock "…dinner."

Her soft skin feeling like a silky manacle around his wrist, she guided him down the wide hallway to the kitchen. Sam pushed away the evocative memories her touch engendered. Exhaled. For once, he was all too willing to let her be in charge of what went on with the two of them. In fact, the knowledge that she had some idea of what to do was reassuring.

His sisters had done all the babysitting when they were growing up. Not him. And the truth was, he had no idea at all how to handle a situation like this.

Sam peeked back into the living room, far enough to be able to surreptitiously check on the three little boys and see they were just where they had been.

Then he moved back toward Lulu. Stood, back braced against the kitchen island, feet crossed at the ankle, arms folded. "You think they're hungry?"

She ran a hand through her sun-streaked honey brown hair, pushing the silky waves off her face. As she squared her shoulders, the luscious curves of her breasts pushed against the bodice of her dress. "I'm sure they are. Thirsty, too." She removed three small cartons of apple juice and a container of Goldfish crackers from the bag, then set them all on the counter.

"I also know they've had a very rough time, being shuffled from home to home for the last two months." She paused to look into Sam's eyes. "They've got to be very confused."

He let his gaze drift over her, surprised at how good

it felt to have her here, in his home, with him. When all they'd done for years was try to stay as far apart from each other as possible. He was beginning to see what a mistake that was. Clearly, there was a lot of unfinished business between them. Aware they were definitely on the same page about one thing—making the triplets happy again—he murmured, "I want them to feel good about being here."

"I'm sure they will," she reassured him softly. "But we have to give them time, Sam."

Without warning, Beauty, who'd been sleeping on her cushion in the corner of the kitchen, lifted her head. Got to her feet. And ever so slowly moved toward the hall.

Wondering what the Saint Bernard had heard, Sam turned in that direction.

There it was.

The unmistakable sound of childlike chatter.

Lulu started in surprise. Pausing to give him a quick, excited glance, she tiptoed down the hallway toward the living room. Sam was right on her heels, moving just as soundlessly.

And there they were. All three boys. Finally sans bucket hats and sunglasses, sitting on the floor, in the middle of their toys.

"You were right," Sam murmured, standing close enough to feel the heat emanating from her slender body. "All we needed to do was give them a little room to maneuver."

Lulu nodded, although to his consternation she didn't look nearly as relieved as he felt to see them up and about.

Figuring it was his turn to comfort her, he reached

over to give her forearm a companionable squeeze. "Maybe acclimating them won't be so difficult after all," he theorized.

Except as it turned out, Lulu noted in despair many times over the next eight hours, it absolutely was.

The three boys all refused their snack, and, except for a few sips of their apple juice, also made a mess of their dinner. Squishing the mac and cheese between their fingers and smearing it on their plates and the table in front of them. Banana slices, applesauce and chopped green beans shared a similar fate. In fact, once they'd finished, it looked as if there had been one heck of a food fight in Sam's kitchen.

Once down from the table, they began to run and climb and shout, while Beauty lay on the floor, watching over them with a sweet maternal grace. As if the Saint Bernard knew exactly what they were thinking and feeling.

Which was good, Lulu thought with increasing disquiet. Because neither she nor Sam had a clue. A fact that really hit home when she decided to take matters in hand and put the overtired little munchkins to bed.

Her old camp-counselor smile plastered on her face, Lulu approached the boys. "Guess what, fellas?" she said. "It's almost bedtime."

"That's right, bedtime," Sam echoed cheerfully.

"Nooooo!" all three boys yelled in unison, then went racing off in all directions.

Sam and Lulu leaped into action. He plucked Andrew off the top of the sofa, then intercepted Ethan, who was scurrying up the stairs to the second floor. Meanwhile, Lulu scooped Theo into her arms before he could reach

the remotes on the third shelf of the entertainment center. "Who wants to take a bubble bath?" she asked, even
more enthusiastically.

Theo wriggled like a tadpole in Lulu's arms. "No
bath!" he shouted.

Ethan and Andrew echoed the sentiment as Sam lowered them onto the living room floor. Lulu followed
suit with Theo.

The mania increased.

Sam looked over at her, clearly at wit's end. "We
have to do something," he said firmly.

Lulu struggled to catch her breath while the boys
began doing somersaults in the middle of the rug.
"Agreed."

"Then...?"

She knew she was the one with all the childcare experience, from her high school and college days. But
even some of the most difficult situations at summer
camp had never been like this. No wonder none of the
other guardians had been able to handle the triplets.

"Maybe we should pass on the baths and just put
them in clean diapers and pajamas before starting the
bedtime routine," she said.

He nodded, clearly ready to comply with anything
she suggested. Which was unusual. He generally liked
to be in charge.

"Got anything to bribe them with?" she asked.

His broad shoulders lifted in an amiable shrug.
"Cookies?"

"Worth a try!"

He disappeared and came back with a transpar-
ent bakery container. "Who wants a chocolate chip
cookie?" he said, holding it aloft.

The boys stopped.

Lulu could see they were about to refuse this, too.

Sam lowered the container so they could get a better look at the confections inside.

Three thumbs immediately went into mouths. They were thinking. Checking with each other silently. Considering.

Good. "All you have to do," Lulu coaxed, "is get ready for bed. Then you can have a cookie *and* a bedtime story. Maybe even a glass of milk, okay?"

The triplets stood still.

Being careful not to spook them, she got out the necessary items, and with Sam's help, swiftly got them all changed. When all were ready, Sam doled out the cookies as promised.

The three of them climbed up onto the center of the sofa and began to chomp away. While Sam watched over them, Lulu raced into the kitchen and brought back three sippy cups of milk.

One by one, they drank that, too.

Pleased she and Sam had been able to work together to bring peace to the household, Lulu smiled. Indicating Sam should take one end of the sofa, she slipped onto the other and began to read a story that—from the well-worn condition of it—appeared to be one of their favorites. It was about a dog who went into his little house to find shelter from the storm and was soon joined by every other animal nearby. By the time the storm passed, the doghouse was full. New friendships had been formed. And everyone was still safe and warm and happy.

As she hoped they would soon be here, at Hidden Creek.

"Would you like another story?" Lulu asked as the triplets blinked sleepily and their heads began to droop.

To her disappointment, there were no nods of agreement.

But no shouts of outright refusal, either. So taking that for a yes, Lulu grabbed another book and then another and another. By the time she hit the fifth story, all three toddlers were sound asleep.

Sam, who'd been hanging out simply listening, gestured toward the three carrying cases in the foyer. "Where do you think I should set up their travel beds?" he whispered.

That was easy, Lulu thought, already thinking about how hard it was going to be to say good-night this evening. But she and Sam had a deal, so...

She drew a deep, bolstering breath. "Close to you, in case they wake up."

He paused, blond brow furrowing. "I know our agreement," he said. "But...are you sure you can't stay? At least for tonight?"

The truth was, Lulu had been hoping like crazy that he'd ask. Partly because she didn't want to leave the boys, given the highly agitated state they'd been in. And also because she wasn't any more confident Sam could handle this on his own than he was.

"I'll have to run home and get a few things," she said, doing her best to hide her elation.

He nodded his assent and rose as she walked over to get her bag. Then, stepping closer, murmured in the same tender tone he had used before, "Think we should get them settled into their beds first?"

Her body tingling at his nearness, she shook her head. "I'd let them get a little deeper into sleep first."

"Okay."

Another silence fell.

He looked so momentarily unsure of himself, her heart went out to him. So she moved in to give him a quick, reassuring hug. "I know we've had a rough start today, but it's all going to work out, Sam," she promised fiercely.

"I know," he whispered back. His arms went around her and he pulled her in close, one hand idly moving down her back, reflexively calming her, too. She sank into his warmth and his strength, wishing things were as simple as they once had been. When need…want…love…were the only things driving them. But they were different people now. She needed to remember that.

Forcing herself to do what was best for all of them, Lulu drew a breath and stepped back from the enticing circle of his arms. She flashed a confident smile she couldn't begin to feel—not when it came to the two of them, anyway.

"I'll be right back," she promised. And while she was gone, for the sake of everyone, she would do her best to get her own feelings in order.

Two hours later, Sam was feeling much better. Lulu had returned with an overnight bag, honey-grilled chicken sandwiches for their dinner and the makings for a pancake breakfast the next morning. He'd cleaned up the kitchen and breakfast room and set up the three toddler travel beds in the master bedroom upstairs in her absence.

Now, with their own hunger sated, all they had to do was figure out how to move the still-snoozing tykes from the sofa to the travel beds on the second floor.

"Want me to go first?" Lulu asked as they stood shoulder to shoulder, gazing down at their little charges.

Doing his best to contain all he was feeling, Sam nodded. "I'll follow your lead."

With an adeptness Sam well remembered, Lulu eased in to remove Theo first. He was sleeping half on Ethan and had one leg beneath Andrew. She slid her hands beneath him, careful as could be not to disturb the other two. Theo shifted and sighed as she lifted him into her arms and then situated him with his head on her shoulder, his body against her middle.

"Wish me luck," she mouthed and glided off toward the stairs.

When she'd made it all the way up without incident, Sam copied her movements and eased Ethan into his arms. The little boy stirred and sighed but did not wake as Sam headed up the stairs. Slowly, he went down the hall, then into the master bedroom where Lulu was still bent over one of the travel cribs, tucking Theo in. She helped him ease Ethan down, and together, they went back to get Andrew. He slept through the move to bed, too.

Ten minutes later, all was set.

They tiptoed into the upstairs hallway. Lulu looked at him in question.

"Take any guest room you want," he said.

She chose the one two doors down. Which was probably an effort to put a little more physical space between them, since the bedroom she passed over, with a queen-size bed and adjoining bath, was almost identical.

When she turned to glance up at him, she looked tired, vulnerable and very much in need of a hug. But a hug would lead to a kiss, and a kiss would lead to everything they didn't need right now.

An electric silence fell between them and his heart kicked against his ribs.

"You'll let me know if you need me?" she said finally.

I need you now, more than I ever thought I would. He returned her half smile, promising, just as kindly, "No question."

Aware there was nothing else to say, he went back down the stairs and retrieved her overnight bag for her. They said good-night quickly, and both turned in.

Sam had no idea if Lulu fell asleep right away or not. He lay there for a while, thinking about all the mistakes they had made, everything they'd lost. How good it had felt to kiss her again the night before.

Still thinking about that, he drifted off. And it was shortly after that when the crying started. First Ethan, then Theo and Andrew.

Heart pounding, Sam threw back the covers and raced over to the travel cribs at the foot of his bed. All three boys were sitting up, distraught, rubbing their eyes.

Lulu rushed in, clad in a pair of blue-and-white-striped linen pajama pants, her hair gloriously mussed. In that instant, giving Sam an insight into what kind of mother she would be, she tenderly scooped up one child.

He reached down and lifted the other two.

"Hush now, baby, it's all right," she cooed, over and over. As did he.

To no avail. The crying continued in concert, long into the night. Sam's only comfort was the fact that Lulu was right there with them, steadfastly weathering the storm.

Chapter 5

Lulu woke slowly, aware of three things. She was incredibly exhausted, curiously weighed down, at least in the region of her midriff, and was that Sam…in all his early-morning glory…sleeping next to her? With two toddlers in his arms?

She blinked. And blinked again.

Yes, it was Sam, clad in a pair of pajama pants and a V-necked T-shirt. With his hair adorably rumpled and a morning beard rimming his chiseled jaw, he looked incredibly masculine and sexy. He was also sound asleep, his breathing as deep and even as that of the two little boys curled up on his chest, their heads nestled between his neck and shoulders.

Better yet, she had a tyke in her arms, too, snuggled up close, his head tucked between her head and shoulder. And all five of them were cozied up in Sam's king-size bed.

Without warning, he stirred slightly. Drew a deep, bolstering breath and opened his eyes.

He turned to look at her, his lips curving up in that sleepy-sexy, good-morning way she recalled so well.

Contentment roared through her, making her feel all warm and cozy inside.

His glance roved her slowly. It seemed like he might be feeling some of that contentment, too. "Some night, huh?" he murmured huskily.

It had been. The boys had cried off and on for hours. Every time they thought they had one asleep, another woke him.

The only thing that had soothed any of them was being walked. And so they'd roamed the master bedroom, crooning softly, Lulu with one toddler in her arms, Sam with two in his.

Until finally, around four in the morning, the boys had drifted off, and wary of disturbing them yet again, Sam and Lulu had eased onto the center of his big bed, children still in their arms. They lay there gently, daring to relax fully and close their eyes. And then, finally, slept.

Admiration shone in Sam's eyes. "You were great with them last night," he said.

She knew the memory of the boys' first night would stick with her. "So were you…"

Theo snuggled close, yawned sleepily, squirmed again and then lifted his head. Andrew and Ethan swiftly followed suit. All looked expectantly in the direction of the open bedroom door. "Mommy?" Theo said.

"Daddy?" Andrew asked.

"Go home?" Ethan demanded.

The plaintive requests, along with the confusion and lack of comprehension in the boys' eyes, tugged on Lulu's heartstrings and filled her with sorrow. She mourned Peter and Theresa, too. She could only imagine how poignant the loss was for the boys. No wonder they were out of control. They didn't understand where their parents were. And at their young age, there was no way to explain.

Her vision blurred.

Sam cleared his throat. "Mommy and Daddy are in heaven," he said gently. "But you know who we do have?" He indicated the stuffed animals scattered around them. "Tiger and Elephant and Giraffe!"

Grinning, the boys picked up their stuffed animals and clutched them to their chests.

"And blankets, too!" Sam declared.

They grabbed those, as well.

Her heart aching with an emotion that was almost primal in its intensity, Lulu did her best to smile, too, and affect an air of normalcy. Her grieving would have to come later, privately. "How about we all go downstairs and I'll rustle up some breakfast?" she suggested.

Sam reached over and squeezed her shoulder. Although the boys' hurt and confusion had affected him, too, he had regained his composure swiftly. "Sounds like a plan to me…"

Sam had to hand it to Lulu. Even though he could see her heart was breaking for the boys, as was his, she pulled it together with feminine grace. Helped with the three diaper changes and, along with Beauty who'd been sleeping on the floor of his bedroom as per usual, escorted the boys downstairs.

While the triplets played with their toys in the living room, she went into the kitchen to start breakfast. He let Beauty outside and put on a pot of coffee. She was still dressed in blue-and-white-striped pajama pants and a white scoop-necked T-shirt that nicely outlined her slender body. Her dark hair was tousled, her cheeks pink with sleep, her turquoise eyes red-rimmed with fatigue.

He cupped a hand over her shoulder as she passed, temporarily stilling her. "Hey. If you want to go back to bed for a while…"

She pivoted another quarter turn, so she was looking up at him directly. Acting as if that were the most ridiculous suggestion she had ever heard, she wrinkled her nose at him. "Ah, no."

"Sure?" he pressed. Aware he was still holding onto her, dropped his hand. Filled with the surprising urge to protect her, too, he said, "You only got two or three hours of sleep."

Propping one hand on her hip, she looked him over, head to toe. "Which, as it turns out, was exactly what you and the boys got," she retorted. "Seriously." Her gaze gentled. "I'm fine. I want to be available to the kids whenever, however they need me."

Before he could respond, the doorbell rang.

"Expecting someone?" she asked.

"No." Sam went to get the door while Lulu remained in the kitchen.

A uniformed Laramie County sheriff's deputy was on his doorstep. And not just any deputy, but Lulu's brother, Dan.

He touched the brim of his hat in an official manner, the grim look in his eyes indicating that although they were longtime acquaintances, this was not a social call. "Sam," Dan said.

Sam nodded back, just as officiously. "Dan."

"My sister here?" Dan asked, looking anything but pleased.

Her brother had to figure that she was, Sam thought, since Lulu's SUV was parked in his driveway. "Yes."

"Can I speak with her?"

Sam wasn't sure how to answer that. Generally, Lulu didn't want her family interfering in her personal business. And this definitely looked personal.

Before he could say anything further, Lulu strode across the living room and into the foyer. She regarded her brother with a mixture of annoyance and concern. "What's going on?" she asked.

Her older brother gave her a look that was strictly family-drama. He compressed his lips, looking over her pajamas. "I could ask you the same thing," he groused.

It didn't help, Sam thought, that with her flushed face and guilty eyes, it appeared as though Lulu had tumbled straight out of bed. *Sam's* bed.

She folded her arms, stubborn as ever. "I asked first."

Dan squinted at her. "I've been trying to get a hold of you since last evening."

"I was busy."

"Yeah, well, that's no reason not to answer your phone," he chastised.

"Actually," Lulu shot back, "it kind of is."

The siblings stared each other down.

Sam cleared his throat. He was all for gallantly coming to Lulu's aid, even if they were no longer a couple. On the other hand, he had no wish to insert himself into another family's drama. Plus, the boys, who were still busily building a block tower, didn't need to witness any quarreling. He cleared his throat and looked back at Lulu, who was still blocking the doorway. "If you'd like, I can step in so you can step out and talk in private," Sam offered mildly.

"Nope." Lulu lounged against the door frame, one ankle crossed over the other. She stared at Dan, nonchalant. "Whatever you have to say to me, big brother, can be said in front of Sam. And how did you know I was here, anyway?"

Dan shrugged. "Simple deduction. Sam was at your place yesterday, helping out and watching over you. Neither of you have been answering your phones. I figured something was going on."

Taken aback, Lulu paused. "That's no reason to spy on me."

"I wasn't spying," Dan continued quietly. "I just wanted to make sure you're safe."

Sam couldn't blame him for that.

And neither, as much as she wanted to, could Lulu. "Well," she said finally, "as you can see, I am."

"Uh-huh. It still doesn't explain why you're here now," Dan said.

"I would think that would be obvious." She pointed to Theo, Andrew and Ethan who were all still playing happily with their toys.

Dan turned to Sam. "So the word in town is true? You've just become legal guardian to three little ones?"

"Yes."

He turned back to his sister. "What do you have to do with this?"

She tensed. "I'm here, helping out."

Dan lifted a curious brow.

"By...um...nannying," she concluded reluctantly.

Her brother eyed her pajamas, which were quite chaste compared to some of the things Sam had once seen Lulu in. And would like to see again.

"Do Mom and Dad know you're now *working* for Sam?"

It felt more like working *with*, but whatever, Sam thought. It was clear they were going to have to renegotiate their deal, anyway.

Meanwhile, Lulu wasn't about to quibble over semantics. "What do you think?"

Dan squinted. "That you were probably afraid to tell them about any of this, never mind your sleeping over, for fear of what they'd say."

Lulu turned to Sam, clearly feeling that was out of line, even if Dan was family. "Would you deck him for me?"

"No." Although he wouldn't mind taking her in his arms again.

Her eyes lit up like firecrackers on the Fourth of July. "Why not?" she demanded, looking both confused and incensed. "You've never had trouble defending my honor before!"

True, Sam thought, but this was different. They weren't a couple now, although for parts of the previous night and this morning it almost felt as if they *could* be again. And because, as the primary caregiving adults in three vulnerable little boys' lives, they had to be adult about all this. She especially had to not care about what others thought, as long as the two of them knew what they were doing was right. "Because there are better ways to resolve conflict," he said wearily.

Lulu flushed again, for an entirely different reason

this time, it seemed. Temper dissipating, she turned back to her brother, contrite. "Okay, sorry for over-reacting."

He lifted a hand, understanding. "It's okay, sis. I know you have a lot going on."

Lulu regarded her brother intently. "Why did you want to talk to me, anyway?"

Dan relaxed as peace returned. "I wanted to tell you there was some news about your hives. The driver of the tractor trailer hauling the off-road forklifts was apprehended last night in Missouri."

Lulu bit her lip. "And the bees?"

"We don't know where they are yet. The two vehicles apparently split up. The guy who loaded the beehives into the refrigeration truck said he thought it was a legal transport."

Her shoulders slumped in disappointment. "What about all the honey that was stolen?"

"The jars are in crates, on the same truck as the beehives. He thought those were authorized to be removed, too."

Appearing distraught, Lulu moved closer to Sam. It was all he could do not to put his arm around her and hug her close. Figuring that was the last thing she would want him to do in front of her protective older brother, he remained where he was.

"Did the officers believe him?" she asked in a low, quavering voice.

Dan's brow furrowed. "Not sure, but the guy is cooperating, so there's a chance we might recover your bees yet."

"Thank heavens." Looking like she needed a moment to compose herself, Lulu went back into the ranch house without another word.

* * *

Dan declined to stay for breakfast. Intuiting Lulu's brother had a few more things he wanted to say, man-to-man, Sam walked him to his squad car.

"You and Lulu an item again?" Dan asked casually.

Sam shook his head. "No." *But after last night, I wish we were*, Sam thought. And how crazy was that?

The lawman slanted him a warning glance. "You know in addition to her usual impulsiveness, Lulu has baby fever..."

"She's also the next and last guardian on the list for the kids. She wants to be involved in this."

"You break her heart again," Dan warned, "friend of the family or not, you're going to be dealing with all five of her brothers. You get that?"

Sam nodded.

For a moment, neither of them spoke.

"So how is it going with the kids?" Dan asked.

Sam gave him the recap of the first eighteen hours.

Dan blinked, then offered empathetically, "I'm off at eleven. If you'd like, Kelly and I could round up our kids and come over this afternoon to lend a hand."

His wife was not only a preschool teacher, but mother to triplets, too. Sam spread his hands, for once open to any assistance offered. "Actually," he said sincerely, "if Kelly would like to visit, whatever tips she can give us would be great."

For the first time since he had arrived, Dan smiled. "I know she'd be glad to help," he said. "As would I."

Kelly, Dan and their triplets arrived shortly after noon, with a picnic lunch and a large box of toys their children had outgrown. Two-year-olds Theo, Andrew and Ethan were immediately taken with four-year-olds Michelle, Michael and Matthew.

Who had *lots* of questions.

"Are these your babies, Aunt Lulu?" Matthew asked.

"No." Looking gorgeous in a pair of coral shorts and a sleeveless white linen blouse, her hair swept up in a clip on the back of her head, Lulu knelt and lined up toy cars and trucks on the floor next to a play garage. Briefly, regret flashed in her long-lashed eyes. "I'm helping to take care of them," she explained, "but they're staying with Sam."

"So you're their daddy," Michael concluded with furrowed brow.

"Guardian," Sam corrected gently. *Although I'm beginning to think I'd like to be more than just that...*

Oblivious to the overemotional nature of his thoughts, Michelle sized up her aunt Lulu, then Sam. "Are you having a romance? 'Cause if you are," she added helpfully, "then you could get *married*."

Sam watched Lulu tense, the way she always did when the subject of her and marriage came up.

Kelly blushed. "Sorry." The lively preschool teacher lifted a hand. "She's been obsessed with love and weddings and marriage since…"

"Forever," Dan chuckled.

Michelle beamed. "Our mommy married Dan so he could be our daddy. They could show you how to fall in love. Then you could become a mommy like you want, Aunt Lulu," she finished sincerely.

So it was true, Sam thought. Dan hadn't been wrong in his analysis. And Lulu hadn't been exaggerating when she'd said she had wanted this forever. She did have baby fever. Enough to skew her judgment? Cause her to behave as recklessly as she had before they'd broken up? Only to regret her overly impulsive actions later? He sure as hell hoped not. Their first breakup had been excruciating enough. And now Theo, Andrew and Ethan were involved.

Seemingly aware of the delicate nature of the circumstances, Kelly took charge. "I think Sam and Aunt Lulu can figure out their own situation, honey."

"Let's show the boys the rest of the stuff we brought for them to play with," Dan said, digging into the big box of toys.

The kids immediately became enthralled, as everything old became new again.

Which was good, because it was only a few minutes later that the small moving van from Houston arrived.

"Where do y'all want this?" the workers asked. The crew boss opened up the back to reveal about twenty cardboard moving boxes, various toddler riding toys, a trio of toddler beds, a bureau, an oversize rocker-glider and a matching footstool.

Sam looked at Lulu, once again very glad she was there. "What do you think?" He had no idea where to put all this stuff.

"If it were me, I'd put the boxes containing Peter and Theresa's belongings in a storage area like…"

"The attic?"

"Yes. And then clear the large bedroom next to yours and set up a nursery for all three boys in there. Maybe figure out where to put the playroom stuff later."

Sam considered the suggestion. "Downstairs, off the kitchen, where my home office is now?"

"That would certainly be practical. You could toddler-proof the space and keep an eye on them while you prepare their meals. Maybe move your home office up-stairs to one of the spare guest rooms you aren't really using. Where it'll be quieter."

Sam nodded gratefully. "Sounds good." He offered to pay the movers a little extra to lend a hand with the reor-ganization efforts. Two hours later, with Dan and Kelly still downstairs supervising both sets of triplets, he and Lulu remained upstairs, unpacking the nursery linens.

"You really don't have to help me with this," Lulu said. "Now that the beds are assembled and put in place, I can get it all set up from here. So, if you want to hook up the stuff in your new office space—" which was at the far end of the hall "—or go downstairs and work on the new playroom area…"

Why was she suddenly in such a hurry to get rid of him, now that the movers had left? Sam could only come up with one reason.

"Afraid what Kelly and Dan will think if you're alone with me for too long?"

"No." Her cheeks lit with embarrassment, she swooped down to pull pillows, mattress pads and sheets out of boxes.

Aware that everything but the possibility of mak-ing love to her again had temporarily left his brain, he lifted his brow. "Uh-huh." He watched her deposit the appropriate stack of linens on the end of each toddler bed with more than necessary care. "Then why didn't you tell anyone in your family that you were going to be the boys' nanny, at least temporarily?"

"Maybe I didn't have time."

He let their glances collide, then linger. "And maybe things haven't really changed since we were together before."

Looking adorably flustered, she whirled away from him and went back to the bed against the far wall. "I know what you thought back then. And apparently now, too," she said, her emotions suddenly as fired up as his. "But I was never ashamed to be with you."

"But you were reluctant to tell them just how serious we were about each other. Isn't that right, darlin'?" He paused to let his words sink in.

Her upright posture emphasized the soft swell of her breasts. His body hardened in response. "You may have been twenty-one," she mused, "but I had just turned nineteen…"

"Which was old enough to go to Tennessee with me for spring break."

"Yes, but my parents didn't know that." She bent to put on the first mattress pad and gestured for him to do the same. "All they knew, or know even to this day, was that I was going to go with Theresa to visit Graceland and Dollywood and Gatlinburg, and then enjoy the music scene in Nashville…"

He tore his eyes from her sensational legs and the sweet curve of her hips, recalling, "They had no idea that you were going to be maid of honor and I was going to be best man at Peter and Theresa's elopement."

Cheeks turning pink, Lulu moved around to the other side of the bed to snap the elastic hem into place. "They wouldn't have approved."

He imagined they would have approved even less if they'd known she was deliberately keeping them in the dark. He finished putting the mattress cover on the second bed, then stood. "Are they going to approve of you nannying here?"

Lulu drew a deep breath. "If you want the truth…"

He did.

She put on the top sheet, then the quilt. "Probably not."

Finished, they both headed for the remaining toddler bed. Her head bent—to avoid his gaze, he imagined—she worked swiftly and methodically. He would have helped had she not edged him out with her hips.

Folding his arms, he moved around so he could see her expression. "You know you can't keep being here a secret from them, don't you?" Laramie County was a close-knit community, where families watched out for other families. Which meant that word would spread quickly.

Finished, Lulu punched the pillow into place. "I wasn't planning to."

"What's going to happen if they do express their displeasure?" he said, goading her. "Will just the *thought* of disappointing them make you run away again?"

She marched toward him, unafraid. "I never ran away." She poked a finger in his chest. "*You* were the one who threw down the gauntlet, *forcing* us to call it all off."

He went toe-to-toe with her and lowered his face until they were nose to nose. "For good reason, Lulu. I wasn't going to hide how I felt!"

"But you did," Lulu whispered, tears gleaming in her eyes. "We both did," she admitted in a choked voice, filled with the kind of heartache he, too, had experienced. "For a long time after that…"

Suddenly, Sam knew, he wasn't the only one who had been carrying a torch for the last ten years.

The next thing he knew, she was all the way in his arms. Her face turned up to his, and in that instant, all the pain of the last decade melted away. Their lips fused. A helpless sound escaped her throat and she pressed herself against him, yielding to him in a way she never had before.

And damn it if he wasn't giving his all to her, too. He gathered her even closer, let the kiss deepen, all the while savoring the sweet womanly taste of her, her fiery temperament, her warmth and her tenderness. Whether or not they'd be able to work it all out in the long haul was still questionable, but there'd never been anyone else for him. Never would be, he knew…

Lulu hadn't meant to let her feelings slip out. It wasn't surprising they had. She'd never been able to be around Sam and keep her guard up for long. He had a way of seeing past her defenses, of giving what was needed, even when she didn't exactly ask for it.

And what she needed right now, she thought as she sank even deeper into his tantalizing embrace, was his strength and his tenderness, his kindness and perceptiveness. She needed to know if there was still something really special between them, or if their all-consuming feelings for each other had faded.

True, they hadn't made things work when they'd had a chance. And there was no way they could go back and undo any of those mistakes, much as she might wish.

They could, however, find a way to forge a new path, one that gave them both what they needed and wanted, she thought as his tongue swept her mouth and mated ever so evocatively with hers. What she wanted right now, she realized, pressing even closer, was a second chance.

For him. For her. Maybe even for the three kids that were legally in his charge and emotionally in hers.

Who knew what would have happened if not for the sounds of a delicately clearing throat? The sight of her sister-in-law in the doorway?

"Sorry to interrupt," Kelly said, her cheeks flushing. "But the kids are all getting hungry. Would you all be up for taking them into town for pizza?"

Chapter 6

"You really think this is going to work?" Sam asked Lulu at seven thirty that evening. He lounged against the bathroom wall, smelling like soap and man and brisk cologne. He also needed a shave. Although, truth be told, the rim of evening shadow on his jaw made him look rakishly sexy.

Trying not to think about how much she wanted to kiss him again, never mind how intimate and somehow right this all felt, Lulu squirted bubble bath soap into the big soaking tub in the master bathroom. As she turned on the warm water, she reflected how much better the triplets' second day at the ranch had gone, compared to the first. It gave her hope the boys might settle in after all. That with a little time and a lot of love and effort, she and Sam *could* handle this.

And if they could handle the boys' adjustment, what else might they be able to handle? she wondered. A real, enduring friendship? An affair? One thing was clear: the hot kiss they'd shared earlier was still resonating within her. And maybe him, too, if the veiled looks he'd been giving her were any indication.

With effort, she forced herself back to the matter at hand. "You heard what Kelly said at dinner. A familiar routine is crucial in helping kids to feel safe and happy."

He cocked a brow, his gaze drifting over her lazily. In the same casual tone, he returned, "And the second thing is making kids *want* to do what they need to do."

"Right." Lulu smiled. Hence, the stop at the discount superstore on the way out of town to let Ethan, Andrew and Theo all pick out new bath toys. The boys had ridden back to the ranch with their treasures clutched in their little arms. And now that Sam had removed the packaging for them, it was time to play.

He walked back into the bedroom, where the triplets were enthusiastically climbing up onto the storage bench at the foot of his bed, and from there, onto the mattress. "Who wants to put their toys in the bubbles?" he asked.

"Me do!" Andrew said, hopping over to the edge and leaping unexpectedly into Sam's arms.

"Me first!" Theo dropped down and scooted over to the edge of the bed, putting his feet over the side of the mattress and onto the wooden bench, then down onto the floor.

Ethan held out his arms joyously and waited to be scooped up. "Me, too!"

"Okay, fellas," Sam said, once they'd all been ushered into the bathroom. "Let's see which new toys like the bath the most."

Andrew dropped his rubber whale and dolphins in.

The creatures shimmied but remained upright. Theo added his waterwheel, sieve and cup. Ethan added his three boats. Sam nodded approvingly at them. "Looking good," he said.

"Play?" Theo asked. He already had one leg up.

"Sure," Lulu said matter-of-factly, "but you have to take your dirty clothes off first, before you get in."

Immediately, all three boys began to undress. Lulu and Sam helped. A minute later, they were all in the tub, playing merrily. And were so entranced by their toys, they endured quick shampoos and rinses, too.

Eventually, they had to get out.

They did not want to do that.

Lulu said, "We have cookies and milk and bedtime stories for three little boys, as soon as they get their jammies on."

They had to think about it. But eventually caved. And by eight thirty, the five of them were on Sam's sofa again, enjoying what was to become their new bedtime routine. She and Sam alternated the reading of the stories, while the boys snuggled close, and cozy contentment flowed through them all.

Once again, the boys fell asleep sprawled together like a pile of puppies on the center of the sofa. Sam looked over at her. The tender regard he bestowed on the boys seemed to include her, too.

A shiver of awareness went through her.

"Move them now, or wait?" he inquired huskily.

It was a toss-up either way. Lulu studied their cherubic faces, then said, "Let's give them a few minutes." Aware her heartbeat had accelerated for no reason she could figure, she gathered up the basket of the boys' laundry that she'd left at the foot of the staircase. "Okay if I use your machine?"

Sam eased away from the sleeping trio, while Beauty dozed nearby, watching over the triplets. "Sure. I'll help."

They went into the laundry room together. Began sorting. Light colors in one pile, darks in another. They added their clothes, too.

He stepped back while she put in the first load, added detergent, switched on the machine. In the small space, it was impossible not to notice the silky smooth skin of her legs beneath the hem of her shorts. He lifted his gaze, taking in the curve of her hips, her slender waist and full breasts, before returning to her face. "It was a much better day," he remarked, aware he hadn't felt this relaxed and happy in a long time.

She smiled back at him. "It was."

As she started to move past him, he captured her in his arms. "On all scores," he rasped, then lowered his head and kissed her tenderly.

She caught her breath, even as she softened against him. Splaying her hands across his hard chest, she submitted to another kiss and then surprised him with a passionate one of her own. "Are we really doing this?" Lulu whispered. "Flirting with romance again?"

They'd be doing more than just flirting if he had his way. Knowing, though, if they were to have any chance at success, they'd have to slow down a bit, Sam gave her waist a playful squeeze. "We really are," he said.

Knowing they could have a rough night ahead, they both turned in shortly after that. Ten hours later, Sam woke slowly, feeling an incredible sense of well-being, a weight on his chest and each shoulder, and the soft press of a female body draped against his right flank. The fragrant scent of citrus and flowers teasing his nostrils, he turned his head slightly as he opened his eyes. Caught a glimpse of Lulu's lustrous hair as the top of her head pressed against his cheek. She shifted slightly, sighing drowsily. Snuggled deeper into the crook of his shoulder. She had a little boy in her arms, too.

In a rush of memory, it all came flooding back to him.

They'd had another night of the kids waking after a few hours with night terrors, crying incessantly, refusing to be soothed. He and Lulu had paced the floor in tandem, toddlers in their arms. Until finally, exhausted, they all climbed into his big bed, and still holding on to each other, slipped one by one into an exhausted sleep.

Made easier by one thing, the fact they were all in this together.

Lulu sighed again and opened her eyes all the way. She appeared to struggle to orient herself, just as he had, then relaxed as the events of the night came flooding back. She turned to gaze into his eyes. "Morning," she mouthed, as if leery of waking the little guy draped across her chest.

"Morning to you," he mouthed back with a grin. There was at least one perk to another stressful, sleepless night. He had forgotten what it had been like to wake up with her beside him. Not that he'd enjoyed it too many times before Tennessee. But the week they'd spent together prior to their breakup, that had been something special.

And now, thanks to the arrival of the triplets, he and Lulu were back to spending lots of time together again.

Without warning, three little heads popped up, one by one. The boys studied Lulu and Sam. Grinned at each other and scrambled upright. "Hungry," Ethan announced.

"Want 'cakes," Andrew said.

Meaning pancakes, Sam thought, recalling how more had been squished between little fingers and smeared across plates than eaten the previous day.

"No. Eggs," Theo declared.

"No, cereal!" Ethan disagreed.

"How about all three?" Lulu said.

Sam grinned. "Given how hungry I am, sounds good to me."

They worked together, cooking and supervising. Of course it was a lot easier, now that they'd moved the boys' toys to the adjacent family room.

"Well, that went better," Sam said half an hour later.

"It did, didn't it?" Lulu replied, pleased.

She looked gorgeous, lounging around his kitchen. He tore his gaze from the flattering fit of her pajamas and moved it to her tousled, honey-brown hair and pink cheeks. "So well," he added expansively, "that if you'd like time off to go to the McCabe family potluck at your brother Jack's house this afternoon, I think it would be okay."

Lulu's brow rose. "You know about that?"

Sam sipped his second mug of coffee. "Dan mentioned it last night at dinner, when he and I went up to the counter to collect our pizzas. He said we would all be welcome, of course, but that if the kids and I were to go with you, there might be…" He paused, unsure how to word it.

"Flack from my parents?" Lulu guessed. She reached

for a bottle of spray cleaner and began wiping down the counters for the second time.

Sam concentrated on the smooth, purposeful movements of her hands. His mouth suddenly dry, he shrugged. "Anyway, I know that they both think I'm a fine enough person, apart from you."

Lulu dropped the used paper towel into the trash. Straightened. "They haven't exactly been your cheerleader, when it comes to me, anyway. Not since we broke up years ago," she concluded.

That was putting it lightly, Sam thought. Maybe it was time they talked about this. "I think they blame me—and the animosity of our breakup—for the fact you've never married anyone else and have yet to get the family of your own that you want." He knew the same could probably be said of him.

"And they're probably right." Lulu raked the edge of her teeth across the soft curve of her lower lip. "You are the reason I've never been serious about anyone else."

She hadn't meant to blurt that out. But now that she had…maybe, given the fact they were trying to get their relationship back on an amiable track…it was time the two of them were more forthright with each other than they had been. She closed the distance between them and slid her hands into his.

"No one has ever compared, in terms of the way you made me feel back then," she confessed. Aware the past tense wasn't entirely accurate, given the whirl her emotions were in.

"Same here," he said gruffly, the expression on his face maddeningly inscrutable.

"But that doesn't mean marriage isn't in both our futures. Someday," she continued hopefully. Even though the only person she could imagine tying the knot with was Sam.

An awkward silence fell.

Lulu reluctantly disengaged their palms and stepped away.

"Back to the potluck at Jack's today," Sam said finally.

She walked over to look out the window. Although rain was predicted for that evening, it was bright and sunny now. "I want you and the boys to go with me."

"Sure?" His gaze roved over her.

Lulu turned back to face him, certain about this much. "If I'm going to be your nanny, my family needs to get used to seeing us together."

The rest of the morning was spent supervising the kids, finishing the laundry they'd started the evening before and showering. They also dealt with their personal responsibilities.

Sam talked to his foreman about the work being done on his ranch.

Lulu called a couple of her beekeeping friends, explaining that in addition to the theft, she was now busy helping out a friend who was weathering a family crisis. She arranged for them to install a new queen and help her tend her remaining hive for the next two weeks.

And of course, they all had to get dressed for the potluck.

By the time they had everyone ready to go, it was nearly one in the afternoon, and the kids, who were sleep deprived, were getting cranky and yawning. Beauty, looking ready for peace and quiet, climbed onto her cushion in the corner of the kitchen.

Sam's hand lightly touched Lulu's waist as they moved through the doorway, then just as easily fell away.

Yet the moment of casual gallantry stayed with her a lot longer than it should have.

Doing her best to disguise the shiver of awareness sifting through her, she guided the boys into the back seat of Sam's extended cab pickup. He went around to the other side and leaned in to help fasten the safety harnesses. "Think they'll sleep on the way into town?" he asked.

Lulu climbed into the pickup, too, then handed the boys the bucket hats and sunglasses they wore in the car. "I hope they can power nap." She smiled as they put them on, then glanced over at Sam, looking across the row of three car seats. "Or will at least behave long enough for me to dash into the market and pick up the loaves of bread I was requested to bring."

Five minutes later, Sam said, "Luck is with us."

Lulu followed his glance.

All three boys had nodded off. Blankets and stuffed animals clutched to their chests. Lulu sighed, the affection she felt for them nearly overwhelming her. "They look so sweet right now," she whispered, stunned by the ferocity of her feelings. She turned back to Sam and, unable to stop herself, asked, "Is it weird for me to be so attached to them already?"

He shook his head. "They need us." His sensual lips took on a pensive curve as his hands tightened on the steering wheel. "And I'm beginning to think we need them, too."

His husky observation sent a thrill down her spine.

She shifted in her seat to better view his ruggedly hand-some profile. "How so?"

"To rekindle our friendship, for one thing."

He was so matter-of-fact, so certain. Her heart skittering in her chest, Lulu drew in a whiff of his tantalizing aftershave. "Do you think this is all part of some big predestined plan for our lives?" That everything they'd experienced up to now had led them to this day?

A muscle ticked in his jaw. He seemed so serious now, in the way that said he wanted the two of them to get closer. The hell of it was, she wanted that, too. "How else to explain it?" he asked.

How else indeed, Lulu wondered, if not fate?

When they stopped at a traffic light at the edge of town, he turned to her. His gaze swept over her, lingering briefly on her lips, before returning to her eyes. "Neither of us had seen Peter or Theresa for years, yet they both put us on the potential guardian list. Everyone else ahead of us failed. And the triplets end up here in Laramie County with us."

What was that, if not some sort of sign? Lulu did her best to keep from overreacting. "According to the will, they were just supposed to be with you, though," she pointed out softly.

He looked deep into her eyes, his gratitude apparent. "But, darlin', you knew without even seeing them that they were going to need both of us. And you stepped in, initially over my reservations. And now—" he reached over to briefly squeeze her hand "—barely three days later, we're together twenty-four-seven and feeling like our own little family unit."

For now, Lulu thought worriedly.

What if they got to the point where he didn't need

her at night? Or left the boys with her, by herself, all day? As they had originally planned?

As much as the hopeless romantic in her wanted to wish otherwise, she had to remember that she was still involved only because he was allowing it. She had no legal standing here. So, if they were to start not getting along again…or decide there was no rekindled romance for them in the cards…their situation could change in a heartbeat.

The light turned green and Sam drove on.

"Um…speaking of destiny…" Lulu drew in a shaky breath.

Sam quirked a brow, listening.

"As heartbreaking…and yet simultaneously incredible…as this has all been for us," she began, knitting her hands together in her lap, "I still feel it's an awfully fragile situation."

Sam turned into the supermarket parking lot. He parked in a space and left the motor running. The boys slept on. One hand resting on the steering wheel, he turned and took in the anguished expression on her face. "Something on your mind?" he asked.

Lulu nodded, her heart in her throat. She didn't want to do this but she knew it had to be said. Sooner, rather than later.

Still holding Sam's eyes, she vowed softly, "I just want you to know that whatever happens…" *between you and me and the rest of it* "…I'm never going to emotionally abandon those boys."

Not exactly a ringing endorsement of their future, Sam thought, stunned by the sudden doubt she was harboring about this situation working out as they hoped.

He was about to ask what had caused her to be so on edge. But before he could speak, she slipped out of the truck, eased the passenger door shut and headed for the supermarket entrance.

As Sam had feared, the lack of forward motion had an effect.

By the time she returned a few minutes later with four bakery-fresh loaves of bread and a basket of fresh Texas peaches in hand, the boys were all awake and kicking their legs rambunctiously. Lulu seemed just as impatient. "On to Jack's!" she said.

Although Sam knew all the McCabes and their loved ones, he had never spent a lot of time in their company. The year he and Lulu had been dating, she had preferred to keep their relationship separate from her family obligations.

And while part of him had felt a little excluded back then, the rest of him had been happy to have Lulu all to himself. So it felt a little different now to be walking in with her and the boys when the rest of her family, sans her parents, was already there in Jack's big shady backyard.

Together, they made the rounds, saying hello to everyone. Her brother Matt was there with the love of his life, Sara Anderson, and her nine-month-old son, Charley. Matt looked happier than Sam had ever imagined he could be again when he'd first returned from war.

Cullen and his newly pregnant wife, Bridgett, introduced their adopted eighteen-month-old son, Robby, to the boys, who were immediately taken with him.

Jack's three daughters, Chloe, Nicole and Lindsay, ages three, four and six, also came over to say hi.

Lulu's brother Chase and his wife, Mitzy, introduced their ten-month-old quadruplet sons.

And of course the triplets were already acquainted with Dan and Kelly's four-year-olds—Matthew, Michael and Michelle.

In no time, the fifteen kids were scattered on the blankets spread across the lawn, playing with the toys that had been set out. Jack had the grill going, and all the other adults were gathered around, talking in small groups.

And Lulu, it seemed, couldn't wait to get away from him, Sam noted, as she touched his arm, her manner pleasant but oddly aloof. Like he was just another random guest in attendance at the barbecue. Not her old friend, not her potential love interest and certainly not her date for the occasion.

"Can I get you anything?" she asked, an officious smile pasted on her face. "A cold drink, maybe?"

He thought of the afternoon ahead. The fact he was suddenly and unexpectedly being pushed out of Lulu's life, just as he had been before.

Aware they had an audience, he smiled back at her in the exact same way. "Sounds great. Thanks."

Lulu made her escape, just as her parents' Escalade pulled up in front of Jack's home. She didn't know what to expect from them when they finally talked. She just knew she was dreading it.

"So what do you ladies have planned for Father's Day?" Kelly was asking when Lulu walked into Jack's kitchen to see what she could do to help.

"Don't know yet." Bridgett sighed.

"Me, either, although the kids and I still have a few days to figure it out," Kelly said.

"Should one of us ask Jack's girls what they'd like to do for him?" Lulu's mother, Rachel, asked as she came in, carrying a large platter of veggies and ranch dip.

Bess Monroe, Jack's friend—and constant platonic companion—smiled shyly and said, "I could probably do that if y'all would like." Although technically not family to anyone here besides her twin, Bridgett, Bess was around enough to be unofficially considered so.

Lulu smiled. "I think that would be great."

Rachel set the platter down, then turned back to Lulu, wasting no time at all in doing what Lulu had feared she might. "Sweetheart," she said softly, "could we have a word?"

"Sure." Lulu followed her mother into Jack's formal living room at the front of the big Victorian. Her dad was waiting there.

"What's this we hear about you becoming a *nanny* for the three kids Sam is guardian to?" Frank asked, his brow furrowed in concern.

Briefly, Lulu explained the situation while her parents listened.

"I understand he's probably got his hands full, but do you really think you should be this involved?" Rachel asked kindly.

Yes, Lulu thought. "I'm next on the list of potential guardians, Mom."

To Lulu's relief, her parents weren't as disappointed in her as she had feared they might be.

"*Next* being the operative word," her father pointed out gently.

"We just don't want to see you get too attached, sweetheart," Rachel said, "since the boys really are Sam's charges."

Frowning worriedly, her dad added, "And the two of you have a history of not getting along…"

That they did, Lulu admitted reluctantly to herself. But all that had changed. The last three days were proof of that. She and Sam had been not only getting along splendidly, but working like a well-rehearsed team. "That was because we were broken up," Lulu explained practically.

Her mother did a double take. "Are you saying you're *not* broken up any more?"

Lulu flushed, not sure how to respond.

Rachel lifted both hands, pleading, "Oh, Lulu." She came forward swiftly to embrace her. "Please don't do anything reckless that you'll regret later!"

"I don't intend to, Mom," Lulu said, returning her mother's hug.

"Good," her dad said in relief. He embraced her, too. Stepped back. "Because the last thing we want to see is you heartbroken the way you were before."

Lulu shoved aside the memories of that awful time. "I'm not going to be." She looked both her parents in the eye.

Her mom paused. "How can you be sure of that?"

Easy, Lulu thought. "Because Sam and I are not the naive kids we were ten years ago. We've grown and matured," she insisted, doing her best to reassure her parents. "There is no way we're making the same mistakes."

Different ones, maybe.

But even those they should be equipped to handle, she promised herself resolutely.

Rachel exhaled. "So you *are* back together?" she pressed.

Knowing a few stolen kisses did not constitute a reconciliation, Lulu shook her head. "No, Mom, we're not." The hell of it was, she just wished they were. And she wasn't sure how any of them, her parents or herself, should feel about that.

Chapter 7

"Are you avoiding me?" Sam asked an hour later, when he finally caught up with Lulu in the walk-in pantry off the kitchen.

Actually, yes, I am.

Determined not to give her parents anything to discuss later, she looked behind him, saw no one in their line of sight and slid him a glance. If only he weren't six feet three inches of masculine perfection, didn't know her inside and out and didn't kiss like a dream, this would be a whole lot easier.

Lulu continued counting out paper plates and putting them in the wicker basket at her hip. Wishing he didn't look so big and strong and immovable standing next to her, she asked, "Why would you think that?"

"Oh, I don't know." His lazy quip brought heat to her cheeks. "Maybe the fact that you've managed to stay as far away from me as possible since your parents got here this afternoon."

Aware he was watching her, gauging her reactions as carefully as she was measuring his, Lulu lifted her chin. "It's just…there's a lot to do," she fibbed, "if we're going to get this meal on before the rain starts…" Hoping to distract him, she asked, "By the way, who's watching the boys?"

"Your mom and dad."

Lulu winced. Of all the people to tell he was going in search of her.

"Why? Is there something wrong with that?" Sam asked. Clad in a blue short-sleeved button-down, jeans and boots, he looked sexy and totally at ease. "They offered, and they've obviously got plenty of experience handling little ones."

"I know."

"Then?" he asked. His gaze roved her knee-length white shorts and sleeveless Mediterranean-blue blouse before returning to her face.

"It's just…the boys can be a lot."

They both stopped as the sound of…was that rain…?

"Oh no!" Lulu exclaimed, pushing past Sam, seeing through the kitchen windows that a sudden downpour had indeed begun. "Everyone's still outside!"

They took off at a run.

Theo was in the sandbox, trying to protect his creation from the torrential downpour to no avail. He was screaming in distress, along with two of Jack's daughters who also did not want to see their castles destroyed. Neither were listening to Lulu's mom, who was trying to coax them inside.

Andrew was standing on the top of the play-fort slide,

along with three-year-old Chloe, enjoying the downpour and also refusing to get down for Bess Monroe—who might have been able to handle one child but definitely could not pick up two simultaneously.

Ethan, wide-eyed with a mixture of surprise and dismay, had taken cover beneath an umbrella table and was also refusing to be coaxed out by Lulu's dad.

Plus, the food on the long picnic tables needed to be rescued. Luckily, it was covered with plastic wrap, but still…

"You get Ethan, I'll get the other two," Sam said.

Every adult jumped in to help.

A frantic five minutes later, their meal had been salvaged, and everyone was inside. And while Jack's Victorian was pretty spacious, the fourteen adults and fifteen children had the first floor bursting at the seams. So, as soon as the meal was over, cleanup done, the great exodus began.

Not surprisingly, the triplets were having so much fun playing with the other kids, they did not want to leave.

"Five more minutes," Lulu said firmly.

"And then we're going back to the ranch to see Beauty," Sam added.

The mention of the beloved pet had all three boys hesitating but not for long.

"No! Stay!" Andrew shouted cantankerously.

"Play! More!" Theo added while Ethan pretended to ignore it all and kept right on driving his toy trucks around in circles.

Sam and Lulu exchanged the kind of looks parents had exchanged forever. A fact that, unfortunately, did not go unnoticed by Lulu's mother.

"One way or another..." Sam murmured.

Lulu nodded. "I agree." The kids had to have boundaries. And when they were overtired, their belligerence only got worse. So even if it meant they were unhappy, they were still going to have to leave when the time was up.

Sam moved off to talk to Dan, to see if there had been any update on Lulu's bees. There had not.

Meanwhile, Kelly noted sympathetically, "The boys really seem to enjoy playing with other children. Did they go to preschool previously? Do you know?"

"From what Sam and I have been able to glean from their records," Lulu said, "Theresa went back to work part-time when the triplets were a year old. They went to school five mornings a week, from nine to one, for about six months, then bumped it up to six hours a day. They usually got picked up right after nap time."

"You could enroll them at the preschool where I teach. Especially if you think that would help them acclimate."

Lulu hesitated.

Kelly continued, "Cece has the two-year-old class, and she's great with them."

Reluctantly, Lulu admitted, "Well, Sam is the one who has the say on that, but I don't know that he'll want to leave them. Especially since they've been moved around so much already in the last two months."

Kelly smiled. "I understand. If you change your mind, let me know because I can really expedite the process for you all."

"Thanks, Kelly."

Sam approached. "Ready to give it another try?"

Feeling as much a mommy as he appeared to be a daddy, Lulu nodded.

They tried reason, cajoling and firmly ordering. No approach worked when it came to getting their way-too-overtired children to cooperate. In the end, they had no choice but to carry all three boys out to Sam's pickup in the still pouring rain. Jack loaned them some beach towels to throw over their heads to keep the boys from getting wet, but Sam and Lulu both got rained on nevertheless.

Sam seemed impervious to the chill. Lulu was not so lucky. Shivering, she draped one of the damp towels across her shoulders and chest, like a shawl, the other over her bare legs as they drove away.

By the time they reached the first stoplight in the downtown area of Laramie, the boys had stopped their protesting and were already yawning. They were sound asleep at the town limits.

Lulu told Sam what Kelly had said about enrolling them in preschool.

"Hmm."

"What does hmm mean?"

He slanted her a self-effacing smile. "It means, like you, I'm on the fence. I think it would be good for their social development, but I worry that more change might make things worse."

Lulu blew out a breath. Not really all that surprised to find them feeling the exact same thing. "Being a parent is hard."

He reached over and squeezed her knee through the towel. "We'll get used to it," he promised.

We'll...

He had said *we'll*.

They really were in this together, Lulu thought.

It was still raining pretty hard fifteen minutes later when they arrived back at the ranch. Sam parked as close as he could to the covered front porch, and they carried the boys in one at a time, with Sam easing the sleeping children from their car seats and Lulu holding a towel over them to keep them dry. They put them all on the sofa, placed their stuffed animals in their arms and covered them with their baby blankets.

Beauty strolled in to say hi. After she'd been let out for a quick potty break, she sank down next to the boys and curled up with her back to the sofa to nap while guarding her little charges.

Arms folded, Sam stood back to look at them. Tenderness sweeping through him, he leaned down to whisper in Lulu's ear, "Boy, they are really out."

"I know," she whispered back fondly.

And it was way too late for them to be taking a long nap. He glanced at his watch. "It's five o'clock."

She wrinkled her nose in concern, a sentiment he shared.

Hand beneath her elbow, he steered her a distance away. "Think we should wake them up? Or let them snooze a little while longer?"

She sent another affectionate look at the boys. As she swung back to him, he couldn't help but admire the sheen of her honey-brown hair. "I don't know." Lulu bit down on her lower lip, and heat pooled through him as she came intimately close. "What do you think?"

As if he were the expert here.

Still, it felt good to be sharing responsibility with her.

To be able to lean on each other, whenever, however, they needed. Had they been able to do that before, they probably never would have broken up.

"Maybe a little while longer?" Sam supposed, inhaling her intoxicating perfume. "Until six?"

Their gazes met and she drew a breath. "Then we can let them play a bit before dinner, give them baths and go through the normal bedtime routine?"

"Sounds good," he said, his gaze dropping to her mouth, then lower, to the damp clothing clinging to her supple curves.

"What isn't good," Lulu said, holding her shirt out away from her breasts before allowing it to fall into place again, "is how I feel."

His body hardening at the sight of her nipples showing through her drenched shirt, he looked down at his own clothes. "We did get a little wet, didn't we, darlin'?"

Lulu grimaced. "I need to change. Unfortunately, I'm out of clean clothes, and I'm reluctant to leave you alone with the boys to make the run back to the Honeybee Ranch."

Not wanting her to go, either, Sam shrugged. "You can borrow one of my shirts." The way she had when they'd spent their spring break in Tennessee. When their attraction to each other was white-hot. Life was so much simpler back then.

Her brow pleated. She didn't appear to be affected with the same memories. "You wouldn't mind?"

"Nah. Besides…" he let his glance sift over the damp, mussed strands of her sun-kissed honey-brown hair "…there's no point in going home to get more clothes when you can throw your laundry in my machines, get it washed and dried in an hour and a half or so. Probably be easier than running back and forth."

"Okay. Thanks." She squared her shoulders and took another deep breath. "You want to get me a shirt, then?"

Sam studied the color that had swept into her fair cheeks. He shrugged. "Just go to my closet and take any one you want. They're all on hangers."

Her flush deepened. "I think I'd feel better about it if you went with me."

Grinning, he gestured broadly. And tried not to think about how much he wanted to make love to her again. "If the lady insists…"

She led the way, with Sam behind her, admiring her every languid, graceful step. When they reached the bedroom doorway, she hesitated. He walked ahead to throw open the closet door, then stepped back. "Take your pick."

Bypassing the nicer ones at the front, she selected a worn blue chambray at the very back. Holding it in front of her, she pivoted back to face him. "This one okay?"

He nodded. "Perfect," he said huskily.

She read his mind, as their eyes met. "Oh, Sam…" she said, her hushed voice sliding like silk over his skin. The shirt she was holding fell to the floor. She stepped into his arms, rose on tiptoe and pressed her lips against his. Her kiss was everything he wanted. Tender. Searching. Sweetly tempting. A rush of molten desire swept through him. This was what he needed. *She* was what he needed. And damn it, he thought as her soft, pliant body surrendered all the more, if she didn't realize it, too.

Kissing Sam again was going to be a risk, Lulu knew. And she had avoided risks like the plague since the two of them had broken up. But the last few days had ignited a fire in her unlike anything she had ever felt, then or now. For good reason, it seemed. Sam was right to think this was all part of some larger destiny that brought them back into each other's lives, just in time to be able to help the boys and resurrect a replacement for the complete family they'd lost.

They were meant to be.

And what better way to prove it than through renewed lovemaking?

Giving in to the passion simmering between them, she dared him to take full advantage of fate and be as impulsive as she was. When he kissed her back with equal fervor, elation flowed through her. Caught up in the moment, she poured everything she had into their embrace. Her knees weakened, her whole body shivered. She hadn't ever felt this much like a woman, or wanted Sam with such unbridled passion. But she wanted him now, wanted him to fill up the aching loneliness deep inside her. She wanted him to help her live her life fully again.

And still he kissed her, hard and wet and deep. Masterfully taking charge, until she shifted restlessly against him, wanting more. His hands slid beneath her blouse to unfasten her bra and caress her erect nipples. His lips parted hers, his tongue sweeping into her mouth, until her entire body was on fire. She moaned at the delicious pressure, the taste and feel of him. Yanked her blouse over her head, let her bra fall to the floor.

His eyes darkened. "So beautiful," he said, his thumbs gently tracing the curves of her breasts, caressing her sensitive nipples. "More so…" he bent to lay a trail of kisses over her throat, collarbone, the tips of her breasts "…than I remember…"

Lord, he was gorgeous, too. All over. She tugged off his shirt, ran her hands over his chest. Explored the satiny warmth of his lean waist, muscled torso and broad shoulders. It had been so long since they'd made love. Too long, she mused as she ran her fingers through the crisp hair arrowing down into the waistband of his jeans.

Quivering with excitement, she slid her hands beneath. Cupped the hot, velvety hardness. He dropped his head, kissing her again, bringing forth another wellspring of desire. Their tongues tangled as surely as their hearts, and he groaned, resting his forehead on hers. "Lulu…" he whispered, the last of his gallantry fading fast.

She knew how easy it would be to fall in love with him all over again. Knew it and welcomed it. "I know what I'm doing, Sam," she whispered. She went to shut the bedroom door, then took him by the hand and led him toward the bed.

"Do you?" Eyes dark, he watched her continue to undress.

She knew what he was thinking; there had been so much hurt between them in the past. Too much. But that was over. It was a new day. One that held the promise of so much more.

There would not be regrets this time, she told herself fiercely. Even if they'd been brought together again by circumstances not of their own making, and were moving a little too fast.

"I know this feels reckless," she whispered. Her heart

skittering in anticipation of the mind-blowing passion to come, she helped him disrobe, too. "But I want you. I've never stopped wanting you," she confessed with a ragged sigh.

Shouldn't that be enough?

Now that they were both adults with another full decade of life experience informing them?

With long-established ways to guard their hearts?

Suddenly, she wasn't the only one shuddering with pent-up need. "Well, in that case..." His sexy grin widened. All too ready to oblige, he dropped a string of kisses down her neck, across the slopes of her breasts to the crests, then he sank to his knees and his lips moved lower still. The white-hot intimacy had her arching in pleasure. Making her feel ravished and cherished all at once.

Closing her eyes, she fisted her hands in his hair and gave herself over to him. Fully. Completely. And she lost what little was left of her restraint as a soft moan and a shudder of overwhelming heat swept through her.

Hands on his shoulders, she urged him upward. Not about to be the only one to find release, she whispered against his shoulder, "My turn now."

Sam laughed quietly, as she'd hoped he would.

Determined to keep it light and sexy between them, she was eager to tantalize his hot, hard body as he had hers. She lay down beside him, kissing and caressing him until everything fell away but the feel and touch and taste of him. Until there was no more holding back.

He found a condom. Together, they rolled it on. Suddenly, she was on her back. One hand was beneath her, lifting her, the other was between her thighs. She surged against him, softness to hardness. He stroked his thumb over her flesh, and she was flying, gone. And still he kissed her, again and again, until there wasn't any place she would rather be.

Needing him to find the same powerful release, Lulu wrapped her arms around him and brought him closer. He groaned, rough and low in his throat, and her muscles tautened as he found his way home in one long, slow, purposeful slide. Allowing her to adjust to the weight and size of him, he went deeper still.

Needing more, she wrapped her legs around his waist, opening up to him, and then there was nothing but the sensation of being taken, possessed. Treasured. And for the first time in an extremely long time, she felt connected to him in that very special man-woman way.

Sam had known it was a mistake to make love to Lulu on a whim. Because it was when Lulu did things on impulse that she was most likely to regret them later. But when she'd reached out to him, he hadn't been able to resist. Now, he was beginning to wish he had, as he watched Lulu silently come to the same conclusion that he had already reached. That once again, they'd let their emotions get the best of them, and had gone too far, too fast. "Us being together this way doesn't have to complicate things unnecessarily," he said, stroking a hand through her hair and soothing her as best he could. "We can still take things one day, one moment at a time, darlin'. Do whatever feels right."

Like make love.

And get closer yet.

"You're right." Lulu let out a long sigh. Pressed her

hand against the center of his chest, insinuating distance between them. As their gazes locked, something came and went in her pretty eyes. "This doesn't have to mean anything more than any other fling would."

He held tight when she would have fled, aware once again she was taking his intentions all wrong. "That's not what I said," he told her gruffly.

"Isn't it?" she returned with a casual smile that did not reach her eyes. Before he could say anything else, she lifted a hand. "It's okay, Sam." With typical grace, she eased away from him. "We're both sophisticated enough to handle just having sex."

Which was obviously all it had been to her.

"And you're right," she finished with a weariness that seemed to come straight from her soul. "It really doesn't have to change anything." She rose and pulled on her panties and his shirt, then, scooping up her damp clothes, padded down the hall to the guest room where she'd been stowing her belongings.

He rose and dressed, too, in dry clothing. Emerging from his bedroom, he caught sight of her as she headed downstairs, small mesh bag of dirty clothes in hand.

Sam went back to gather up his own laundry, then found her in the utility room, sorting clothes, her head averted. He noted she had added an above-the-knee denim skirt and pretty sandals to her ensemble.

"Are we really just going to leave it like this?" he said, dumping his own clothing into a separate hamper.

Cheeks slightly pink, she kept her attention on her task. "What's there to say?" They both reached for the detergent at the same time. Their shoulders and arms brushed before they could draw back.

Wishing he could make love to her again—without

driving her further away than she was at this moment—
he stepped back to give her the physical space she craved.
He focused on the tumult in her eyes.

"Maybe you should tell me."

She looked at him for a long moment. "Well, it was
probably important for us to satisfy our curiosity, given
the situation."

She focused on her task, added soap, set the dials
and closed the lid. Turned on the machine.

He stayed his ground. "Curiosity," he repeated. *So
that's what they were calling it now.*

"We probably also needed to find out if the sparks
we used to have still existed." She drew in a deep breath
and finally pivoted to meet his gaze. Her chin lifted.
"And now we know."

Now they did know. Though he had the intuition that
they had arrived at completely different conclusions…

"Meaning what?"

She walked past him, down the hall, peered around
the corner into the living room. The triplets were all
still fast asleep. She returned to the kitchen, still not
clarifying what she meant.

Knowing nothing would ever be solved by pretending there wasn't a problem, he edged closer. Needing to
know where he stood with her. Guessed, "Meaning…
it's not going to happen again?" Or it would?

She leaned against the kitchen island, her back to the
still-pouring rain, and let out a slow breath. "I'm not
sure."

He switched on the overhead lights, bringing light to
the gloomy room. He moved so she had no choice but
to look at him. "Hey," he said softly, not about to let her
deny it. His gaze roved her. "I know it was good for you."

She blushed at his needling tone. "I know it was good for you, too." Seeing Beauty heading for the back door, she moved to open it. Stepped out under the overhang. "But as you noted earlier, our life is pretty complicated right now, with the kids and all," she said, keeping her voice low as the damp warmth surrounded them.

Sam gave his pet room to move down the steps, into the yard, then eased next to Lulu. "And making love just now makes it even more so. I get that. It doesn't mean we can pretend it didn't happen," he pointed out. Or that he even wanted to.

Regret pinched the corners of her mouth. "Sure about that?"

Because she sure seemed able to do so, Sam noted bitterly as Beauty came back up the deck steps and walked on into the house.

Lulu grabbed a dog towel off the hook and bent to dry off Beauty's thick coat. When she was done, she gave the Saint Bernard a fond pat on the head and watched as the dog padded soundlessly back to the living room, to stand guard once again over the kids.

Lulu hung up the towel, then, glancing over at the family room, zeroed in on the toys that had been left all over the place. She breezed past him and began picking them up. Although he didn't care whether the toys were neatly put away or not, he followed and began to help.

An even more conflicted silence fell. Which was a shame, Sam thought, since they didn't often have time to themselves. "You really don't want to talk about this any more?" he said, wishing like hell that she would.

Still bearing the glow of their lovemaking, she bit her lip. Ambivalence flooded her expression. "I really don't," she returned, just as softly.

And suddenly, Sam knew what the real problem likely was.

"Then how about you tell me what happened at the picnic today, when you and your parents went off for a private chat?"

Chapter 8

The last thing Lulu wanted to do was tell Sam her folks' doubts about her ability to make wise decisions in her life. On the other hand, he was involved, too, if only by circumstance.

She knelt beside the wooden toy box emblazoned with the triplets' names. He knelt on the other side. Wearing a washed-till-it-was-soft cotton shirt, much the same as the one she had borrowed and was still wearing, and faded jeans, he was every inch the indomitable Texan.

Trying not to notice how sated and relaxed he looked post-lovemaking, she forced a smile and an attitude of nonchalance. "My mom and dad cornered me."

Handsome jaw tautening, he regarded her. "And?" His voice dropped another husky notch, in a way that sent heat flashing through her.

She flushed under his scrutiny. As always, his ultramasculine presence made her feel intensely aware of him. "Bottom line? They're concerned I'm getting too involved with you and the kids."

Something flickered in his gold-flecked eyes, then maddeningly disappeared as he watched her drop more toys into the storage container.

"Is that what you think?" he asked, his expression closed and uncommunicative.

No, I think I've had the brakes on for way too long. But maybe that was the old Lulu talking. The reckless, restless, impulsive Lulu who once fell in love with Sam and ran off with him and then panicked and made the biggest mistake of her life...

The Lulu who was ruled more by emotion and the fear of disappointing anyone than logical, practical thought.

The Lulu who just gave in to the buildup from the most emotional four days of her life and recklessly made love with Sam again.

And worse, she couldn't quite bring herself to regret it. Much as the practical side of her wished that she could.

Not that he looked as if he were lamenting it, either...

Even though, as he said, none of this had to change anything between them.

When to her, it already had...

Oblivious to the conflicted nature of her thoughts, Sam persisted, "What did you say to them?"

Feeling a little unsteady, she drew a deep breath, glad to have someone to confide in about this. "I told them they were wrong," she said softly, lifting her chin. "That the kids need us both."

"They do." Finished picking up, he lifted the box and

carried it over to the corner where it usually sat. Taking her by the hand, he led her to the breakfast room table. The corners of his eyes crinkled. "Which is why I've been thinking, you shouldn't just be their nanny, Lulu. Or a concerned friend helping out." He waited for her to take a seat and then settled opposite her.

He paused to look her in the eye, then said, even more resolutely, "You should be their legal guardian, too."

Legal guardian!

She caught her breath, feeling thrilled and stunned. Still, this was awfully sudden. Too sudden, maybe?

Swallowing, she lifted a halting hand. "Sam..."

He reached across the table to take her hands in his. "I'm serious, Lulu. Your parents were right. It isn't fair for you to be so involved if you're not a guardian. So why not be a co-guardian with me? It's obvious I can't do it alone."

Lulu sighed. "Neither could I."

Sam nodded his agreement, all matter-of-fact rancher now. "Even more important, you love the kids and they love you. They need a mom." Warmth spread throughout her body as his fingers tightened on hers. "I need a partner..."

Aware his grip felt as masculine and strong as the rest of him, she withdrew her hands from his. "Are you saying that because I just put the moves on you?"

A look of hurt flashed in his eyes, then disappeared. "Our lovemaking just now has nothing to do with this."

"Doesn't it?" she returned.

He kept his gaze locked with hers. "No." His expression sobered, becoming all the more sincere. "These are two separate issues."

For him, maybe. But for her?

Her desire for him seemed an integral part of her. Aware she could fall way too hard for him if she wasn't careful, she folded her arms.

"You say that now." She drew a deep breath, wishing he weren't so sexy and capable and kind. So tender and good with the kids. "But what happens if you and I start down that road again and then don't work out as a couple again?" she challenged, feeling self-conscious, as he zeroed in on her nervousness. "How would you feel about sharing guardianship duties with me then?"

"If that happens, and I don't think it will, we'll do exactly what we're doing now and figure out how to continue to make things work—as friends," Sam said firmly. "But instinct tells me that we will work out, Lulu. And if you listen to yours, I imagine you'll be convinced of the same thing."

He was right about that. Only it wasn't her feminine instinct doing the talking. It was her heart that wanted to be with Sam and the kids...

"So what do you say, darlin'?" he proposed softly, gripping her hands again and looking deep into her eyes. "Will you be their co-guardian with me?"

Lulu might still be confused about what she wanted when it came to Sam, but there was no doubt at all about what her heart wanted in regard to the three little boys. Or what would be best for them. They needed both a mother figure and a father figure in their lives.

Joy bubbled up inside her. She'd imagined she would have to fight to make this happen. Instead, once again, she and Sam were on the exact same page.

She returned his searching gaze and said, ever so

softly, "Yes, I'd love to be legally responsible for the triplets, too."

Their new deal would inadvertently solve another problem she had not been looking forward to contending with. She pushed back her chair and rose, aware it was time for them to wake the children for dinner. "This way, you won't have to pay me for caring for them."

"I'll still owe you…"

"No," she cut him off, feeling vaguely insulted by his insistence, although she wasn't sure why, "you won't."

Their stare-down continued.

"This isn't about the money, Lulu," he warned.

"I know it isn't," she agreed. "For you." But for her… the thought of him being her boss…giving her a paycheck… Well, that might have been their *initial* agreement, the only way she'd gotten herself in the door to help. Yet from the first moment the children arrived at Hidden Creek Ranch, she hadn't felt like his employee so much as she'd felt like his comrade in arms.

"But I still prefer it this way," she reiterated, "with us equally responsible. And absolutely zero money changing hands."

"I owe you…"

"And you've paid me," she stated, just as vehemently, "in room and board."

His eyes glinted, the way they always did when he let her have what she wanted. He exhaled, his gaze drifting over her with lazy male appreciation before finally returning to her face. "I'm not going to win on this. Am I, darlin'?"

"No, cowboy," Lulu shot back sassily. Knowing the only way they would ever truly be able to come together was as equals. She whirled on her heel and marched off. "You are not!"

As for the rest…

She sighed.

Sam was right. They could figure it all out later. In the meantime, the first thing they needed to do was take care of the legal formalities.

"I think that's wonderful," Hiram said when Lulu and Sam called his office the following morning, just after breakfast.

Sam looked over at Lulu, who was smiling from ear to ear. He felt relieved and happy about their new agreement, too. As far as it went, anyway. They still had a lot to work out about their own relationship, but he could be patient on that front. In the meantime, as far as the caretaking went, he and Lulu were in this together. And as they'd already more than proved, he thought, returning her excited grin, they made a very good team.

As unaware as Lulu of the romantic nature of Sam's thoughts, Hiram concluded, "I'll send the appropriate papers to Liz and Travis. You can go to their law office to sign them."

"Thank you, we will," Lulu replied.

They all signed off.

And just in time, too, Sam thought. Behind them, a cacophony of toddler voices sounded.

"Horsey!" Theo yelled.

"Me ride!" Andrew insisted.

"No! Doggy," Ethan disagreed. Not sure what was going on, since the boys had escaped to the living room while they were on the phone, Sam and Lulu headed off in their direction. They found Beauty standing parallel to the big leather sofa. Ethan was standing just in front of her and petting her face gently while Theo and Andrew tried to simultaneously climb on her back and ride her like a horse.

"Oh dear!" Lulu rushed to rescue the remarkably patient Saint Bernard.

Sam plucked both little cowboys off her back and deposited them on the far end of the sofa, out of harm's way. "Fellas, Beauty is not a horse," he scolded. "So you *cannot* climb on her back." He gave his dog a consoling pat on the head, then lifted Ethan out of the way, too. With a beleaguered sigh and the way now clear, Beauty lumbered down the hall, over to her cushion in the corner of the kitchen, and sank into the bed.

All three boys began jumping on the sofa, as hard and high as they could. "Want friends," Theo shouted loudly.

"Play now!" Andrew agreed.

"Go car," Ethan explained.

Lulu went to her phone. "I'll see if I can arrange a playdate," she called over her shoulder.

She came back five minutes later. The triplets had given up jumping but were now attempting to climb onto and slide down the bannister. Every time Sam plucked one off, another climbed on.

"Everyone is at preschool," Lulu informed him, lifting her brow at the boys. Like magic, they all stopped climbing on the stair railing. Only to resume jumping and shouting from the sofa. Lulu shouted to be heard above the bedlam. "Kelly said the triplets could be visitors in her three-year-old class today, which in the summer runs from nine to one o'clock."

Knowing the only thing that ever entertained the

boys for long was other children, Sam replied, "Sounds good."

The boys were even more delighted.

While they drove to town, Lulu called their attorney and arranged to visit their office to sign the guardianship papers Hiram had sent.

"You sure you don't want to think about this?" Liz and Travis asked them, after they'd dropped the kids off.

To Sam's relief, Lulu shook her head, looking prettier and more determined than ever. "No. Sam and I agree they need both of us."

They walked out of the office building into the late-morning sunlight. For a moment, they just looked at each other. He studied the rosy color in her cheeks and the shimmer of excitement in her eyes. He was happy she was finally getting the children she had wanted, too. They were all lucky to have each other.

Her gaze swept over his form, making him glad he had taken the time to iron his shirt instead of just shave and shower and put on the first set of clean clothes he pulled from his closet.

Instead of going to the passenger side of his pickup, she remained in the sunlight. "You know," Lulu mused, "this is the first time we've been without chaperones in almost five days. I almost don't know what to do with myself."

He had to fight not to reach out and touch the silky strands of her honey-brown hair. "I know."

An awkward silence fell. He observed the pulse throbbing in her throat.

She raked her teeth across the lush softness of her lower lip. "I don't want to go too far, though, in case the triplets suddenly decide they don't want to be at pre-school after all."

"No kidding," Sam said, wishing it were appropriate to take her in his arms and kiss her.

She cocked her head to one side, as if thinking the same thing. He was about to reach for her, figuring they could at least hug each other in congratulations, when Lulu's phone rang.

"Oh no," Lulu said, plucking it from her purse.

"Don't tell me it's the school already," Sam said. Which in one sense would not be surprising, since the drop-off had been almost *too* easy to be believed, with the kids going right in without batting an eye.

"No." She exhaled, looking distressed. "It's not them. It's Dan."

To Lulu's relief, Sam was happy to accompany her to the sheriff's station.

Her brother ushered them into a conference room and, as usual, got straight to the point as soon as she and Sam sat down. "We found your bees."

Lulu had figured as much, when he'd said he had *news*. "Where are they?"

"A commercial melon farm in Wisconsin. The owner thought it was a legitimate lease. When he saw your brand listed as stolen on the state agricultural website, he notified authorities there immediately. They, in turn, contacted us."

"Thank goodness for that," Lulu said as Sam reached over and squeezed her hand. "How are my hives doing?"

Dan looked down at his notes. "Apparently, there was some loss, but the majority of the hives seem to be doing well. The question is what to do now. The farm owner still needs your bees for his crops, but he understands if you want them shipped back immediately."

Her heart racing, Lulu asked, "Do you have his contact information?"

Dan handed her a piece of paper.

Lulu called the melon farmer. They talked at length. Finally, she hung up. Her brother had gone off to attend to other law enforcement business. But Sam was still there, waiting. Patient and calm as ever.

"Everything okay?" he asked, his handsome face etched with concern.

Her emotions still in turmoil, Lulu nodded and led the way into the hall. She waved to the front desk and, aware it would soon be time to pick up the triplets, headed out into the summer sunshine. "The farm owner is going to pay the going rate, which will be negotiated through our lawyers, and keep the hives until late August."

Easing a hand beneath her elbow, Sam matched his steps to hers. "And then what?"

"I'll either ship them back home or sell them outright to a beekeeper where they are now."

Sam stopped in midstride. "You'd really do that?"

Not willingly. She also knew she had to be practical here, now that she was co-guardian to the triplets. "It might make the most sense."

"Those bees are your life's work," he reminded her, clearly disappointed.

Lulu tensed. She didn't like him judging or second-guessing her. Shifting her bag higher on her arm, she returned in a cool tone, "That's true. They were." She paused to look him straight in the eye. "But things are different now I'm going to be raising the triplets. Already, I've had to ask beekeeping friends to install a new queen for me, and tend my remaining hive on an emergency basis, because I just don't have time to get over to the ranch. That being the case, it might be better for me to pocket the cash from the sale and concentrate on the kids for now. Worry about resuming my beekeeping career later."

Sam stared at her. Feeling like he had gone back in time to their college years, when Lulu had flitted from one thing to another, changing her major almost as often as she changed hairstyles. A pattern that had continued for at least three years after the two of them had broken up.

In fact, to date, beekeeping was the one thing, the *only* thing, she seemed to have stuck with.

Her lips slid out in a seductive pout. "You don't approve?" she challenged.

He rubbed his jaw, considering. The last thing he wanted to do was make an emotional situation worse. "I know it's hard now, but I think if you give it all up you might regret it, darlin'."

Her eyes turned dark and heated. "Exactly why I'm putting off the decision for a couple of months, so I will have time to think about what I want to do."

With a scowl, she pivoted and continued on to the parking lot, walking briskly ahead of him. "I'm not going to lean on you financially, if that's what you're worried about. Whatever I decide to do, I'll have enough to pay my share of the kids' expenses. And of course all my own, too."

He caught up with her, sliding his hand beneath her elbow once again. "That's not what I'm worried about and you know it."

She whirled, coming close enough he could inhale her tantalizing floral scent and feel her body heat radiating off of her. "Then...?"

His gaze drifted over her pretty turquoise sundress and silver necklace. It was all he could do not to touch her.

Aware this was something they did need to discuss, even if it was unpleasant, he stuck his hands into the back pockets of his jeans instead. "I just wouldn't want you to change your mind about other things down the road, too."

"Like...?"

He shrugged. Was she really going to make him say it? Apparently, she was. "The kids."

Color swept into her high, sculpted cheeks. "Did you *really* just say that to me?"

"Look, I wasn't trying to insult you—"

"So you did accidentally?"

He tracked the silky spill of hair across her bare shoulders. Figuring if they were going to be co-guardians, they ought to be able to talk everything out together, he shrugged. Given what she'd just said about the business she'd spent the last seven years building... which was also the one thing, the only thing, he'd seen her feel maternal toward, up to now. "It's a legitimate worry."

Hurt sparked in her gaze. "No, it isn't, Sam," she disagreed quietly. "And if you really feel that way..."

What he really felt was the intense urge to haul her close and kiss her until the tension between them went away. The fact he'd been brought up a Texas gentleman kept him from doing so, but—

Her phone pinged to signal an incoming text.

She paused, brow furrowing, and read the screen. "It's Kelly," she said in concern. She looked up at Sam. "She said there may be trouble at the preschool. She wants us to come now to get the kids."

Fortunately, they were only a couple of minutes away. Sam climbed behind the wheel and Lulu settled in the passenger seat. He stretched his arm along the back of the seat and looked behind them as he backed his truck out of the space. He paused before he put it in gear. "She didn't say anything more?"

She shook her head. "Nope."

Sam drove through the lot and turned onto the street. Hands gripping the wheel, he asked, "You don't think they caused some sort of ruckus, do you?"

Lulu sighed, and put a hand over her eyes, looking like a harried mother. She pressed her soft lips together ruefully. "I wish I could say no, but you know how they are when they're overtired."

He did, indeed.

It seemed to take forever to make it to the school, a fact hampered by the number of cars lining up in the driveway and down the street. They bypassed the drop-off and parked. Still not speaking to each other, they headed inside.

There were no sounds of crying or wild behavior as they moved through the hall.

When they cleared the doorway to Kelly's classroom, the boys were huddled together anxiously, watching the portal. Other kids were being escorted out by their moms and dads.

"Hey, guys." Lulu knelt down to say hello. Sam hunkered down beside her. "How's it going?"

"Want *Mommy*," Theo said fiercely.

Andrew folded his arms militantly. "Want *Daddy*."

"Go *home*," Ethan said, his lower lip trembling.

Too late, Sam realized it might have been a mistake to bring them to a setting that so closely mirrored the place where they'd been when they'd received the news that something terrible had happened and their parents weren't coming back.

Sam started to engulf them in a reassuring hug. "We're going to take you home, fellas," he said.

"No!" Theo shouted, pushing him away. "Want Mommy!"

"Want Daddy," Andrew agreed, wriggling free.

"Me scared," Ethan collapsed to the floor in a limp heap and sobbed outright.

The hysteria spread. Within seconds, other preschoolers were welling up. Some sobbing. Others loudly demanding their own parents take them home. And so it went, well after the classroom was cleared.

The triplets, it seemed, weren't going anywhere. Not willingly, it seemed.

Kelly disappeared, then came back a few minutes later. "I called the head of grief counseling over at the hospital. She's on her way over now."

"Thank heavens," Lulu whispered, moving closer to Sam as if for protection while the boys clustered together on the play rug on the floor, stubbornly waiting.

Kate Marten-McCabe breezed in.

The silver-haired therapist had a small cooler and a big bag of books and toys. "I've got some things for us to do," she announced with soothing candor. She glanced at the three adults remaining. "Could y'all could give us a little time to talk? Maybe wait for us on the playground, where we'll have Popsicles later?"

Sam and Lulu nodded.

They walked to a bench beneath a shady tree in silence. "Well, you were right," Sam admitted ruefully as they took a seat side by side.

Lulu slanted him a questioning glance.

He cleared his throat. "Maybe we're both going to have to step back from our jobs for a while." He paused to look deep into her eyes, intensifying the intimacy between them. He took her hand in his and squeezed it affectionately. "And I'm sorry I didn't realize that as quickly as you did."

Lulu knew it was a big step, and an important one, for Sam to say he was wrong when they differed. He had never done so in the past. Instead, had just expected her to come around to his way of thinking or accept he wasn't going to change his opinion and deal with it.

She looked down at their entwined fingers. Realizing she could have done more to intuit the reason behind his worry and reassure him on the spot that she would never ever abandon him or the kids, rather than simply go on the defensive.

"Apology accepted," she said quietly. She turned to face him, her bent knee nudging his thigh. "But as for your work, running Hidden Creek… Could you really step back for more than a week or two?"

The reservation was back in his eyes, along with a lingering desire she felt, too. "My foreman and the other ranch hands can handle everything day-to-day until the boys are really settled."

"That could take a while."

He exhaled roughly. "I know." But seemed prepared to make the sacrifice nevertheless.

Silence fell between them.

"What do you think is going on in there?" he asked finally.

Lulu turned toward the school, saw no sign of anyone coming outside. "Kate's probably explaining to them that their parents aren't coming back."

His expression turned brooding. "You think they'll accept that?"

Recalling the raw grief the triplets had exhibited, their emotional expectation that their parents would magically appear to take them home, Lulu drew in another jagged breath. She looked down at her and Sam's entwined hands. Realized they really did need each other to see the boys through this rough patch. "At their age? I don't know."

Another silence fell.

This time they didn't talk.

Finally, Kelly came out of the school with two sets of triplets, hers and theirs. All six had Popsicles. As she neared, Sam and Lulu disengaged their hands and stood.

Kelly gave them a smile. "Kate would like to talk to you inside."

They found the grief counselor in the classroom, packing up. She gestured for them to have a seat. "I explained to the boys that their parents are in heaven, but they don't really comprehend what that is yet. They just know their parents won't be coming to pick them up today." She brought a notebook and pen out of her bag. "How have the kids been doing at home?" she asked kindly.

"Better every day," Sam said.

"Is there any hyperactivity?" Kate asked.

Reluctantly, Lulu admitted, "Pretty much all the time."

"Their sleeping?"

"Fitful at best," Lulu said.

They went on to explain about the night terrors and their inability to get them to lie down in their own beds.

"In fact," Lulu added, "the only way they will rest at all, for any length of time, is if we're holding them."

Kate did not look surprised. "How is their eating?"

"They like sweets," Sam replied, "but when it comes to anything else, they're pretty picky."

Lulu nodded. "They'll ask for something, like pancakes or scrambled eggs, but then they don't really eat much of it."

"Have they had any temper tantrums?"

Sam and Lulu nodded in tandem. "At least once a day."

"These are all signs of toddler grief. Healing is going to take time. But the good news is, we have programs at the hospital for all of you that will help."

Sam and Lulu exchanged relieved glances. Feeling more like a team than ever, Lulu asked, "What can we do in the meantime?"

"Reinstate as many familiar routines from their old life as you can, including preschool. Get them on a schedule and sleeping in their own beds. Help them remember their parents and the love they received in a way that is comforting and heartwarming rather than grief-provoking. And…" Kate handed them a storybook for orphaned children and a packet of information with her card attached "…bring them to the children's grief group at the hospital on Saturday morning. The two of you can attend the one for guardians and caretakers."

"Thank you." Sam and Lulu shook her hand, promising in unison, "We will."

Kate smiled. "Call me if you have any questions or concerns." She slipped out of the classroom.

Sam and Lulu turned to face each other. Aware what a sticky situation they had found themselves in, it was hard not to feel completely overwhelmed. Especially when the two of them were still privately mourning the loss of their friends, too. "Looks like we have our hands full, cowboy," she murmured in an attempt to lighten the mood and dispel some of the grief they were both feeling.

He returned her quavering smile. "And then some." His gaze stroked her features, every one, ending with her eyes. With his customary confidence, he promised, "Together, we'll make it all work out. But first things first. You've got to move in."

Chapter 9

Lulu gaped at Sam. His thick blond hair rumpled, his gold-flecked eyes filled with worry, he looked a little ragged around the edges. Which, after the afternoon they'd had, was exactly how she felt. And they still had the rest of the day, and night, to get through.

"You want me to actually move in?" she repeated in astonishment, not sure she'd understood him correctly. "With you?"

"And the boys, obviously," Sam said. He appeared perfectly at ease with the idea of them residing together under one roof, full-time.

"Temporarily," Lulu ascertained.

He shook his head, correcting, "From here on out."

Lulu was still trying to wrap her mind around that when he moved closer. His gaze caressed her face. "You heard what Kate said." He tucked his hand in hers, gave it a tender squeeze. "If we want the boys to recover, we have to give them as much security as possible. Get back to familiar routines." He paused to let his words sink in. Once again, a thoughtful silence brought them together.

"And what was normal to them," he continued practically, "was living with a mom and a dad under one roof."

A tingle of awareness sweeping through her, Lulu hitched in a breath. "That's true," she managed around the sudden dryness of her throat. The thought of making love with him again dominated her mind. "But..." It would be impossible to ignore their attraction for long under such intimate circumstances. A fact she guessed he knew very well!

Dropping his grip on her, he stepped back. Cocked a brow. "What?" he prodded.

This was the kind of impulsive thing *she* would do. Not him. Doing her best to control her soaring emotions, she studied him from beneath her lashes. "Are you sure you really want to do this?" Thus far, their arrangement had been only temporary. Meant to last only until the boys adjusted and were sleeping peacefully through the night.

They'd yet to discuss what would happen after that.

"If we're going to raise them together, as full-time co-guardians, we need to be *permanently* under one roof." He lifted a hand. "We could do it at your place, of course, but it's so much smaller..."

They would be tripping all over each other.

"And the boys are already sort of used to staying at Hidden Creek. I don't think it would be smart to uproot them again, do you? Especially after what happened a little while ago." He jerked his head in the direction of the classroom floor.

Aware that Kelly and the two sets of triplets were waiting for them on the playground, Lulu began moving about the classroom, gathering up the boys' things. "No. Of course it wouldn't be wise to move them again," she said.

He held her carryall open while she slid their belongings inside. "Then...?"

The two of them hesitated just inside the door. Lulu hated to admit it, but she was worried about how it would look. "If I actually move in," she murmured, looking up at him, "people are going to probably assume, because of our romantic history, that you and I are a couple again."

Sam lounged, arms folded, with one brawny shoulder braced against the wall. His glance drifted over her intimately. "So?"

"So," Lulu said before she could stop herself, "that could put a crimp in your dating life." *Oh my god! Where did that thought come from?*

To her embarrassment, her flash of jealousy did not go unnoticed.

Male satisfaction tugging at the corners of his lips, he stepped closer, gently cupped her shoulders and told her exactly what she had hoped to hear. "I'm not going to have any dating life when I have three kids to take care of."

A thrill swept through her. She forced herself to calm down. Just because they'd had a brief fling did not mean he would ever fall in love with her again, or vice versa. And from what she'd seen in the time since they'd broken up, he'd suffered no shortage of attractive female dinner companions.

Shrugging, she stepped back, away from the enticing feel of his warm, calloused hands on her bare skin. "You might be surprised. A lot of women my age have baby fever." *A lot of women lust after you.* She pretended an insouciance she couldn't begin to feel. "Three adorable toddlers could make you a very hot prospect."

Just that suddenly, something came and went in the air between them. The slightest spark of hope of renewed passion and a rekindling of the love they had once shared.

"Is that why you made love with me?" he chided, in a tone that was half joking, half serious. "Because you have a well-known case of baby fever? And wanted in on the bounty of family I suddenly found myself blessed with?"

Wondering just what it was about him that made her unable to get over him, she said, "Of course not."

To her chagrin, he looked skeptical.

"As I said before, I made love with you because I was…" *nostalgic for what we once shared*, she wanted to say "…curious," she fibbed instead.

His eyes darkened with a mixture of masculine pride and intense interest. Oblivious to the leaping of her heart, he mused in a low, husky voice that made her want to kiss him passionately, "You wanted to see if it was as good as we both recalled."

"Yes," she replied in a strangled voice.

Seemingly in no hurry to leave until he had the answers he wanted, Sam tucked a hand behind her ear. "And was it?"

Lulu swallowed around the building tightness in her

throat. "Physically, you know it was." She shoved her hands into the pockets of her sundress skirt. In an attempt to appear oh-so-casual, she leaned against the bulletin board decorated with pictures of family. Children, parents, grandparents, pets... The sum of which made her want him, and everything he offered, all the more.

"And emotionally?" His gaze dropped to her lips and he came closer still.

She planted a hand on the center of his chest before she gave in to the temptation to kiss him again. "Whoa there, cowboy." She stepped aside. "I'm not going there."

Sam shrugged. And straightened. "We're going to have to eventually, if we plan to adopt the kids."

Wow. The man just didn't stop. But then, she remembered that about him, too. When he wanted something, he worked single-mindedly until he achieved his goal.

Her eyes widened. "If *we* plan to *adopt*?" she echoed.

Talk about acting impulsively and going way too far way too fast! Had the two of them exchanged personality flaws or what?

Shrugging, he straightened to his full six feet three inches. "You didn't think I'd be content to be just guardians forever. Did you?"

Honestly, she'd been so busy trying to keep pace with the swift moving events she hadn't given it any thought. Although in the back of her mind, she had always thought, if she were lucky enough to be given the chance to raise the kids, she would certainly adopt.

None of that meant, however, that she and Sam should rush into anything again. No matter how selfless the reason.

She folded her arms. "First of all, Sam, at this point, the boys are so young they don't know the difference between us being their guardians versus their adoptive parents."

"But they will, probably before we know it. And if we want to give them the most stable family possible, we should probably be married, too."

Of course he would throw in a matter-of-fact proposal. Sam was a get-things-done kind of person. He never put off for tomorrow what could be done right now.

The thing was, to her surprise, she could see them eventually deciding to get married, too, if it meant giving the three little boys more security.

Still, she had to make sure she and Sam were on the exact same wavelength when it came to their future. That she wasn't jumping to erroneous conclusions. "And we would eventually do this as a convenience," she said, trying not to think what his steady appraisal and deep voice did to her.

"Yes. And a way to ensure sexual exclusivity."

Leave it to him, she thought with a mixture of excitement and exasperation, to spell it out when she would rather have left it undecided.

"Because you're right, Lulu," he continued in a way that seemed designed to curtail her emotional vulnerability. And maybe his, too. "If we're just living together, acting as guardians and taking care of the kids without having made a formal public commitment to each other, people will speculate about the state of our relationship."

And that could hurt the kids at some point down the road, Lulu realized.

"So, if we find we have needs..." She kept her eyes locked with his, even as her heart raced like a wild thing in her chest.

He squared his shoulders. "Then we satisfy them with each other."

It was certainly a practical, adult approach to what could be a very thorny situation. There was also no doubt they'd both lost the naivete that had once made them believe in fairy-tale romance and happy endings.

Even so, thinking about adoption and eventual marriage was a risk. One she wasn't sure she was ready to take, even if he wanted to go ahead and get everything settled. "What makes you think a marriage of convenience would work?" she challenged. Were they even really discussing this? "When our previous romance crashed and burned?" *Big-time.*

"There would be less pressure on us, as a couple and a family, if you and I went into it from a practical standpoint, as friends and co-parents."

And less pressure, at least in his view, meant it might work.

"And maybe, at some point, lovers, too." Doing her best to protect them both, she went back to his previous point.

A corner of his mouth quirked. "Yes." He looked as pleased as she was by the prospect of never having to imagine each other with anyone else. His gaze drifted over her lovingly. "I could see that happening," he rasped, taking her hand and rubbing his thumb along the inside of her wrist, starting a thousand tiny fires. "Especially after what happened yesterday."

Lulu flushed. Their lovemaking had been spectacular. No question. All she had to do was think about what it had felt like to be with him again, and renewed need pulsed inside her. Pushing aside the lingering thrill, she cautioned, "We need to slow down, Sam. Take it one day, one step at a time."

He glanced at her, as if his heart were on the line, too. "But you'll think about it?" he pressed.

Was he kidding? She wouldn't be able to do anything but!

An hour and a half later, all three boys shouted and giggled as they bounced wildly up and down on the center of Lulu's queen-size bed.

"Whoo whee!"

"Jump!"

"Me fun!"

Keeping watch to make sure the boys remained somewhat contained and didn't tumble off the mattress, Sam asked, "Can I help you?"

Lulu could tell he wanted her to go faster. It wasn't easy to pack when she was so completely distracted.

"Yes," she said, getting a handful of frilly bras and panties from her drawer and stashing them as unobtrusively as possible in the duffel she had looped over her arm. Noting Sam's glance tracking a silky burgundy thong hanging over the side, she hastily stuffed it out of sight. In an effort to direct his attention elsewhere, she inclined her head toward the boys. "Make sure they don't fall off and land on their heads."

"Okay, guys, settle down a little bit. We don't want anyone getting hurt."

The triplets responded by hopping around even higher.

Lulu sighed. What was it about guys and danger?

"I've got this," Sam said, scooping them up into his arms. "Time to sing the monkey song!"

The boys, who'd been hyperactive since their expression of grief earlier in the day, paused. All three tilted their head at Sam.

He sat down on the bed and gathered them onto his lap. "Everybody knows the monkey song," Sam said. He sang, "One little monkey jumping on the bed. He fell off and bumped his head. Momma called the doctor and the doctor said…" he wagged his finger in theatrical admonishment "…no more monkeys jumping on the bed!"

The boys began to grin. Clearly, they'd heard this children's song before.

He glanced over at her. "You could join in."

Still gathering shirts, shorts, pajamas and the occasional summer dress or skirt, Lulu winked at the guys in her life and, as requested, added her voice to Sam's baritone. "Two little monkeys…"

The boys chimed in, too, their words and tune garbled and mostly nonsensical but cute.

To Lulu and Sam's mutual relief, the switch in activity helped bring about much needed calm. They were up to ten monkeys by the time Lulu had what she needed for the rest of the week in two clothes baskets.

"Sure that's all?" Sam asked when she showed him what he would need to carry down to her Lexus for her while she shepherded the boys outside.

"Yep."

He quirked a brow.

She knew what he was thinking. If she was really moving in, she should be taking a lot more with her. For lots of reasons she preferred not to examine too closely, she needed to keep one foot out the door. Leaving the majority of her summer clothes at the Honeybee Ranch would accomplish that.

That evening, they closely followed their nighttime routine. Dinner, bath and then, at long last, story time. With Lulu and Sam sitting side by side on the sofa and all three boys sprawled across their laps, they read a few of the favorite tales. Then injected the book Kate Marten-McCabe had given them, about children whose parents had gone to heaven.

The boys listened, but did not seem to connect it to Peter and Theresa or themselves.

Sam and Lulu continued reading, alternating stories, until the boys fell asleep, then carried them one by one upstairs to their toddler beds.

With the boys asleep, Sam went to take Beauty out while Lulu stayed nearby, putting her things away. Shortly after Sam returned, the boys awakened. And once again, Sam and Lulu walked the floor with them, only to end up for the rest of the night snuggled with all five of them together in Sam's big bed, Beauty sleeping on the floor next to them.

The following morning, as per Kate's advice, they went into town and formally enrolled the boys in pre-school, from nine to one o'clock every day.

"So what's next on the list Kate gave us?" Sam asked as they walked out of the preschool.

Relieved the drop-off had been so easy and feeling a lot like the co-parents they aspired to be, Lulu fell into step beside him. "We need to find a way to help the boys remember Peter and Theresa."

Sam matched his long strides to her shorter ones. "All their belongings are in the boxes in my attic."

Lulu pushed aside the dread she felt at having to tackle such an emotional chore. They had to do this for the kids. "Want to go have a look?"

He nodded.

Like the rest of Sam's home, the third floor of the ranch house was clean, well lit and spacious. They pulled the boxes to the rug on the center of the wood floor and wordlessly began going through them, finding clothes of Theresa's and Peter's. A huge cache of old photos. Theresa's perfume. Peter's aftershave. Photos of their Memphis elopement.

"Here's a few with us in the picture, too," Sam said thickly. He handed over a photo of the four of them. The guys were in suits and ties, the gals in pretty white spring dresses. The guys wore boutonnieres, the girls carried bouquets.

"We were so young," Lulu murmured.

"And happy and idealistic," Sam said, studying their smiling faces.

If only they could have stayed that way, Lulu thought wistfully. But they hadn't, so…

She handed the photo back to Sam. And took out another. This one of Peter and Theresa at the hospital with their three newborns. Their first Christmas, the boys' first and second birthdays. One from Easter that year, which had to have been taken just before Theresa and Peter's death. A folder of the children's artwork from school. Another with newspaper articles detailing the eight-car pileup on the Houston freeway during morning rush hour that had killed them and seriously injured a dozen others.

Suddenly, the loss was too much. The grief hit Lulu hard, and she began to cry.

"Hey," Sam said, folding her close. After reading the articles, his eyes were wet, too. "Hey…" He stroked a hand through her hair. "I've got you…"

Needing the comfort only he could give, she snuggled into the reassuring safety of his strong arms. "Oh, Sam," she sobbed. "This is all just so unfair!" Her chin quivering, tears still streaming down her face, she struggled to get her emotions under control. "How are we ever going to fill the void their parents' deaths have left?"

Sorrow etched the handsome contours of Sam's face. "The only way we can," he countered, cupping her face between his big hands. "By taking it one day, one moment at a time. And becoming a real family in every possible way."

Lulu thought of the boys' meltdown the previous day, their sad little faces, the heartrending sounds of their sobs when they awakened at night.

"But what if we fail them?" she asked, knowing she'd never been so scared and so overwhelmed. "The way we once failed each other?"

Chapter 10

"We're not going to fail them, darlin'," Sam said.

The depth of her despair only made her look more vulnerable. He wiped away her tears, cuddling her even closer. Still caging her loosely in his arms, he gently kissed her temple. "We never fail when we're together. It's only when we split up that we make a mess of things."

For a brief second, she seemed to take his assertion at face value. Then worry clouded her eyes. "I wish I shared your confidence."

But she didn't. She didn't believe in herself. In him. Or in the two of them.

So he showed her the only way he could what an excellent team they made. Determined to convince her, he lowered his mouth to hers and delivered a deep and sensual kiss. As he hoped, she opened herself up to his embrace just as swiftly. Wreathing her arms about his neck, she let out an involuntary moan and curled against him. Returning the hot, riveting kiss again and again and again. Blood rushing hot and needy through his veins, he slid his hands beneath her shirt and her nipples pearled against the centers of his palms.

"Oh, Sam," Lulu whispered, as he trailed kisses along the shell of her ear, down the nape of her neck. The tears she'd shed still damp across her face.

She whimpered, another helpless little sound that sent his senses swimming even more. Aware he had never wanted a woman as much as he wanted her, he deepened the kiss. Her mouth was pliant beneath his, warm and sexy, her body soft, surrendering. And still they kissed, sweetly and languidly, hotly and passionately, slowly and tenderly. Until worries faded and pleasure reigned.

Not about to take advantage, though, Sam reluctantly drew back. "Now's the time," he teased, looking deep into her eyes. "Tell me to stop." He caressed the damp curves of her lip with his fingertip. "Or go."

Her turquoise eyes smoldered. "Go," she said, smiling and taking him by the hand and leading him down the stairs, away from everything that had been so upsetting, to her bedroom. She shut the door behind them. She plucked a brand-new box of condoms from the nightstand drawer.

"Definitely go." She shimmied out of her skirt. Drew her blouse off, too.

"Gotta say," he drawled, enjoying the view of her in a peach bra and panties set, knowing she had obviously planned ahead. "I like the way this is going." The fact she'd known, just as he had, that despite all the problems still facing them, they would make love again.

She toed off her sandals. "Good." She motioned toward his clothes. "Your turn, cowboy."

Appreciating the reckless, sexy side of her, he stripped down to his boxers.

Her delicate brow lifted. "Keep going."

He didn't need to glance down to know he was getting pretty far ahead of her. "Ah…sure?"

Mischief and her typical zest for life sparkled in her smile. Tilting her head to one side, she gave him a lusty once-over. "Mmm-hmm."

"What the lady wants." He obliged and saw her eyes go wide.

Rationally, Lulu knew they shouldn't be making love again, at least not so soon, when the last time he'd been so casual, and she'd felt so inexplicably conflicted, afterward. But for now, as she sauntered toward him, took him in her arms and kissed him again, all she could think about was how much every one of them had been through in such a brief span of time, how short life was. How unpredictable. The only thing she could count on, besides this very moment they were in, was how good she felt whenever she was with him. How grateful that they had found each other again.

With a low murmur of appreciation, Sam stopped kissing her long enough to ease off her bra and panties. Her hands rested on his shoulders while he helped her step out. Still kneeling, he savored the sight of her, then kissed her most sensitive spot. She quivered, clinging to him like a lifeline, aware that she was on the brink.

He left her just long enough to retrieve a condom and

then roll it on. Then he settled her against the wall. She wrapped her legs around his waist and they were kissing again. Touching. Caressing. Finding and discovering every pleasure point.

She was wet and open. He was hot and hard. So hard. And then there was no more waiting. He surged inside her and she welcomed him home. All was lost in blazing passion and overwhelming need. Pleasure spiraled. Soared. And then they floated blissfully down into a satisfaction unlike anything she had ever known.

Afterward, they clung together, still pressed up against the wall, their bodies still entwined and shuddering with release. Eventually, he let her down. Sam kissed her shoulder tenderly as her feet touched the floor, and she continued leaning up against him, snuggled into the warm, strong embrace of his arms. "Feeling better?" Sam asked.

Suddenly realizing that she and Sam and their three little boys might comprise the perfect family after all, Lulu murmured against his shoulder, "Always, when we make love."

"Same here." Sam gave her another angel-soft kiss, then drew back just far enough to see her face. "Anything else on your mind?"

"I was thinking about what you said, about us never failing when we're together."

He tucked a strand of hair behind her ear. "It's true."

Lulu thought about what else she had learned from growing up McCabe. Mindful of the time, she eased away from him and began to dress. "When you add the reality that the foundation of every happy family is the relationship of the couple at its heart." She drew a deep, bolstering breath, as she shimmied into her panties. "It makes sense that we need to be united in every way we can be."

Sam pulled on his boxers and stepped behind her to help her fasten her bra. Grinning, he said, "Including bed?"

Lulu sighed luxuriantly. "Definitely including bed. Though I'm still not sold on the two of us actually getting married in order to make that happen," she cautioned candidly while she pulled on her blouse.

Sam tensed, as if an old wound was reopened. "Because you don't want to be married to me?"

Lulu flushed self-consciously, warning herself she had nothing to feel guilty about as long as she was being completely honest with him. "Because I don't think that legal formality is even necessary these days," she clarified.

An indecipherable emotion came and went in Sam's eyes.

"But," she went on with heartfelt enthusiasm, "I am definitely on board with co-adopting the children with you." She paused to look him in the eye. "And I want to start that process as soon as possible."

To get things moving, Sam called their attorneys that same afternoon. Liz and Travis agreed to meet with Lulu and Sam the following day while the triplets were in preschool. Their two attorneys listened while Sam and Lulu outlined their plans, occasionally exchanging lawyerly looks and appearing concerned about the speed with which Lulu and Sam had reached their decision.

"Travis and I understand you want to protect the triplets," Liz said gently. "But there is a big difference between being co-guardians and adoptive parents, at least in terms of the court."

"Meaning?" Lulu asked nervously.

Sam reached over and squeezed her hand. A week ago, Lulu would have pulled away. However, today, feeling like they were members of the same family unit, she relaxed into his reassuring grip.

Both their attorneys noticed. Sobering all the more, Travis said, "To become a guardian, when you've been named by the parents in their will, is a fairly simple matter. You express a willingness to do so, papers are signed, and it's a done deal. Unless of course, there is some obvious reason why it shouldn't happen."

"But when you petition to adopt," Liz continued where her husband left off, "you have to complete a formal application and petition the court, undergo home studies and background checks."

"What are they looking for?" Sam asked.

Liz spread her hands. "Any signs of potential problems. Or instability."

"You mean mental instability?" he asked, perplexed.

"Or personal," Liz explained. "Like if someone's had multiple marriages or ones that only lasted a day, has been consistently fired from or quit their jobs, things like that…"

Lulu froze.

Travis jumped in. "Everything is looked at. Your finances, your family histories, your lifestyle. You have to provide character references and show proof of any marital history or divorce. It's a lot to undergo. Particularly when you already have your hands full just trying to acclimate the kids to their new circumstances."

Liz lifted a soothing hand. "It's not that we're expecting anything problematic to come up."

Unable to prevent herself from worrying, Lulu tried to figure out how to ask the question without revealing what she was really stressed about. "But what if it did? What if there were, I don't know, say, unpaid parking tickets? Or a noise violation?" *Or other evidence of reckless behavior.* "From years ago?"

Sam turned to look at Lulu. Poker-faced, but concerned.

"Then we'd address it," Liz said soothingly.

"But of course it would be better if we knew about any potential issues before making any formal application or getting social services involved," Travis said.

"Agreed." Sam suddenly looked every bit as on edge as Lulu felt. Still, he sounded calm when he added, "Which is why we should probably go ahead and have your law firm do complete background checks on both of us. Just so we can see what does come up, and if there is anything, deal with it."

"I agree with Sam." Lulu did her best to mimic Sam's laid-back attitude.

Liz and Travis seemed a little surprised by their request, but readily agreed.

Trying not to look at Sam, for fear she would give away what it was they were both trying like hell to hide, Lulu asked, "How long will it take?"

Travis shrugged. "Depends on how far back you want our investigator to go."

"As far back as they can," Sam said. He was no longer looking at Lulu, either.

Travis made a note on the legal pad in front of him. "Probably seven to ten days."

"Relax." Liz smiled. She got up to walk them out. "Knowing the two of you and your squeaky-clean reputations, I'm sure it will be fine."

But would it? Given Lulu and Sam's rocky romantic past?

Sam looked over at her as they left their attorneys' office. "I think we need to talk."

"I agree."

They walked over to The Cowgirl Chef and picked up a couple of cold drinks—a mocha frappé for her and a black iced coffee for him—and then headed for the park in the center of town. As they moved across the grass toward one of the benches in the shade, Lulu sent him an anxious glance. "Do you think that what happened in Tennessee is likely to come up?"

Sam sat down beside her and draped his arm along the back of the bench. He kept his voice low as she settled beside him. "No idea if it will or not, darlin', since there was never any follow-through on our part and therefore nothing put on record. But it will probably be good to know for sure."

Lulu worked her straw back and forth between her fingertips. "What about my business? The theft I just had?" She took a long sip of her drink, then dropped her hand and ran her fingertip along the hem of her pretty cotton skirt. It had ridden up above her knee and showed several inches of bare, silky skin. "Will that make me look irresponsible for not having had a security system installed on the property?"

He moved his gaze upward, past the scoop-necked knit top cloaking her slender midriff and the swell of her breasts, to the flushed pink color in her face. She had put her honey-brown hair up in a neat knot on the back of her head before the meeting. She looked beautiful and kissable and frustrated as all get-out. He moved his hand from the back of the bench to cup her shoulder gently.

"It's Laramie County, Lulu. We don't usually need security systems here since pretty much everyone who resides here is honest and neighborly. The court will understand that."

She shifted toward him, her bare knee brushing up against his jean-clad thigh. "Yes, but will they understand I haven't decided whether or not I even want all my bees back?"

"The court will probably want to know what your plans are in that regard. If you decide not to work, at least for now in order to take better care of the kids, I'm sure the court would be okay with that. Especially since we can well afford to take care of them on my income alone."

Lulu met his eyes, then shifted forward again. "I know but I really don't want to look like a dilettante. And we both know, during college and for a couple years after, I was pretty flighty."

Sam liked the idea of her leaning on him, even if it was just for moral support. "And you worked through that and built a business to be proud of. I really don't see it as a problem."

Shame flushed her cheeks. "I really don't want anyone to find out about the choices we made on spring break."

"Hopefully, they won't."

Lulu crossed her arms beneath the soft curves of her breasts and took another sip of her coffee. "And if they do?"

He paused, taking in the anxious twist of her lips. Unlike her, he didn't regret what they had done, not then and not now, just how they had let it end. But he had been older at the time of what she had once referred to as Their Big Mistake.

He squeezed her shoulder. Knowing he would do whatever he had to do to protect her, he leaned down to whisper in her ear. "Then we'll deal with it, Lulu. The best way we know how."

"Well, there's one good thing about having the kids in preschool five half days a week," Lulu said the following morning. They'd returned to the ranch after drop-off, ready to tackle that day's To Do list. "It gives us time to do the things we couldn't do otherwise."

Sam followed her up to the second floor. "Which would normally be sleep," he joked.

"No kidding." Lulu walked into the boys' room, where the beds were still unmade. She reached for the covers on one bed. Sam, another. "I never thought I'd want just *one* solid night of shut-eye so badly."

Looking sexy as could be in a T-shirt and jeans, he arranged blankets and stuffed animals against the pillows. "That's what being a parent is all about, isn't it?" He straightened and waggled his eyebrows at her. "Losing sleep? For the best possible reason?"

To comfort them. And each other. Speaking of which… Lulu glided into Sam's arms. Hugged him fiercely. "I love those little guys."

Squeezing her back, he rasped, "So do I." They stayed that way another long moment. Sam stole a few kisses, as Lulu knew he would. Then gave her another long, affectionate hug. "Now, if we could just figure out how to get them sleeping through the night, in their own bed," he murmured against her hair.

Lulu thought for a moment. "Maybe it would help if we set up their bedroom more like it used to be. We have photos." She went to get some.

Sam studied the layout with her. "Definitely worth a try."

Together, they shifted the three toddler beds from the U shape they had been in, with the beds pushed up along the sides of the bedroom, into a neat dormitory-style row, with all the headboards against the same wall. They took the rocker glider out of the corner, as well as the box of toys, and put both out into the upstairs hall for later rearranging.

Hands on her hips, Lulu studied their handiwork, lamenting, "They won't be able to play in here at all."

Sam moved behind her. He wrapped his arms around her and rested his chin on the top of her head. "Well, maybe that was the idea," he said, bringing her softer form back against his hard body. He pressed a kiss into the top of her hair, the shell of her ear. "Theresa and Peter wanted their bedroom to be a dedicated sleeping space and nothing more."

"Maybe." Lulu leaned against Sam another long moment, then went over to stack their bedtime storybooks on top of the room's lone bureau containing their clothing. Among them was the one Kate Marten-McCabe had given them.

Sam frowned, and, as was happening more and more these days, seemed to read her mind. "I know the grief specialists said reading this to the kids would help," he ruminated, "but I get the feeling they think it's just another story, and one they don't really want to hear."

"I know what you mean." Lulu sighed. "I don't think they make the connection between their own grief and the loss the little boy and girl in the storybook experience."

Sorrow clouded Sam's eyes. "Me, either."

For a long moment, neither of them spoke.

"Maybe it will come in time," he offered finally.

"And maybe," Lulu said, knowing they needed more than hope, they needed action, "what we really need is a book about the boys and their journey."

Crinkling his brow, he walked over to look at the book she was holding. "You mean superimpose their pictures and names in this storybook?"

"Actually, I think we should go one better." Lulu gestured for Sam to follow her and walked into the guest room she was using, where she had stashed several of the boxes of old photos and mementos.

"Maybe we should put together a story about Peter and Theresa. How they fell in love. Had the triplets. And all lived together happily. And then there was an accident. Their parents went to heaven. The boys went to stay with a number of other people. Before they ended up with the two of us and Beauty."

Sam ran his palm across his jaw. "So they would understand."

Eager to get him fully on board with the idea, she clamped her hands on his biceps. "Maybe we could end it with them blowing kisses at their parents in heaven, and their parents looking down on them, happy they are okay. So they can see there is still, and will always be, some connection."

"That could work." Sam grinned down at her, his enthusiasm building.

"It *will* work," Lulu said. Happy she and Sam were becoming such a good team, she rose on tiptoe and kissed his cheek.

He squeezed her waist affectionately. "Then let's get to it!" he said.

Lulu downloaded self-publishing software that helped her write and format the custom story that evening, after the kids were asleep, while Sam sorted through the photos, selecting the ones she needed.

Together, they put the book together, and while it would never make bestseller status, it did explain with words and pictures how many people loved the triplets and how they had come to live at Hidden Creek Ranch.

They printed it out, took it into town the following day to have it laminated and bound at the copy shop, and read it to them that evening after their baths. Sam and Lulu sat together with the three boys sprawled across their laps, the homemade storybook held out in front of them.

"Again," Theo said enthusiastically when Lulu had finished.

Ethan pointed to the photos of Theresa and Peter. "Mommy," he said. "Daddy!"

Andrew leaned his head on Sam's shoulder. "Heaven," he murmured.

Beauty, who had been stretched out at their feet, sat up. As she looked from one triplet to another, she seemed to be offering comfort and condolence.

The only problem was, all three boys wanted to take the new book to bed with them. To the point where there was almost a free-for-all.

"Hang on, guys," Lulu said, rushing off. She returned with a photo of Peter and Theresa for each of them. "Would you like to sleep with these tonight?" she said.

Three little heads nodded.

"Okay, then, up you go." Sam picked up Ethan and Andrew. Lulu hefted Theo in her arms. They went up the stairs.

Although the new bedroom arrangement hadn't done much to relax the boys the night before, they weren't giving up. Lulu put on a CD of lullabies she had found in one of the moving boxes. As the soft orchestral music filled the room, the boys perked up, listening, then snuggled down on their pillows, photos, stuffed animals and blankets in their arms.

Sam sat, his back to the wall, between beds one and two, while Lulu planted herself between beds two and three.

The boys continued listening. Child by child, eyes shuttered closed.

Sam and Lulu turned on the monitor and eased from the room.

"We should do more of this," she whispered. "Helping them remember, like Kate suggested. I think it really might help."

Sam took her hand and led her down the hall. He bussed her cheek. "Maybe you and I should do some remembering, too."

Chapter 11

"What are we going to be remembering?" Lulu asked, her heart fluttering in her chest. The look in his eyes was so incredibly romantic!

Sam walked into his bedroom, shut the door and turned on the monitor on the bedside table. Then, pivoting back to her, he lifted her up, so she was sitting on his bureau, arms wrapped around his neck, his strong, hard body ensconced in the open V of her legs. The insides of her thighs rubbed the outsides of his. "Our first date," he murmured.

She trembled as his palms molded her breasts through the knit of her shirt and the lace of her bra, his thumbs rubbing over the tender crests. His mouth hovered above hers and Lulu felt herself surge to life.

"Our first kiss," he whispered as their lips met in a melding of want and need.

Yearning spiraled through her and she ran her hands through his hair, giving back, meeting him kiss for kiss. The feel of his mouth on hers imbuing her with the kind of love she had wanted all her life. The kind of love only he could give.

She kissed him passionately, adoring the way his tongue stroked hers, once and then again and again, all while he never stopped touching her. Caressing her breasts, the curve of her hips, cupping her buttocks in his palms, before moving around to trace the lines of her pelvic bones and the sensitive area between her thighs.

Aware it was her turn, Lulu reached between them to unclasp his belt. Dropping hot kisses along his neck, she slid her hand inside his jeans. Felt the velvety heat and hardness, even as his mouth moved on hers in a way that was shattering in its possessive sensuality. "The first time I touched you," Lulu whispered, when they finally came up for air.

He found his way beneath her panties. "And the first time I touched you."

Deciding it was time they both got naked, she lifted his shirt over his head and tossed it aside. Taking a moment to admire him, she let her glance sift over his bare chest. His skin was golden and satiny smooth, covered with curling tufts of golden-brown hair that spread across his pecs, before angling down toward his navel. Lower still, his hardness pressed against the front of his jeans. "The first time we were together all night, in Tennessee."

Sam grinned, recalling. He helped her off with her shirt, bra, skirt. "If I could do that entire trip over, I would."

Lulu lifted up enough so he could dispense with her

panties. "So would I," she admitted huskily, as the rest of his clothing followed suit. He came back to her once again, and she wound her arms about his neck. "But I'd make sure we had a different ending this time." One rife with love and tenderness, instead of heartbreak and anger.

Sam smiled over at her in a way that made her feel beautiful inside and out. He tucked an errant strand of hair behind her ear. "We may not be able to go back in time and have a do-over," he said, kissing her thoroughly and claiming her as his. "But we can certainly put all our mistakes behind us and start fresh again."

Lulu luxuriated in the feel of his mouth on hers. "I'd like that, Sam," she whispered back, pulling him close once again. "I really would…"

Sam knew Lulu was still afraid their reconciliation would turn out to be short-lived. But *he* knew better. He'd lost her once; he wasn't going to make the same mistake again. He set about showing her that he was in this for the long haul as they resumed kissing again, long and deep, soft and slow, sweet and tender.

She ran her hands over his back, across his hips. He luxuriated in the soft, silky feel of her. Caressing, exploring, entering and withdrawing in slow, shallow strokes that soon had her arching against him, clamoring for more.

And still they kissed. Taking up the rhythm he started. Until their breath caught and their hearts thundered in unison, and there was no more playing and delaying. She held fast, claiming him as he claimed her. Giving and taking everything. Tumbling into the sweet, hot abyss.

Afterward, they snuggled together, the aftershocks

every bit as potent as their lovemaking had been. "This was nice." She sighed, looking utterly fulfilled as they moved from bureau to bed.

Aware he felt the same, he lay on his back. With her draped over top of him, her head nestled against his chest, he stroked a hand languidly down her spine. "Ah. You mean Sam-and-Lulu time?" he teased. Knowing he never wanted to be without her again.

She bantered back, "Where we see to our own... very adult...needs."

Realizing she looked for comfort from him as much as he yearned to receive it from her, Sam nodded. A contemplative silence fell. Moments drew out. He could feel Lulu drifting away from him, the way she usually did when her guard went back up, but he was determined not to let their closeness fade. "What are you thinking, darlin'?" Sam rasped, still enjoying how beautiful and utterly ravished she looked.

Lulu drew the sheet up over her breasts and rolled onto her side, facing him. Her honey-brown hair spilling over her shoulders, she rested her arm on the mattress and propped her head up on her hand. She met his gaze equably and drew in a bolstering breath. "That maybe we should just stop fighting our attraction to each other and accept it."

Glad she'd told him what was eating away at her, he traced the curve of her lips with his fingertip. "I haven't been fighting mine."

"I know." Their glances met, held. Her turquoise eyes sparkled ruefully. "But up to now, cowboy, I have."

How well he knew that! He took her free hand and lifted it to his mouth. Gently kissing her knuckles, he felt comfortable enough to ask, "Any particular reason why?"

She wrinkled her nose at him and let out a beleaguered sigh. "I just don't want either of us to be disappointed if things don't work out in the end."

The fact that she was beginning to feel the kind of heartfelt emotion that had drawn them to each other in the first place, in addition to the sizzling physical attraction that had always existed between them, made Sam very happy. To his frustration, however, beneath her outward pragmatism and acceptance, Lulu still seemed somewhat ambivalent.

Up one moment. And fully on board with their increasing intimacy. Wary—and down—the next.

"You don't sound deliriously pleased with the situation," he deadpanned, trying to make light of the maelstrom of emotions running through him.

"No, it's not that at all," Lulu explained. "I've just been trying really hard to keep our situation from becoming overly complicated." She shifted slightly, and the sheet moved lower, giving him a seductive glimpse of her breasts.

He felt himself grow hard again.

She raked her teeth across her lower lip and shyly admitted, "And I don't want us to have expectations of each other that we can't possibly meet, the way we did before."

He could see why she didn't want them to be disappointed in each other. Again. But it bothered him that she always expected less of them than they were capable of giving.

Still, this was progress. It was the first time they'd made love that she had expressed acceptance instead of worry or regret, at least since they had come together to care for the triplets.

"So." She waggled her brows at him mischievously, looking happy and relaxed again. "As long as this is good…for the both of us…"

"We can make love however, whenever, wherever you want," Sam promised her gently, folding her close. And as her body began to respond to the urgency of his, he made love to her all over again.

Saturday morning, Lulu and Sam attended the grief group for parents of orphaned children. As was her custom with new attendees, psychologist Kate Marten-McCabe asked them to stay after for a few minutes. "So how are things going?" the silver-blond therapist asked.

"Better." Lulu explained what they had done thus far to help the children remember their parents.

"The storybook sounds wonderful." Kate smiled.

"We still can't get them to spend the night in their own beds though," Sam said.

"Although we did get them to actually go to sleep in their beds last night," Lulu added.

"It'll come," Kate promised, and then gave them a few more tips.

"Kate's right," Lulu's brother Jack said. Sam, Lulu and the triplets had stopped by his home for lunch and an afternoon playdate with his three little girls and Jack's old friend, rehab nurse Bess Monroe. "Progress does come. But it's often in infinitesimal degrees."

"Are you trying to encourage me or discourage me?" Lulu joked while making lunch with Bess. Her famous honey-grilled chicken salads for the adults, PB&J and apple slices for the kids.

Sam and Jack stood in the doorway of the kitchen and kept an eye on the six nicely playing kids. "I'm just saying the sleep thing is a hard thing to work out," Jack retorted, sadness creasing his face.

Concerned, Lulu went over to hug her brother. His surgical skills were legendary among the returning veterans that he and Bess both helped. However, he was not so great at dealing with the grief left by the death of his wife, Gayle.

Lulu stepped back to take him in. "Are you okay?"

"It's Father's Day," Bess put in.

Jack shot her a massively irritated look.

She raised both hands. "Well, it is. You get like this every year."

Lulu turned back to Jack. "Why would this make you sad? Your children love you! I'm sure they made you gifts at school."

"They do and did," Bess put in.

Pushing aside his usual stoicism, Jack said thickly, "It's just that Father's Day reminds me of Mother's Day. Which makes me think about Gayle. And all the holidays she's never going to celebrate with us."

Lulu understood, and she knew Sam did, too. Her eyes suddenly glistening, Bess slipped from the room. She disappeared down the hall and into the bathroom. Which was no surprise, Lulu noted, since Bess and Gayle had been very good friends.

Lulu wrapped Jack in another consoling hug. "I miss her, too," she admitted, tears welling.

Sam walked over to clap Jack on the shoulder. "We all do. She was a real force of nature."

A recuperative silence fell.

Seconds later, Bess emerged. Her nose was red and her eyes too bright, but she had a cheerful smile plastered on her face. Completely ignoring what had just happened, she asked, "What do you all think? Should we eat lunch inside or outside?"

The rest of the afternoon went pleasantly. Mostly because the kids played well and the adults avoided talk of anything the least bit sensitive or uncomfortable.

As they were getting the kids ready to leave, Jack took Lulu and Sam aside. "About the nighttime travails... My only advice is to comfort them when they wake and then always put them back in their own beds for the remainder of the night, even if it means you're stretched out on the floor next to them, so they get the idea that *their* beds are for sleeping, not yours. Unless it's very special circumstances, like they're running a fever or there's a big thunderstorm or something."

"And that works?" Lulu asked as Bess came to stand next to Jack.

Jack smiled. "It does."

The events of the day stayed with Lulu.

On the way back to Hidden Creek, Lulu said to Sam, as casually as possible, "Hey. What do you think about stopping by the Honeybee and letting me and the kids off for a few minutes, and then going and getting lost for, oh, an hour or so?"

He slanted her a quick glance. Clad in his usual snug jeans, custom-fitted boots and solid-colored cotton shirt, he looked so ruggedly masculine and handsome it was enough to make her go weak in the knees. "You serious?"

She shrugged and checked out the kids in the rearview mirror. They were all wearing their bucket hats and sunglasses, looking cute as could be, and were surprisingly wide-awake. "You must have some stuff to check on at your ranch."

"Tons."

Which was no surprise, Lulu thought. Since they'd taken custody of the triplets, Sam had been all kids, all the time.

He made the turn into the Honeybee Ranch and drove up to the house. He put the pickup in Park, then turned to look at her with a mixture of curiosity and affection. "You sure you can handle them by yourself?"

She was going to have to if she wanted to succeed with her secret plan. Lulu smiled. "Yep."

Sam reached over to cup her face in one hand. He rubbed his thumb across the curve of her cheekbone. Said admiringly, "Your older brother sure did infuse you with confidence."

Tingling all over, Lulu smiled back at him. "And good ideas," she said mysteriously.

As Lulu expected, the boys were delighted to sit at her kitchen table and play with the kids' craft stuff that she kept for her preschool-age nieces and nephews when they visited. The triplets were covered with washable glue and glitter and colorful markers and still working on their "projects" when Sam came back an hour later.

"Surprise!" they shouted in unison. "Happy Day!"

They rushed at him, wet and sticky artwork in tow. "Here! For you! Sam!"

Looking surprised and touched, Sam hunkered down and wrapped them all in a hug. "You fellas did all this for me?"

For the second time that day, Lulu felt herself welling up. She edged closer to indulge in the group embrace. Knelt down. "Even though we're technically still guardians, they wanted you to know what a fabulous father figure you've become to them," she said hoarsely.

Sam wrapped an arm about her waist and drew her in close. He pressed a kiss to the top of her head. "Right back at you, darlin'."

One day, they would be Mommy and Daddy. But for now, Lulu thought, returning Sam's warm hug and cuddling the boys, this life they'd fashioned was more than enough.

Chapter 12

"Congratulations." Lulu toasted Sam three days later.

Aware how right it all felt, having her and the boys in his home, he clinked his coffee mug against hers. Who would have thought the five of them could become a family so fast? Or that mornings would become so blissful? "To you, too, darlin'."

"Can you believe it?" she whispered. Fresh from the shower and clad in yellow linen shorts, a striped tee and sneakers, she looked pretty and ready to take on their day. "The boys spent the whole night in their beds!"

His gaze drifted over her appreciatively. She'd put on makeup sparingly. Damp honey-brown hair twisted in a knot on the back of her head, she smelled of the citrus-and-flowers shampoo and soap she favored. Lower still, he could see her sleek and sexy legs.

Doing his best to tamp down his desire and focus

on the conversation at hand, he lingered next to her. Enjoying their camaraderie, he leaned over to buss the top of her head and reminded her, "We did have to go back in and sit propped against the wall next to them, twice, to get them to fall back asleep."

"I know," she acknowledged. As she shifted toward him, the soft swell of her breasts rubbed against his arm. She stepped back to gaze up at him, and the absence of her touch had him feeling bereft. "But they stopped crying almost immediately and we didn't have to pick them up and walk the floor with them to calm them down. All we had to do was reassure them."

He nodded with a depth of parental satisfaction that surprised him and set his coffee mug aside. "It was a lot better than it ever has been."

She put her own mug down, then splayed her hands across his chest. "Jack's advice is really working."

He wrapped his arms around her waist and tugged her so they were touching in one long, tensile line. Burying his face in her hair, he thought of all they'd managed to accomplish in just under two weeks. Then murmured, "A lot of things are really working out."

She drew back. Smiling, she looked up at him as if she were tempted to kiss him. Would have, if not for the three little boys playing in the adjacent room.

Later, he promised himself.

They would make up for lost time. And when they did, she would understand how much she meant to him.

As she gazed up at him, a wealth of feelings was in her eyes. He realized he had never seen her looking so happy. "Oh, by the way." She snapped her fingers. "I almost forgot. It's show-and-tell at the preschool this morning."

"They have that for two-year-olds?"

Lulu slipped out of the loose circle of his arms. She grabbed the three insulated lunch sacks they'd purchased for the boys, then opened up the fridge, removed three drinks and three premade PB&J sandwiches. Before he could get there to assist, she closed the door with a sexy swivel of her hip.

"Half the kids in their group are nearly three," she said.

"Oh. Right." Knowing they needed individual packs of graham crackers and dried fruit the boys were convinced was candy, Sam got those out of the pantry and added them to the bags. Noting what a good team they made, he went to get the school backpacks, too.

"Anyway." Lulu paused to match the lunch bags to the right backpacks. Finished, she and Sam zipped them all shut. "I talked to the kids yesterday after school, while you were out talking to your foreman, about what they were going to bring today to show their classmates."

Motioning for him to follow, she strode into the adjacent playroom. "Boys! Remember? It's show-and-tell today. So, do you want to get the toys you picked out?"

Three little heads tilted. They looked up at her, seeming slightly puzzled.

Sam sympathized. For a two-year-old, what happened yesterday might as well have been eons ago. They were usually so "in the moment."

Looking sweet and maternal, Lulu knelt to their level. Gently, she reminded them, "Ethan, you were going to take your stuffed panda bear. Andrew, you were going to take your Frisbee. And, Theo, you were going to take the wall you made with your snap-together building set."

The triplets turned to each other, once again communicating visually the way only multiples could. "No," they said firmly in unison.

All three went over to their beloved Saint Bernard, who was sprawled out on the floor, as per usual, watching over them.

"Take Beauty!" they chorused.

"Ah, guys," Sam said reluctantly, hunkering down. He hated disappointing them. "I'm sorry," he informed them as kindly as he could. "But that's not possible."

"Take Beauty!" they shouted again.

Uh-oh, Sam thought, catching Lulu's warily astonished expression. They were headed for meltdown territory.

Wondering if there were any exceptions to be made, Sam tilted his head. "Are they permitted to bring pets into the preschool?" he asked Lulu.

Her cheeks pink with distress, she shrugged. "I don't know. Let me call and ask."

Sam stayed with the kids and got them involved in helping straighten their toys. A few minutes later, Lulu returned. "I spoke with their teacher, Miss Cece. Apparently, it is possible, as long as the pet is up to date on all their vaccinations, is good with kids and the visit is brief."

"How much advance notice do they need?"

"If you've got the right vet records, today is good."

"I do."

Lulu's grin widened. Looking extremely happy they hadn't had to disappoint the boys, she declared, "Well then, kids, looks like your best friend is going to school with you today."

"Yay!" The boys clapped and danced with excitement.

She made another phone call, confirming the visit. Because Beauty was so big and couldn't arrive until midmorning, Sam agreed to follow later and drive his dog separately. Anticipating they might need extra help, Lulu pledged to stay on in the classroom as a volunteer.

When the time came, Sam headed into town. He got there a little early, so he walked Beauty up and down the shady town streets. Pausing to give her water from her travel bowl and making sure she had time to take care of necessities. Finally, Lulu texted that they were ready.

Aware he was almost as excited as the kids, Sam entered the school, stopped by the front office to check in and say hello and then headed back down the hall.

The two-year-olds were buzzing with excitement. Their eyes widened when they saw the extremely gentle brown-and-white dog that stood twice as high as them.

Confessed dog lover Cece Taylor welcomed them into the classroom. The fifty-five-year-old educator directed Sam to take his pet to the open space next to the bulletin board. The rest of the kids sat cross-legged in a semicircle on the carpet.

"Okay, Theo, Andrew, Ethan," Miss Cece said. "Do you boys want to come up here and show us your dog and tell us about her?"

The boys stood importantly. Little chests puffed out, they walked up to Beauty.

"And who is this?" Miss Cece prompted.

"Beauty. Doggy," Theo explained.

"Soft. Pet." Ethan demonstrated how to stroke her fur.

"No ride," Andrew explained gravely, pointing at her back.

Miss Cece flashed an inquisitive look their way.

Sam told the assembled group, "Andrew is telling us we don't ever try to ride the doggy like a horse. Because that's not good. We can pet Beauty, though, because she really likes that."

Enthralled, the kids took this in.

"Are there any questions?" Miss Cece asked.

One of the older little girls in the class raised her hand. When called on, she pointed at Lulu. "Who is that?" she asked.

"And that?" Another child jumped in to point at Sam.

Sam bit down on an oath. A land mine. One that none of the adults in the room had expected. Luckily, the triplets were taking the queries in stride. All three boys grinned proudly.

Theo walked over to Lulu, who was seated on a small chair next to Beauty. He took her face in his hands. Gazed happily into her eyes. "Lulu. *Mommy*," he declared.

Was he calling Lulu Mommy? Sam wondered, barely suppressing a sharp inhalation of surprise and delight.

Andrew walked over to Sam. He motioned for Sam to bend down. When Sam did, Andrew took Sam's face in his hands. "Sam. *Daddy*," he said clearly.

Sam felt himself begin to mist up. He wasn't the only one, either. Lulu's eyes were moist with unshed tears, too.

Ethan walked over to stand between Lulu and Sam. He put one hand on each of them and then walked over to Beauty. He took the big dog's face in his hands. "Family," he said reverently, before taking another big breath and puffing out his little chest.

Andrew and Theo echoed the sentiment. Her lower lip trembling, barely stifling a sob, Lulu flashed a smile as wide as Texas. Tears streaming down her face, she engulfed all three little boys, then Beauty and then Sam, in hug after hug. "That's right, boys, Beauty, Sam and I are all part of your family now," she said huskily.

Not sure when he'd ever felt such joy, Sam swallowed the knot in his throat and embraced them all. The boys had been right. They were a family, and a darned good one. He swallowed around the lump in his throat and held them close.

Hours later, Lulu still felt herself welling up from time to time. To her satisfaction, Sam seemed overwhelmed with happiness, too. In fact, they were brimming with joy as they headed downstairs to finish the dinner dishes.

Lulu picked up where she'd left off an hour earlier. It had become clear their little darlings were in desperate need of their bedtime routine a good forty-five minutes earlier than usual. Which, as it happened, was a good thing, because the cuddling and storybook reading took longer and were rife with more mutual affection than ever.

Sighing contentedly, Lulu began loading the dishwasher. "Whoever said good things come when you least expect them was right."

The fabric of his shirt stretching across his broad shoulders and nicely delineating the muscles in his chest, Sam knelt to pick up green beans and potatoes from the floor. His snug jeans did equally nice things to his lower half.

Gold-flecked eyes twinkling, he slanted her a fond glance. "That was some show-and-tell, wasn't it?" he ruminated softly.

Finished, Lulu wiped down the counters. Sam took out the trash. When he came back, they both stood at the sink and washed their hands. Lulu ripped off a paper towel and handed him one. Now that they finally had a quiet moment alone, she asked what had been nagging at her. "Do you think they were trying to call us Lulu-Mommy and Sam-Daddy, or just explain what our role was in their lives?"

He came closer, gently cupped her face in his large, warm palms. "Both."

Lulu released an uneven breath. "I do love them."

He wrapped his arms around her, inundating her with his steady masculine warmth. "I do, too, sweetheart."

Aware how close she was to falling for him all over again, she released a reluctant, admiring sigh. "And I think they're beginning to love and trust us."

The question was, when would she and Sam ever love and trust each other as much as they needed to, to have the kind of forever-family she still yearned for? Or would they? Had that window closed? If not for her, for him? And if it had, would it be okay if they were just really great friends and lovers and co-parents to three adorable little boys? Although she knew she was happy as is—wildly happy, in fact—the romantic side of her still wanted more, and that disappointed her. She didn't want to ruin everything by being greedy. They had so very much as it was.

Sam's cell rang. He glanced at the screen. Reluctantly stepped away from her and answered. "Hey, Travis," he said. "Thanks for returning my call."

He had called his attorney? And not mentioned it to her?

Oblivious to her shock, he continued speaking in

his husky baritone, "I've got Lulu here with me, too, so I'm going to put you on speakerphone." Sam hit the button and set his cell on the counter in front of them.

Lulu and Travis exchanged greetings. Then Sam said, "We were wondering if there had been news about the background check yet."

Lulu tensed.

Travis replied, "I just talked with the private investigator. He's still tracking something down."

Oh no, Lulu thought.

Sam reached over to take her hand. Gave it a reassuring squeeze. "Any idea what he's looking at?" Sam asked his attorney.

Matter-of-factly, Travis replied, "Liz and I never discuss anything with our clients until we receive the final report. Otherwise, people can get upset for no reason other than records somewhere that weren't complete, or some such."

Sam wrapped his arm around Lulu's shoulders and drew her against his side. "Makes sense," he said. Seeming to understand her silence for the apprehension that it was, he continued, "I'm sure everything will be fine."

Maybe...or maybe not, Lulu thought, worried her and Sam's reckless actions in the past could come back to haunt them now.

"That's our assumption, too," Travis said. "Although..." his voice took on a teasing lilt "...Liz and I did hear what happened in preschool, Lulu-Mommy and Sam-Daddy."

Recalling, Sam and Lulu chuckled in tandem. It was all she could do not to tear up again. "It was definitely a moment," she said proudly.

"A moment that's apparently all over the school,"

Travis continued. "And since our kids are enrolled there, too, Liz heard about it when she went to pick our girls up. I have to tell you, stuff like that is really going to help your petition to adopt."

"Let's hope so," Lulu said.

It certainly helped her heart.

Hugging her close, Sam drawled, "Speaking of our plans to adopt. Any idea when we *can* expect the report from the investigator?"

"Early next week," his attorney said.

"Okay. Thanks, Travis." Sam ended the call. Satisfaction turned up the corners of his lips. "When we clear that hurdle, we'll be one step closer," he vowed.

Lulu bit her lip, still not so sure. "You really think we're going to be in the clear?" she asked nervously. "That no one will ever know what happened when we were in Tennessee?"

He rocked forward on the toes of his boots. "How could they? For there to be a record of it, there had to be follow-through on our part." His gaze drifted over her. "And we didn't…so there should be absolutely nothing standing in our way."

"And we'll be able to move forward with the adoption! Oh, Sam, it's really going to happen, isn't it?" Lulu threw her arms around his neck. "We're all going to be together! We're going to be a family."

"We really are. In the meantime, I'm thinking I'd like a shower." He fit his lips to hers and kissed her seductively. "Want to join me?"

She splayed her hands across his chest. Felt his heart beat in tandem with hers. "You're serious."

"As can be." He kissed her again, leisurely.

"Then so am I." She kissed him back, then took him by the hand and led him upstairs.

The master bath featured an old claw-foot tub that had been nicely refinished, two sinks and a large modern shower. They stripped down, each helping the other, and climbed in. And although it wasn't the first time they had showered together, it was the first time since they had gotten back together, and definitely the most exciting. Water sluiced down upon them from the rainfall shower fixture above.

They lathered each other from head to toe, taking their time, then stood together under the spray to rinse. Then kissed, fiercely and evocatively, until they were both trembling and groaning for more.

He turned her so she was facing the tile, and he slipped in behind her. One hand explored her breasts, the other moved across her tummy and downward. "So soft and sweet," he murmured against her ear.

She arched her throat, to give him better access. "So hot and hard…"

He laughed and brought her back around to face him. Moved her against the wall. And then they were kissing again, barely stopping to come up for air. Quivering with sensation, she felt her body surrendering all the more.

Sam exited the shower just long enough to get a condom, roll it on. He sank onto the bench built into the shower wall, then pulled her down so she was straddling his lap.

She was wet and open. He seemed intent on giving her what she needed. Kissing her deeply. Finding her with his fingertips, possessing her body and soul, until she felt his desire in every kiss and caress.

He loved her as an equal. As a friend. As a lover, and maybe, just maybe, something more. And she adored him, too. Opening herself up to him in a way she never had before. Celebrating the occasion and possessing him as well, with the tenderness and need and singularity of purpose they both deserved.

Afterward, as they cuddled together in bed, Lulu knew this was what it felt like when it was right, when her life was finally on the brink of being complete.

All she had to do was trust in fate. Trust in Sam. And the love that would bring their new little family together.

Chapter 13

The rest of the week passed blissfully, and on Saturday morning, Sam made his famous blueberry pancakes while they all lounged around in their pajamas. Not surprisingly, the boys picked up on the lack of urgency. As if realizing they would normally be rushing around, looking for shoes and getting dressed, Theo cocked his head. "Me. School?"

Sam knelt down so they were eye to eye. He was still in loose-fitting pajama pants and a short-sleeved gray T-shirt. Thick wheat-colored hair rumpled and standing on end, morning stubble rimming his jaw, he looked slightly on edge. Same as Lulu.

They'd made plans for that afternoon, but this morning it was going to be just the five of them again. That arrangement had not worked out well previously. They were hoping that the boys had been with them long enough that they wouldn't need the distraction of constantly playing with other children to make them happy. That the five of them would be able to feel like the complete family they aspired to be.

Sam smiled down at their little charges. If he was disappointed the boys were already starting to feel restless and on the verge of being unhappy, he did not show it. "Not today, fellas," he said soothingly. "It's Saturday."

Briefly, the boys looked as crestfallen as Sam and Lulu had feared they might be, upon learning there was no school that day. "But we can do other fun things," Sam said cheerfully, rising.

Like what? Lulu wondered. They hadn't discussed this. She moved close enough to feel his body heat. "What did you have in mind?" she asked.

The boys, already bored, wandered back to the play area in the reconfigured family room and began jumping on the sofa.

Keeping one eye on them, to make sure they didn't get too wild, Sam lounged against the counter. "There's a custom backyard play set company over in San Angelo. They've got an air-conditioned sales facility with all the different possibilities set up for kids and their parents to explore. I thought we all might mosey over there and let the boys run around and pick out a swing set for the backyard."

It would sure beat having them jump on and climb all over everything inside the ranch house, Lulu thought. Still… "That sounds like a pretty big investment." Were they getting ahead of themselves? They hadn't even cleared the background check.

Sam glanced over at the boys. They had abandoned the sofa and were now doing somersaults on the rug. He grinned and shook his head in amusement, as the gymnastics turned to a poorly executed game of leapfrog.

He turned back to Lulu. "And a very necessary one, when you think about the fact the closest playground is a good twenty minutes away by car. Convenient to us only when we're already in town."

Winded, the boys collapsed and, lying on their backs, began to talk gibberish among themselves.

Relaxing, Lulu took up a place opposite Sam. She let her gaze drift over the rugged planes of his face. "True."

He looked over at her, as protective as ever. "We're not tempting fate, darlin'." His gaze lingered briefly on her lips before returning to her eyes.

A spiral of heat swept through her, flushing her cheeks. "How did you know that was what I was thinking?" she asked, attempting to keep her mind on the mundane instead of the sizzling chemistry between them.

"That little pleat right here." Sam traced the line between her brows, just above her nose. He caught her around the waist and drew her all the way into his arms. "It always appears when you worry."

Lulu turned her head to check on the boys. Noting they were now calmly playing with their cars and trucks, and that it was safe to give Sam her full attention, she murmured, "I just wish I knew what the PI was still looking into."

"Like Travis said, it's probably nothing to worry about."

She swallowed around the ache in her throat. Aware she thought she'd had it all, one time, only to lose it all, just as swiftly. She released an uneven breath. "But if it is…"

His gaze gentled. "Then we'll fret when the time comes. Right now, we're going to have fun," he promised, a mischievous glint in his eyes. He flattened a soothing palm over her spine. "Otherwise the boys will worry, and we don't want them getting anxious."

She leaned into his reassuring touch, unable to help but think what a good husband and father he would be. "You're right. We don't."

As Sam had predicted, the triplets loved the sales facility. They raced from one sample play yard to another in air-conditioned comfort while Sam and Lulu simultaneously watched over them and checked out the outdoor equipment. The more time went on, the more content she felt.

"You have a beautiful family," the salesman said.

Looking as proud and happy as Lulu felt, Sam wrapped his arm around Lulu's shoulders. Gave her an affectionate squeeze. "We do."

Was this what their weekends would be like when it all did become official? Lulu wondered. Or would they be even better?

She only knew what she hoped.

And what Sam appeared to be counting on, too, she thought, tucking her hand in Sam's.

Together, they went to round up the boys. Eventually, they picked out a sandbox with plenty of room for driving excavators and dump trucks around and an A-frame swing set that held three swings. It came with toddler bucket seats for now, flexible plank-style child seats for later. They agreed that the climbing fort and slide could come later when the boys were big enough to safely handle both.

From there, they went to have dinner with Lulu's brother Matt, and his fiancée, Sara Anderson, and her son.

Although they had napped in the pickup truck, the boys were tuckered out when they finally arrived home and went through the usual bath time routine.

"Stories!" Theo shouted as they headed for the big leather sofa.

Lulu picked up the stack of favorites, as well as their own homemade book about the changes in the boys' life. With her and Sam sitting cozily side by side and the triplets sprawled across their two laps, they took turns reading through the stack of familiar books. It all felt as comfy and family-oriented as usual, yet when they had finished, the boys looked surprisingly restless. "New. Story," Andrew demanded.

Were they getting bored with the same old tales? Apparently so. Lulu looked at Sam, wanting his input.

"They might have a point," he said, still snuggling close. "Since they do know all the endings."

Aware their bright and lively little boys might need more intellectual stimulation, Lulu suggested, "We could hit the library tomorrow afternoon."

Unfortunately, that did not seem to solve the immediate problem.

Ethan frowned in displeasure. "Story. *Beauty.*"

Not sure what the boys were talking about, although as usual all three seemed to be of the same mind-set, Lulu looked to Sam for help.

Taking her cue, he attempted to clarify. "You want to read a story about a doggy?"

"No. Beauty," Theo insisted vehemently.

"Story. Beauty," Andrew repeated.

Abruptly, it all clicked. "You want us to make our own storybook about Beauty, with pictures of her?" Lulu asked.

"Yay!" the boys shouted in unison.

She and Sam exchanged grins of relief. These were the kinds of problems they could easily handle. "I think we can do that," she promised. Now that she had experience using the publishing software, it wasn't hard at all.

Pleased their wish was going to be granted, the boys headed to bed. That night, they fell asleep easily.

"I think we're getting a handle on this parenting thing," Lulu mused happily as she and Sam tiptoed from the room.

"I think we're getting a handle on a lot of things," Sam murmured, taking her in his arms and dancing her back toward her bedroom.

Wishing more than ever that the two of them had never called it quits, Lulu asked coyly, "Got something specific in mind, cowboy?"

Lulu was looking at him that way again. The way she once had years ago, every time they were together. The way that said she was his for the taking. But she hadn't been before, and wary of making the same mistake again by assuming too much too soon, he kept to the pace they had agreed upon and the deal they had made.

They were co-parents, first and foremost. Friends. And sometimes lovers.

Although the first time around, they had wanted to get married. Now she saw getting hitched as something to be avoided. He had to remember that.

Take it day by day, moment by moment. Night by

night. So he pulled her into his arms. Bent his head to kiss her thoroughly. Showing her all he felt, all they could have, if only she would open up her heart.

Until she moaned deep and low in her throat, arching up against him, and kissed him back with even less restraint than he had shown.

"Beginning to get the idea?" he said. Taking her by the hand, he continued leading her down the hall to her bed.

Eyes glittering with anticipation, she swayed toward him, clearly wanting more. She pressed her lips to his. "Very much so," she whispered.

Prepared to be as relentless as he needed to be in pursuit of her, he drew her flush against him, so she could feel his hardness. He wanted her to know how much she excited him, and he wanted to arouse her, too.

"Because I want you," he ground out against her mouth. "So much…"

She hitched in a breath as they divested each other of their clothes. When they were naked, she murmured, "Oh, Sam, I want you, too…"

He laid her back on the bed, settling between her thighs, sliding lower. Caressing her with the flat of his palms, his fingertips, his lips. Studiously avoiding the part he most wanted to touch. Until she arched and made a soft, helpless sound that sent his desire into overdrive.

She caught his head between her trembling palms. He lifted her against his mouth, circling, retreating, moving up, in. Until at last she fell apart in his arms.

Burning with a need he could no longer deny, he took control of their mesmerizing embrace. Making it as hot and wanton as the kisses she was giving. Finding protection. Lifting and entering her with excruciating slowness and care, making her his in a way that had her surrendering against him. Reveling in the erotic yearning and sweet, hot need. Knowing that this night, this time, she was his, in a way she had never been before. And, if he had his way, always would be.

To Lulu's delight, Sam had plans for their little family Sunday afternoon, as well. Regarding her fondly, he said, "I thought we might drive around the ranch and go see the horses, cattle and cowboys. Then head over to Monroe's Western Wear to get tyke-size cowboy hats and comfy boots and jeans."

"Sounds good to me," she said, returning his affectionate glance. They were feeling more and more like a family with each passing day. So what if they hadn't said they loved each other? She and Sam might not be a traditional couple, but they were a team. And a very good one at that. It was going to have to be enough.

That night, they had dinner with Lulu's brother Cullen, his wife Bridgett and their son Robby. To Lulu's relief, neither her brother nor his new wife inquired into the status of Lulu and Sam's relationship. On the other hand, Beauty, who was back at Hidden Creek and absent from the gathering, was quite the center of focus. The Saint Bernard's name came up a lot while the triplets and eighteen-month-old Robby played with their family dog.

"Beauty. *Play*," Theo explained, petting the top of Riot's head.

"Beauty. *Friend*," Andrew added helpfully.

"Play. *Fun*," Ethan stroked the beagle mix's silky tricolored fur.

In frustration, Theo turned to Sam and Lulu. "Beauty. Here?" he asked.

Abruptly, Lulu realized what the boys were asking, in their abbreviated way.

"I think they want the two of them to meet," Sam said.

Bridgett smiled. "We can probably make that happen."

And that swiftly, a new canine friendship was arranged.

That evening, the boys listened raptly to the new story about Beauty that Lulu and Sam had pulled together the previous night. They were delighted and insisted on hearing it not one but three times before Lulu finally called a halt.

"More," Andrew demanded earnestly, pointing to the storybook. *"New."*

His two brothers nodded. "Sam-Daddy," Ethan said, affectionately patting Sam's chest.

"Lulu-Mommy," Theo added, snuggling close.

"You want us to make a story about us?" Lulu asked.

The boys responded by getting up to give them great big hugs and smacking kisses. "Yay!" they shouted. More hugs followed. And then they reared back and said the words to both of them that Lulu had never expected to hear, at least not for a very long time.

Wrapping their arms around Lulu's and Sam's necks, in turn, they chorused, *"Me. Love. Sam-Daddy. Lulu-Mommy."*

"You can stop crying now," Sam teased two hours later. He and Lulu were putting the finishing touches on the story about themselves, complete with pictures from their current ranches and of themselves and the boys.

"Oh hush, cowboy! You've been welling up all evening, too."

He grinned, guilty as charged. He folded his arms across his broad chest. Tilting his head, he said thickly, "It was pretty great, wasn't it? To hear them try to tell us they loved us?"

Lulu's happiness increased a million fold. "It sure was."

A brief, contented silence fell. Aware she had never imagined being so happy, she reached over and took his hand. "Oh, Sam, I love them so much."

His eyes glistened once again. Using the leverage of their entwined hands, he brought her closer. "Me, too. More and more each day."

The joyful tears Lulu had been holding back rolled down her cheeks.

"Ah, darlin'." Sam stroked a hand through her hair and pressed a kiss to her temple.

Her spirits soared as he shifted her onto his lap and went about showing her that the affection in the Thompson-Kirkland-McCabe household did not end with the kids and the family's adorable Saint Bernard.

For the first time in a very long time, Lulu felt her life was really and truly complete. Or at least very, very close to being so. Now, if only they'd get the go-ahead from their attorneys, so they could get the adoption process started!

"You want me to drive the kids to school this morning?" Sam asked her the next morning. Since the triplets had adapted to the new routine, it was no longer necessary for both of them to do the drop-off and pickup. They were now alternating.

But the rest of the day, they were still together. Or at least they had been for the last two and a half weeks. Lulu knew that, too, was going to have to end. They both had work responsibilities to honor. Speaking of which…she hadn't been doing as much as she should with hers.

Lulu bit her lip. Sighed. And felt warmth pool through her as she watched Sam's gaze devour her head to toe.

Trying not to think how much she'd like to spend the morning making love with him, Lulu said, "If you don't mind, I'd like to head over to the Honeybee Ranch this morning and tend my remaining hive."

"No problem," he said, his gold-flecked eyes twinkling.

Telling herself he couldn't possibly have known what she was wishing, Lulu said goodbye to everyone, made sure the boys had their backpacks and lunches and then headed out herself.

As she drove onto her property, what had once been her sanctuary felt slightly alien. Definitely overly quiet, now that she no longer had honey to sell and customers coming in.

Even her food truck sat idle inside the locked barn.

It was funny, she thought, suiting up and putting on her beekeeper's hat and veil, how much her life had changed since she had first learned about the orphaned boys and began helping Sam care for them. In fact, she was pretty sure it was her most eventful June ever.

Thanks to the help she had received from her beekeeping friends, the bee colony was making progress. The new queen had been accepted by the hive. The brood combs looked healthy. There were adequate honey and pollen stores.

She added water, then replaced the lid on the hive. Picking up her smoker, she headed for the gate. She was just emerging from the mostly empty apiary when Sam's familiar truck drove up.

Alarmed, because he was supposed to be at his ranch checking on things with his crew, she ripped off her hat, veil and gloves and strode toward him. "Everything okay?" she called out.

Sam opened up the door, his cowboy hat slanted sexily across his brow, a fistful of gorgeous flowers in his hand. "It will be," he drawled, heading for her with a seductive grin, "if you'll agree to go on a date with me."

Chapter 14

Sam watched Lulu walk across the lawn toward him, her honey-brown hair cascading over her shoulders. As she got closer, she stepped out of the white bee suit, revealing a pair of thigh-length shorts and a scoop-necked tank that highlighted her stunning curves and long, lissome legs.

Soft lips curving into a smile that spoke volumes about her sassy attitude, she strolled right up to him. Turquoise eyes sparkling, she tossed out, "Hey, cowboy, didn't you know you're supposed to give a gal some notice before you show up, ready to take her out, looking handsome as can be?"

His heart jackhammered in his chest. "You think I'm handsome?" Still clutching the flowers, he flirted shamelessly.

She let out a slow breath that drew his attention to her full shapely breasts. "Oh, yeah." Poking back the brim of an imaginary cowgirl hat, she wickedly looked him up and down.

Figuring he'd kept his distance long enough, he hooked an arm about her waist and tugged her against him. "Nice to hear," he murmured, pressing the bouquet in her hands.

Their fingers brushed as she accepted the first of many gifts he planned to give her. She wrinkled her nose. "Lots of things are nice to hear." She paused. Their eyes met. Emotion shimmered between them. And once again, he was reminded of all the things they didn't yet have.

Like commitment.

Not for the boys. They had that in spades.

But for each other.

He leaned down to kiss her, giving in to instinct and claiming her as his. When the smoldering caress ended, she pulled away, pouting playfully. "You really should have given me notice."

He shrugged, still way too turned on for the beginning of a daytime date. As was she, if the tautness of her nipples was any indication. He rubbed his thumb down the nape of her neck, felt her quiver in response. "Hey, I love you in a bee suit. And out," he couldn't help but tease.

Her eyes sparkled. "I bet." With a frown, she glanced down at her watch. "Seriously, we've only got two hours before pickup."

Taking her by the hand, he led her toward the porch. "Actually, a little more." Wrapping his arm around her waist, he brought her in close to his side. "I called Kelly yesterday and explained that I hadn't had enough time to do the kind of courting I'd like to do and asked if she and Dan would consider taking the kids this afternoon for a playdate."

Lulu chuckled softly. "I am sure it didn't take much coaxing. They're always willing to help romance along…"

Sam nodded. He held the door for her as Lulu moved inside ahead of him. His gaze drifted over the taut, sexy curves of her derriere. "They said yes. Dan's off today. So it won't be a problem to have them all at their place after school."

Lulu led the way into the kitchen. Perspiration dotted her neck, hairline. She set the flowers down on the island, reached into the fridge and brought out two bottles of ice-cold water. "Nice work."

He accepted his with a thanks. Leaning against the counter opposite her, he matched her drink for thirsty drink. "So what did you want to do?"

Grinning, Lulu wiped her damp lips with the back of her hand, then let the nearly empty bottle fall to her side. "You really want me to answer that?"

He nodded, serious now. "Yes. I do. You've worked so hard to help make my dreams come true."

She furrowed her brow, looking suddenly wary again. "What kind of dreams?"

"Of having a family," he said casually. *And having you back in my life, to stay*, he wanted to add. Leery she would consider that to be pushing her again, or God forbid, taking her for granted, he went on, "I wanted to say thank you."

Lulu reached for a vase. "You're welcome." Looking abruptly way too serious, she slid the bouquet into the neck and added water. Set it in a prominent place on the kitchen counter.

With a bolstering breath, she turned to him again. "Although I should say thank you, too," she said with the careful politeness usually reserved for strangers, "for welcoming me into your home and making my dreams of family come true, too."

Not sure how his attempt to woo her had gone so awry so fast, Sam forced a smile. Yes, they were great co-parents, lovers and friends, but he wanted more. A *lot* more.

"So…" he said, clearing his throat. "Want to do lunch out?" He cast around for anything that might please her. And get this day date back on track.

To his frustration, she was looking as oddly off-her-game as he was.

"A movie?" he proposed. "Shopping?"

That got her. "Shopping? Come on! You hate shopping!"

Didn't he know it. He shrugged, determined to make this her day. Spreading his hands accommodatingly wide, he flashed her a sexy smile. "Your wish is my command today."

Her cheeks lit up with a rosy blush.

He had the feeling she was about to tell him she wanted to make love. But before she could utter another word, her cell phone chimed at the exact same time as his. Lulu started, recalling as swiftly as Sam the last time that had happened. Alarmed, she said, "I hope it's not the school."

It was not.

It was their attorneys.

Lulu knew by what Liz and Travis would not say to them on the phone that their worst fears were being realized, so she went upstairs to hurriedly shower and change into business casual clothes. Then she and Sam drove into town.

Liz and Travis were waiting for them in the conference room. "Why don't you both have a seat?" Liz said.

Sam held Lulu's chair for her, then sat down beside her. As usual, he wasted no time cutting to the chase. "You found something problematic, didn't you?"

Travis grimaced. "Definitely something interesting."

"The two of you are still married," Liz said.

"Still?" Lulu croaked.

Sam asked, "What are you talking about?"

"More to the point, how do you know this?" Lulu demanded, the news hitting her like a gut punch.

Travis looked down at the papers in front of him. "Official state records show you eloped in the Double Knot Wedding Chapel in Memphis, Tennessee, on Monday, March 14, over ten years ago. Alongside another couple, Peter and Theresa Thompson, in a double wedding ceremony."

Lulu gulped. "But our union was never legal," she pointed out, trying to stay calm while Sam sat beside her in stoic silence.

Liz countered, "Ah, actually, it is legal. In fact, it's still valid to this day."

Sam reached over and took her hand in his, much as he had the first time they had been in this room together. "How is that possible?" Lulu asked weakly.

"We never mailed in the certificate of marriage, or the license, to the state of Tennessee," Sam said.

"And for our union to be recorded and legal, we would have had to have done that," Lulu reiterated.

"Well, apparently, the owners of the Double Knot

Wedding Chapel did, and your marriage was recorded," Travis said. "And is still valid to this day, near as we can tell. Unless you two got a divorce or an annulment somewhere else? Say, another country?"

"Why would we do that? We didn't know we were married," Sam returned.

Lulu noted her "husband" did not appear anywhere near as upset as she was. She forced herself to settle down. With a dismissive wave of her hand, she told everyone in the room, "It doesn't matter. We'll just explain we were too young, or at least at nineteen I was too young to know what I was doing," she amended hastily, "and get an annulment now."

Again, Liz shook her head. "Sorry. It's been too long. It would have to be a divorce."

Lulu groaned. Talk about a day going all wrong! First, Sam had completely knocked her off guard by impulsively asking her out on a date. And now this! She twisted her hands and asked, "Is it possible we could obtain a divorce, without anyone finding out?"

"You mean like social services or the court?" Travis asked. "No."

Beside her, Sam went into all-business mode. "How does this development affect our proposed petition to adopt?"

Lulu noticed he hadn't said *mistake*.

Liz tapped her pen against the table. "It certainly makes it a great deal more complicated."

Lulu tried to get a grip and adopted Sam's no-nonsense tone. "In what sense?" she asked.

Travis sat back in his chair. "To become guardians, the bar is not that high, if the parents named you in their will. Mostly because guardianship can be terminated rather easily, for any number of reasons. However, adoption is permanent and cannot easily be undone." He cleared his throat. "So when it comes to that process of qualifying, social services and the courts want to see a stable, loving environment for the children. Anything that points to the opposite, like your secret elopement, equally impulsive breakup, and the fact you did not properly follow-through with either an annulment or a divorce and had no idea you were still married, can send up a red flag."

Lulu gulped. "How do we fix this?"

"You could admit you made a mistake, get an amicable divorce and prove you can get along in the aftermath."

Frowning, Sam asked, "How long would all that take?"

Travis made a seesawing gesture. "Potentially months, if not years, to satisfy the court."

Sam leaned forward, gaze narrowing. "And if we stay married, then what kind of detrimental impact will it have on our proposal to adopt?"

"Less of one. But," Liz said firmly, "if you two choose to go that route, you have to show real commitment to each other, as well as the children."

Lulu's anxiety rose. More and more this seemed like an impossible predicament. "How do we do that?" she asked.

Their lawyers exchanged telltale glances, then shrugged. "That is up to the two of you."

At Sam's suggestion, he and Lulu picked up some sandwiches and coffees from the bistro in town, and then retreated to Lulu's ranch to come up with a strategy for dealing with the marital crisis they suddenly found themselves in.

"I can't believe it," Lulu said miserably, burying her face in her hands.

Sam could. He'd always felt married to Lulu in his heart, ever since they said their vows. It was what had made it so hard for him to move on. What Lulu was feeling, though, he had no clue.

"Can't?" he asked before he could stop himself, realizing he had to know where he stood with her. "Or *don't* want to believe it?"

She jumped out of her seat and whirled to face him. Hands on her hips. Like him, she'd barely touched her food. "Would you please stop doing that?" she asked with icy disdain.

The resentment he'd stuffed deep inside rose to the surface. "Stop doing what?" *Wanting you?*

She winced. Looking guilty as all get-out, which of course, she should, since it was her abrupt change of heart, not his, that had ultimately put them in this mess.

She huffed in answer to his question. "Stop bringing up all the angst we felt back then!"

"Can't help it." Within him, anger and irritation surged. "It was a lousy thing to do, insist we get married, along with our friends. And then," he continued, the words coming out along with the hurt, "four days later, tell me the only way we could continue as husband and wife was if we kept it a secret!"

She took another deep breath, suddenly appearing oddly vulnerable. "I wasn't saying permanently!" She gestured broadly, then started to pivot away from him.

Not about to let her run away from him again, he stopped her with a light hand to her shoulder. Turned her slowly back to face him. And finally asked what he'd wanted to know for years. "Why say it at all?"

An emotional silence stretched between them.

He let his hand fall to his side. "You either loved me or you didn't, and apparently you didn't."

"It's more complicated than that, and you know it."

A muscle ticked in his jaw. "Then why, Lulu?" He gritted out. "Why did you run scared?"

Another long, awkward silence fell. "My parents would not have understood."

Aggravated to find her still using that lame excuse, he gave her a chastising glance. "There's no way to know that, because we never gave them a chance to support us."

"It's not like you told anyone in your family!" Lulu said, just as bitterly. Reminding him she wasn't the only one who had suffered from a hefty dose of pride. She stepped forward and jabbed an accusing finger at his chest. "Since you said we'd either go public with our marriage immediately, or it was all over. And no one would ever have to know!"

Seeing she was about to bolt again, he let out a rough breath and stepped closer. "Can you blame me?"

She tossed her head, silky hair flying in every direction. "For having a 'my way or the highway' approach?" she shot back. "Yes, I can, since marriage is supposed to be a fair and equal partnership."

Her words hit their target. She had a point. He shouldn't be lashing out. He shook his head. "I'm sorry," he said guiltily. "I'm upset." They had been so close to having everything they wanted. And now...

Lulu released a deep breath and grew quiet once again. "We're both upset, Sam." She shoved her hair away from her face. Shook her head in misery. "The big issue is where do we go from here?"

That, at least, was easy, Sam thought. "Isn't it obvious? We stay married."

Lulu's day went from bad to worse in sixty seconds. She stared at the handsome cowboy opposite her, wondering how she had ever imagined the two of them were living in some sort of fairy tale. "Are you serious?"

Looking more resolute than ever, he replied, "We want to adopt the kids. Our best shot at doing that is by being married. And since we already are, why not just leave it as is and go forward as husband and wife?"

How about because we don't love each other? Lulu thought. But not about to reveal the direction of her thoughts, she countered sarcastically, "Just like that? Presto, change-o, snap our fingers, and we're a happily married couple?"

Even though, if she were honest, she would have to admit that lately she had been feeling as if they were on the verge of being just that.

"Why not? We're already spending time together every day. Sleeping together. Raising three kids together and living under the same roof. Why not just admit that staying married is the best avenue for raising the kids and making them feel safe and secure and loved?"

Because, Lulu thought, *if I do that, then I'm one step away from opening up my heart and admitting the real reason why I've never really been able to get serious about anyone else but you, Sam.* "Because we'd have to tell everyone what we did back then," she blurted out.

Again, he clearly did not see what the problem was.

"So?" His gruff response was a direct hit to her carefully constructed defenses.

"It's embarrassing," she whispered, the heat moving from her chest into her face. She threw up her hands and paced. "It makes us look idiotic and reckless."

Sam crossed his arms. Determined, it seemed, to win this argument. His gaze sifted over her before returning ever so slowly to her eyes. "Or wildly in love. I mean, isn't that why people usually elope?"

"Except we weren't wildly in love, Sam." If they had been, they never would have split up and stayed apart for almost a decade. Would they?

He sobered, looking pensive. "Well, what do you want to do, Lulu?" he asked in exasperation. "Split up again and go through the hell of divorce, because even an uncontested one is just that, and then try to adopt?"

Put that way, it did sound unreasonable.

"And what if getting divorced not only ruins our chances of ever adopting the triplets," he said, in an increasingly rusty voice, "but also casts a bad light on our character and gets them removed from our guardianship, too?"

Lulu swallowed around the lump in her throat. "I couldn't bear that." The thought of losing the triplets was on par with how she had felt losing Sam. Heartbreakingly awful.

Sam compressed his lips. "Well, neither could I."

A stony silence fell.

Lulu weighed the possibilities. Life with Sam and the kids. Life without. There really was no other choice. Not if they didn't want to disappoint literally everyone. "So we're in agreement," she said, trying not to cry. She swallowed hard, aware she had never felt so trapped or miserable. She lifted her gaze to his. "We bite the bullet and stay married for the sake of the kids."

Sam locked eyes with her, looking no happier than she felt. He exhaled grimly, ran a hand through his hair. "I really don't see any other way out of this. Do you?"

Chapter 15

Unfortunately, Lulu did not see any other way out. So they asked Dan and Kelly to keep the kids a little longer and went to see her parents first, figuring they could then leave it to Rachel and Frank to spread the word.

As they sat down together at the kitchen table, Lulu said, "Y'all remember spring break, my sophomore year of college, when I went on a country music tour with some of my best girlfriends?"

Her parents nodded, perplexed, unable to see where this was going.

Hating to disappoint them, Lulu knotted her hands in front of her. "Well, I lied to you," she admitted shamefully. "I *was* in Tennessee. But I was staying with Sam that week, not a group of girls."

Her parents looked at Sam. "I apologize for that," he said with gruff sincerity. "We should have told you the truth."

Her parents paused. "I assume there is a reason you're telling us all this now?" her father said.

Lulu nodded. "There is." She explained how she and Sam had accompanied their friends Peter and Theresa to Tennessee to be the witnesses for their secret wedding ceremony.

Sam reached over and took her hand. Buoyed by the warmth and security of his touch, she plunged on, "I was so caught up in the romance of it all—" *and my incredible, overwhelming feelings for Sam*, she added silently "—that I suggested we make it a double wedding."

Sam lifted a hand. "For the record, I was all too ready to jump in."

"So we eloped, too," Lulu confessed. "And for the rest of our spring break," she admitted wistfully as Sam's hand tightened over hers, "everything was wonderful." For a few heady days, she'd felt all her dreams had come true.

"What happened to change all that?" her dad asked. "And make you break up?"

"When it came time to go home, the reality of what we had done set in for me." Hard.

The memory of that last horrible fight was not a good one. Sam withdrew his hand, sat back.

Tears blurred her vision once again. Embarrassed, she continued, "I knew we'd acted recklessly and I was afraid to tell anyone else what we'd done. And I especially didn't want to disappoint the two of you." Unable to look her "husband" in the eye, she related sadly, "Sam refused to live our marriage in the shadows, so we broke up."

"And got the marriage annulled?" her mother assumed.

"Actually…" Sam went on to explain the confusion over the paperwork that had followed. "We just found out we're still legally married."

Her parents took a moment to absorb that information. "Which puts us in a little bit of a quandary," Lulu said.

"Little?" her father echoed, finally appearing as upset with her as Lulu had initially expected him to be.

"Okay. It's a pretty big problem," she conceded, chagrined. "But Sam and I are going to figure this out."

"Well." Her mother sighed. "First, I wish you had come to us at the time and told us what was going on, so we could have made sure there were no lingering legal snafus. And supported you. And we *would* have supported you, Lulu, no matter what you thought then. Or think now…"

Her dad, calming down, nodded.

"Second," Rachel said, with a gentle firmness, "as for you being fearful of our opinion, when it comes to your life—" she paused to look long and hard at the two of them "—it only matters what *you* two feel in *your* hearts, not what anyone else thinks." She reached across the table to take Lulu's and Sam's hands. Squeezed. "Furthermore, your family will defend your right to make those choices for yourself, by yourselves, even when we don't approve or understand them."

Her dad covered their enjoined hands with his own. "Your mother and brothers and I want you to be happy, sweetheart. And the same goes for you, Sam." He regarded them both with respect.

"It's up to you to figure out what will make you feel that way and then go for it," Rachel added gently.

Everyone disengaged hands. Another silence fell, even more awkward and fraught with untenable emotions.

"Do you know what you're going to do?" her mom asked finally.

Lulu and Sam looked at each other. "Stay married," they answered in unison.

Sam draped his arm across the back of Lulu's chair and continued with the same steady affability that made him such a good leader. "We think it would provide a more stable environment for the kids."

Frank pushed back his chair and got up to make coffee. Once again, he seemed loaded for bear. "You really think you can make an arrangement like this work?"

Lulu didn't see any choice if they wanted to help the kids. But sensing it would be a mistake to tell her parents that, she answered, "Yes." She hauled in another breath, admitting a little more happily, "Sam and I have recently gotten back together, anyway, so it just makes sense for us to stay married and build on that."

Beside her, Sam seemed calm and accepting of the predicament they found themselves in. Her parents regarded them with equal parts doubt and consideration. Which amped up her own wariness. But to her surprise, Frank and Rachel didn't try to talk them out of it.

"Okay, then," her mom said finally. "But if you're going to stay married—" her regard was stern, unrelenting "—your dad and I want you to be as serious as the institution of marriage requires this time. And do it right by officially and publicly recommitting to each other and saying your vows before all your family and friends. That way, everyone—including and especially the two of you—will know it is not just a whim that can be easily discarded. But an honorable, heartfelt promise you can both be proud of."

"I don't see why you're so upset," Sam said, late into the following week.

Lulu pushed away from her laptop, where she had been dutifully compiling the expected guest lists for her parents. "Because it's all so unnecessary!" she fumed, stepping out back where the newly installed swings and sandbox sat in the warmth of a perfect summer night.

With the triplets soundly asleep and now snoozing happily through most nights, she should be relaxing and getting to know Sam again. Instead, she was slaving away on the endless To Do lists her parents kept giving her.

She swung around to face Sam, her shoulder knocking into his. "I don't see why we even have to have a wedding, when everyone in the whole county—heck, probably the whole state, thanks to the McCabe-Laramie grapevine!—knows our story."

He reached out to steady her, then lounged beside her against the deck railing. His hands braced on either side of him, he continued to study her face, his expression as inscrutable as his mood the last few days.

Unable to quell the emotions riding roughshod inside her, she challenged softly, "Why do we have to go through the motions of getting married again?" If he'd just told her parents no…

He leaned toward her earnestly. "Because the kids deserve it," he returned with a chivalry that grated on her nerves even more than his calculated calm.

The heat of indignation climbed from her chest, into her face. "They're not old enough to realize—"

"But they will be one day," he countered. "Do we really want them to have to weather not just the tragic loss of their parents and the chaos that ensued regarding their guardianship, but a scandal regarding their adoptive parents, too?"

She curled her hands over his biceps, finding much needed solace in his masculine warmth. "It's not like getting married all over again erases the elopement and paperwork snafu that followed."

He wrapped both arms about her waist. "But it brings closure and a well-respected, time-honored path to the future stability of our family." Tugging her closer still, he reached up to tuck a strand of hair behind her ear. "And proving we are serious about staying together," he continued tenderly, "not just as co-guardians or lovers and friends but as husband and wife, *will* bolster our efforts to adopt."

Abruptly feeling as trapped as she had during their conversation with her parents, she pivoted away and stepped farther into the warm and breezy summer night. Stars sparkled in the black velvet sky overhead. A quarter moon shone bright. "That's assuming we *can* still adopt after all this."

He clamped his lips together, as if he was not going to continue, then did, anyway. "You heard what Liz and Travis said about this." He followed her down into the grass. "We will be able to, we're just going to have to wait a little while and prove we have a solid relationship before submitting our application."

Lulu breathed in the minty scent of his breath. "I get all that," she said grumpily.

His eyes tracked her as she paced restlessly back and forth. "But...?"

She came closer and tipped her chin up at him. "I just don't see why I have to have a wedding dress and a whole big reception complete with a live band and a harpist and a flute and five attendants, when we could just as easily say our I dos in jeans and T-shirts."

He gave her a quelling look. "You really want to give people the impression that this means so little to us we couldn't even bother to get properly dressed?"

Okay, so maybe she was taking her resistance to all the hoopla too far.

"Your attendants are all family, and your sisters-in-laws and your brothers all want to participate in this day. So why not let them be members of the wedding party? Plus, as your mom has pointed out on *numerous* occasions for the last several weeks, you are their *only* daughter. They want the privilege and pleasure of seeing you get married on the ranch, the way you all used to envision, when you were growing up."

Damn, why did he have to be so reasonable when making his points?

Recalling how much she hated arguing with him and coming out the loser, she steered the conversation in another direction. "Your family isn't making such a fuss."

His stoicism took on a tinge of sadness. "That's because we're all scattered all over the world now, since all five of my sisters opted for demanding international jobs. And none of them can get here till the very last moment."

Lulu sensed there was more. "And...?" she prodded gently.

One corner of his lips turned down. "No one's actually said it, but I think it's hard for them, having the first wedding, without either of my parents still here with us on earth."

Lulu drew in a breath, guilt washing over her. She hadn't meant to be so insensitive. "Oh, Sam. I'm so sorry about that."

"It's okay." He squared his broad shoulders, dealing with trouble the way he always did. Head-on. He flashed her a grin. "I think they're still looking down on us from up above. And what they are telling us, Lulu… is that you need to get yourself in gear."

Lulu knew Sam was right.

So she tried.

She went to her final dress fitting. Approved the tuxes Sam had picked out for him and the boys. Went with Sam to taste wedding cake and pick out a band. And sat down with the florist.

But when it came to the last and final thing, she balked.

"I don't want to be married by a minister or say traditional wedding vows."

Sam gave her the long-suffering look that had become way too commonplace during the weeks of wedding prep. He continued getting ready for bed. "How come?"

Because this all still felt like a travesty. Like the romance and the enthralling passion was gone, and now all they had left was the duty of recommitment.

Leery of admitting that out loud, though, for fear of hurting his feelings, Lulu washed off her makeup. "I'd prefer a justice of the peace."

Sam stripped down to his boxers and a T-shirt, then walked into the bathroom. "And why's that?"

Trying not to notice how buff he looked or how much she always seemed to want to make love to him, Lulu layered toothpaste onto her brush. "Because when we got married before, we were too young to know what we were doing."

"And now it's different?" he prompted.

"Yes, totally different. Now that we're old enough to know what we are doing, we are going in with clearer heads and are on the same page about the fact that our nuptials aren't romantically or spiritually motivated." She lounged against the marble counter. "Rather, it's just more of a…an optimal agreement about how we're going to live in the future. So." She drew in a deep breath. "That being the case, it seems like we should use a justice of the peace instead of a minister."

That look again. A very long exhalation. Another heartfelt pause.

"Okay," he said finally. "A justice of the peace it is. What do you want to do about the vows?"

Lulu brushed her teeth, rinsed, spit. As did he. "Maybe we could each write our own."

She expected an argument. Instead, he set his toothbrush back in the holder next to hers and said, "That'll work."

Aware all over again how cozy and right it felt to share space with him like this, Lulu said, "You don't mind?"

"Not at all." Coming close enough to take her in his arms, he gazed down at her lovingly and sifted his hand through her hair. "In fact, I kind of like the idea."

As it turned out, however, Lulu did not enjoy writing her vows to Sam any more than she had liked any of the other wedding preparations. Mostly because she could not figure out what to say. Reciting poetry just wasn't *them*. Everything she wrote sounded either disingenuous or lame. Or both.

Finally, there were just three days left before the big event. And she was nowhere close to having anything to say.

She moaned over her laptop, where she had been continuously typing…and deleting…and typing…and deleting.

Sam sank down on the big leather sofa next to her. With the kids and Beauty asleep upstairs in the nursery, the house was oddly quiet. He draped his arm around her shoulders. "What's wrong, sweetheart?"

Aware this part of her life felt more out of control than ever, Lulu buried her face in her hands. "I'm never going to get my vows written."

Settling closer, he gave her an encouraging squeeze. "Do you want my help?"

Briefly, she turned her head and rested her face against his shoulder. She loved snuggling up to him, especially when her emotions were in turmoil. He made her feel so protected. "No." She sighed. "It has to come from me."

Looking devilishly handsome with the hint of evening beard rimming his face, he bussed the top of her head. "Give it time. It'll come."

Would it? "What if it doesn't?" Lulu lamented, her mood growing ever more troubled. She looked deep into Sam's eyes. "What then?"

They had been down this road before, Sam thought, at the end of their passion-filled Tennessee honeymoon.

Then, it had been post-wedding jitters. Was this the pre-wedding jitters?

He hadn't talked her out of making a mistake the last time and heartbreak had ensued. He wouldn't let her run away again.

Tilting her face toward his, he gently stroked her cheek. "There is no rule that says we have to write our own vows, Lulu. We can just go back to the tried and true." Which would be a heck of a lot easier, since he hadn't written his vows yet, either. Although he wasn't stressing out about it.

Lulu shot to her feet. Her eyes were steady but her lower lip trembled. "I can't stand up in front of everyone we love and say traditional vows, Sam."

He rose, too. "Why not?"

Regret glimmered briefly in her gaze. She seemed to think she had failed on some level. "Because they're not true!"

He stepped closer and took her rigid body in his arms. "You'd leave me if I was sick? Or poor?"

She lifted her chin and speared him with an outraged look. "No, of course not," she conceded.

"You don't plan to take me as your lawfully wedded husband?" he asked, his own temper beginning to flare.

As she spoke, her face grew pale, her shoulders even stiffer. She shook her head, determined, it seemed, to think the worst of them. "We're already legally hitched."

He stared at her in frustration. "You don't want to love and cherish me?"

"I…" She sent him a confused glance, making no effort at all to hide her reluctance to further their romance. "You mean love like a friend?" she asked warily.

His heart rate accelerated. "Like a wife loves a husband."

She swallowed, looking miserable all over again. Shoving a hand through her hair, she paced away from him. "See? This is why I don't like this!"

"You've lost me, darlin'." He followed her over to the fireplace. "Don't like what?"

She spun around to face him, the soft swell of her breasts lifting and lowering with every anxious breath she took. "Having to analyze our relationship and spell everything out."

These were not the words of a bride who was blissfully in love. These were the words of a woman who was desperately trying to find a way out of getting hitched. He positioned himself so she had no choice but to look at him. "Our relationship won't stand the test of time, is that what you're saying?"

"Of course we'll be together for the kids' sake. For as long as they need us," she said, her eyes glittering. "But we don't have to go through all this rigmarole to do that, Sam. We could just continue on, as we have been, as we would have, had we not become aware we were still legally married."

Sam forced himself to show no reaction. He might not want to hear this but he had half expected her to say something similar. "You're saying you want a divorce?"

"No!" Still holding his eyes—even more reluctantly now, he noticed—she gulped. "I'm saying I don't want to go through with this wedding." Tears blurred her eyes, and her lower lip trembled all the more. "If they need us to restate our vows, and honestly I don't see why in the world we need to go to the trouble to do that since our marriage is legal just as it is, then I'd rather just elope again. And make the statement that way."

Sam stood, arms crossed. "Thereby proving what, exactly, Lulu? That we're still the impulsive idiots we were before?"

Huffing out a breath, she went back to her laptop and closed it with more care than necessary. "No," she said. She slid her computer back into its case, zipped it shut. "We would be doing what other couples do when they decide the hoopla is all too much and that life has gotten too crazy. They run off and elope."

He took her by the shoulders and held her in front of him. "We did that, Lulu. It didn't work out so well."

Case held against her chest, she eased away. "I was a lot younger." She stalked into the kitchen.

He watched her set the case down. "True. But still just as skittish when it comes to making an actual commitment."

She opened the fridge. "I'm *completely* committed to the children."

"Just not to me."

She spun back to face him, a riot of color filling her cheeks. "Please don't misinterpret this."

He reached past her to get a beer for himself. His gut tightened as he twisted off the cap. "What other way is there to interpret it, darlin'? You want to stay married to me, so long as you don't have to publicly act like you mean it."

She took a sip of water. He took a swig of beer.

"I'm *living here*, aren't I?"

He grimaced. "As a matter of convenience."

Her gaze narrowing, she set her bottle down with a

thud. "Well, that makes sense, because you invited me to *bunk here* as a matter of convenience."

An accusatory silence fell.

She came nearer, her hurt obvious. "I don't understand why you're so upset with me. For once in my life, I don't care what people think about this situation we've found ourselves in. I don't care if my parents are going to be disappointed or mad at me."

There was a time when that would have pleased him immensely, to know that she put their relationship above all else. Now, it felt like a booby prize.

"I only care what *we* think and feel is right for us."

He tore his eyes away from the way her knee-length shorts hugged her hips, her cotton T-shirt her breasts. "Which would be...?"

Noticing her hair was falling out of the clip, she undid the clasp and let her mane fall across her shoulders. "To just skip this whole travesty of a wedding and leave things as is."

"Meaning married."

"Technically." She ran her fingers through the silky strands, pushing them into place, then leaned against the opposite counter, her hands braced on either side of her. "And living together."

He definitely felt burned by her casual attitude. "As co-parents."

"Yes." She caught his hand. "Don't you see, Sam? Everything was great until we found we were still legally hitched."

It had been—and it hadn't. The feel of her smooth fingers in his brought only partial comfort. He tried and failed to summon up what little gallantry he had left. "Just like it was great when we were on a honeymoon." A muscle ticked in his jaw. "But then when we had to go home and tell our families what we had done, it was not so great."

She flushed and shook her head in silent remonstration. "There's no comparison between then and now, Sam," she warned.

"Isn't there?" he asked bitterly. Their glances meshed, held. "You're doing exactly what you did before."

She looked at him, incredulous.

"Recklessly jump all in with me—all the while swearing your devotion—only to jump all out."

Her eyes shone even as her low tone took on a defiant edge. "I won't leave the kids, Sam, if that's what you're worried about."

He knew that. Was even grateful for it.

"But you would be right back out that door if the kids weren't here," he countered, before he could stop himself. "Wouldn't you?"

She stared at him, as if feeling every bit as boxed in—and deeply disappointed—as he felt. Like they needed to take a step back. Give each other time to breathe. Figure out what they really felt. "I don't know how to answer that," she said finally, her chin quivering.

"Sadly, I do." He paused to give her a slow, critical once-over. Wondering all the while how they ever could have deluded themselves into thinking this would work. "We never should have told your parents we would renew our vows. Or fooled ourselves into thinking we could carry off this charade," he said, pain knotting his gut. "And this is what any marriage between us is to you, isn't it, Lulu? A charade?"

Her disillusionment grew. "Given the way this wedding has come about, how could it be anything but?" she asked, her face a polite, bland mask.

She moved closer still, imploring now. "Which is why I can't seem to write my vows no matter how hard I try." She lifted her chin. In control, again. "And why we should cancel it, Sam. So we can go back to the way things were before marriage entered the mix."

It wasn't the legality of the situation that was destroying them. It was her refusal to open up her heart. "I asked you this before but I am going to ask you again. And this time, I want an honest answer." He propped his hands on her shoulders and bore his eyes into hers. "You want a divorce?"

She flinched. "No, of course I don't want a divorce now!"

Now…

Which meant…

Releasing her, his feelings for her erupted in a storm of anger and sorrow. "But you will, won't you?" he concluded bitterly, wishing like hell he had seen this coming. Like their second time around would end any other way. "Maybe not tomorrow. Or the next. But one day…"

She compressed her lips. "You're twisting everything I've said."

He told himself he was immune to her hurt. He had to be. For everyone's sake, one of them needed to be reasonable. "Well, one thing is clear. For us, marriage is and always has been a mistake. We can be co-parents, Lulu, but that is all."

She blinked. "*You're* throwing down the gauntlet and issuing an ultimatum to me? *Again?*"

Not happily.

He shook his head, and with a heavy sigh, said, "No. I'm doing what you've been trying to do, indirectly, for weeks now, Lulu. I'm calling an end to our romantic relationship. This time, for good." Heart aching, he stormed out.

Chapter 16

With a heavy heart, Lulu went to see her parents at their ranch. They took one look at her face and sat her down with them at the kitchen table. "Tell us what's going on," her mom urged gently while her father made them all a pot of coffee.

Pushing away the dreams of what might have been, Lulu knotted her hands in front of her. "Sam and I are still planning to adopt the kids together, but we're not going to have a wedding on Saturday afternoon after all." Lulu swallowed around the lump in her throat. "So it would help me out a lot," she continued, swiping at a tear slipping down her cheek, "if you could help me notify everyone."

"Of course we'll help out, honey." Her dad got out the cream and sugar. Added three mugs to the table. "But…?" He looked at her mom, with the same kind of parental telepathy she and Sam had been sharing.

"...are you sure?" Rachel interjected, handing her a box of tissues.

Wiping away a fresh onslaught of tears, Lulu forced herself to be honest. "I really thought I could do it." Her heart aching, she paused to look her folks in the eye. "Build on everything I feel for Sam and the kids and marry him strictly as a matter of convenience. But—" she felt the hot sting of shame that she ever could have been so shortsighted "—when we started trying to work on our vows, I realized there was no way we could really do this without it all being a lie. And I couldn't base our entire relationship on that. Never mind pretend," she continued thickly, "in front of everyone that it was going to be a real marriage." Her voice trembled. "When I knew in my heart it was all a sham."

"And Sam thinks it's a sham, too?" Her dad brought the carafe over to the table and poured coffee into mugs. Not surprisingly, he was more focused on fixing this problem than consoling her.

Aware she hadn't a clue what Sam was thinking or feeling, Lulu stuttered, "I...ah..."

"Did he actually *say* that it was untruthful for him, too?" her attorney-mom asked, in her cross-examination voice.

"No," Lulu admitted miserably.

"Then what *did* he say?" Rachel persisted.

Sam's angry words still reverberating in her mind, Lulu admitted grimly, "That if I couldn't find some wedding vows that would work for us and go through with the wedding on Saturday, our romantic relationship was off. Permanently this time."

Her dad shook his head in mute remonstration, for

once not taking her side. "Honestly, Lulu. Can you blame the guy?"

"Hey!" Lulu scowled, feeling indignant. To calm herself, she stirred cream and sugar into her coffee and lifted the mug to her lips, breathing in the fragrant steam. "He never once said he loved me. Not this time around, anyway…!" So what choice had she had, no matter what her feelings were? A fraud was a fraud! And that was no example to set for the kids, never mind a foundation to base a marriage on.

"So." Her mother sighed in regret. "You don't trust the two of you to be able to sustain a romantic relationship that will go the distance."

Softly, Lulu admitted this was so.

Her mom studied her over the rim of her mug. "Will you be able to be friends?"

Lulu took another sip, and finally said, albeit a little uneasily, "When the dust clears, I think so."

Her dad sat down beside her mom. "What about the children?" he asked.

"We still plan to adopt them."

"Together?" he questioned.

"Yes."

"Living separately," he continued to press, "or under one roof?"

Lulu flushed. Aware that hadn't been completely worked out, but she could assume. "Under one roof, just the way we have been."

Her mom picked up where her dad left off. "And you have faith this arrangement will work."

Lulu replied without hesitation. "Yes."

Rachel's eyes narrowed. "Why?"

Lulu struggled to find the words that would explain what she knew in the deepest recesses of her soul to be true. She looked both her parents in the eye. "Because that part of our life together just works and works really well. And we never ever disappoint each other in that regard."

Her mom's brow furrowed. "And you think not disappointing each other is key."

Lulu lifted a hand. "Of course."

"Oh, honey," Rachel said, getting up to engulf Lulu in a hug. Her dad came around the other side and joined in. "Disappointment is part of life."

They drew back to face her once again. "The more you love someone, the more likely it is that you will disappoint each other from time to time," her dad said gently but firmly.

Her mom nodded. "It's those highs and lows and the ability to weather each storm and come back even stronger, as a couple and a family, that make loving worthwhile."

Thursday morning, Sam had just dropped the kids off at preschool and returned to his ranch, when a caravan of five pickup trucks and SUVs came up the lane.

All five of Lulu's brothers got out and walked toward him. None looked the least bit happy.

Sam bit down on an oath. Great. This was all he needed after the week he'd had. With him and Lulu more or less alternating care of the kids when possible, and doing the polite-strangers dance around each other when it wasn't.

Thus far, they'd manage to keep the boys from picking up on the breech between them, but whenever he and Lulu faced off alone, even for a few minutes, the residual hurt and anger was palpable. To the point they'd more or less taken to completely avoiding each other.

"Told you that you'd be seeing us if you hurt our sister again," Dan drawled.

This would be comical if he hadn't spent the entire night nursing a broken heart.

"I didn't hurt her." Sam pushed the words through his teeth.

Dan adopted a law officer's stance. "Then why is she over at Mom and Dad's ranch, crying her heart out over a potentially canceled wedding?"

Potentially?

Did that mean Lulu was having second thoughts about calling their love affair quits, too? Or just that her folks weren't willing to let her off the hook?

There was no way to tell without speaking to Lulu about it in person.

Sam glared back at the McCabe posse. He curtailed the urge to put his fist through something, anything. "You'll have to ask her that, since she's the one who found it impossible to stand up in front of family and friends and say I do."

"Then what was she going to say?"

"That was the problem. She couldn't figure it out. And was apparently tired of trying."

A contemplative silence fell among the six men.

Chase squinted, his calm, analytical CEO temperament coming to the fore. "I can't believe she would react that way without a very good reason."

Well, she had, Sam thought grimly.

"What aren't either of you telling us?"

A lot of things actually. Like the fact I opened up my heart and soul to her and it still wasn't enough. Or the fact I still don't want a divorce, even though Lulu all but came out and admitted in a roundabout way that her only attraction to me is physical.

Looking very much like the chivalrous ex-soldier he was, Matt rubbed the flat of his hand beneath his jaw. "Are you protecting her?"

Yes, Sam thought, *I am*. Which on the surface wasn't surprising. Like the McCabes, he had been raised to be a Texas gentleman, too. And gentlemen didn't tell a woman's secrets.

Ever. But this went deeper than that. For the first time, he found himself caring about what people thought. Not about him. But about Lulu. He didn't want anyone thinking less of her because of mistakes they'd both made. So he remained mum.

Jack analyzed the situation with a physician's empathy. "One thing's clear. You're both miserable."

Sam tried not to hang any hope on that. "That's kind of hard to believe since she's been dragging her heels," he scoffed. "And doing everything possible to show her resistance to renewing our marriage vows, for several weeks now."

Matt squinted. "Why would she do that?"

Sam shrugged. "Isn't it obvious? She has a real problem with commitment."

At least to me.

It couldn't be anything else.

The brothers didn't believe that any more than he wanted to. "Is she abandoning the kids, too?" Dan asked.

Sam frowned. "No, of course not. She loves those little guys."

"Then it's just you that's the problem?" Cullen taunted.

Actually, Sam thought, even more miserably, *I don't know what the problem is.* The two of them clicked. They had always clicked. Until it came time to take their love public in an everlasting way. Then she just started putting up roadblocks even he couldn't get past.

"Is there a point to all this?" Sam asked with a great deal more patience than he felt.

The five men nodded.

"The fact Lulu is trying to call the wedding off," Chase said finally, "when it's clear how crazy she is about you, should point you toward some pretty big deficit in your behavior. And if you're smart—" he paused meaningfully, to let his words sink in "—you'll figure out what that is. Pronto."

Friday afternoon, Lulu had just finished taking care of her lone remaining hive when Sam's truck turned into her ranch. Her heart pounding, because she wasn't sure she was quite ready to say all the things she needed to say to him, she drew off her beekeeper's gloves and veil, stepped outside the apiary gate and began moving toward him.

He walked toward her, too, and as he did, she couldn't help but admire how good he looked in the usual jeans, boots, chambray work shirt and stone-colored Resistol slanted across his brow. As he neared, the masculine determination she so admired glinted in his gold-flecked eyes.

Her heart thundered in her chest, as her spirits rose and fell, then rose again.

When she reached him, she stripped off her protective suit and hung it over the porch railing, feeling suddenly achingly vulnerable. "I thought we were going to meet up later," she said with as much feminine cool as she could muster. When she'd had time to clean up and put on something besides an old Texas A&M T-shirt and shorts.

He acknowledged this was so with a dip of his head. "I know what we said before I left to take the kids to preschool."

"But?" Lulu inhaled the brisk masculine fragrance of his aftershave.

"I didn't want to waste any more time."

Funny, she didn't, either. But would they be able to work it out? The way they hadn't before?

In that instant, she decided they would.

Taking her by the hand, he led her up the steps to the front porch. Sat down with her in the wooden rocking chairs she'd inherited from her late grandmother and brought his chair around until they were facing each other, knee to knee.

His eyes were full of the things she'd almost been afraid to hope for, his gaze leveled on hers. "I want to start over, Lulu," he continued, his voice a sexy rumble. His hands tightened protectively on hers. "And this time keep working at it, until we get it right." He looked at her with so much tenderness she could barely breathe.

Her heart somersaulted in her chest. She drew in a shuddery breath. "You mean that?" she whispered.

He nodded soberly and hauled in a rough breath. Shaking his head in regret, confessed, "I never should have pressured you into staying married to me. Like it was some kind of social contract or means to an end. Because you're right, Lulu." He stood and pulled her to her feet. Wrapping his arms around her, he brought her even closer, so they were touching in one long, comforting line. "A real marriage is so much more than that. It's about promising your whole heart and soul."

He paused, all the love and commitment she had ever wanted to see shining in his eyes. "It's about vowing to stay together no matter what for the rest of your lives. And that's what I want with you, Lulu," he confessed. "To be with you for the rest of our lives. Because I love you. I've always loved you. And I always will."

Tears of joy and relief blurred her vision. "Oh, Sam," she said, hugging him tight. "I love you, too."

He paused to kiss her, demonstrating the depth of his feelings in a most effective way.

She kissed him back, sweetly and tenderly, letting him know she felt the same.

When they finally drew apart, Lulu confessed raggedly, "But I've made so many mistakes, too."

His gaze holding hers, he listened.

She swallowed around the lump in her throat and pushed on. "The biggest one was not letting you know that I never fell out of love with you. Not at the time we broke up. Not during all those years when we were apart." Her lips curving ruefully, she shifted even closer. "And certainly not the last couple of months."

His hand slid down her spine, soothing, massaging, giving her the courage to finally convey what was in her heart. "Then why didn't you want to say that in your vows to me?"

She drew a shuddery breath and clutched at him, reveling in his heat and his strength. "I was so happy, just living with you and the triplets. I was afraid to upset the status quo. Afraid if I told you how I really felt, only to find that you didn't still love me the way you once had, that it would change things or put too much pressure on us. Somehow ruin things, the way our elopement did."

He sat down again, pulling her onto his lap. "I take the responsibility for that." Regret tightened the corners of his lips. "I knew you weren't ready to marry me at nineteen."

Looking back reluctantly, she remembered his initial hesitation. Realized, too late, it was a warning she should have heeded. "Then why *did* you say yes, when I suggested eloping with Peter and Theresa?" she asked curiously.

His mouth twisted in a rueful line. "It was selfishness. I was so damn in love with you, and I was graduating college and about to head back to Laramie. I wanted you with me, even if it wasn't the right thing for you. And deep down, you knew we were too young to make that kind of lifelong commitment, too."

"Otherwise I wouldn't have been so afraid and ashamed to tell everyone we'd gotten hitched."

A contemplative silence fell while they both came to terms with the past.

"Even so…" She put her hands across the warm, solid wall of his chest. "I shouldn't have asked you to hide our marriage. Especially when I know now it made you feel like I was ashamed of my feelings for you. I wasn't. I was just afraid of what people would think… that they'd assume I was being reckless and impulsive again." She sighed. "And most of all? I was afraid of disappointing you and ruining everything between us. And *that* I really couldn't take."

"We both made mistakes." The pain in his low tone matched the anguish she'd felt in her heart. "Years ago. And recently, too." He pressed a kiss to her temple, her brow. "I never should have walked out on you when you told me you didn't want to go through with our re-commitment ceremony. I should have given you all the time you needed."

Tingles sliding through her head to toe, Lulu called on the perspective she, too, had gained. "I had enough time to figure out what was in my heart."

His brow lifted.

Feeling the thud of his heart beneath her questing fingertips, she confessed in a tone overflowing with soul-deep affection, "You taught me how to love. How to be vulnerable. And how to risk."

He grinned with the shared realization that they'd finally found the happiness they'd both been craving.

"And that being the case…" She recited her feelings in an impromptu version of the vows he'd been wanting her to pen, "I pledge my past, my present and my future to you. I promise to be your wife and take you as my husband forevermore. And—" she hitched in a bolstering breath, looking deep into his eyes "—I promise to do everything I can to make you happy, Samuel Kirkland. To give love and accept it in return. Because I do love you," she finished thickly, knowing she'd never be able to say it enough, "so very, very much…"

Sam's eyes gleamed. "I love you, too, sweetheart," he murmured, bending her backward from the waist and bestowing on her the kind of jubilant kiss couples engaged in at the end of their nuptials.

Grinning, he brought her upright. "And as long as we're speaking about what's in our hearts... I want to thank you for teaching me what love is and making my life so much happier and brighter than I thought it could ever be. For giving us...and the boys...a future." Voice rusty, he went down on one knee. "So, if you'll have me, Lulu McCabe, I vow to love, cherish and protect you for as long as we both shall live." He reached into his pocket and brought out a diamond engagement ring.

"Oh, I'll have you, Sam Kirkland!" Tenderness streaming through her, Lulu drew him to his feet. She gave him another long kiss. "For the rest of my life!"

"You know," Sam teased, when the steamy caress had ended and the ring was on her finger, "our spur of the moment vows were really spectacular."

And heartfelt, Lulu thought. On both sides. "So much so that I kind of feel married again," she teased. Even without the wedding rings.

"Really married," he agreed. Sobering, he went on, "But I still think we should make our union as strong and official as it can be."

And that meant going public with their commitment.

"I'm with you, cowboy." Lulu beamed, excited to tell him the rest. "Luckily for us, there's still a wedding planned for tomorrow at my parent's ranch."

He grinned his sexy, mischievous smile that she loved so much. "You didn't cancel it?"

Lulu wreathed her arms about his shoulders and gazed up at him adoringly. "I couldn't. Not when I still wanted to spend the rest of my life with you so very much."

He sifted a hand through her hair, then drawled happily, "Sounds like we'd better get a move on then, darlin', as I imagine there's still a lot to do."

"We'll handle it," Lulu told him confidently. "And while we're at it, we'll enjoy every moment, every step of the way. Because this time, my love—" she rose on tiptoe to give him another lengthy reunion kiss "—we're doing it right."

Epilogue

One year later

"Mommy, can we take Beauty to court with us?" Ethan asked.

Lulu wasn't surprised the triplets wanted their beloved pet to accompany them. It was going to be an exciting day.

"No, honey." She knelt to help him clip on the tie he had insisted on wearing, because he wanted to be just like Daddy. Who was looking mighty fine, in a dark suit, pale blue shirt and tie.

Sam assisted Andrew with his neckwear. Theo had figured his tie out on his own and didn't need any assistance.

"How come?" Andrew asked, gently petting the top of Beauty's head.

"Dogs aren't allowed in court," Sam explained. "Unless they're service dogs. Like the ones some of Uncle Matt's friends have."

"That wear the special vests," Ethan said. "And help the old soldiers."

"Ex-soldiers, and yes, that's right." Sam grinned.

The boys thought about that for a minute. "Then could we take some of Mommy's bees with us?" Ethan asked.

Sam shook his head. "They need to stay on the Honeybee Ranch."

"So they can make more honey," Andrew said.

"Right." Lulu smiled.

"How many hives do you have?" asked Theo, who was always counting something.

"About three hundred and ten."

Sam had not only created an auxiliary membership that allowed her and other ranchers who did not specialize in cattle to join the Laramie County Cattleman's Association, he had also convinced her she could do more than one thing. So she'd brought the colony back from Wisconsin, nurtured them through the stress of post-travel and added a few more boxes in the spring.

She'd also hired an assistant beekeeper to stay on the property and do a lot of the day-to-day work for her business, so she could concentrate on caring for Sam and the boys, who altogether were quite the handful. Especially now that the triplets had gone from two-word sentences to nonstop chatter and endless questions.

As they prepared to leave, Beauty followed them to the door.

"Ahhh," Ethan pouted. "She's going to be lonely without us!"

"Are you sure we can't take her?" Andrew asked.

"She was in the wedding!"

"That was outside, on Grandma and Grandpa's ranch, and she had special permission to be there."

"Yes, but she was really good."

She had been. As had the boys. And it had been a glorious day, full of the promise of a lifetime of love ahead.

Sam got out a dog biscuit for each boy to give the Saint Bernard. "She'll be waiting for us when we get back," he said.

"And we're going to have a huge party!" Andrew spread his hands wide.

"Yes, we are," Lulu promised.

All the McCabes were going to be there in court to witness the big day. And all of Sam's sisters, as well.

Outside the courtroom in the marble-floored hallway, Lulu and Sam paused to speak to the boys. "This is very important," Lulu said gently.

"So you all need to be on your best behavior," Sam continued. "Do you understand?"

The boys nodded.

Sam and Lulu escorted them into the courtroom and took a seat at the table. The clerk announced the adoption procedure.

Hearing their names, all three boys jumped up onto the seats of their chairs, unable to contain themselves.

Andrew yelled, "Do we take this Mommy? Yes!"

Ethan shouted, too. "Do we take this Daddy? Yes!"

Theo clapped his hands. "You may kiss!"

The courtroom full of family erupted in a flood of laughter and tears. Sam and Lulu shot to their feet, too. Together, they lovingly contained their three little charges.

"Sorry, Your Honor," Sam said with as much solemnity as he could manage, "they have wedding and adoption formalities mixed up."

"Well." The judge cleared her throat, looking a little teary-eyed, too. "It's understandable. The depth of commitment is the same."

It absolutely was, Lulu thought.

"So, if y'all think we can continue…?"

Sam and Lulu bent and whispered a new set of instructions to the boys. They nodded solemnly, raised their hands and when called upon, said, "Sorry, Your Honors. We're going to be quiet until we're *allowed* to cheer."

And they were.

Afterward, they gathered outside the courtroom in the hallway. Hugs and congratulations were exchanged all around.

Hours later, when their company was gone and the kids were finally asleep in their beds, Sam and Lulu met up on the back deck for a glass of champagne in the starlight.

He clinked glasses with her and smiled victoriously. "We did it."

She linked arms with him, sipped. "We sure did."

They took a moment to ruminate on all they had accomplished in coming together. Sam slanted her a deadpan glance. "Think we'll ever get that honeymoon?" he teased.

"Oh, maybe twenty years from now," Lulu joked.

They both laughed.

"Seriously." She rose up on tiptoe and kissed him,

sweetly and tenderly. With a contented sigh, she drew back just enough to be able to see his face. "It feels like we've been on one since we got back together."

Bliss flowed between them.

Sam gave her waist an affectionate squeeze. His gold-flecked eyes sparkling with joy, he mimed writing in the sky. "Hashtag. Best Life Ever."

* * * * *

"Wait, what?" he interrupted again. "Logan worked for a
tech firm?"

Although his brother had taught himself to code when he
was still in middle school, and he'd been a good hacker of
the dirty tricks variety when they were teenagers, Chance
couldn't see him ever living the cubicle lifestyle for a steady
paycheck.

"Yes," Poppy said. "And he developed a computer program
several years ago that allowed companies to legally plunder
and sell all kinds of personal information and online habits of
anyone who used their websites. It goes without saying that it
was worth a gold mine to corporate America. And corporate
America paid your brother a gold mine for it."

Okay, that did actually sound like something Logan would
have been able to do. Chance probably shouldn't be surprised
that his brother would turn his gift for hacking into making a
pile of money.

Poppy pulled another piece of paper from the collection in front of her. "I have another statement that's been prepared for your trust, Mr. Foley."

He started to correct Poppy's "Mr. Foley" again, but the other part of her statement sank in too quickly. "What do you mean my trust?"

"I mean your brother and sister-in-law have put funds into a trust for you, as well."

He didn't know what to say. So he said nothing, only gazed back at Poppy, confused as hell.

When he said nothing, she continued. "The children's trust will begin to gradually revert to them when they reach the age of twenty-two. That's when the funds in your trust will revert entirely to you."

Out of nowhere, a thought popped up in the back of Chance's brain, and he was reminded of something he hadn't thought about for a long time—a wish he'd made to a comet when he was fifteen years old. A wish, legend said, that should be coming true about now, since Endicott had been celebrating the "Welcome Back, Bob" comet festival for a few weeks. Something cool and unpleasant wedged into his throat at the memory.

He eyed Poppy warily. "H-how much money is in that trust?"

Her serious green eyes had never looked more serious. "A million dollars, Mr. Foley. Once the children have reached the age of twenty-two, that million dollars will be yours."

Love Harlequin romance?

DISCOVER.

Be the first to find out about promotions, news and exclusive content!

f Facebook.com/HarlequinBooks

𝕏 Twitter.com/HarlequinBooks

◎ Instagram.com/HarlequinBooks

ⓟ Pinterest.com/HarlequinBooks

You Tube YouTube.com/HarlequinBooks

ReaderService.com

EXPLORE.

Sign up for the Harlequin e-newsletter and download a free book from any series at **TryHarlequin.com**

CONNECT.

Join our Harlequin community to share your thoughts and connect with other romance readers!
Facebook.com/groups/HarlequinConnection

◆HARLEQUIN

Heartfelt or thrilling, passionate or uplifting—Harlequin is more than just happily-ever-after.

With twelve different series to choose from and new books available every month, you are sure to find stories that will move you, uplift you, inspire and delight you.